TEN NIGHTS IN A BAR-ROOM

IN HIS STEPS

$1.50

COMPLIMENTS OF
THE ODYSSEY PRESS · INC ·
55 FIFTH AVENUE   NEW YORK 10003

TEN NIGHTS IN A BAR-ROOM
T. S. Arthur

AND

IN HIS STEPS
Charles M. Sheldon

EDITED BY C. HUGH HOLMAN

University of North Carolina

THE ODYSSEY PRESS · INC · NEW YORK

INTRODUCTION

From its earliest beginnings, fiction has put on respectability with the masses by wrapping about itself the chaste robes of morality; and, with equal earnestness, the moralist has employed fiction as a confectionery to make palatable truths that in plainer form might be bitter. Although the protagonist of Daniel Defoe's *Moll Flanders* (1722) had supposedly reported her numerous acts of immorality in order to instruct the young lest they follow her course, Samuel Richardson's *Pamela*, which Benjamin Franklin published in Philadelphia in 1744, introduced the combination of moral earnestness, titillating plot, and authorial admonition which has been characteristic of popular writing in America ever since. These moralistic *exempla* had an early imitator in William Hill Brown, whose *The Power of Sympathy; or, The Triumph of Nature* (1789), the first American novel, addressed itself, in the words of its dedication, "To the Young Ladies of United Columbia, These Volumes, Intended to represent the specious Causes, and to Expose the fatal Consequences, of Seduction; To inspire the female mind with a Principle of Self Complacency, and to Promote the Economy of Human Life." Writers of American fiction from that time to the present have attempted to persuade their readers to take as serious examples the misfortunes which befall the ungodly.

Thus, from its beginnings, American fiction has taught private morality and voiced protests against social wrongs, using its devices to elicit attention and its sentimentality to provoke heightened emotional involvement by its readers. These efforts have justified the pleasures of fiction to readers skeptical of "lies" and in their broad sentimental appeals have found very large audiences. From the first "cheap book" period in the 1840's, through the dime novels of the 1860's and later, and in the "Sunday School Libraries" of the end of the century, the sentimental novel of social protest and private morality shared with the "Western," the detective story, the boy's adventure book, and the "success" story a mass appeal. At least two such books, *Ten Nights in a Bar-room* and *In His Steps*, achieved individual reading audiences of massive size.

America in the nineteenth century had many of the aspirations and much of the optimism of the Utopian dreamers and believed that a social order could be created that would remove the sources of evil from the center of human action. By the middle of the century, the combination of this belief in a remediable society and the urge toward humanitarian actions had substituted reform for religion and social theory for theology in a substantial section of America. On the part of many men, a central motive for their existence could be found in the seeking of various solutions to the human dilemma. An amusing account of this kind of attitude is Ralph Waldo Emerson's record of the Chardon Street Convention, which occurred in Boston in 1840 and which was "a Convention of Friends of Universal Reform." In Emerson's words, "If the assembly was disorderly, it was picturesque. Madmen, madwomen, men with beards, Dunkers, Muggletonians, Comeouters, Groaners, Agrarians, Seventh-day Baptists, Quakers, Abolitionists, Calvinists, Unitarians and Philosophers,—all came successively to the top, and seized their moment, if not their hour, wherein to chide, or pray, or preach, or protest. . . . If there was not parliamentary order, there was life, and the assurance of that constitutional love for religion and religious liberty which, in all periods, characterizes the inhabitants of this part of America."

This urge toward social reform was wedded to individual morality most effectively in the pursuit of temperance, for among the most obvious evils in an imperfect society, these reformers found alcohol to be the major one and one where social wrong followed from individual error. From the 1830's until the twentieth century, much of America thought that it saw in Demon Rum the doom of civilized man and was confident that nothing short of absolute prohibition could rescue from moral decay a society that hoped for perfection. Protestant and dissenter groups have always placed a strong emphasis on behavior, conventional standards of conduct, and questions of public morality. It was, therefore, by no means surprising that intemperance became an issue of major importance in America. There had been voices raised against the drinking of spirituous liquors from the seventeenth century on; but by 1826, when the American Society for the Promotion of Temperance was organized, a movement which rapidly became enormous had begun. By 1833 there were over 4,000 active temperance societies and a half million members. There seemed to be an almost endless number of kinds of temperance groups ranging from the "Cold Water Army" to those active in securing moral commitments of total abstinence and to those seeking legal coercion to prevent the manufacture and sale of alcoholic drinks. In 1851 the first genuine law prohibiting the manufacture and sale of alcohol was passed by the State of Maine, and promptly it precipitated the charge of legal coercion of the individual's private actions, and the charge of unconstitutionality was leveled against it. Movements wrestling with alcohol in many different ways continued until they finally reached their epitome of success in this century with the passage of the Eighteenth Amendment to the Constitution and the Volstead Act.

The idea of the legal control of moral and social issues was extremely attractive to a pietistic audience such as the masses of Americans formed in the nineteenth century. Thus temperance proved to be, in many ways, the simplest and most obvious device by which the impact of moral attitudes could be brought to bear upon the issues of social conduct. Undoubtedly, the number of those who believed that the true way to the creation of an ideal moral state rested primarily in the control of drinking and drunkenness was small, but the number who found in such control a telling symbol of the imposition of moral judgments upon public conduct was very large indeed, and it continues to this day. In Truman Capote's *In Cold Blood*, a Midwestern rural world is portrayed which still uses abstinence as a barometer of virtue, for the community of Holcomb, Kansas, held the ill-fated Clutter family in high repute, in part at least, because of their abhorrence of strong drink. Alcohol thus is still used as an external measure of moral rectitude, a point of view which the civilized European has always regarded as barbaric. That this should be true is in part the result of certain aspects of American culture and certain tendencies toward violence in the American character and in American history. This oversimplified view of moral and social issues was obviously very usable to the writer of sentimental reform fiction, and the "temperance novel" appeared in great quantities.

The representation of the dangers that followed inevitably upon the drinking of alcohol absorbed the interest of many writers of fiction—and among them one distinguished poet, Walt Whitman, whose only novel, *Franklin Evans; or, The Inebriate* (1846) is plainly a temperance tale. But of all the writers of temperance novels, the most prolific and, in certain respects, the most influential was Timothy Shay Arthur, who employed stereotype characters, simple and over-stated plot situations, and a semi-literate but sometimes powerful prose style to show the inevitable route which led from the first drink to the drunkard's grave and which stripped innocence of its joy, money of its meaning, and made man the mad victim of his appetites. And of all Timothy Shay Arthur's many works—he is believed to have written himself five percent of all the volumes of fiction sold in the United States between 1840 and 1850—the most successful was *Ten Nights in a Bar-room* (1854). This novel exists not only as a terrifying pamphlet but also has worked its way into the American consciousness through the presentation of its theme and its story in a play version prepared by William

W. Pratt in 1858. The play was one of the most popular items of the repertory theater, and it wove its way into the imagination not only through its action but especially through a song in it in which Mary Morgan, invading the "Sickle and Sheaf" to plead with her drunken father, sings heartbreakingly, "Father, dear father, come home with me now."

Seldom have violence and rectitude reached more obvious interplay than they do in *Ten Nights in a Bar-room*. Not even in Mark Twain's and Bernard De Voto's violent midwestern frontier have Puritanism and melodramatic violence been so vigorously but so unhappily wedded as they are in the downward progress of those who frequent the "Sickle and the Sheaf," whether that tavern is seen in Arthur's book or Pratt's play.

At the end of the century, the attempt to resolve the issues of society not through law but through humanitarian religion, with temperance again playing a central role, found vigorous expression in Charles M. Sheldon's almost incredibly popular novel *In His Steps*. Although this book with its persistent question "What would Jesus do?" by no means centered its attention exclusively on the temperance issue, that question was certainly one of the major and most recurrent issues with which it dealt in its exploration of Christian socialism.

These two books, like hundreds of those addressed to an audience with little literary taste and small education, differed primarily from others of their class in the enormous success which they had in the marketplace and in the minds of their readers. In nineteenth-century America only one issue was more pervasively present to the reforming mind than temperance. That issue was slavery; and only *Uncle Tom's Cabin*, which employed the sentimental, domestic tradition to attack that evil, surpassed these two books in popularity.

Timothy Shay Arthur was born in New York City in 1809. Although poorly educated, he was an effective magazine editor and a remarkably successful writer of books of all sorts. The more than 100 books which he produced—many of them fiction designed as *exempla*—included children's stories, manuals of advice for adolescents, hints to the married, and instruction on many moral points. He was also the author of domestic sentimental novels dealing with marital maladjustment—frequently as a result of intemperance on the part of the husband, as in *The Two Wives* (1851); but he also argued for the importance of there being only one head in any household in *The Withered Heart* (1861) and *Out in the World* (1864); and he may have been the first American novelist to treat the problem of divorce seriously, as he did in *The Hand But Not the Heart* (1858). But the great subject

which called forth from him the best that he had to offer in the way
of melodramatic instruction was temperance. In addition to *Ten
Nights in a Bar-room*—by all means his best novel and the best known
temperance novel in American writing—he produced *Six Nights with
the Washingtonians: A Series of Original Temperance Tales* (1842), in
which a group of reformed drunkards known as "the Washingtonians"
were celebrated as a kind of nineteenth-century Alcoholics Anonymous. This record of the horrors of drink sold 175,000 copies by 1850,
although the entire publishing industry was in a state of deep depres-
sion as a result of the lingering effects of the financial disaster known
as "The Panic of 1837." *Ten Nights* was ultimately to sell at least
400,000 copies.

Arthur wrote many other well-known temperance works. *Three
Years in a Man-Trap* (1872) was laid in a large city and depicted the
evils of drink; its publisher called it a sequel to *Ten Nights in a Bar-
room* and said that in it Arthur "grapples again with the monster intemperance, but in a new field and with enemies more thoroughly dis-
ciplined and organized." The field was the big city saloon as opposed
to the country inn. These saloons Arthur picturesquely called "nurser-
ies of vice and crime." In the same year he also published *Women to
the Rescue*, a story of the new crusade which celebrated the beginnings of the Women's Christian Temperance Union and made a heroine of its leader Carry Nation, who attacked saloons through direct
physical action in what she accurately but picturesquely called
"hatchetations." Arthur's war with Demon Rum did not cease, though
by this time it had certainly had its most effective expressions. In 1875
he launched a battle against moderate drinking in a novel called *Danger; or, Wounded in the House of a Friend*, which he designed, he
said, as "an exhibition of the fearful disasters which flow from our social drinking customs." In 1877 he attacked the saloons again in *The
Barrooms at Brantly*. In the same year he compiled statistical and his-
torical data in *Grappling with the Monster; or, The Curse and the
Cure of Strong Drink;* and at the age of seventy-two he fired his final
volley at a still impervious enemy in *Saved as by Fire* (1881).

While this amount of writing would absorb the major attention of
most people, it did not prevent Arthur's effective career as the publisher of magazines addressed to various audiences but, most frequently, to ladies and the family. A magazine which began as a weekly in
1850 under the title *Arthur's Home Gazette* and continued under the
briefer title of *The Home Magazine* until Arthur's death in 1885 was
enormously successful. He also published children's magazines, magazines representing monthly selections from foreign periodicals, magazines addressed to the working man and his family—in fact, a host of

lower middle-class and proletariat journals. His brief association in his youth with the *Baltimore Saturday Visiter,* and through it with Edgar Allan Poe, is one of the major ironies of American literary history. Although Poe might have served as an example for one of Arthur's books, to think of him as being edited by the author of *Ten Nights in a Bar-room* makes one feel as though he were involved in a drama of the absurd.

Charles M. Sheldon (1857-1946) was a Congregational clergyman in Topeka, Kansas, and for a brief time in the 1920's the editor of the *Christian Herald.* He turned to fiction in an effort to deal with social issues and at the same time maintain interest in his Sunday evening sermons. The result was that his particular brand of "social gospel" was the basis for a kind of "sermon-serial" in which fictional accounts demonstrating social and religious theses were presented in installments each Sunday evening. In 1890 he delivered from his pulpit the first of these theological "cliff-hangers," *His Brother's Keeper,* the story of a miners' strike, in which the first installment ends with the hero at the bottom of a mine with water already at his knees and rising rapidly. The next Sunday evening, an even larger audience was in the same place to find out how the protagonist got out of the mine; and for twelve weeks this story was continued to steadily mounting numbers of people, so that the application of Christian principles to the labor problem filled the Central Congregational Church to overflowing. In the fall of the next year he tried it again, and in the following fall he presented *The Crucifixion of Philip Strong,* which was serialized in a church weekly and then published in book form. Its sales were moderate but large enough to justify the appearance of *His Brother's Keeper* in book form the following year.

By that time, the Reverend Dr. Sheldon was already embarked upon another serial and one which was destined for worldwide sales. Its title was *In His Steps.* Its theme was clearly defined by the question, "What would Jesus do?" It belongs to the Utopian literature of the last quarter of the nineteenth century in which altruism, brotherhood, and humanitarian sympathy are portrayed as combining to create a world of ideal principles. The cutting edge of the question "What would Jesus do?" is examined as it affects newspaper publishing, manufacturing, settlement houses, education, politics, and almost every other movement that the social gospel was concerned with. But to a greater extent than anything else, it was aimed at the liquor question.

The Reverend Dr. Sheldon was deeply committed to the temperance movement; and after the publication of *In His Steps* he continued this interest, traveling to Great Britain in 1900 to participate in a prohibition campaign, traveling to Australia and New Zealand for a similar campaign in 1914, being a member of the "Flying Squadron" in the interest of national prohibition in 1914 and 1915, and conducting a campaign during the First World War for "national prohibition to protect American boys from drinking en route to France."

In His Steps began in a middle-sized city very much like Topeka, Kansas, and, when it was two-thirds finished, it shifted to Chicago. The shift does substantial violence to unity of plot but is an inevitable extension of the concern with the problems of an industrial, urban society. Dr. Sheldon was not alone in asking his persistent question and in attempting to apply the principles of Christian love to the problems of the world of the Robber Barons. The novel *Robert Elsmere* by Mrs. Humphrey Ward, one of the most controversial books of the nineteenth century, had not only stimulated discussion in its native England but had put a social challenge to the smug Christians of middle-class America by pointing its finger toward the slums and the ghettos. In 1894 William T. Stead in *If Christ Came to Chicago* had sensationally attacked the moral structure of the Midwest metropolis, an attack that was responded to in 1895 by Edward Everett Hale in *If Jesus Came to Boston*, which pleasantly suggested that if He did He would probably feel at home; and in the year 1896, Hall Caine, in *The Christian*, attacked the church as being inadequate to meet the problems of the modern world.

Sheldon's *In His Steps* is a worthy member of this group of Utopian and socialistic novels. It was a vigorous weapon in the warfare for the social gospel and one which proved almost unbelievably acceptable to church-going America. The book, according to its author, was enthusiastically received by Christian Endeavor societies, temperance organizations, and YMCA's. It went through many different editions, most of them in paper or in cheap cloth, selling at a price ranging from as little as eight cents to $2 or more. Unfortunately for the young minister, the copyright was improperly applied for and the book passed into public domain. How many copies actually have been published and sold is a matter of major debate. Dr. Sheldon believed that eight million copies had been sold in America up to 1924, ten million in Great Britain, four million in other countries, a total of over twenty-two million copies by 1924. This rather ambitious figure has crept upward as others have repeated it, and the claim is often made that *In His Steps* sold more than thirty million copies, the largest sale of any book ever printed except for *The Bible*. Frank Luther Mott has made a serious effort to track down figures which would be more accurate. He has concluded that about two million copies were sold in the United States and some six million in other nations. Though eight million

copies is an astounding sale for any book, the figure, if accepted by
Dr. Sheldon, would have forced him to a disappointing conclusion
about the measure of his success; for apparently, since royalty was not
involved, people told the minister what he wanted to hear about the
popularity of his book; and in all honesty—and some understandable
vanity—he arrived at a figure three times its probable sale, high
though that figure was.

There are many characteristics which *Ten Nights in a Bar-room* and
In His Steps share with better books and with each other. These books
were like Harriet Beecher Stowe's *Uncle Tom's Cabin,* which warred
against slavery, Upton Sinclair's *The Jungle,* which warred against the
evils that capitalism created for immigrant workers, and John Steinbeck's *The Grapes of Wrath,* which portrayed the evils of the modern
world as they oppressed the drought-stricken Okies—the three most
successful social protest novels written by Americans. Timothy Shay
Arthur and Charles M. Sheldon used characters who represented attitudes, placed them in actions which tended to use these attitudes to
make moral statements, and then, not content with meaning conveyed
through the narrative, stepped in themselves through one or another
guise to comment upon the meaning of what they had portrayed. Mrs.
Stowe does this as an omniscient author and through the person of
George Harris, who gives what most people regard as her solution to
the problem at the end of *Uncle Tom's Cabin.* Upton Sinclair, pleading
for the institution of socialism in place of capitalism, concludes *The
Jungle* as his protagonist listens to a long address setting forth the logic
and the humanity of the socialistic point of view—an address taken directly from a tract which Sinclair himself had written and circulated. In
The Grapes of Wrath, John Steinbeck was confined to an objective
scenic method in recounting the disasters which befell the Joad family,
but in alternate chapters he dropped the Joad narrative and picked up
in its stead an authorial commentary cast in the language of Isaiah and
Amos. T. S. Arthur, through his anonymous narrator in *Ten Nights in
a Bar-room,* makes everywhere obvious the odium in which drink is
held, and on numerous occasions he has the narrator and other characters give passionate expression to the protest theme of the book.
Charles M. Sheldon in *In His Steps* writes as an omniscient author;
and the hortatory tone is everywhere present, for the events of the
book are not so much presented as commented upon.

Most of the books of social protest in the nineteenth century owed
unmistakable debts to Charles Dickens; but like many other American
novelists writing on social issues, Arthur and Sheldon borrowed Dickens' melodramatic and sentimental plots, his exaggerated characters,

his oppressed people, and his lachrymose death scenes without borrowing also his rich imagination, his exuberance, his command of character, and his endlessly marvelous invention. The result is undiluted and often offensive sentimentality pursued for its own sake and unredeemed by style or plot or originality of character.

Neither Arthur nor Sheldon had any firm sense of plot. Their stories consist of disjointed scenes threaded together on the string of theme. *Ten Nights in a Bar-room* recounts what happens over a period of years as a nameless traveler persists in spending the night in a country town where the "Sickle and the Sheaf" is the only hostelry. One may wonder about how it was that he continued to subject himself to scenes so obviously repulsive to his moral nature, but that he does constitutes almost the only thread that binds together the horrendous episodes that he witnesses.

In His Steps has as its unifying principle the application of the question "What would Jesus do?" to the problems of modern society in a Midwestern city and then in Chicago. Its unity is artificial beyond this theme, for it is a very loosely linked sequence of events tied together only by the fact that the events happen to the members of a single church congregation as that congregation accepts the challenge of literal discipleship. In order to achieve the "cliff-hanging" conclusions to his Sunday evening sermons, Dr. Sheldon had to break off in the middle of an episode and conclude it the following Sunday, at which time he also began another episode.

The styles of both writers are flat, almost ungrammatical, simple in diction, direct in sentence structure, and stridently rhetorical when the writers decide to reach for authorial authority. There is in this process little to commend either author as a craftsman with the language, though Arthur's style is simpler, more direct, and more attractive than the heavy periods of Dr. Sheldon.

The characters, too, survive in our minds not as human beings but as overdrawn types. Out of both the books the only figures that will be remembered with any pleasure by the reader are Mrs. Slade, Simon's poor wife in *Ten Nights in a Bar-room,* and the man who interrupts the sermon and asks the penetrating question of the congregation and its minister, Henry Maxwell, in *In His Steps.* Neither of these, in fact, are triumphs of characterization; but both of them appear to me to strike reasonably convincing postures that linger at least briefly in the mind.

Bad though these two novels are, each of them reached an audience of substantial size and called forth from that audience a response which was pietistic, optimistic, humanitarian, and finally egalitarian. The address which they made to the reading public is perhaps effectively summed up in the passage in *In His Steps* when the music of Rachel's voice works on the slums so that "It lay like some wild beast at her feet and she sang it into harmlessness. Ah! What were the flippant, perfumed, critical audiences in concert halls compared with this dirty, drunken, impure, besotted mass of humanity that trembled and wept and grew strangely, sadly thoughtful, under the touch of this divine ministry of this beautiful young woman. Mr. Maxwell, as he raised his head and saw the transformed mob, had a glimpse of something that Jesus would probably do with a voice like Rachel Winslow's. Jasper Chase sat with his eyes on the singer, and his greatest longing as an ambitious author was swallowed up in the thought of what Rachel Winslow's love might some time mean to him. And over in the shadow, outside, stood the last person anyone might have expected to see at a gospel tent service—Rollin Page, who, jostled on every side by rough men and women who stared at the swell in the fine clothes, seemed careless of his surroundings and at the same time evidently swayed by the power that Rachel possessed."

In their differing ways, these two immensely popular works helped to define a change in American culture and a growing despair about legal solutions to social problems. Both novels dealt with unsuccessful elections involving the control of alcohol; yet their views of the world differed sharply. *Ten Nights in a Bar-room* in 1854 reflected confidence in legal political structures and portrayed the world in terms of the agrarian countryside and the small town. *In His Steps* in 1896 moved from the small town to the city, from an agrarian culture to an industrial capitalistic culture, and saw the solution to these problems in the religious and humanitarian dedication of the individual man rather than in the efforts of groups of men to change the legal structure.

These fictionalized sermons reached a wider audience, attracted a greater attention, and may have had a more marked influence than almost any other works produced in America, aside from *Uncle Tom's Cabin* and Edward Bellamy's *Looking Backward;* and while they may give us an alarming picture of American aesthetic ideals, they demonstrate America's moral commitments and the firmness with which it attempted to pursue them.

University of North Carolina   C. Hugh Holman
Chapel Hill

BIBLIOGRAPHY

The best general study of American domestic fiction is Herbert Ross Brown's *The Sentimental Novel in America, 1789-1860* (Durham, N. C., 1940). Brown is excellent on the sentimental social protest novel, although his study stops before Sheldon's period. Two studies of popular books in America give significant treatment to *Ten Nights in a Bar-room* and *In His Steps:* Frank Luther Mott's *Golden Multitudes: The Story of Best Sellers in the United States* (New York, 1947) and James D. Hart's *The Popular Book: A History of America's Taste* (New York, 1950). Edward Wagenknecht, in *Cavalcade of the American Novel* (New York, 1952), gives good discussions of both books. Alexander Cowie, in *The Rise of the American Novel* (New York, 1948), is excellent on the sentimental novel and on Arthur, but he does not deal with Sheldon. Leslie Fiedler's *Love and Death in the American Novel* (New York, 1960) is interesting on the novel of sentimental protest and on Arthur.

The temperance movement is treated in John Allen Krout's *The Origins of Prohibition* (New York, 1925) and Alice Felt Tyler's *Freedom's Ferment* (Minneapolis, 1944). Edmund Pearson, in *Queer Books* (Garden City, N. Y., 1928), writes entertainingly of temperance novels, including *Ten Nights in a Bar-room.*

An excellent brief treatment of Christian socialism in the American novel is in Walter Fuller Taylor's *The Economic Novel in America* (Chapel Hill, N. C., 1942). Henry Steele Commager's *The American Mind: An Interpretation of American Thought and Character Since the 1880's* (New Haven, 1950) has a good short discussion of the social gospel in America.

The best single study of Arthur and of *Ten Nights in a Bar-room* is Donald A. Koch's long and fine introduction to "The John Harvard Library" edition of the novel (Cambridge, Mass., 1964). The only detailed biographical treatment of Sheldon is his clumsily written autobiography, *Charles M. Sheldon: His Life Story* (New York, 1925).

NOTE ON TEXTS

The texts of both *Ten Nights in a Bar-room* and *In His Steps* are corrupt in all their forms, and show the signs of hasty writing, type-setting, and proof-reading. None has any serious "authority." In the following reprintings, the 1854 text of *Ten Nights* has been followed, with only slight corrections. The texts of *In His Steps* are generally undated; the one here reproduced follows, with slight changes, an undated text published in Chicago by Hurst & Co., probably around 1900. In neither book has an attempt been made to regularize the author's punctuation, syntax, grammar, or diction.

CONTENTS

TEN NIGHTS IN A BAR-ROOM

AND WHAT I SAW THERE

By T. S. ARTHUR

PUBLISHER'S PREFACE

[From the 1854 Edition]

This new temperance volume, by Mr. Arthur, comes in just at the right time, when the subject of restrictive laws is agitating the whole country, and good and true men everywhere are gathering up their strength for a prolonged and unflinching contest. It will prove a powerful auxiliary in the cause.

"Ten Nights in a Bar-Room" gives a series of sharply drawn sketches of scenes, some of them touching in the extreme, and some dark and terrible. Step by step the author traces the downward course of the tempting vender and his infatuated victims, until both are involved in hopeless ruin. The book is marred by no exaggerations, but exhibits the actualities of bar-room life, and the consequences flowing therefrom, with a severe simplicity, and adherence to truth, that gives to every picture a Daguerrean vividness.

Night the First

THE "SICKLE AND SHEAF"

Ten years ago, business required me to pass a day in Cedarville. It was late in the afternoon when the stage set me down at the "Sickle and Sheaf," a new tavern, just opened by a new landlord, in a new house, built with the special end of providing "accommodations for man and beast." As I stepped from the dusty old vehicle in which I had been jolted along a rough road for some thirty miles, feeling tired and hungry, the good-natured face of Simon Slade, the landlord, beaming as it did with a hearty welcome, was really a pleasant sight to see, and the grasp of his hand was like that of a true friend.

I felt, as I entered the new and neatly furnished sitting-room adjoining the bar, that I had indeed found a comfortable resting-place after my wearisome journey.

"All as nice as a new pin," said I, approvingly, as I glanced around the room, up to the ceiling—white as the driven snow—and over the handsomely carpeted floor. "Haven't seen any thing so inviting as this. How long have you been open?"

"Only a few months," answered the gratified landlord. "But we are not yet in good going order. It takes time, you know, to bring everything into the right shape. Have you dined yet?"

"No. Every thing looked so dirty at the stage-house where we stopped to get dinner, that I couldn't venture upon the experiment of eating. How long before your supper will be ready?"

"In an hour," replied the landlord.

"That will do. Let me have a nice piece of tender steak, and the loss of dinner will soon be forgotten."

"You shall have that, cooked fit for an alderman," said the landlord. "I call my wife the best cook in Cedarville."

As he spoke, a neatly dressed girl, about sixteen years of age, with rather an attractive countenance, passed through the room.

"My daughter," said the landlord, as she vanished through the door. There was a sparkle of pride in the father's eyes, and a certain tenderness in the tones of his voice, as he said—"My daughter," that told me she was very dear to him.

"You are a happy man to have so fair a child," said I, speaking more in compliment than with a careful choice of words.

"I am a happy man," was the landlord's smiling answer; his fair, round face, unwrinkled by a line of care or trouble, beaming with self-satisfaction. "I have always been a happy man, and always expect to

3

be. Simon Slade takes the world as it comes, and takes it easy. My son, sir"—he added, as a boy in his twelfth year, came in. "Speak to the gentleman."

The boy lifted to mine a pair of deep blue eyes, from which innocence beamed, as he offered me his hand, and said, respectfully—"How do you do, sir?" I could not but remark the girl-like beauty of his face, in which the hardier firmness of the boy's character was already visible.

"What is your name?" I asked.

"Frank, sir."

"Frank is his name," said the landlord—"we called him after his uncle. Frank and Flora—the names sound pleasant to our ears. But, you know, parents are apt to be a little partial and over fond."

"Better that extreme than its opposite," I remarked.

"Just what I always say. Frank, my son"—the landlord spoke to the boy, "there's some one in the bar. You can wait on him as well as I can."

The lad glided from the room, in ready obedience.

"A handy boy that, sir; a very handy boy. Almost as good in the bar as a man. He mixes a toddy or a punch just as well as I can."

"But," I suggested, "are you not a little afraid of placing one so young in the way of temptation."

"Temptation!" The open brows of Simon Slade contracted a little. "No, sir!" he replied, emphatically. "The till is safer under his care than it would be in that of one man in ten. The boy comes, sir, of honest parents. Simon Slade never wronged anybody out of a farthing."

"Oh," said I, quickly, "you altogether misapprehend me. I had no reference to the till, but to the bottle."

The landlord's brows were instantly unbent, and a broad smile circled over his good-humoured face.

"Is that all? Nothing to fear, I can assure you. Frank has no taste for liquor, and might pour it out for months without a drop finding its way to his lips. Nothing to apprehend there, sir—nothing."

I saw that further suggestions of danger would be useless, and so remained silent. The arrival of a traveller called away the landlord, and I was left alone for observation and reflection. The bar adjoined the neat sitting-room, and I could see, through the open door, the customer upon whom the lad was attending. He was a well-dressed young man—or rather boy, for he did not appear to be over nineteen years of age—with a fine, intelligent face, that was already slightly marred by sensual indulgence. He raised the glass to his lips, with a quick, almost eager motion, and drained it at a single draught.

"Just right," said he, tossing a sixpence to the young bar-tender. "You are first-rate at a brandy-toddy. Never drank a better in my life."

The lad's smiling face told that he was gratified by the compliment. To me the sight was painful, for I saw that this youthful tippler was on dangerous ground.

"Who is that young man in the bar?" I asked, a few minutes afterward, on being rejoined by the landlord.

Simon Slade stepped to the door and looked into the bar for a moment. Two or three men were there by this time; but he was at no loss in answering my question.

"Oh, that's a son of Judge Hammond, who lives in the large brick house just as you enter the village. Willy Hammond, as everybody familiarly calls him, is about the finest young man in our neighbourhood. There is nothing proud or put-on about him—nothing—even if his father is a judge, and rich into the bargain. Every one, gentle or simple, likes Willy Hammond. And then he is such good company. Always so cheerful, and always with a pleasant story on his tongue. And he's so high-spirited withal, and so honourable. Willy Hammond would lose his right hand rather than be guilty of a mean action."

"Landlord!" The voice came loud from the road in front of the house, and Simon Slade again left me to answer the demands of some new comer. I went into the bar-room, in order to take a closer observation of Willy Hammond, in whom an interest, not unmingled with concern, had already been awakened in my mind. I found him engaged in a pleasant conversation with a plain-looking farmer, whose homely, terse, common sense was quite as conspicuous as his fine play of words and lively fancy. The farmer was a substantial conservative, and young Hammond a warm admirer of new ideas and the quicker adaptation of means to ends. I soon saw that his mental powers were developed beyond his years, while his personal qualities were strongly attractive. I understood better, after being a silent listener and observer for ten minutes, why the landlord had spoken of him so warmly.

"Take a brand-toddy, Mr. H——?" said Hammond, after the discussion closed, good humouredly. "Frank, our junior bar-keeper here, beats his father, in that line."

"I don't care if I do," returned the farmer; and the two passed up to the bar.

"Now, Frank, my boy, don't belie my praises," said the young man; "do your handsomest."

"Two brandy-toddies, did you say?" Frank made the inquiry with quite a professional air.

"Just what I did say; and let them be equal to Jove's nectar."

Pleased at this familiarity, the boy went briskly to his work of mixing the tempting compound, while Hammond looked on with an approving smile.

"There," said the latter, as Frank passed the glasses across the counter, "if you don't call that first-rate, you're no judge." And he handed one of them to the farmer, who tasted the agreeable draught, and praised its flavour. As before, I noticed that Hammond drank eagerly, like one athirst—emptying his glass without once taking it from his lips.

Soon after the bar-room was empty; and then I walked around the premises, in company with the landlord, and listened to his praise of everything and his plans and purposes for the future. The house, yard, garden, and out-buildings were in the most perfect order; presenting, in the whole, a model of a village tavern.

"Whatever I do, sir," said the talkative Simon Slade, "I like to do well. I wasn't just raised to tavern-keeping, you must know; but I'm one who can turn his hand to almost any thing."

"What was your business?" I inquired.

"I'm a miller, sir, by trade," he answered—"and a better miller, though I say it myself, is not to be found in Bolton county. I've followed milling these twenty years, and made some little money. But I got tired of hard work, and determined to lead an easier life. So I sold my mill, and built this house with the money. I always thought I'd like tavern-keeping. It's an easy life; and, if rightly seen after, one in which a man is sure to make money."

"You were still doing a fair business with your mill?"

"Oh yes. Whatever I do, I do right. Last year, I put by a thousand dollars above all expenses, which is not bad, I can assure you, for a mere grist mill. If the present owner comes out even, he'll do well!"

"How is that?"

"Oh, he's no miller. Give him the best wheat that is grown, and he'll ruin it in grinding. He takes the life out of every grain. I don't believe he'll keep half the custom that I transferred with the mill."

"A thousand dollars, clear profit, in so useful a business, ought to have satisfied you," said I.

"There you and I differ," answered the landlord. "Every man desires to make as much money as possible, and with the least labour. I hope to make two or three thousand dollars a year, over and above all expenses, at tavern-keeping. My bar alone ought to yield me that sum. A man with a wife and children very naturally tries to do as well by them as possible."

"Very true; but," I ventured to suggest, "will this be doing as well by them as if you had kept on at the mill?"

"Two or three thousand dollars a year against one thousand! Where are your figures, man?"

"There may be something beyond the money to take into the account," said I.

"What?" inquired Slade, with a kind of half credulity.

"Consider the different influences of the two callings in life—that of a miller and a tavern-keeper."

"Well! say on."

"Will your children be as safe from temptation here as in their former home?"

"Just as safe," was the unhesitating answer. "Why not?"

I was about to speak of the alluring glass in the case of Frank, but remembering that I had already expressed a fear in that direction, felt that to do so again would be useless, and so kept silent.

"A tavern-keeper," said Slade, "is just as respectable as a miller—in fact, the very people who used to call me 'Simon,' or 'Neighbour Dustycoat,' now say 'Landlord,' or Mr. Slade, and treat me in every way more as if I were an equal than ever they did before."

"The change," said I, "may be due to the fact of your giving evidence of possessing some means. Men are very apt to be courteous to those who have property. The building of the tavern has, without doubt, contributed to the new estimation in which you are held."

"That isn't all," replied the landlord. "It is because I am keeping a good tavern, and thus materially advancing the interests of Cedarville, that some of our best people look at me with different eyes."

"Advancing the interests of Cedarville! In what way?" I did not apprehend his meaning.

"A good tavern always draws people to a place, while a miserable old tumbledown of an affair, badly kept, such as we have had for years, as surely repels them. You can generally tell something about the condition of a town by looking at its taverns. If they are well kept, and doing a good business, you will hardly be wrong in the conclusion that the place is thriving. Why, already, since I built and opened the 'Sickle and Sheaf,' property has advanced over twenty per cent. along the whole street, and not less than five new houses have been commenced."

"Other causes, besides the simple opening of a new tavern, may have contributed to this result," said I.

"None of which I am aware. I was talking with Judge Hammond only yesterday—he owns a great deal of ground on the street—and he did not hesitate to say, that the building and opening of a good tavern here had increased the value of his property at least five thousand dollars. He said, moreover, that he thought the people of Cedarville ought to present me with a silver pitcher; and that, for one, he would contribute ten dollars for the purpose."

The ringing of the supper bell here interrupted further conversation; and with the best of appetites, I took my way to the room, where a plentiful meal was spread. As I entered, I met the wife of Simon Slade, just passing out, after seeing that everything was in order. I had not observed her before; and now could not help remarking that she had a flushed, excited countenance, as if she had been over a hot fire, and was both worried and fatigued. And there was, moreover, a peculiar expression of the mouth, never observed in one whose mind is entirely at ease—an expression that once seen is never forgotten. The face stamped itself, instantly, on my memory; and I can even now recall it with almost the original distinctness. How strongly it contrasted with that of her smiling, self-satisfied husband, who took his place at the head of his table with an air of conscious importance. I was too hungry to talk much, and so found greater enjoyment in eating than in conversation. The landlord had a more chatty guest by his side, and I left them to entertain each other, while I did ample justice to the excellent food with which the table was liberally provided.

After supper I went to the sitting-room, and remained there until the lamps were lighted. A newspaper occupied my time for perhaps half an hour; then the buzz of voices from the adjoining bar-room, which had been increasing for some time, attracted my attention, and I went in there to see and hear what was passing. The first person upon whom my eyes rested was young Hammond, who sat talking with a man older than himself by several years. At a glance, I saw that this man could only associate himself with Willy Hammond as a tempter. Unscrupulous selfishness was written all over his sinister countenance; and I wondered that it did not strike every one, as it did me, with instant repulsion. There could not be, I felt certain, any common ground of association, for two such persons, but the dead level of a village bar-room. I afterward learned, during the evening, that this man's name was Harvey Green, and that he was an occasional visitor at Cedarville, remaining a few days, or a few weeks at a time, as appeared to suit his fancy, and having no ostensible business or special acquaintance with anybody in the village.

"There is one thing about him," remarked Simon Slade, in answering some question that I put in reference to the man, "that I don't object to; he has plenty of money, and is not at all niggardly in spending it. He used to come here, so he told me, about once in five or six months; but his stay at the miserably kept tavern, the only one then in Cedarville, was so uncomfortable, that he had pretty well made up his mind never to visit us again. Now, however, he has engaged one of my best rooms, for which he pays me by the year, and I am to charge him full board for the time he occupies it. He says that there is something about Cedarville that always attracts him; and that his health is better while here than it is anywhere, except South during the winter season. He'll not leave less than two or three hundred dollars a year in our village—there is one item, for you, of advantage to a place in having a good tavern."

"What is his business?" I asked. "Is he engaged in any trading operations?"

The landlord shrugged his shoulders, and looked slightly mysterious, as he answered—

"I never inquire about the business of a guest. My calling is to entertain strangers. If they are pleased with my house, and pay my bills on presentation, I have no right to seek further. As a miller, I never asked a customer whether he raised, bought, or stole his wheat. It was my business to grind it, and I took care to do it well. Beyond that, it was all his own affair. And so it will be in my new calling. I shall mind my own business and keep my own place."

Besides young Hammond and this Harvey Green, there were, in the bar-room, when I entered, four others besides the landlord. Among these was a Judge Lyman,—so he was addressed—a man between forty and fifty years of age, who had a few weeks before received the Democratic nomination for member of Congress. He was very talkative and very affable, and soon formed a kind of centre of attraction to the bar-room circle. Among other topics of conversation that came up was the new tavern, introduced by the landlord, in whose mind it was, very naturally, the uppermost thought.

"The only wonder to me is," said Judge Lyman, "that nobody had wit enough to see the advantage of a good tavern in Cedarville ten years ago, or enterprise enough to start one. I give our friend Slade the credit of being a shrewd, far-seeing man; and, mark my word for it, in ten years from to-day he will be the richest man in the county."

"Nonsense—Ho! ho!" Simon Slade laughed outright. "The richest man! You forget Judge Hammond."

"No, not even Judge Hammond, with all deference for our clever friend Willy"—and Judge Lyman smiled pleasantly on the young man.

"If he gets richer, somebody will be poorer!" The individual who uttered these words had not spoken before; and I turned to look at him more closely. A glance showed him to be one of a class seen in all bar-rooms; a poor, broken-down inebriate, with the inward power of resistance gone—conscious of having no man's respect, and giving respect to none. There was a shrewd twinkle in his eyes, as he fixed them on Slade, that gave added force to the peculiar tone in which his brief, but telling sentence was uttered. I noticed a slight contraction on the landlord's ample forehead, the first evidence I had yet seen of ruffled feelings. The remark, thrown in so untimely, (or, timely, some will say,) and with a kind of prophetic malice, produced a temporary pause in the conversation. No one answered, or questioned the intruder, who, I could perceive, silently enjoyed the effect of his words. But soon the obstructed current ran on again.

"If our excellent friend, Mr. Slade," said Harvey Green, "is not the richest man in Cedarville at the end of ten years, he will at least enjoy the satisfaction of having made his town richer."

"A true word that," replied Judge Lyman—"as true a word as ever was spoken. What a dead-and-alive place this has been until within the last few months. All vigorous growth had stopped, and we were actually going to seed."

"And the graveyard too"—muttered the individual who had before disturbed the self-satisfied harmony of the company, remarking upon the closing sentence of Harvey Green. "Come, landlord," he added, as he strode across to the bar, speaking in a changed, reckless sort of a way, "fix me up a good hot whisky-punch, and do it right; and there's another sixpence toward the fortune you are bound to make. It's the last one left—not a copper more in my pockets"—and he turned them inside-out, with a half-solemn, half-ludicrous air. "I send it to keep company in your till with four others that have found their way into that snug place since morning, and which will be lonesome without their little friend."

I looked at Simon Slade, his eyes rested on mine for a moment or two, and then sunk beneath my earnest gaze. I saw that his countenance flushed, and that his motions were slightly confused. The incident, it was plain, did not awaken agreeable thoughts. Once I saw his hand move toward the sixpence, that lay upon the counter; but, whether to push it back, or draw it toward the till, I could not determine. The whisky-punch was in due time ready, and with it the man retired to a table across the room, and sat down to enjoy the tempting beverage. As he did so, the landlord quietly swept the poor unfortunate's last sixpence into his drawer. The influence of this strong potation was to render the man a little more talkative. To the free conversation passing around him he lent an attentive ear, dropping in a word, now and then, that always told upon the company like a well-directed blow. At last, Slade lost all patience with him, and said, a little fretfully,—

"Look here, Joe Morgan, if you will be ill-natured, pray go somewhere else, and not interrupt good feeling among gentlemen."

"Got my last sixpence," retorted Joe, turning his pockets inside-out again. "No more use for me here tonight. That's the way of the world. How apt a scholar is our good friend Dustycoat, in this new school!

Well, he was a good miller—no one ever disputed that—and it's plain to see that he is going to make a good landlord. I thought his heart was a little too soft; but the indurating process has begun; and, in less than ten years, if it isn't as hard as one of his old millstones, Joe Morgan is no prophet. Oh, you needn't knit your brows so, friend Simon, we're old friends; and friends are privileged to speak plain."

"I wish you'd go home. You're not yourself, tonight," said the landlord, a little coaxingly—for he saw that nothing was to be gained by quarrelling with Morgan. "Maybe my heart *is* growing harder," he added, with affected-good humour; "and it is time, perhaps. One of my weaknesses, I have heard even you say, was being too woman-hearted."

"No danger of that now," retorted Joe Morgan. "I've known a good many landlords in my time, but can't remember one that was troubled with the disease that once afflicted you."

Just at this moment the outer door was pushed open with a slow, hesitating motion; then a little pale face peered in, and a pair of soft blue eyes went searching about the room. Conversation was instantly hushed, and every face, excited with interest, turned toward the child, who had now stepped through the door. She was not over ten years of age; but it moved the heart to look upon the saddened expression of her young countenance, and the forced bravery therein, that scarcely overcame the native timidity so touchingly visible.

"Father!" I have never heard this word spoken in a voice that sent such a thrill along every nerve. It was full of sorrowful love—full of a tender concern that had its origin too deep for the heart of a child. As she spoke, the little one sprang across the room, and laying her hands upon the arm of Joe Morgan, lifted her eyes, that were ready to gush over with tears, to his face.

"Come, father! won't you come home?" I hear that low, pleading voice even now, and my heart gives a quicker throb. Poor child! Darkly shadowed was the sky that bent gloomily over thy young life.

Morgan arose, and suffered the child to lead him from the room. He seemed passive in her hands. I noticed that he thrust his fingers nervously into his pocket, and that a troubled look went over his face as they were withdrawn. His last sixpence was in the till of Simon Slade!

The first man who spoke was Harvey Green, and this not for a minute after the father and his child had vanished through the door.

"If I was in your place, landlord"—his voice was cold and unfeeling —"I'd pitch that fellow out of the bar-room the next time he stepped through the door. He's no business here, in the first place; and, in the second, he doesn't know how to behave himself. There's no telling how much a vagabond like him injures a respectable house."

"I wish he would stay away," said Simon, with a perplexed air.

"I'd *make* him stay away," answered Green.

"That may be easier said than done," remarked Judge Lyman. "Our friend keeps a public-house, and can't just say who shall or who shall not come into it."

"But such a fellow has no business here. He's a good-for-nothing sot. If I kept a tavern, I'd refuse to sell him liquor."

"That you might do," said Judge Lyman—"and I presume your hint will not be lost on our friend Slade."

"He will have liquor, so long as he can get a cent to buy it with," remarked one of the company; "and I don't see why our landlord here, who has gone to so much expense to fit up a tavern, shouldn't have the sale of it as well as anybody else. Joe talks a little freely sometimes; but no one can say that he is quarrelsome. You've got to take him as he is, that's all."

"I'm one," retorted Harvey Green, with a slightly ruffled manner, "who is never disposed to take people as they are when they choose to render themselves disagreeable. If I was Mr. Slade, as I remarked in the beginning, I'd pitch that fellow into the road the next time he put his foot over my door-step."

"Not if I were present," remarked the other coolly.

Green was on his feet in a moment; and I saw, from the flash of his eyes, that he was a man of evil passions. Moving a pace or two in the direction of the other, he said sharply—

"What is that, sir?"

The individual against whom his anger was so suddenly aroused was dressed plainly, and had the appearance of a working-man. He was stout and muscular.

"I presume you heard my words. They were spoken distinctly," he replied, not moving from where he sat, nor seeming to be in the least disturbed. But there was cool defiance in the tones of his voice and in the steady look of his eyes.

"You're an impertinent fellow, and I'm half tempted to chastise you."

Green had scarcely finished the sentence, ere he was lying at full length upon the floor! The other had sprung upon him like a tiger, and with one blow from his heavy fist, struck him down as if he had been a child. For a moment or two, Green lay stunned and bewildered —then, starting up with a savage cry, that sounded more bestial than human, he draw a long knife from a concealed sheath, and attempted to stab his assailant; but the murderous purpose was not accomplished, for the other man, who had superior strength and coolness, saw the design, and with a well-directed blow almost broke the arm of Green, causing the knife to leave his hand and glide far across the room.

"I'm half tempted to wring your neck off," exclaimed the man, whose name was Lyon, now much excited; and seizing Green by the throat, he strangled him until his face grew black. "Draw a knife on me, ha! You murdering villain!" And he gripped him tighter.

Judge Lyman and the landlord now interfered, and rescued Green from the hands of his fully aroused antagonist. For some time they stood growling at each other, like two parted dogs, struggling to get free, in order to renew the conflict, but gradually cooled off. In a little while Judge Lyman drew Green aside, and the two men left the bar-room together. In the door, as they were retiring, the former slightly nodded to Willy Hammond, who soon followed them, going into the sitting-room; and from thence, as I could perceive, upstairs, to an apartment above.

"Not after much good," I heard Lyon mutter to himself. "If Judge Hammond don't look a little closer after that boy of his, he'll be sorry for it, that's all."

"Who is this Green?" I asked of Lyon, finding myself alone with him in the bar-room, soon after.

"A black-leg, I take it," was his unhesitating answer.

"Does Judge Lyman suspect his real character?"

"I don't know any thing about that; but, I wouldn't be afraid to bet ten dollars, that if you could look in upon them now, you would find cards in their hands."

"What a school, and what teachers for the youth who just went with them!" I could not helping remarking.

"Willy Hammond?"

"Yes."

"You may well say that. What can his father be thinking about to leave him exposed to such influences!"

"He's one of the few who are in raptures about this tavern, because its erection has slightly increased the value of his property about here; but, if he is not the loser of fifty per cent. for every one gained, before ten years go by, I'm very much in error."

"How so?"

"It will prove, I fear, the open door to ruin for his son."

"That's bad," said I.

"Bad! It is awful to think of. There is not a finer young man in the country; nor one with better mind and heart than Willy Hammond. So much the sadder will be his destruction. Ah, sir! this tavern-keeping is a curse to any place."

"But I thought, just now, that you spoke in favour of letting even the poor drunkard's money go into our landlord's till, in order to encourage his commendable enterprise in opening so good a tavern."

"We all speak with covert irony sometimes," answered the man, "as

I did then. Poor Joe Morgan! He is an old and early friend of Simon
Slade. They were boys together, and worked as millers under the
same roof for many years. In fact, Joe's father owned the mill, and the
two learned their trade with him. When old Morgan died, the mill
came into Joe's hands. It was in rather a worn-out condition, and Joe
went in debt for some pretty thorough repairs and additions of machinery. By and by, Simon Slade, who was hired by Joe to run the
mill, received a couple of thousand dollars at the death of an aunt.
This sum enabled him to buy a share in the mill, which Morgan was
very glad to sell in order to get clear of his debt. Time passed on, and
Joe left his milling interest almost entirely in the care of Slade, who, it
must be said in his favour, did not neglect the business. But it somehow happened—I will not say unfairly—that, at the end of ten years,
Joe Morgan no longer owned a share in the mill. The whole property
was in the hands of Slade. People did not much wonder at this; for
while Slade was always to be found at the mill, industrious, active,
and attentive to customers, Morgan was rarely seen on the premises.
You would oftener find him in the woods, with a gun over his shoulder, or sitting by a trout brook, or lounging at the tavern. And yet everybody liked Joe; for he was companionable, quick-witted, and very
kind-hearted. He would say sharp things, sometimes, when people
manifested little meannesses; but there was so much honey in his gall,
that bitterness rarely predominated.

"A year or two before his ownership in the mill ceased, Morgan
married one of the sweetest girls in our town—Fanny Ellis, that was
her name, and she could have had her pick of the young men. Everybody affected to wonder at her choice; and yet nobody really did
wonder, for Joe was an attractive young man, take him as you would,
and just the one to win the heart of a girl like Fanny. What if he had
been seen, now and then, a little the worse for drink! What if he
showed more fondness for pleasure than for business! Fanny did not
look into the future with doubt or fear. She believed that her love was
strong enough to win him from all evil allurements; and, as for this
world's goods, they were matters in which her maiden fancies rarely
busied themselves.

"Well. Dark days came for her, poor soul! And yet, in all the darkness of her earthly lot, she has never, it is said, been any thing but a
loving, forbearing, self-denying wife to Morgan. And he—fallen as he
is, and powerless in the grasp of the monster intemperance—has never,
I am sure, hurt her with a cruel word. Had he added these, her heart
would, long ere this, have broken. Poor Joe Morgan! Poor Fanny! Oh,
what a curse is this drink!"

The man, warming with his theme, had spoken with an eloquence I had not expected from his lips. Slightly overmastered by his feelings, he paused for a moment or two, and then added.

"It was unfortunate for Joe, at least, that Slade sold his mill, and became a tavern-keeper; for Joe had a sure berth, and wages regularly paid. He didn't always stick to his work, but would go off on a spree every now and then; but Slade bore with all this, and worked harder himself to make up for his hand's shortcoming. And no matter what deficiency the little store-room at home might show, Fanny Morgan never found her meal barrel empty without knowing where to get it replenished.

"But, after Slade sold the mill, a sad change took place. The new owner was little disposed to pay wages to a hand who would not give him all his time during working hours; and in less than two weeks from the day he took possession, Morgan was discharged. Since then, he has been working about at one odd job and another, earning scarcely enough to buy the liquor it requires to feed the inordinate thirst that is consuming him. I am not disposed to blame Simon Slade for the wrong-doing of Morgan; but here is a simple fact in the case— if he had kept on at the useful calling of a miller, he would have saved this man's family from want, suffering, and a lower deep of misery than that into which they have already fallen. I merely state it, and you can draw your own conclusion. It is one of the many facts, on the other side of this tavern question, which it will do no harm to mention. I have noted a good many facts besides, and one is, that before Slade opened the "Sickle and Sheaf," he did all in his power to save his early friend from the curse of intemperance; now he has become his tempter. Heretofore, it was his hand that provided the means for his family to live in some small degree of comfort; now he takes the poor pittance the wretched man earns, and dropping it in his till, forgets the wife and children at home who are hungry for the bread this money should have purchased.

"Joe Morgan, fallen as he is, sir, is no fool. His mind sees quickly yet; and he rarely utters a sentiment that is not full of meaning. When he spoke of Slade's heart growing as hard in ten years as one of his old millstones, he was not uttering words at random, nor merely indulging in a harsh sentiment, little caring whether it were closely applicable or not. That the indurating process had begun, he, alas! was too sadly conscious."

The landlord had been absent from the room for some time. He left soon after Judge Lyman, Harvey Green, and Willy Hammond withdrew, and I did not see him again during the evening. His son Frank was left to attend at the bar; no very hard task, for not more than half a dozen called in to drink from the time Morgan left until the bar was closed.

While Mr. Lyon was giving me the brief history just recorded, I noticed a little incident that caused a troubled feeling to pervade my mind. After a man, for whom the landlord's son had prepared a fancy drink, had nearly emptied his glass, he sat it down upon the counter and went out. A tablespoonful or two remained in the glass, and I noticed Frank, after smelling at it two or three times, put the glass to his lips and sip the sweetened liquor. The flavour proved agreeable; for after tasting it, he raised the glass again and drained every drop.

"Frank!" I heard a low voice, in a warning tone, pronounce the name, and glancing toward a door partly opened, that led from the inside of the bar to the yard, I saw the face of Mrs. Slade. It had the same troubled expression I had noticed before, but now blended with more of anxiety.

The boy went out at the call of his mother; and when a new customer entered, I noticed that Flora, the daughter, came in to wait upon him. I noticed, too, that while she poured out the liquor, there was a heightened colour on her face, in which I fancied that I saw a tinge of shame. It is certain that she was not in the least gracious to the person on whom she was waiting; and that there was little heart in her manner of performing the task.

Ten o'clock found me alone and musing in the bar-room over the occurrences of the evening. Of all the incidents, that of the entrance of Joe Morgan's child kept the most prominent place in my thoughts. The picture of that mournful little face was ever before me; and I seemed all the while to hear the word "Father," uttered so touchingly, and yet with such a world of childish tenderness. And the man, who would have opposed the most stubborn resistance to his fellow men, had they sought to force him from the room, going passively, almost meekly out, led by that little child—I could not, for a time, turn my thoughts from the image thereof! And then thought bore me to the wretched home, back to which the gentle, loving child had taken her father, and my heart grew faint in me as imagination busied itself with all the misery there.

And Willy Hammond. The little that I had heard and seen of him greatly interested me in his favour. Ah! upon what dangerous ground was he treading. How many pitfalls awaited his feet—how near they were to the brink of a fearful precipice, down which to fall was certain destruction. How beautiful had been his life-promise! How fair the opening day of his existence! Alas! the clouds were gathering already, and the low rumble of the distant thunder presaged the coming of a fearful tempest. Was there none to warn him of the danger? Alas! all might now come too late, for so few who enter the path in which his steps were treading will hearken to friendly counsel, or heed the solemn warning. Where was he now? This question recurred over and over again. He had left the bar-room with Judge Lyman and Green early in the evening, and had not made his appearance since. Who and what was Green? And Judge Lyman, was he a man of principle? One with whom it was safe to trust a youth like Willy Hammond?

While I mused thus, the bar-room door opened, and a man past the prime of life, with a somewhat florid face, which gave a strong relief to the gray, almost white hair that, suffered to grow freely, was pushed back, and lay in heavy masses on his coat collar, entered with a hasty step. He was almost venerable in appearance; yet, there was in his dark, quick eyes the brightness of unquenched loves, the fires of which were kindled at the altars of selfishness and sensuality. This I saw at a glance. There was a look of concern on his face, as he threw his eyes around the bar-room; and he seemed disappointed, I thought, at finding it empty.

"Is Simon Slade here?"

As I answered in the negative, Mrs. Slade entered through the door that opened from the yard, and stood behind the counter.

"Ah, Mrs. Slade! Good evening, madam!" he said.

"Good evening, Judge Hammond."

"Is your husband at home?"

"I believe he is," answered Mrs. Slade. "I think he's somewhere about the house."

"Ask him to step here, will you?"

Mrs. Slade went out. Nearly five minutes went by, during which time Judge Hammond paced the floor of the bar-room uneasily. Then the landlord made his appearance. The free, open, manly, self-satisfied expression of his countenance, which I had remarked on alighting from the stage in the afternoon, was gone. I noticed at once the change, for it was striking. He did not look steadily into the face of Judge Hammond, who asked him in a low voice, if his son had been there during the evening.

"He was here," said Slade.

"When?"

"He came in some time after dark and stayed, maybe, an hour."

"And hasn't been here since?"

"It's nearly two hours since he left the bar-room," replied the landlord.

Judge Hammond seemed perplexed. There was a degree of evasion in Slade's manner that he could hardly help noticing. To me it was all apparent, for I had lively suspicions that made my observation acute.

Judge Hammond crossed his arms behind him, and took three or four strides about the floor.

"Was Judge Lyman here to-night?" he then asked.

"He was," answered Slade.

"Did he and Willy go out together?"

The question seemed an unexpected one for the landlord. Slade appeared slightly confused, and did not answer promptly.

"I—I rather think they did," he said, after a brief hesitation.

"Ah, well! Perhaps he is at Judge Lyman's. I will call over there."

And Judge Hammond left the bar-room.

"Would you like to retire, sir?" said the landlord, now turning to me, with a forced smile—I saw that it was forced.

"If you please," I answered.

He lit a candle and conducted me to my room, where, overwearied with the day's exertion, I soon fell asleep, and did not awake until the sun was shining brightly into my windows.

I remained at the village a portion of the day, but saw nothing of the parties in whom the incidents of the previous evening had awakened a lively interest. At four o'clock I left in the stage, and did not visit Cedarville again for a year.

☞ *Night the Second* ☜

THE CHANGES OF A YEAR

A cordial grasp of the hand and a few words of hearty welcome greeted me as I alighted from the stage at the "Sickle and Sheaf," on my next visit to Cedarville. At the first glance, I saw no change in the countenance, manner, or general bearing of Simon Slade, the landlord. With him, the year seemed to have passed like a pleasant summer day. His face was round, and full, and rosy, and his eyes sparkled with that good-humour which flows from intense self-satisfaction. Everything about him seemed to say—"All right with myself and the world."

I had scarcely expected this. From what I saw during my last brief sojourn at the "Sickle and Sheaf," the inference was natural, that elements had been called into activity, which must produce changes adverse to those pleasant states of mind that threw an almost perpetual sunshine over the landlord's countenance. How many hundreds of times had I thought of Joe Morgan and Willy Hammond—of Frank, and the temptations to which a bar-room exposed him. The heart of Slade must, indeed, be as hard as one of his old mill-stones, if he could remain an unmoved witness of the corruption and degradation of these.

"My fears have outrun the actual progress of things," said I to myself, with a sense of relief, as I mused alone in the still neatly arranged sitting-room, after the landlord, who sat and chatted for a few minutes, had left me. "There is, I am willing to believe, a basis of good in this man's character, which has led him to remove, as far as possible, the more palpable evils that ever attach themselves to a house of public entertainment. He had but entered on the business last year. There was much to be learned, pondered, and corrected. Experience, I doubt not, has led to many important changes in the manner of conducting the establishment, and especially in what pertains to the bar."

As I thought thus, my eyes glanced through the half open door, and rested on the face of Simon Slade. He was standing behind his bar—evidently alone in the room—with his head bent in a musing attitude. At first I was in some doubt as to the identity of the singularly changed countenance. Two deep perpendicular seams lay sharply defined on his forehead—the arch of his eyebrows was gone, and from each corner of his compressed lips, lines were seen reaching halfway to the chin. Blending with a slightly troubled expression, was a strongly marked selfishness, evidently brooding over the consummation of its purpose. For some moments I sat gazing on this face, half doubting at times if it were really that of Simon Slade. Suddenly, a gleam flashed over it—an ejaculation was uttered, and one clenched hand brought down, with a sharp stroke, into the open palm of the other. The landlord's mind had reached a conclusion, and was resolved upon action. There were no warm rays in the gleam of light that irradiated his countenance—at least none for my heart, which felt under them an almost icy coldness.

"Just the man I was thinking about," I heard the landlord say, as some one entered the bar, while his whole manner underwent a sudden change.

"The old saying is true," was answered in a voice, the tones of which were familiar to my ears.

"Thinking of the old Harry?" said Slade.

"Yes."

"True, literally, in the present case," I heard the landlord remark, though in a much lower tone; "for, if you are not the devil himself, you can't be farther removed than a second cousin."

A low, gurgling laugh met this little sally. There was something in it so unlike a human laugh, that it caused my blood to trickle, for a moment, coldly along my veins.

I heard nothing more except the murmur of voices in the bar, for a hand shut the partly opened door that led from the sitting-room.

Whose was that voice? I recalled its tones, and tried to fix in my thought the person to whom it belonged, but was unable to do so. I was not very long in doubt, for on stepping out upon the porch in front of the tavern, the well-remembered face of Harvey Green presented itself. He stood in the bar-room door, and was talking earnestly to Slade, whose back was toward me. I saw that he recognised me, although I had not passed a word with him on the occasion of my former visit; and there was a lighting up of his countenance as if about to speak—but I withdrew my eyes from his face to avoid the unwelcome greeting. When I looked at him again, I saw that he was regarding me with a sinister glance, which was instantly withdrawn. In what broad, black characters was the word TEMPTER written on his face! How was it possible for any one to look thereon, and not read the warning inscription!

Soon after, he withdrew into the bar-room, and the landlord came and took a seat near me on the porch.

"How is the Sickle and Sheaf coming on?" I inquired.

"First-rate," was the answer—"First-rate."

"As well as you expected?"

"Better."

"Satisfied with your experiment."

"Perfectly. Couldn't get me back to the rumbling old mill again, if you were to make me a present of it."

"What of the mill?" I asked. "How does the new owner come on?"

"About as I thought it would be."

"Not doing very well?"

"How could it be expected, when he didn't know enough of the milling business to grind a bushel of wheat right. He lost half of the custom I transferred to him in less than three months. Then he broke his main shaft, and it took over three weeks to get in a new one. Half of his remaining customers discovered by this time, that they could get far better meal from their grain at Harwood's mill near Lynwood, and so did not care to trouble him any more. The upshot of the whole matter is, he broke down next, and had to sell the mill at a heavy loss."

"Who has it now?"

"Judge Hammond is the purchaser."

"He is going to rent it, I suppose?"

"No; I believe he means to turn it into some kind of a factory—and, I rather think, will connect therewith a distillery. This is a fine grain-growing country, as you know. If he does set up a distillery, he'll make a fine thing of it. Grain has been too low in this section for some years: this all the farmers have felt, and they are very much pleased at the idea. It will help them wonderfully. I always thought my mill a great thing for the farmers; but what I did for them was a mere song compared to the advantage of an extensive distillery."

"Judge Hammond is one of your richest men?"

"Yes—the richest in the county. And what is more, he's a shrewd, far-seeing man, and knows how to multiply his riches."

"How is his son Willy coming on?"

"Oh! first-rate."

The landlord's eyes fell under the searching look I bent upon him.

"How old is he now?"

"Just twenty."

"A critical age," I remarked.

"So people say; but I didn't find it so," answered Slade, a little distantly.

"The impulses within and the temptations without, are the measure of its dangers. At his age, you were, no doubt, daily employed at hard work."

"I was, and no mistake."

"Thousands and hundred of thousands are indebted to useful work, occupying many hours through each day, and leaving them with wearied bodies at night, for their safe passage from yielding youth to firm, resisting manhood. It might not be with you as it is now, had leisure and freedom to go in and out when you pleased, been offered at the age of nineteen."

"I can't tell as to that," said the landlord, shrugging his shoulders. "But I don't see that Willy Hammond is in any especial danger. He is a young man with many admirable qualities—is social—liberal—generous almost to a fault—but has good common sense, and wit enough, I take it, to keep out of harm's way."

A man passing the house at the moment, gave Simon Slade an opportunity to break off a conversation, that was not, I could see, altogether agreeable. As he left me, I arose and stepped into the bar-room. Frank, the landlord's son, was behind the bar. He had grown considerably in the year—and from a rather delicate, innocent-looking boy, to a stout, bold lad. His face was rounder, and had a gross, sensual expression, that showed itself particularly about the mouth. The man Green was standing beside the bar talking to him, and I noticed that Frank laughed heartily, at some low, half obscene remarks that he was making. In the midst of these, Flora, the sister of Frank, a really beautiful girl, came in to get something from the bar. Green spoke to her familiarly, and Flora answered him with a perceptibly heightening colour.

I glanced toward Frank, half expecting to see an indignant flush on his young face. But no—he looked on with a smile! "Ah!" thought I, "have the boy's pure impulses so soon died out in this fatal atmosphere? Can he bear to see those evil eyes—he knows they are evil—rest upon the face of his sister? or to hear those lips, only a moment since polluted with vile words, address her with the familarity of friend?"

"Fine girl, that sister of yours, Frank! Fine girl!" said Green, after Flora had withdrawn—speaking of her with about as much respect in his voice as if he were praising a fleet racer or favourite hound.

The boy smiled, with a pleased air.

"I must try and find her a good husband, Frank. I wonder if she wouldn't have me?"

"You'd better ask her," said the boy, laughing.

"I would, if I thought there was any chance for me."

"Nothing like trying. Faint heart never won fair lady," returned Frank, more with the air of a man than a boy. How fast he was growing old!

"A banter, by George!" exclaimed Green, slapping his hands together. "You're a great boy, Frank! a great boy! I shall have to talk to your father about you. Coming on too fast. Have to be put back in your lessons—hey!"

And Green winked at the boy, and shook his finger at him. Frank laughed in a pleased way, as he replied—

"I guess I'll do."

"I guess you will," said Green, as, satisfied with his colloquy, he turned off and left the bar-room.

"Have something to drink, sir?" inquired Frank, addressing me in a bold, free way.

I shook my head.

"Here's a newspaper," he added.

I took the paper and sat down—not to read, but to observe. Two or three men soon came in, and spoke in a very familiar way to Frank, who was presently busy setting out the liquors they had called for. Their conversation, interlarded with much that was profane and vulgar, was of horses, horse-racing, gunning, and the like, to all of which the young bar-keeper lent an attentive ear, putting in a word now and then, and showing an intelligence in such matters quite beyond his

age. In the midst thereof, Mr. Slade made his appearance. His presence caused a marked change in Frank, who retired from his place
among the men, a step or two outside of the bar, and did not make a
remark while his father remained. It was plain from this, that Mr.
Slade was not only aware of Frank's dangerous precocity, but had already marked his forwardness by rebuke.

So far, all that I had seen and heard impressed me unfavourably,
notwithstanding the declaration of Simon Slade, that everything
about the "Sickle and Sheaf" was coming on "first-rate," and that he
was "perfectly satisfied" with his experiment. Why, even if the man
had gained, in money, fifty thousand dollars by tavern-keeping in a
year, he had lost a jewel in the innocence of his boy that was beyond
all valuation. "Perfectly satisfied?" Impossible! He was not perfectly
satisfied. How could he be? The look thrown upon Frank when he entered the bar-room, and saw him "hale fellow, well met," with three or
four idle, profane, drinking customers, contradicted that assertion.

After supper, I took a seat in the bar-room, to see how life moved
on in that place of rendezvous for the surface-population of Cedarville. Interest enough in the characters I had met there a year before
remained, for me to choose this way of spending the time, instead of
visiting at the house of a gentleman who had kindly invited me to
pass an evening with his family.

The bar-room custom, I soon found, had largely increased in a year.
It now required, for a good part of the time, the active services of
both the landlord and his son to meet the calls for liquor. What
pained me most, was to see the large number of lads and young men
who came in to lounge and drink; and there was scarcely one of them
whose face did not show marks of sensuality, or whose language was
not marred by obscenity, profanity, or vulgar slang. The subjects of
conversation were varied enough, though politics was the most prominent. In regard to politics, I heard nothing in the least instructive; but
only abuse of individuals and dogmatism on public measures. They
were all exceedingly confident in assertion; but I listened in vain for
exposition, or even for demonstrative facts. He who asseverated in the
most positive manner, and swore the hardest, carried the day in the
petty contests.

I noticed, early in the evening, and at a time when all the inmates
of the room were in the best possible humour with themselves, the entrance of an elderly man, on whose face I instantly read a deep concern. It was one of those mild, yet strongly marked faces, that strike
you at a glance. The forehead was broad, the eyes large and far back
in their sockets, the lips full but firm. You saw evidences of a strong,
but well balanced character. As he came in, I noticed a look of intelli-

gence pass from one to another; and then the eyes of two or three were fixed upon a young man who was seated not far from me, with his back to the entrance, playing at dominos. He had a glass of ale by his side. The old man searched about the room for some moments, before his glance rested upon the individual I have mentioned. My eyes were full upon his face, as he advanced toward him, yet unseen. Upon it was not a sign of angry excitement, but a most touching sorrow.

"Edward!" he said, as he laid his hand gently on the young man's shoulder. The latter started at the voice, and crimsoned deeply. A few moments he sat irresolute.

"Edward, my son!" It would have been a cold, hard heart indeed that softened not under the melting tenderness of these tones. The call was irresistible, and obedience a necessity. The powers of evil had, yet, too feeble a grasp on the young man's heart to hold him in thrall. Rising with a half-reluctant manner, and with a shamefacedness that it was impossible to conceal, he retired as quietly as possible. The notice of only a few in the bar-room was attracted by the incident.

"I can tell you what," I heard the individual, with whom the young man had been playing at dominos, remark—himself not twenty years of age—"if my old man were to make a fool of himself in this way—sneaking around after me in bar-rooms—he'd get only his trouble for his pains. I'd like to see him try it, though! There'd be a nice time of it, I guess. Wouldn't I creep off with him, as meek as a lamb! Ho! ho!"

"Who is that old gentleman who came in just now?" I inquired of the person who thus commented on the incident which had just occurred.

"Mr. Hargrove is his name."

"And that was his son?"

"Yes; and I'm only sorry he doesn't possess a little more spirit."

"How old is he?"

"About twenty."

"Not of legal age, then?"

"He's old enough to be his own master."

"The law says differently," I suggested.

In answer, the young man cursed the law, snapping his fingers in its imaginary face as he did so.

"At least you will admit," said I, "that Edward Hargrove, in the use of a liberty to go where he pleases, and do what he pleases, exhibits but small discretion."

"I will admit no such thing. What harm is there, I would like to know, in a social little game such as we were playing? There were no stakes—we were not gambling."

I pointed to the half-emptied glass of ale left by young Hargrove.

"Oh! oh!" half sneered, half laughed a man, twice the age of the one I had addressed, who sat near by, listening to our conversation. I looked at him for a moment, and then said—

"The great danger lies there, without doubt. If it were only a glass of ale and a game of dominos—but it doesn't stop there, and well the young man's father knows it."

"Perhaps he does," was answered. "I remember him in his younger days; and a pretty high boy he was. He didn't stop at a glass of ale and a game at dominos; not he! I've seen him as drunk as a lord many a time; and many a time at a horse-race, or cock-fight, betting with the bravest. I was only a boy, though a pretty old boy; but I can tell you, Hargrove was no saint."

"I wonder not, then, that he is anxious for his son," was my remark. "He knows well the lurking dangers in the path he seems inclined to enter."

"I don't see that they have done him much harm. He sowed his wild oats—then got married, and settled down into a good, substantial citizen. A little too religious and pharisaical, I always thought; but upright in his dealings. He had his pleasures in early life, as was befitting the season of youth—why not let his son taste of the same agreeable fruit? He's wrong, sir—wrong! And I've said as much to Ned. I only wish the boy had showed the right spunk this evening, and told the old man to go home about his business."

"So do I," chimed in the young disciple in this bad school. "It's what I'd say to my old man, in double-quick time, if he was to come hunting after me."

"He knows better than to do that," said the other, in a way that let me deeper into the young man's character.

"Indeed he does. He's tried his hand on me once or twice during the last year, but found it wouldn't do, no how; Tom Peters is out of his leading-strings."

"And can drink his glass with any one, and not be a grain the worse for it."

"Exactly, old boy!" said Peters, slapping his preceptor on the knee. "Exactly! I'm not one of your weak-headed ones. Oh no!"

"Look here, Joe Morgan!"—the half angry voice of Simon Slade now rung through the bar-room,—"just take yourself off home!"

I had not observed the entrance of this person. He was standing at the bar, with an emptied glass in his hand. A year had made no improvement in his appearance. On the contrary, his clothes were more worn and tattered; his countenance more sadly marred. What he had said to irritate the landlord, I know not; but Slade's face was fiery with passion, and his eyes glared threateningly at the poor besotted one, who showed not the least inclination to obey.

"Off with you, I say! And never show your face here again. I won't have such low vagabonds as you are about my house. If you can't keep decent and stay decent, don't intrude yourself here."

"A rum-seller talk of decency!" retorted Morgan. "Pah! You were a decent man once, and a good miller into the bargain. But that time's past and gone. Decency died out when you exchanged the pick and facing-hammer for the glass and muddler. Decency! Pah! How you talk! As if it were any more decent to sell rum than to drink it."

There was so much of biting contempt in the tones, as well as the words of the half intoxicated man, that Slade, who had himself been drinking rather more freely than usual, was angered beyond self-control. Catching up an empty glass from the counter, he hurled it with all his strength at the head of Joe Morgan. The missive just grazed one of his temples, and flew by on its dangerous course. The quick sharp cry of a child startled the air, followed by exclamations of alarm and horror from many voices.

"It's Joe Morgan's child!" "He's killed her!" "Good heavens!" Such were the exclamations that rang through the room. I was among the first to reach the spot where a little girl, just gliding in through the door, had been struck on the forehead by the glass, which had cut a deep gash, and stunned her into insensibility. The blood flowed instantly from the wound, and covered her face, which presented a shocking appearance. As I lifted her from the floor, upon which she had fallen, Morgan, into whose very soul the piercing cry of his child had penetrated, stood by my side, and grappled his arms around her insensible form, uttering as he did so heart-touching moans and lamentations.

"What's the matter? Oh, what's the matter?" It was a woman's voice, speaking in frightened tones.

"It's nothing! Just go out, will you, Ann!" I heard the landlord say.

But his wife—it was Mrs. Slade—having heard the shrieks of pain and terror uttered by Morgan's child, had come running into the bar-room—heeded not his words, but pressed forward into the little group that stood around the bleeding girl.

"Run for Doctor Green, Frank," she cried in an imperative voice, the moment her eyes rested on the little one's bloody face.

Frank came around from behind the bar, in obedience to the word; but his father gave a partial countermand, and he stood still. Upon observing which, his mother repeated the order, even more emphatically.

"Why don't you jump, you young rascal!" exclaimed Harvey Green. "The child may be dead before the doctor can get here."

Frank hesitated no longer, but disappeared instantly through the door.

"Poor, poor child!" Almost sobbed Mrs. Slade, as she lifted the insensible form from my arms. "How did it happen? Who struck her?"

"Who? Curse him! Who but Simon Slade?" answered Joe Morgan, through his clenched teeth.

The look of anguish, mingled with bitter reproach, instantly thrown upon the landlord by his wife, can hardly be forgotten by any who saw it that night.

"Oh, Simon! Simon! And has it come to this already?" What a world of bitter memories, and sad forebodings of evil, did that little sentence express. "To this already"—Ah! In the downward way, how rapidly the steps do tread—how fast the progress!

"Bring me a basin of water, and a towel, quickly!" she now exclaimed.

The water was brought, and in a little while the face of the child lay pure and white as snow against her bosom. The wound from which the blood had flowed so freely was found on the upper part of the forehead, a little to the side, and extending several inches back, along the top of the head. As soon as the blood stains were wiped away, and the effusion partially stopped, Mrs. Slade carried the still insensible body into the next room, whither the distressed, and now completely sobered father, accompanied her. I went with them, but Slade remained behind.

The arrival of the doctor was soon followed by the restoration of life to the inanimate body. He happened to be at home, and came instantly. He had just taken the last stitch in the wound, which required to be drawn together, and was applying strips of adhesive plaster, when the hurried entrance of some one caused me to look up. What an apparition met my eyes! A woman stood in the door, with a face in which maternal anxiety and terror blended fearfully. Her countenance was like ashes—her eyes straining wildly—her lips aparts, while the panting breath almost hissed through them.

"Joe! Joe! What is it? Where is Mary? Is she dead?" were her eager inquiries.

"No, Fanny," answered Joe Morgan, starting up from where he was actually kneeling by the side of the reviving little one, and going quickly to his wife. "She's better now. It's a bad hurt, but the doctor says it's nothing dangerous. Poor, dear child!"

The pale face of the mother grew paler—she gasped—caught for breath two or three times—a low shudder ran through her frame—and then she lay white and pulseless in the arms of her husband. As the doctor applied restoratives, I had opportunity to note more particularly the appearance of Mrs. Morgan. Her person was very slender, and her face so attenuated that it might almost be called shadowy. Her hair, which was a rich chestnut brown, with a slight golden lustre, had fallen from her comb, and now lay all over her neck and bosom in beautiful luxuriance. Back from her full temples it had been smoothed away by the hand of Morgan, that all the while moved over her brow and temples with a caressing motion that I saw was unconscious, and which revealed the tenderness of feeling with which, debased as he was, he regarded the wife of his youth, and the long suffering companion of his later and evil days. Her dress was plain and coarse, but clean and well fitting; and about her whole person was an air of neatness and taste. She could not now be called beautiful; yet in her marred features—marred by suffering and grief—were many lineaments of beauty; and much that told of a pure, true woman's heart beating in her bosom. Life came slowly back to the stilled heart, and it was nearly half an hour before the circle of motion was fully restored.

Then, the twain, with their child, tenderly borne in the arms of her father, went sadly homeward, leaving more than one heart heavier for their visit.

I saw more of the landlord's wife on this occasion than before. She had acted with a promptness and humanity that impressed me very favourably. It was plain, from her exclamations on learning that her husband's hand inflicted the blow that came so near destroying the child's life, that her faith for good in the tavern-keeping experiment had never been strong. I had already inferred as much. Her face, the few times I had seen her, wore a troubled look; and I could never forget its expression, nor her anxious, warning voice, when she discovered Frank sipping the dregs from a glass in the bar-room.

It is rarely, I believe, that wives consent freely to the opening of taverns by their husbands; and the determination on the part of the latter to do so, is not infrequently attended with a breach of confidence and good feeling, never afterward fully healed. Men look close to the money result; women to the moral consequences. I doubt if there be one dram-seller in ten, between whom and his wife there exists a good understanding—to say nothing of genuine affection. And, in the exceptional cases, it will generally be found that the wife is as mercenary, or careless of the public good, as her husband. I have known some women to set up grog-shops; but they were women of bad principles and worse hearts. I remember one case, where a woman, with a sober, church-going husband, opened a dram-shop. The husband opposed, remonstrated, begged, threatened—but all to no purpose. The wife, by working for the clothing stores, had earned and saved about three hundred dollars. The love of money, in the slow process of accumulation, had been awakened; and, in ministering to the depraved appetites of men who loved drink and neglected their families, she saw a quicker mode of acquiring the gold she coveted. And so the dram-shop was opened. And what was the result? The husband quit going to church. He had no heart for that; for, even on the Sabbath-day, the fiery stream was stayed not in his house. Next he began to tipple. Soon, alas! the subtle poison so pervaded his system that morbid desire came; and then he moved along quick-footed in the way to ruin. In less than three years, I think, from the time the grog-shop was opened by his wife, he was in a drunkard's grave. A year or two more, and the pit that was digged for others by the hand of the wife, she fell into herself. Ever breathing an atmosphere, poisoned by the fumes of liquor, the love of tasting it was gradually formed, and she too, in the end, became a slave to the Demon of Drink. She died, at last, poor as a beggar in the street. Ah! this liquor-selling is the way to ruin; and they who open the gates, as well as those who enter the downward path, alike go to destruction. But this is digressing.

After Joe Morgan and his wife left the "Sickle and Sheaf," with that gentle child, who, as I afterward learned, had not, for a year or more, laid her little head to sleep until her father returned home—and who, if he stayed out beyond a certain hour, would go for him, and lead him back, a very angel of love and patience—I re-entered the bar-room, to see how life was passing there. Not one of all I had left in the room remained. The incident which had occurred was of so painful a nature, that no further unalloyed pleasure was to be had there during the evening, and so each had retired. In his little kingdom the landlord sat alone, his head resting on his hand, and his face shaded from the light. The whole aspect of the man was that of one in self-humiliation. As I entered he raised his head, and turned his face toward me. Its expression was painful.

"Rather an unfortunate affair," said he. "I'm angry with myself, and sorry for the poor child. But she'd no business here. As for Joe Morgan, it would take a saint to bear his tongue when once set a going by liquor. I wish he'd stay away from the house. Nobody wants his company. Oh dear!"

The ejaculation, or rather groan, that closed the sentence, showed how little Slade was satisfied with himself, notwithstanding this feeble effort at self-justification.

"His thirst for liquor draws him hither," I remarked. "The attraction of your bar to his appetite is like that of the magnet to the needle. He cannot stay away."

"He *must* stay away!" exclaimed the landlord, with some vehemence of tone, striking his fist upon the table by which he sat. "He *must* stay away! There is scarcely an evening that he does not ruffle my temper, and mar good feelings in all the company. Just see what he provoked me to do this evening. I might have killed the child. It makes my blood run cold to think of it! Yes, sir—he must stay away. If no better can be done, I'll hire a man to stand at the door and keep him out."

"He never troubled you at the mill," said I. "No man was required at the mill door?"

"No!" And the landlord gave emphasis to the word by an oath, ejaculated with a heartiness that almost startled me. I had not heard him swear before. "No! the great trouble was to get him and keep him there, the good-for-nothing, idle fellow!"

"I'm afraid," I ventured to suggest, "that things don't go on quite so smoothly here as they did at the mill. Your customers are of a different class."

"I don't know about that; why not?" He did not just relish my remark.

"Between quiet, thrifty, substantial farmers, and drinking bar-room loungers, are many degrees of comparison."

"Excuse me, sir!" Simon Slade elevated his person. "The men who visit my bar-room, as a general thing, are quite as respectable, moral, and substantial as any who came to the mill—and I believe more so. The first people in the place, sir, are to be found here. Judge Lyman and Judge Hammond; Lawyer Wilks and Doctor Maynard; Mr. Grand and Mr. Lee; and dozens of others—all our first people. No, sir; you mustn't judge all by vagabonds like Joe Morgan."

There was a testy spirit manifested that I did not care to provoke. I could have met his assertion with facts and inferences of a character to startle any one occupying his position, who was in a calm, reflective state; but to argue with him then would have been worse than idle: and so I let him talk on until the excitement occasioned by my words died out for want of new fuel.

☞ *Night the Third* ☜

JOE MORGAN'S CHILD

"I don't see any thing of your very particular friend, Joe Morgan, this evening," said Harvey Green, leaning on the bar and speaking to Slade. It was the night succeeding that on which the painful and exciting scene with the child had occurred.

"No," was answered—and to the word was added a profane imprecation. "No; and if he'll just keep away from here, he may go to—— on a hard trotting horse and a porcupine saddle as fast as he pleases. He's tried my patience beyond endurance, and my mind is made up, that he gets no more drams at this bar. I've borne his vile tongue and seen my company annoyed by him just as long as I mean to stand it. Last night decided me. Suppose I'd killed that child?"

"You'd have had trouble then, and no mistake."

"Wouldn't I? Blast her little picture! What business has she creeping in here every night?"

"She must have a nice kind of a mother," remarked Green, with a cold sneer.

"I don't know what she is now," said Slade, a slight touch of feeling in his voice—"heart-broken, I suppose. I couldn't look at her last night; it made me sick. But, there was a time when Fanny Morgan was the loveliest and best woman in Cedarville. I'll say that for her. Oh dear! What a life her miserable husband has caused her to lead."

"Better that he were dead and out of the way."

"Better a thousand times," answered Slade. "If he'd only fall down some night and break his neck, it would be a blessing to his family."

"And to you in particular," laughed Green.

"You may be sure it wouldn't cost me a large sum for mourning," was the unfeeling response.

Let us leave the bar-room of the "Sickle and Sheaf," and its cold-hearted inmates, and look in upon the family of Joe Morgan, and see how it is in the home of the poor inebriate. We will pass by a quick transition.

"Joe!" The thin white hand of Mrs. Morgan clasps the arm of her husband, who has arisen up suddenly, and now stands by the partly opened door. "Don't go out to-night, Joe. Please, don't go out."

"Father!" A feeble voice calls from the corner of an old settee, where little Mary lies with her head bandaged.

"Well, I won't then!" is replied—not angrily, nor even fretfully—but in a kind voice.

"Come and sit by me, father." How tenderly, yet how full of concern is that low, sweet voice. "Come, won't you?"

"Yes, dear."

"Now hold my hand, father."

Joe takes the hand of little Mary, that instantly tightens upon his.

"You won't go away and leave me to-night, will you, father? Say you won't."

"How very hot your hand is, dear. Does your head ache?"

"A little; but it will soon feel better."

Up into the swollen and disfigured face of the fallen father, the large, earnest blue eyes of the child are raised. She does not see the marred lineaments; but, only the beloved countenance of her parent.

"Dear father!"

"What, love?"

"I wish you'd promise me something."

"What, dear?"

"Will you promise?"

"I can't say until I hear your request. If I can promise, I will."

"Oh! you can promise—you can, father!"

"How very hot your hand is, dear. Does your head ache?"

"What is it, love?"

"That you'll never go into Simon Slade's bar any more."

The child raises herself, evidently with a painful effort; and leans nearer to her father.

Joe shakes his head, and poor Mary drops back upon her pillow with a sigh. Her lids fall, and the long lashes lie strongly relieved on her colourless cheeks.

"I won't go there to-night, dear. So let your heart be at rest."

Mary's lids unclose, and two round drops, released from their clasp, glide slowly over her face.

"Thank you, father—thank you. Mother will be so glad."

The eyes closed again; and the father moved uneasily. His heart is touched. There is a struggle within him. It is on his lips to say that he will never drink at the "Sickle and Sheaf" again; but resolution just lacks the force of utterance.

"Father!"

"Well, dear!"

"I don't think I'll be well enough to go out in two or three days.

You know the doctor said that I would have to keep very still, for I had a great deal of fever."

"Yes, poor child."

"Now, won't you promise me one thing?"

"What is it, dear?"

"Not to go out in the evening until I get well."

Joe Morgan hesitated.

"Just promise me that, father. It won't be long. I shall be up again in a little while."

How well the father knows what is in the heart of his child. Her fears are all for him. Who is to go after her poor father, and lead him home when the darkness of inebriety is on his spirit, and external perception so dulled that not skill enough remains to shun the harm that lies in his path.

"Do promise just that, father, dear."

He cannot resist the pleading voice and look.

"I promise it, Mary; so shut your eyes now and go to sleep. I'm afraid this fever will increase."

"Oh! I'm so glad—so glad!"

Mary does not clasp her hands, nor show strong external signs of pleasure; but how full of a pure, unselfish joy is that low murmured ejaculation, spoken in the depths of her spirit, as well as syllabled by her tongue!

Mrs. Morgan has been no unconcerned witness of all this; but knowing the child's influence over her father, she has not ventured a word. More was to be gained, she was sure, by silence on her part; and so she has kept silent. Now she comes nearer to them, and says, as she lets a hand rest on the shoulder of her husband—

"You feel better for that promise, already; I know you do."

He looks up to her, and smiles faintly. He does feel better, but is hardly willing to acknowledge it.

Soon after Mary is sleeping. It does not escape the observation of Mrs. Morgan that her husband grows restless; for he gets up suddenly, every now and then, and walks quickly across the room, as if in search of something. Then sits down, listlessly—sighs—stretches himself, and says—"Oh dear!" What shall she do for him? How is the want of his accustomed evening stimulus to be met? She thinks, and questions, and grieves inwardly. Poor Joe Morgan! His wife understands his case, and pities him from her heart. But, what can she do? Go out and get him something to drink? "Oh, no! no! no! Never!" She answered the thought audibly almost, in the excitement of her feelings. An hour has passed—Joe's restlessness has increased instead of diminishing. What is to be done? Now Mrs. Morgan has left the room. She has resolved upon something, for the case must be met. Ah! here she comes, after an absence of five minutes, bearing in her hand a cup of strong coffee.

"It was kind and thoughtful in you, Fanny," says Morgan, as with a gratified look he takes the cup. But his hand trembles, and he spills a portion of the contents as he tries to raise it to his lips. How dreadfully his nerves are shattered! Unnatural stimulants have been applied so long, that all true vitality seems lost.

And now the hand of his wife is holding the cup to his lips, and he drinks eagerly.

"This is dreadful—dreadful! Where will it end? What is to be done?"

Fanny suppresses a sob, as she thus gives vent to her troubled feelings. Twice, already, has her husband been seized with the drunkard's madness; and, in the nervous prostration consequent upon even a brief withdrawal of his usual strong stimulants, she sees the fearful precursor of another attack of this dreadful and dangerous malady. In the hope of supplying the needed tone she has given him strong coffee; and this, for the time, produces the effect desired. The restlessness is allayed, and a quiet state of body and mind succeeds. It needs but a suggestion to induce him to retire for the night. After being a few minutes in bed, sleep steals over him, and his heavy breathing tells that he is in the world of dreams.

And now there comes a tap at the door.

"Come in," is answered.

The latch is lifted, the door swings open, and a woman enters.

"Mrs. Slade!" The name is uttered in a tone of surprise.

"Fanny, how are you this evening?" Kindly, yet half sadly, the words are said.

"Tolerable, I thank you."

The hands of the two women are clasped, and for a few moments they gaze into each other's face. What a world of tender commiseration is in that of Mrs. Slade!

"How is little Mary to-night?"

"Not so well, I'm afraid. She has a good deal of fever."

"Indeed! Oh, I'm sorry! Poor child! what a dreadful thing it was. Oh, Fanny! you don't know how it has troubled me. I've been intending to come around all day to see how she was, but couldn't get off until now."

"It came near killing her," said Mrs. Morgan.

"It's in God's mercy she escaped. The thought of it curdles the very blood in my veins. Poor child! is this her on the settee?"

"Yes."

Mrs. Slade takes a chair, and sitting by the sleeping child, gazes long upon her pale, sweet face. Now the lips of Mary part—words are murmured—what is she saying?

"No, no, mother; I can't go to bed yet. Father isn't home. And it's so dark. There's no one to lead him over the bridge. I'm not afraid. Don't—don't cry so, mother—I'm not afraid! Nothing will hurt me."

The child's face flushes. She moans, and throws her arms about uneasily. Hark again.

"I wish Mr. Slade wouldn't look so cross at me. He never did when I went to the mill. He doesn't take me on his knee now, and stroke my hair. Oh dear! I wish father wouldn't go there any more. Don't! don't, Mr. Slade. Oh! oh!"—the ejaculation prolonged into a frightened cry, "My head! my head!"

A few choking sobs are followed by low moans; and then the child breathes easily again. But the flush does not leave her cheek; and when Mrs. Slade, from whose eyes the tears come forth drop by drop, and roll down her face, touches it lightly, she finds it hot with fever.

"Has the doctor seen her to-day, Fanny?"

"No, ma'am."

"He should see her at once. I will go for him;" and Mrs. Slade starts up and goes quickly from the room. In a little while she returns with Doctor Green, who sits down and looks at the child for some moments with a sober, thoughtful face. Then he lays his fingers on her pulse and times its beat by his watch—shakes his head, and looks graver still.

"How long has she had fever?" he asks.

"All day."

"You should have sent for me earlier."

"Oh doctor! She is not dangerous, I hope?" Mrs. Morgan looks frightened.

"She's a sick child, madam."

"You've promised, father."—The dreamer is speaking again.—"I'm not well enough yet. Oh, don't go, father; don't! There! He's gone! Well, well! I'll try and walk there—I can sit down and rest by the way. Oh dear! How tired I am! Father! Father!"

The child starts up and looks about her wildly.

"Oh, mother, is it you?" And she sinks back upon her pillow, looking now inquiringly from face to face.

"Father—where is father?" she asks.

"Asleep, dear."

"Oh! Is he? I'm glad."

Her eyes close wearily.

"Do you feel any pain, Mary?" inquired the doctor.

"Yes, sir—in my head. It aches and beats so."

The cry of "Father" has reached the ears of Morgan, who is sleeping in the next room, and roused him into consciousness. He knows the doctor's voice. Why is he here at this late hour? "Do you feel any pain, Mary?" The question he hears distinctly, and the faintly uttered reply also. He is sober enough to have all his fears instantly excited. There is nothing in the world that he loves as he loves that child. And so he gets up and dresses himself as quickly as possible; the stimulus of anxiety giving tension to his relaxed nerves.

"Oh father!" The quick ears of Mary detect his entrance first, and a pleasant smile welcomes him.

"Is she very sick, doctor?" he asks, in a voice full of anxiety.

"She's a sick child, sir; you should have sent for me earlier." The doctor speaks rather sternly, and with a purpose to rebuke.

The reply stirs Morgan, and he seems to cower half-timidly under the words, as if they were blows. Mary has already grasped her father's hand, and holds on to it tightly.

After examining the case a little more closely, the doctor prepares some medicine, and, promising to call early in the morning, goes away. Mrs. Slade follows soon after; but, in parting with Mrs. Morgan, leaves something in her hand, which, to the surprise of the latter, proves to be a ten-dollar bill. The tears start to her eyes; and she conceals the money in her bosom—murmuring a fervent "God bless her!"

A simple act of restitution is this on the part of Mrs. Slade, prompted as well by humanity as a sense of justice. With one hand her husband has taken the bread from the family of his old friend, and thus with the other she restores it.

And now Morgan and his wife are alone with their sick child. Higher the fever rises, and partial delirium seizes upon her over-excited brain. She talks for a time almost incessantly. All her trouble is about her father; and she is constantly referring to his promise not to go out in the evening until she gets well. How tenderly and touchingly she appeals to him; now looking up into his face in recognition; and now calling anxiously after him, as if he had left her and was going away.

"You'll not forget your promise, will you, father?" she says, speaking so calmly, that he thinks her mind has ceased to wander.

"No, dear; I will not forget it," he answers, smoothing her hair gently with his hand.

"You'll not go out in the evening again, until I get well?"

"No, dear."

"Father!"

"What, love?"

"Stoop down closer; I don't want mother to hear; it will make her feel so bad."

The father bends his ear close to the lips of Mary. How he starts and shudders! What has she said?—only these brief words—

"I shall not get well, father; I'm going to die."

The groans, impossible to repress, that issued through the lips of Joe Morgan, startled the ears of his wife, and she came quickly to the bed-side.

"What is it? What is the matter, Joe?" she inquired with a look of anxiety.

"Hush, father. Don't tell her. I only said it to you." And Mary put a finger on her lips, and looked mysterious. "There, mother—you go away; you've got trouble enough, anyhow. Don't tell her, father."

But the words, which came to him like a prophecy, awoke such pangs of fear and remorse in the heart of Joe Morgan, that it was impossible for him to repress the signs of pain. For some moments he gazed at his wife—then stooping forward, suddenly, he buried his face in the bed-clothes, and sobbed bitterly.

A suggestion of the truth now flashed through the mind of Mrs. Morgan, sending a thrill of pain along every nerve. Ere she had time to recover herself, the low, sweet voice of Mary broke upon the hushed air of the room, and she sung—

> Jesus can make a dying bed
> Feel soft as downy pillows are,
> While on his breast I lean my head,
> And breathe my life out, sweetly, there.

It was impossible for Mrs. Morgan longer to repress her feelings. As the softly breathed strain died away, her sobs broke forth, and for a time she wept violently.

"There," said the child,—"I didn't mean to tell you. I only told father, because—because he promised not to go to the tavern any more until I got well; and I'm not going to get well. So, you see, mother, he'll never go again—never—never—never. Oh dear! how my head pains. Mr. Slade threw it so hard. But it didn't strike father; and I'm so glad. How it would have hurt him—poor father! But he'll never go there any more; and that will be so good, won't it, mother?"

A light broke over her face; but seeing that her mother still wept, she said—

"Don't cry. Maybe I'll be better."

And then her eyes closed heavily, and she slept again.

"Joe," said Mrs. Morgan, after she had in a measure recovered herself—she spoke firmly. "Joe, did you hear what she said?"

Morgan only answered with a groan.

"Her mind wanders; and yet she may have spoken only the truth."

He groaned again.

"If she should die, Joe—"

"Don't; oh, don't talk so, Fanny. She's not going to die. It's only because she's a little light-headed."

"Why is she light-headed, Joe?"

"It's the fever—only the fever, Fanny."

"It was the blow, and the wound on her head, that caused the fever. How do we know the extent of injury on the brain? Doctor Green looked very serious. I'm afraid, husband, that the worst is before us. I've borne and suffered a great deal—only God knows how much,—I pray that I may have strength to bear this trial also. Dear child! She is better fitted for heaven than for earth; and it may be that God is about to take her to himself. She's been a great comfort to me—and to you, Joe, more like a guardian angel than a child."

Mrs. Morgan had tried to speak very firmly; but as sentence followed sentence, her voice lost more and more of its even tone. With the closing words all self-control vanished; and she wept bitterly. What could her feeble erring husband do, but weep with her?

"Joe,"—Mrs. Morgan aroused herself as quickly as possible, for she had that to say which she feared she might not have the heart to utter —"Joe, if Mary dies, you cannot forget the cause of her death."

"Oh, Fanny! Fanny!"

"Nor the hand that struck the cruel blow."

"Forget it? Never! And if I forgive Simon Slade——"

"Nor the place where the blow was dealt," said Mrs. Morgan, interrupting him.

"Poor—poor child!" moaned the conscience-stricken man.

"Nor your promise, Joe—nor your promise given to our dying child."

"Father! Father! Dear father!" Mary's eyes suddenly unclosed, as she called her father eagerly.

"Here I am, love. What is it?" And Joe Morgan pressed up to the bed-side.

"Oh! it's you, father! I dreamed that you had gone out, and—and— but you won't, will you, dear father?"

"No, love—no."

"Never any more until I get well."

"I must go out to work, you know, Mary."

"At night, father. That's what I mean. You won't, will you?"

"No, dear, no."

A soft smile trembled over the child's face; her eyelids drooped wearily, and she fell off into slumber again. She seemed not so restless as before—did not moan, nor throw herself about in her sleep.

"She's better, I think," said Morgan, as he bent over her, and listened to her softer breathing.

"It seems so," replied his wife. "And now, Joe, you must go to bed again. I will lie down here with Mary, and be ready to do any thing for her that she may want."

"I don't feel sleepy. I'm sure I couldn't close my eyes. So let me sit up with Mary. You are tired and worn out."

Mrs. Morgan looked earnestly into her husband's face. His eyes were unusually bright, and she noticed a slight nervous restlessness about his lips. She laid one of her hands on his, and perceived a slight tremor.

"You must go to bed," she spoke firmly. "I shall not let you sit up with Mary. So go at once." And she drew him almost by force into the next room.

"It's no use, Fanny. There's not a wink of sleep in my eyes. I shall lie awake anyhow. So do you get a little rest."

Even as he spoke there were nervous twitchings of his arms and shoulders; and as he entered the chamber, impelled by his wife, he stopped suddenly and said—

"What is that?"

"Where?" asked Mrs. Morgan.

"Oh, it's nothing—I see. Only one of my old boots. I thought it a great black cat."

Oh! what a shudder of despair seized upon the heart of the wretched wife. Too well she knew the fearful signs of that terrible madness from which, twice before, he had suffered. She could have looked on calmly and seen him die—but, "Not this—not this! Oh, Father in heaven!" she murmured, with such a heart-sinking that it seemed as if life itself would go out.

"Get into bed, Joe; get into bed as quickly as possible."

Morgan was now passive in the hands of his wife, and obeyed her almost like a child. He had turned down the bedclothes, and was about getting in, when he started back, with a look of disgust and alarm.

"There's nothing there, Joe. What's the matter with you?"

"I'm sure I don't know, Fanny," and his teeth rattled together, as he spoke. "I thought there was a great toad under the clothes."

"How foolish you are!"—yet tears were blinding her eyes as she said this. "It's only fancy. Get into bed and shut your eyes. I'll make you another cup of strong coffee. Perhaps that will do you good. You're only a little nervous. Mary's sickness has disturbed you."

Joe looked cautiously under the bedclothes, as he lifted them up still farther, and peered beneath.

"You know there's nothing in your bed; see!"

And Mrs. Morgan threw, with a single jerk, all the clothes upon the floor.

"There now! look for yourself. Now shut your eyes," she continued, as she spread the sheet and quilt over him, after his head was on the pillow. "Shut them tight and keep them so until I boil the water and make a cup of coffee. You know as well as I do that it's nothing but fancy."

Morgan closed his eyes firmly, and drew the clothes over his head.

"I'll be back in a very few minutes," said his wife, going hurriedly to the door. Ere leaving, however, she partly turned her head and glanced back. There sat her husband, upright and staring fearfully.

"Don't, Fanny! don't go away!" he cried, in a frightened voice.

"Joe! Joe! why will you be so foolish? It's nothing but imagination. Now do lie down and shut your eyes. Keep them shut. There now."

And she laid a hand over his eyes, and pressed it down tightly.

"I wish Doctor Green was here," said the wretched man. "He could give me something."

"Shall I go for him?"

"Go, Fanny! Run over right quickly."

"But you won't keep in bed."

"Yes, I will. There now." And he drew the clothes over his face. "There; I'll lie just so until you come back. Now run, Fanny, and don't stay a minute."

Scarcely stopping to think, Mrs. Morgan went hurriedly from the room, and drawing an old shawl over her head, started with swift feet for the residence of Doctor Green, which was not very far away. The kind doctor understood, at a word, the sad condition of her husband, and promised to attend him immediately. Back she flew at even a wilder speed, her heart throbbing with vague apprehension. Oh! what a fearful cry was that which smote her ears as she came within a few paces of home. She knew the voice, changed as it was by terror, and a shudder almost palsied her heart. At a single bound she cleared the intervening space, and in the next moment was in the room where she had left her husband. But he was not there! With suspended breath, and feet that scarcely obeyed her will, she passed into the chamber where little Mary lay. Not here!

"Joe! husband!" she called in a faint voice.

"Here he is, mother." And now she saw that Joe had crept into the bed behind the sick child, and that her arm was drawn tightly around his neck.

"You won't let them hurt me, will you, dear?" said the poor, frightened victim of a terrible mania.

"Nothing will hurt you, father," answered Mary, in a voice that showed her mind to be clear, and fully conscious of her parent's true condition.

She had seen him thus before. Ah! what an experience for a child!

"You're an angel—my good angel, Mary," he murmured, in a voice yet trembling with fear. "Pray for me, my child. Oh, ask your Father in heaven to save me from these dreadful creatures. There now!" he cried, rising up suddenly, and looking toward the door. "Keep out! Go away! You can't come in here. This is Mary's room; and she's an angel. Ah, ha! I knew you wouldn't dare come in here—

> A single saint can put to flight,
> Ten thousand blustering sons of night."

He added in a half wandering way, yet with an assured voice, as he laid himself back upon his pillow, and drew the clothes over his head.

"Poor father!" sighed the child, as she gathered both arms about his neck. "I will be your good angel. Nothing shall hurt you here."

"I knew I would be safe where you were," he whispered back.—"I knew it, and so I came. Kiss me, love."

How pure and fervent was the kiss laid instantly upon his lips! There was a power in it to remand the evil influences that were surrounding and pressing in upon him like a flood. All was quiet now, and Mrs. Morgan neither by word nor movement disturbed the solemn stillness that reigned in the apartment. In a few minutes the deepened breathing of her husband gave a blessed intimation that he was sinking into sleep. Oh, sleep! sleep! How tearfully, in times past, had she prayed that he might sleep; and yet no sleep came for hours and days —even though powerful opiates were given—until exhausted nature yielded, and then sleep had a long, long struggle with death. Now the sphere of his loving, innocent child seemed to have overcome, at least for the time, the evil influences that were getting possession even of his external senses. Yes, yes, he was sleeping! Oh, what a fervent "Thank God!" went up from the heart of his stricken wife.

Soon the quick ears of Mrs. Morgan detected the doctor's approaching footsteps, and she met him at the door with a finger on her lips. A whispered word or two explained the better aspect of affairs, and the doctor said, encouragingly,

"That's good, if he will only sleep on."

"Do you think he will, doctor?" was asked anxiously.

"He may. But we cannot hope too strongly. It would be something very unusual."

Both passed noiselessly into the chamber. Morgan still slept, and by his deep breathing it was plain that he slept soundly. And Mary, too, was sleeping, her face now laid against her father's, and her arms still about his neck. The sight touched even the doctor's heart and moistened his eyes. For nearly half an hour he remained; and then, as Morgan continued to sleep, he left medicine to be given immediately, and went home, promising to call early in the morning.

It is now past midnight, and we leave the lonely, sad-hearted watcher with her sick ones.

I was sitting, with a newspaper in my hand—not reading, but musing—at the "Sickle and Sheaf," late in the evening marked by the incidents just detailed.

"Where's your mother?" I heard Simon Slade inquire. He had just entered an adjoining room.

"She's gone out somewhere," was answered by his daughter Flora.

"Where?"

"I don't know."

"How long has she been away?"

"More than an hour."

"And you don't know where she went to?"

"No, sir."

Nothing more was said, but I heard the landlord's heavy feet moving backward and forward across the room for some minutes.

"Why, Ann! where have you been?" The door of the next room had opened and shut.

"Where I wish you had been with me," was answered in a very firm voice.

"Where?"

"To Joe Morgan's."

"Humph!" Only this ejaculation met my ears. But something was said in a low voice, to which Mrs. Slade replied with some warmth,

"If you don't have his child's blood clinging for life to your garments, you may be thankful."

"What do you mean?" he asked, quickly.

"All that my words indicate. Little Mary is very ill!"

"Well, what of it."

"Much. The doctor thinks her in great danger. The cut on her head has thrown her into a violent fever, and she is delirious. Oh, Simon! if you had heard what I heard to-night."

"What?" was asked in a growling tone.

"She is out of her mind, as I said, and talks a great deal. She talked about you."

"Of me! Well, what had she to say?"

"She said—so pitifully—'I wish Mr. Slade wouldn't look so cross at me. He never did when I went to the mill. He doesn't take me on his knee now, and stroke my hair. Oh dear!' Poor child! She was always so good."

"Did she say that?" Slade seemed touched.

"Yes, and a great deal more. Once she screamed out, 'Oh don't! don't, Mr. Slade! don't! My head! my head!' It made my very heart ache. I can never forget her pale, frightened face, nor her cry of fear. Simon—if she should die!"

There was a long silence.

"If we were only back to the mill." It was Mrs. Slade's voice.

"There, now! I don't want to hear that again," quickly spoke out the landlord. "I made a slave of myself long enough."

"You had at least a clear conscience," his wife answered.

"Do hush, will you!" Slade was now angry. "One would think, by the way you talk sometimes, that I had broken every command of the Decalogue."

"You will break hearts as well as commandments, if you keep on for a few years as you have begun—and ruin souls as well as fortunes."

Mrs. Slade spoke calmly, but with marked severity of tone. Her husband answered with an oath, and then left the room, banging the door after him. In the hush that followed I retired to my chamber, and lay for an hour awake, pondering on all I had just heard. What a revelation was in that brief passage of words between the landlord and his excited companion!

☞ Night the Fourth ☜

DEATH OF LITTLE MARY MORGAN

"Where are you going, Ann?" It was the landlord's voice. Time—a little after dark.

"I'm going over to see Mrs. Morgan," answered his wife.

"What for?"

"I wish to go," was replied.

"Well, *I* don't wish you to go," said Slade, in a very decided way.

"I can't help that, Simon. Mary, I'm told, is dying, and Joe is in a dreadful way. I'm needed there—and so are you, as to that matter. There was a time when, if word came to you that Morgan or his family were in trouble——"

"Do hush, will you!" exclaimed the landlord, angrily. "I won't be preached to in this way any longer."

"Oh, well; then don't interfere with my movements, Simon; that's all I have to say. I'm needed over there, as I just said, and I'm going."

There were considerable odds against him, and Slade, perceiving this, turned off, muttering something that his wife did not hear, and she went on her way. A hurried walk brought her to the wretched home of the poor drunkard, whose wife met her at the door.

"How is Mary?" was the visitor's earnest inquiry.

Mrs. Morgan tried to answer the question; but, though her lips moved, no sounds issued therefrom.

Mrs. Slade pressed her hands tightly in both of hers; and then passed in with her to the room where the child lay. A glance sufficed to tell Mrs. Slade that death had already laid his icy fingers upon her brow.

"How are you, dear?" she asked, as she bent over and kissed her.

"Better, I thank you," replied Mary, in a low whisper.

Then she fixed her eyes upon her mother's face, with a look of inquiry.

"What is it, love?"

"Hasn't father waked up yet?"

"No, dear."

"Won't he wake up soon?"

"He's sleeping very soundly. I wouldn't like to disturb him."

"Oh, no; don't disturb him. I thought, maybe, he was awake."

And the child's lids dropped languidly, until the long lashes lay close against her cheeks.

There was silence for a little while, and then Mrs. Morgan said, in a half-whisper to Mrs. Slade,

"Oh, we've had such a dreadful time with poor Joe. He got in that terrible way again last night. I had to go for Doctor Green and leave him all alone. When I came back, he was in bed with Mary; and she, dear child! had her arms around his neck, and was trying to comfort him; and would you believe it, he went off to sleep and slept in that way for a long time. The doctor came, and when he saw how it was, left some medicine for him, and went away. I was in such hopes that he would sleep it all off. But about twelve o'clock he started up, and sprung out of bed with an awful scream. Poor Mary! she too had fallen asleep. The cry wakened her, and frightened her dreadfully. She's been getting worse ever since, Mrs. Slade.

"Just as he was rushing out of the room, I caught him by the arm, and it took all my strength to hold him.

" 'Father! father!' Mary called after him, as soon as she was awake enough to understand what was the matter—'Don't go out, father; there's nothing here.'

"He looked back toward the bed, in a frightful way.

"'See, father!' and the dear child turned down the quilt and sheet, in order to convince him that nothing was in the bed. 'I'm here,' she added. 'I'm not afraid. Come, father. If there's nothing here to hurt me, there's nothing to hurt you.'

"There was something so assuring in this, that Joe took a step or two toward the bed, looking sharply into it as he did so. From the bed his eyes wandered up to the ceiling, and the old look of terror came into his face.

"'There it is now! Jump out of bed, quick! Jump out, Mary!' he cried. 'See! it's right over your head.'

"Mary showed no sign of fear as she lifted her eyes to the ceiling, and gazed steadily, for a few moments, in that direction.

"'There's nothing there, father,' said she, in a confident voice.

"'It's gone now,' Joe spoke in a tone of relief. 'Your angel-look drove it away. Aha! There it is now, creeping along the floor!' he suddenly exclaimed, fearfully; starting away from where he stood.

"'Here, father! Here!' Mary called to him, and he sprung into the bed again; while she gathered her arms about him tightly, saying, in a low, soothing voice,—'Nothing can harm you here, father.'

"Without a moment's delay, I gave him the morphine left by Doctor Green. He took it eagerly, and then crouched down in the bed, while Mary continued to assure him of perfect safety. So long as he was clearly conscious as to where he was, he remained perfectly still. But, as soon as partial slumber came, he would scream out, and spring from the bed in terror, and then it would take us several minutes to quiet him again. Six times during the night did this occur; and as often, Mary coaxed him back. The morphine I continued to give, as the doctor had directed. By morning, the opiates had done their work, and he was sleeping soundly. When the doctor came, we removed him to his own bed. He is still asleep; and I begin to feel uneasy, lest he should never awake again. I have heard of this happening."

"See if father isn't awake," said Mary, raising her head from the pillow. She had not heard what passed between her mother and Mrs. Slade, for the conversation was carried on in low voices.

Mrs. Morgan stepped to the door, and looked into the room where her husband lay.

"He is still asleep, dear," she remarked, coming back to the bed.

"Oh! I wish he was awake. I want to see him so much. Won't you call him, mother?"

"I have called him a good many times. But you know the doctor gave him opium. He can't wake up yet."

"He's been sleeping a very long time; don't you think so, mother?"

"Yes, dear, it does seem a long time. But it's best for him. He'll be better when he wakes."

Mary closed her eyes, wearily. How deathly white was her face—how sunken her eyes—how sharply contracted her features!

"I've given her up, Mrs. Slade," said Mrs. Morgan, in a low, rough, choking whisper, as she leaned nearer to her friend. "I've given her up! The worst is over; but, oh! it seemed as though my heart would break in the struggle. Dear child! In all the darkness of my way, she has helped and comforted me. Without her, it would have been the blackness of darkness."

"Father! father!" The voice of Mary broke out with a startling quickness.

Mrs. Morgan turned to the bed, and laying her hand on Mary's arm said—

"He's still sound asleep, dear."

"No, he isn't, mother. I heard him move. Won't you go in and see if he is awake?"

In order to satisfy the child, her mother left the room. To her surprise, she met the eyes of her husband as she entered the chamber where he lay. He looked at her calmly.

"What does Mary want with me?" he asked.

"She wishes to see you. She's called you so many, many times. Shall I bring her in here?"

"No. I'll get up and dress myself."

"I wouldn't do that. You've been sick."

"Oh, no. I don't feel sick."

"Father! father!" The clear, earnest voice of Mary was heard calling.

"I'm coming, dear," answered Morgan.

"Come quick, father, won't you?"

"Yes, love." And Morgan got up and dressed himself—but with unsteady hands, and every sign of nervous prostration. In a little while, with the assistance of his wife, he was ready, and, supported by her, came tottering into the room where Mary was lying.

"Oh, father!"—What a light broke over her countenance.—"I've been waiting for you so long. I thought you were never going to wake up. Kiss me, father."

"What can I do for you, Mary?" asked Morgan, tenderly, as he laid his face down upon the pillow beside her.

"Nothing, father. I don't wish for any thing. I only wanted to see you."

"I'm here, now, love."

"Dear father!" How earnestly, yet tenderly she spoke, laying her small hand upon his face. "You've always been good to me, father."

"Oh, no. I've never been good to anybody," sobbed the weak, broken-spirited man, as he raised himself from the pillow.

How deeply touched was Mrs. Slade, as she sat, the silent witness of this scene!

"You haven't been good to yourself, father—but you've always been good to us."

"Don't, Mary! don't say anything about that," interposed Morgan. "Say that I've been very bad—very wicked. Oh, Mary, dear! I only wish that I was as good as you are; I'd like to die, then, and go right away from this evil world. I wish there was no liquor to drink—no taverns—no bar-rooms. Oh dear! Oh dear! I wish I was dead."

And the weak, trembling, half-palsied man laid his face again upon the pillow beside his child, and sobbed aloud.

What an oppressive silence reigned for a time through the room!

"Father." The stillness was broken by Mary. Her voice was clear and even. "Father, I want to tell you something?"

"What is it, Mary?"

"There'll be nobody to go for you, father." The child's lips now quivered, and tears filled into her eyes.

"Don't talk about that, Mary. I'm not going out in the evening any more until you get well. Don't you remember I promised?"

"But, father"—She hesitated.

"What, dear?"

"I'm going away to leave you and mother."

"Oh, no—no—no, Mary! Don't say that."—The poor man's voice was broken.—"Don't say that! We can't let you go, dear."

"God has called me." The child's voice had a solemn tone, and her eyes turned reverently upward.

"I wish he would call me! Oh, I wish he would call me!" groaned Morgan, hiding his face in his hands. "What shall I do when you are gone? Oh dear! Oh dear!"

"Father!" Mary spoke calmly again. "You are not ready to go yet. God will let you live here longer, that you may get ready."

"How can I get ready without you to help me, Mary? My angel child!"

"Haven't I tried to help you, father, oh, so many times?" said Mary.

"Yes—yes—you've always tried."

"But it wasn't any use. You would go out—you would go to the tavern. It seemed almost as if you couldn't help it."

Morgan groaned in spirit.

"Maybe I can help you better, father, after I die. I love you so much, that I am sure God will let me come to you, and stay with you always, and be your angel. Don't you think he will, mother?"

But Mrs. Morgan's heart was too full. She did not even try to answer, but sat, with streaming eyes, gazing upon her child's face.

"Father, I dreamed something about you, while I slept to-day." Mary again turned to her father.

"What was it, dear?"

"I thought it was night, and that I was still sick. You promised not to go out again until I was well. But you did go out; and I thought you went over to Mr. Slade's tavern. When I knew this, I felt as strong as when I was well, and I got up and dressed myself, and started out after you. But I hadn't gone far, before I met Mr. Slade's great bull-dog Nero, and he growled at me so dreadfully that I was frightened and ran back home. Then I started again, and went away round by Mr. Mason's. But there was Nero in the road, and this time he caught my dress in his mouth and tore a great piece out of the skirt. I ran back again, and he chased me all the way home. Just as I got to the door, I looked around, and there was Mr. Slade, setting Nero on me. As soon as I saw Mr. Slade, though he looked at me very wicked, I lost all my fear, and turning around, I walked past Nero, who showed his teeth, and growled as fiercely as ever, but didn't touch me. Then Mr. Slade tried to stop me. But I didn't mind him, and kept right on, until I came to the tavern, and there you stood in the door. And you were dressed so nice. You had on a new hat and a new coat; and your boots were new, and polished just like Judge Hammond's. I said—'O father! is this you?' And then you took me up in your arms and kissed me, and said—'Yes, Mary, I am your real father. Not old Joe Morgan—but Mr. Morgan now.' It seemed all so strange, that I looked into the bar-room to see who was there. But it wasn't a bar-room any longer; but a store full of goods. The sign of the 'Sickle and Sheaf' was taken down; and over the door I now read your name, father. Oh! I was so glad, that I awoke—and then I cried all to myself, for it was only a dream."

The last words were said very mournfully, and with a drooping of Mary's lids, until the tear-gemmed lashes lay close upon her cheeks. Another period of deep silence followed—for the oppressed listeners gave no utterance to what was in their hearts. Feeling was too strong for speech. Nearly five minutes glided away, and then Mary whispered the name of her father, but without opening her eyes.

Morgan answered, and bent down his ear.

"You will only have mother left," she said—"only mother. And she cries so much when you are away."

"I won't leave her, Mary, only when I go to work," said Morgan, whispering back to the child. "And I'll never go out at night any more."

"Yes; you promised me that."

"And I'll promise more."

"What, father?"

"Never to go into a tavern again."

"Never!"

"No, never. And I'll promise still more."

"Father?"

"Never to drink a liquor as long as I live."

"Oh, father! dear, dear father!" And with a cry of joy Mary started up and flung herself upon his breast. Morgan drew his arms tightly around her, and sat for a long time, with his lips pressed to her cheek —while she lay against his bosom as still as death. As death? Yes; for, when the father unclasped his arms, the spirit of his child was with the angels of the resurrection!

It was my fourth evening in the bar-room of the "Sickle and Sheaf." The company was not large, nor in very gay spirits. All had heard of little Mary's illness; which followed so quickly on the blow from the tumbler, that none hesitated about connecting the one with the other. So regular had been the child's visits, and so gently exerted, yet powerful, her influence over her father, that most of the frequenters at the "Sickle and Sheaf" had felt for her a more than common interest; which the cruel treatment she received, and the subsequent illness, materially heightened.

"Joe Morgan hasn't turned up this evening," remarked some one.

"And isn't likely to for a while," was answered.

"Why not?" inquired the first speaker.

"They say, the man with the poker is after him."

"Oh, dear! that's dreadful. It's the second or third chase, isn't it?"

"Yes."

"He'll be likely to catch him this time."

"I shouldn't wonder."

"Poor devil! It won't be much matter. His family will be a great deal better without him."

"It will be a blessing to them if he dies."

"Miserable, drunken wretch!" muttered Harvey Green, who was present. "He's only in the way of everybody. The sooner he's off, the better."

The landlord said nothing. He stood leaning across the bar, looking more sober than usual.

"That was rather an unlucky affair of yours, Simon. They say the child is going to die."

"Who says so?" Slade started, scowled, and threw a quick glance upon the speaker.

"Doctor Green."

"Nonsense! Doctor Green never said any such thing."

"Yes, he did, though."

"Who heard him?"

"I did."

"You did?"

"Yes."

"He wasn't in earnest?" A slight paleness overspread the countenance of the landlord.

"He was, though. They had an awful time there last night."

"Where?"

"At Joe Morgan's. Joe has the mania, and Mrs. Morgan was alone with him and her sick girl all night."

"He deserves to have it; that's all I've got to say." Slade tried to speak with a kind of rough indifference.

"That's pretty hard talk," said one of the company.

"I don't care if it is. It's the truth. What else could he expect?"

"A man like Joe is to be pitied," remarked the other.

"I pity his family," said Slade.

"Especially little Mary." The words were uttered tauntingly, and produced murmurs of satisfaction throughout the room.

Slade started back from where he stood, in an impatient manner, saying something that I did not hear.

"Look here, Simon, I heard some strong suggestions over at Lawyer Phillip's office to-day."

Slade turned his eyes upon the speaker.

"If that child should die, you'll probably have to stand a trial for manslaughter."

"No—girl-slaughter," said Harvey Green, with a cold, inhuman chuckle.

"But, I'm in earnest," said the other. "Mr. Phillips said that a case could be made out of it."

"It was only an accident, and all the lawyers in Christendom can't make anything more of it," remarked Green, taking the side of the landlord, and speaking with more gravity than before.

"Hardly an accident," was replied.

"He didn't throw at the girl."

"No matter. He threw a heavy tumbler at her father's head. The intention was to do an injury; and the law will not stop to make any nice discriminations in regard to the individual upon whom the injury was wrought. Moreover, who is prepared to say, that he didn't aim at the girl?"

"Any man who intimates such a thing is a cursed liar!" exclaimed the landlord, half maddened by the suggestion.

"I won't throw a tumbler at your head," coolly remarked the individual whose plain speaking had so irriated Simon Slade. "Throwing tumblers I never thought a very creditable kind of argument—though, with some men, when cornered, it is a favourite mode of settling a question. Now, as for our friend the landlord, I am sorry to say, that his new business doesn't seem to have improved either his manners or his temper a great deal. As a miller, he was one of the best-tempered men in the world, and wouldn't have harmed a kitten. But, now, he can swear, and bluster, and throw glasses at people's heads, and all that sort of thing, with the best of brawling rowdies. I'm afraid he's taking lessons in a bad school—I am."

"I don't think you have any right to insult a man in his own house," answered Slade, in a voice dropped to a lower key than the one in which he had before spoken.

"I had no intention to insult you," said the other. "I was only speaking suppositiously, and in view of your position on a trial for manslaughter, when I suggested, that no one could prove, or say, that you didn't mean to strike little Mary, when you threw the tumbler."

"Well, I didn't mean to strike her; and I don't believe there is a man in this bar-room who thinks that I did—not one."

"I'm sure I do not," said the individual with whom he was in controversy. "Nor I"—"Nor I"—went round the room.

"But, as I wished to set forth," was continued, "the case will not be so plain a one when it finds its way into court, and twelve men, to each of whom you may be a stranger, come to sit in judgment upon the act. The slightest twist in the evidence, the prepossessions of a witness, or the bad tact of the prosecution, may cause things to look so dark on your side as to leave you but little chance. For my part, if the child should die, I think your chances for a term in the state's prison are as eight to ten; and I should call that pretty close cutting."

I looked attentively at the man who said this, all the while he was speaking, but could not clearly make out whether he were altogether in earnest, or merely trying to worry the mind of Slade. That he was successful in accomplishing the latter, was very plain; for the landlord's countenance steadily lost colour, and became overcast with alarm. With that evil delight which some men take in giving pain, others, seeing Slade's anxious looks, joined in the persecution, and soon made the landlord's case look black enough; and the landlord himself almost as frightened as a criminal just under arrest.

"It's bad business, and no mistake," said one.

"Yes, bad enough. I wouldn't be in his shoes for his coat," remarked another.

"For his coat? No, not for his whole wardrobe," said a third.

"Nor for the 'Sickle and Sheaf' thrown into the bargain," added a fourth.

"It will be a clear case of manslaughter, and no mistake. What is the penalty?"

"From two to ten years in the penitentiary," was readily answered.

"They'll give him five, I reckon."

"No—not more than two. It will be hard to prove malicious intention."

"I don't know that. I've heard him curse the girl and threaten her many a time. Haven't you?"

"Yes"—"Yes"—"I have, often," ran around the bar-room.

"You'd better hang me at once," said Slade, affecting to laugh.

At this moment, the door behind Slade opened, and I saw his wife's anxious face thrust in for a moment. She said something to her husband, who uttered a low ejaculation of surprise, and went out quickly.

"What's the matter now?" asked one of another.

"I shouldn't wonder if little Mary Morgan was dead," was suggested.

"I heard her say dead," remarked one who was standing near the bar.

"What's the matter, Frank?" inquired several voices, as the landlord's son came in through the door out of which his father had passed.

"Mary Morgan is dead," answered the boy.

"Poor child! Poor child!" sighed one, in genuine regret at the not unlooked for intelligence. "Her trouble is over."

And there was not one present, but Harvey Green, who did not utter some word of pity or sympathy. He shrugged his shoulders, and looked as much of contempt and indifference as he thought it prudent to express.

"See here, boys," spoke out one of the company, "can't we do something for poor Mrs. Morgan? Can't we make up a purse for her?"

"That's it," was quickly responded; "I'm good for three dollars; and there they are," drawing out the money and laying it upon the counter.

"And here are five to go with them," said I, quickly stepping forward, and placing a five-dollar bill along side of the first contribution.

"Here are five more," added a third individual. And so it went on, until thirty dollars were paid down for the benefit of Mrs. Morgan.

"Into whose hands shall this be placed?" was next asked.

"Let me suggest Mrs. Slade," said I. "To my certain knowledge, she has been with Mrs. Morgan to-night. I know that she feels in her a true woman's interest."

"Just the person," was answered. "Frank, tell your mother we would like to see her. Ask her to step into the sitting-room."

In a few moments the boy came back, and said that his mother would see us in the next room, into which we all passed. Mrs. Slade stood near the table, on which burned a lamp. I noticed that her eyes were red, and that there was on her countenance a troubled and sorrowful expression.

"We have just heard," said one of the company, "that little Mary Morgan is dead."

"Yes—it is too true," answered Mrs. Slade, mournfully. "I have just left there. Poor child! she has passed from an evil world."

"Evil it has indeed been to her," was remarked.

"You may well say that. And yet, amid all the evil, she has been an angel of mercy. Her last thought in dying was of her miserable father. For him, at any time, she would have laid down her life willingly."

"Her mother must be nearly broken-hearted. Mary is the last of her children."

"And yet the child's death may prove a blessing to her."

"How so?"

"Her father promised Mary, just at the last moment—solemnly promised her—that, henceforth, he would never taste liquor. That was all her trouble. That was the thorn in her dying pillow. But he plucked it out, and she went to sleep, lying against his heart. Oh, gentlemen! it was the most touching sight I ever saw."

All present seemed deeply moved.

"They are very poor and wretched," was said.

"Poor and miserable enough," answered Mrs. Slade.

"We have just been taking up a collection for Mrs. Morgan. Here is the money, Mrs. Slade—thirty dollars—we place it in your hands for her benefit. Do with it, for her, as you may see best."

"Oh, gentlemen!" What a quick gleam went over the face of Mrs. Slade. "I thank you, from my heart, in the name of that unhappy one, for this act of true benevolence. To you the sacrifice has been small; to her the benefit will be great indeed. A new life will, I trust, be commenced by her husband, and this timely aid will be something to rest upon, until he can get into better employment than he now has. Oh, gentlemen! let me urge on you, one and all, to make common cause in favour of Joe Morgan. His purposes are good now; he means to keep his promise to his dying child—means to reform his life. Let the good impulses that led to this act of relief, further prompt you to watch over him, and, if you see him about going astray, to lead him kindly back into the right path. Never—oh! never encourage him to drink; but rather take the glass from his hand, if his own appetite lead him aside, and by all the persuasive influence you possess, induce him to go out from the place of temptation.

"Pardon my boldness in saying so much," added Mrs. Slade, recollecting herself, and colouring deeply as she did so. "My feelings have led me away."

And she took the money from the table where it had been placed, and retired toward the door.

"You have spoken well, madam," was answered. "And we thank you for reminding us of our duty."

"One word more—and forgive the earnest heart from which it comes"—said Mrs. Slade, in a voice that trembled on the words she uttered. "I cannot help speaking, gentlemen! Think if some of you be not entering the road wherein Joe Morgan has so long been walking. Save him, in heaven's name!—but see that ye do not yourselves become cast-aways!"

As she said this, she glided through the door, and it closed after her.

"I don't know what her husband would say to that," was remarked after a few moments of surprised silence.

"I don't care what *he* would say; but I'll tell you what *I* will say," spoke out a man whom I had several times noticed as rather a free tippler. "The old lady has given us capital advice, and I mean to take it, for one. I'm going to try to save Joe Morgan, and—myself too. I've already entered the road she referred to; but I'm going to turn back. So good-night to you all; and if Simon Slade gets no more of my sixpences, he may thank his wife for it—God bless her!"

And the man drew his hat with a jerk over his forehead, and left immediately.

This seemed the signal for dispersion, and all retired—not by way of the bar-room, but out into the hall, and through the door leading upon the porch that ran along in front of the house. Soon after the bar was closed, and a dead silence reigned throughout the house. I saw no more of Slade that night. Early in the morning, I left Cedarville; the landlord looked very sober when he bade me good-by through the stage-door, and wished me a pleasant journey.

☞ *Night the Fifth* ☜

SOME OF THE CONSEQUENCES
OF TAVERN-KEEPING

Nearly five years glided away before business again called me to Cedarville. I knew little of what passed there in the interval, except that Simon Slade had actually been indicted for manslaughter, in causing the death of Morgan's child. He did not stand a trial, however, Judge Lyman having used his influence, successfully, in getting the indictment quashed. The judge, some people said, interested himself in Slade more than was just seemly—especially, as he had, on several occasions, in the discharge of his official duties, displayed what seemed an over-righteous indignation against individuals arraigned for petty offences. The impression made upon me by Judge Lyman had not been favourable. He seemed a cold, selfish, scheming man of the world. That he was an unscrupulous politician, was plain to me, in a single evening's observation of his sayings and doings among the common herd of a village bar-room.

As the stage rolled, with a gay flourish of our driver's bugle, into the village, I noted here and there familiar objects, and marked the varied evidences of change. Our way was past the elegant residence and grounds of Judge Hammond, the most beautiful and highly cultivated in Cedarville. At least, such it was regarded at the time of my previous visit. But, the moment my eyes rested upon the dwelling and its varied surroundings, I perceived an altered aspect. Was it the simple work of time? or, had familiarity with other and more elegantly arranged suburban homes, marred this in my eyes by involuntary contrast? Or had the hand of cultivation really been stayed, and then marring fingers of neglect suffered undisturbed to trace on every thing disfiguring characters?

Such questions were in my thoughts, when I saw a man in the large portico of the dwelling, the ample columns of which, capped in rich Corinthian, gave the edifice the aspect of a Grecian temple. He stood leaning against one of the columns—his hat off, and his long gray hair thrown back and resting lightly on his neck and shoulders. His head was bent down upon his breast, and he seemed in deep abstraction. Just as the coach swept by, he looked up, and in the changed features I recognised Judge Hammond. His complexion was still florid, but his face had grown thin, and his eyes were sunken. Trouble was written in every lineament. Trouble? How inadequately does the word express my meaning! Ah! at a single glance, what a volume of suffering was opened to the gazer's eye. Not lightly had the foot of time rested there, as if treading on odorous flowers, but heavily, and with iron-shod heel. This I saw at a glance; and then, only the image of the man was present to my inner vision, for the swiftly rolling stage-coach had borne me onward past the altered home of the wealthier denizen of Cedarville. In a few minutes our driver reined up before the "Sickle and Sheaf," and as I stepped to the ground, a rotund, coarse, red-faced man, whom I failed to recognise as Simon Slade until he spoke, grasped my hand, and pronounced my name. I could not but contrast, in thought, his appearance with what it was when I first saw him, some six years previously; nor help saying to myself—

"So much for tavern-keeping!"

As marked a change was visible everywhere in and around the "Sickle and Sheaf." It, too, had grown larger by additions of wings and rooms; but it had also grown coarser in growing larger. When built, all the doors were painted white, and the shutters green, giving to the house a neat, even tasteful appearance. But the white and green had given place to a dark, dirty brown, that to my eyes was particularly unattractive. The bar-room had been extended, and now a polished brass rod, or railing, embellished the counter, and sundry ornamental attractions had been given to the shelving behind the bar—such as mirrors, gilding, etc. Pictures, too, were hung upon the walls, or more accurately speaking, coarse coloured lithographs, the subjects of which, if not really obscene, were flashing or vulgar. In the sitting-room, next to the bar, I noticed little change of objects, but much in their condition. The carpet, chairs, and tables were the same in fact, but far from being the same in appearance. The room had a close, greasy odour, and looked as if it had not been thoroughly swept and dusted for a week.

A smart young Irishman was in the bar, and handed me the book in which passenger's names were registered. After I had recorded mine, he directed my trunk to be carried to the room designated as the one I was to occupy. I followed the porter, who conducted me to the chamber which had been mine at previous visits. Here, too, were evidences of change; but not for the better. Then the room was as sweet and clean as it could be; the sheets and pillow-cases as white as snow, and the furniture shining with polish. Now all was dusty and dingy, the air foul, and the bed linen scarcely whiter than tow. No curtain made softer the light as it came through the window; nor would the shutters entirely keep out the glare, for several of the slats were broken. A feeling of disgust came over me, at the close smell and foul appearance of everything; so, after washing my hands and face, and brushing the dust from my clothes, I went down-stairs. The sitting-room was scarcely more attractive than my chamber; so I went out upon the porch and took a chair. Several loungers were here; hearty, strong-looking, but lazy fellows, who, if they had any thing to do, liked idling better than working. One of them had leaned his chair back against the wall of the house, and was swinging his legs with a half circular motion, and humming "Old Folks at Home." Another sat astride of his chair, with his face turned toward, and his chin resting upon, the back. He was in too lazy a condition of body and mind for motion or singing. A third had slidden down in his chair, until he sat on his back, while his feet were elevated above his head, and resting against one of the pillars that supported the porch; while a fourth lay stretched out on a bench, sleeping, his hat over his face to protect him from buzzing and biting flies.

Though all but the sleeping man eyed me, inquisitively, as I took my place among them, not one changed his position. The rolling of eyeballs cost but little exertion; and with that effort they were contented.

"Hallo! who's that?" one of these loungers suddenly exclaimed, as a man went swiftly by in a light sulky; and he started up, and gazed down the road, seeking to penetrate the cloud of dust which the fleet rider had swept up with hoofs and wheels.

"I didn't see." The sleeping man aroused himself, rubbed his eyes, and gazed along the road.

"Who was it, Matthew?" The Irish bar-keeper now stood in the door.

"Willy Hammond," was answered by Matthew.

"Indeed! Is that his new three hundred dollar horse?"

"Yes."

"My! but he's a screamer!"

"Isn't he! Most as fast as his young master."

"Hardly," said one of the men, laughing. "I don't think anything in creation can beat Hammond. He goes it, with a perfect rush."

"Doesn't he! Well; you may say what you please of him, he's as good-hearted a fellow as ever walked; and generous to a fault."

"His old dad will agree with you in the last remark," said Matthew.

"No doubt of that, for he has to stand the bills," was answered.

"Yes, whether he will or no, for I rather think Willy has, somehow or other, got the upper hand of him."

"In what way?"

"It's Hammond and Son, over at the mill and distillery."

"I know; but what of that?"

"Willy was made the business man—ostensibly—in order, as the old man thought, to get him to feel the responsibility of the new position, and thus tame him down."

"Tame *him* down! Oh, dear! It will take more than business to do that. The curb was applied too late."

"As the old gentleman has already discovered, I'm thinking, to his sorrow."

"He never comes here any more; does he, Matthew?"

"Who?"

"Judge Hammond."

"Oh, dear, no. He and Slade had all sorts of a quarrel about a year ago, and he's never darkened our doors since."

"It was something about Willy and——." The speaker did not mention any name, but winked knowingly and tossed his head toward the entrance of the house, to indicate some member of Slade's family.

"I believe so."

"D'ye think Willy really likes her?"

Matthew shrugged his shoulders, but made no answer.

"She's a nice girl," was remarked in an under tone, "and good enough for Hammond's son any day; though, if she were my daughter, I'd rather see her in Jericho than fond of his company."

"He'll have plenty of money to give her. She can live like a queen."

"For how long?"

"Hush!" came from the lips of Matthew. "There she is now."

I looked up and saw, at a short distance from the house, and approaching a young lady, in whose sweet, modest face, I at once recognised Flora Slade. Five years had developed her into a beautiful woman. In her alone, of all that appertained to Simon Slade, there was no deterioration. Her eyes were as mild and pure as when first I met her at gentle sixteen, and her father said "My daughter," with such a mingling of pride and affection in his tone. She passed near where I was sitting, and entered the house. A closer view showed me some marks of thought and suffering; but they only heightened the attractions of her face. I failed not to observe the air of respect with which all returned her slight nod and smile of recognition.

"She's a nice girl, and no mistake—the flower of this flock," was said, as soon as she passed into the house.

"Too good for Willy Hammond, in my opinion," said Matthew. "Clever and generous as people call him."

"Just my opinion," was responded. "She's as pure and good, almost, as an angel; and he?—I can tell you what—he's not the clear thing. He knows a little too much of the world—on its bad side, I mean."

The appearance of Slade put an end to this conversation. A second observation of his person and countenance did not remove the first unfavourable impression. His face had grown decidedly bad in expression, as well as gross and sensual. The odour of his breath, as he took a chair close to where I was sitting, was that of one who drank habitually and freely; and the red, swimming eyes evidenced, too surely, a rapid progress toward the sad condition of a confirmed inebriate. There was, too, a certain thickness of speech, that gave another corroborating sign of evil progress.

"Have you seen any thing of Frank this afternoon?" he inquired of Matthew, after we had passed a few words.

"Nothing," was the bar-keeper's answer.

"I saw him with Tom Wilkins as I came over," said one of the men who was sitting in the porch.

"What was he doing with Tom Wilkins?" said Slade, in a fretted tone of voice. "He doesn't seem very choice of his company."

"They were gunning."

"Gunning!"

"Yes. They both had fowling-pieces. I wasn't near enough to ask where they were going."

This information disturbed Slade a good deal. After muttering to himself for a little while, he started up and went into the house.

"And I could have told him a little more, had I been so inclined," said the individual who mentioned the fact that Frank was with Tom Wilkins.

"What more?" inquired Matthew.

"There was a buggy in the case; and a champagne basket. What the latter contained you can easily guess."

"Whose buggy?"

"I don't know any thing about the buggy; but if 'Lightfoot' doesn't sink in value a hundred dollars or so before sundown, call me a false prophet."

"Oh, no," said Matthew, incredulously. "Frank wouldn't do an outrageous thing like that. Lightfoot won't be in a condition to drive for a month to come."

"I don't care. She's out now; and the way she was putting it down when I saw her, would have made a locomotive look cloudy."

"Where did he get her?" was inquired.

"She's been in the six-acre field, over by Mason's Bridge, for the last week or so," Matthew answered. "Well; all I have to say," he added, "is that Frank ought to be slung up and well horsewhipped. I never saw such a young rascal. He cares for no good, and fears no evil. He's the worst boy I ever saw."

"It would hardly do for you to call him a boy to his face," said one of the men, laughing.

"I don't have much to say to him in any way," replied Matthew, "for I know very well, that if we ever do get into a regular quarrel, there'll be a hard time of it. The same house will not hold us afterward—that's certain. So I steer clear of the young reprobate."

"I wonder his father don't put him to some business," was remarked. "The idle life he now leads will be his ruin."

"He was behind the bar for a year or two."

"Yes; and was smart at mixing a glass—but——"

"Was himself becoming too good a customer?"

"Precisely. He got drunk as a fool before reaching his fifteenth year."

"Good gracious!" I exclaimed, involuntarily.

"It's true, sir," said the last speaker, turning to me. "I never saw any thing like it. And this wasn't all. Bar-room talk, as you maybe know, isn't the most refined and virtuous in the world. I wouldn't like my son to hear much of it. Frank was always an eager listener to everything that was said, and in a very short time became an adept in slang and profanity. I'm no saint myself; but it's often made my blood run cold to hear him swear."

"I pity his mother," said I; for my thought turned naturally to Mrs. Slade.

"You may well do that," was answered. "I doubt if Cedarville holds a sadder heart. It was a dark day for her, let me tell you, when Simon Slade sold his mill and built this tavern. She was opposed to it in the beginning."

"I have inferred as much."

"I know it," said the man. "My wife has been intimate with her for years. Indeed, they have always been like sisters. I remember very well her coming to our house, about the time the mill was sold, and crying about it as if her heart would break. She saw nothing but trouble and sorrow ahead. Tavern-keeping she had always regarded as a low business; and the change from a respectable miller to a lazy tavern-keeper, as she expressed it, was presented to her mind as something disgraceful. I remember, very well, trying to argue the point with her—assuming that it was quite as respectable to keep tavern as to do any thing else; but I might as well have talked to the wind. She was always a pleasant, hopeful, cheerful woman before that time; but, really, I don't think I've seen a true smile on her face since."

"That was a great deal for a man to lose," said I.

"What?" he inquired, not clearly understanding me.

"The cheerful face of his wife."

"The face was but an index of her heart," said he.

"So much the worse."

"True enough for that. Yes, it was a great deal to lose."

"What has he gained that will make up for this?"

The man shrugged his shoulders.

"What has he gained?" I repeated. "Can you figure it up?"

"He's a richer man, for one thing."

"Happier?"

There was another shrug of the shoulders. "I wouldn't like to say that."

"How much richer?"

"Oh, a great deal. Somebody was saying, only yesterday, that he couldn't be worth less than thirty thousand dollars."

"Indeed? So much."

"Yes."

"How has he managed to accumulate so rapidly?"

"His bar has a large run of custom. And, you know, that pays wonderfully."

"He must have sold a great deal of liquor in six years."

"And he has. I don't think I'm wrong in saying, that in the six years which have gone by since the 'Sickle and Sheaf' was opened, more liquor has been drank than in the previous twenty years."

"Say forty," remarked a man who had been a listener to what we said.

"Let it be forty then," was the according answer.

"How come this?" I inquired. "You had a tavern here before the 'Sickle and Sheaf' was opened."

"I know we had, and several places besides where liquor was sold. But, everybody far and near knew Simon Slade the miller, and everybody liked him. He was a good miller, and a cheerful, social, chatty sort of a man, putting everybody in a good humour who came near him. So it became the talk everywhere, when he built this house, which he fitted up nicer than anything that had been seen in these parts. Judge Hammond, Judge Lyman, Lawyer Wilson, and all the big-bugs of the place at once patronised the new tavern; and, of course, everybody else did the same. So, you can easily see how he got such a run."

"It was thought in the beginning," said I, "that the new tavern was going to do wonders for Cedarville."

"Yes," answered the man laughing, "and so it has."

"In what respect?"

"Oh, in many. It has made some men richer, and some poorer."

"Who has it made poorer?"

"Dozens of people. You may always take it for granted, when you see a tavern-keeper, who has a good run at his bar, getting rich, that a great many people are getting poor."

"How so?" I wished to hear in what way the man, who was himself, as was plain to see, a good customer at somebody's bar, reasoned on the subject.

"He does not add to the general wealth. He produces nothing. He takes money from his customers, but gives them no article of value in return—nothing that can be called property, personal or real. He is just so much richer and they just so much poorer for the exchange. Is it not so?"

I readily assented to the position as true, and than said—

"Who, in particular, is poorer?"

"Judge Hammond, for one."

"Indeed! I thought the advance in his property, in consequence of the building of this tavern, was so great, that he was reaping a rich pecuniary harvest."

"There was a slight advance in property along the street after the 'Sickle and Sheaf' was opened, and Judge Hammond was benefited thereby. Interested parties made a good deal of noise about it; but it didn't amount to much, I believe."

"What has caused the judge to grow poorer?"

"The opening of this tavern, as I just said."

"In what way did it affect him?"

"He was among Slade's warmest supporters, as soon as he felt the advance in the price of building lots; called him one of the most enterprising men in Cedarville—a real benefactor to the place—and all that stuff. To set a good example of patronage, he came over every day and took his glass of brandy, and encouraged everybody else that he could influence to do the same. Among those who followed his example was his son Willy. There was not, let me tell you, in all the country for twenty miles around, a finer young man than Willy, nor one of so much promise, when this man-trap"—he let his voice fall, and glanced around, as he thus designated Slade's tavern—"was opened; and now, there is not one dashing more recklessly along the road to ruin. When too late, his father saw that his son was corrupted, and that the company he kept was of a dangerous character. Two reasons led him to purchase Slade's old mill, and turn it into a factory and a distillery. Of course, he had to make a heavy outlay for additional buildings, machinery, and distilling apparatus. The reasons influencing him were the prospect of realizing a large amount of money, especially in distilling, and the hope of saving Willy, by getting him closely engaged and interested in business. To accomplish, more certainly, the latter end, he unwisely transferred to his son, as his own capital, twenty thousand dollars, and then formed with him a regular copartnership —giving Willy an active business control.

"But the experiment, sir," added the man, emphatically, "has proved a failure. I heard yesterday, that both mill and distillery were to be shut up, and offered for sale."

"They did not prove as money-making as was anticipated?"

"No, not under Willy Hammond's management. He had made too many bad acquaintances—men who clung to him because he had plenty of money at his command, and spent it as freely as water. One half of his time he was away from the mill, and while there, didn't half attend to business. I've heard it said—and I don't much doubt its truth—that he's squandered his twenty thousand dollars, and a great deal more besides."

"How is that possible?"

"Well; people talk, and not always at random. There's been a man staying here, most of his time, for the last four or five years, named Green. He does not do anything, and don't seem to have any friends in the neighbourhood. Nobody knows where he came from, and he is not at all communicative on that head himself. Well, this man became acquainted with young Hammond after Willy got to visiting the bar here, and attached himself to him at once. They have, to all appearance, been fast friends ever since; riding about, or going off on gunning or fishing excursions almost every day, and secluding themselves somewhere nearly every evening. That man, Green, sir, it is whispered, is a gambler; and I believe it. Granted, and there is no longer a mystery as to what Willy does with his own and his father's money."

I readily assented to this view of the case.

"And so assuming that Green is a gambler," said I, "He has grown richer, in consequence of the opening of a new and more attractive tavern in Cedarville."

"Yes, and Cedarville is so much the poorer for all his gains; for I've never heard of his buying a foot of ground, or in any way encouraging productive industry. He's only a blood-sucker."

"It is worse than the mere abstraction of money," I remarked; "he corrupts his victims, at the same time that he robs them."

"True."

"Willy Hammond may not be his only victim," I suggested.

"Nor is he, in my opinion. I've been coming to this bar, nightly, for a good many years—a sorry confession for a man to make, I must own," he added, with a slight tinge of shame; "but so it is. Well, as I was saying, I've been coming to this bar, nightly, for a good many years, and I generally see all that is going on around me. Among the regular visitors are at least half a dozen young men, belonging to our best families—who have been raised with care, and well educated. That their presence here is unknown to their friends, I am quite certain—or, at least, unknown and unsuspected by some of them. They do not drink a great deal yet; but all try a glass or two. Toward nine o'clock, often at an earlier hour, you will see one and another of them go quietly out of the bar, through the sitting-room, preceded, or soon followed, by Green and Slade. At any hour of the night, up to one or two, and sometimes three o'clock, you can see light streaming through the rent in a curtain drawn before a particular window, which I know to be in the room of Harvey Green. These are facts, sir; and you can draw your own conclusion. I think it a very serious matter."

"Why does Slade go out with these young men?" I inquired. "Do you think he gambles, also?"

"If he isn't a kind of a stool-pigeon for Harvey Green, then I'm mistaken again."

"Hardly. He cannot, already, have become so utterly unprincipled."

"It's a bad school, sir, this tavern-keeping," said the man.

"I readily grant you that."

"And it's nearly seven years since he commenced to take lessons. A great deal may be learned, sir, of good or evil, in seven years, especially if any interest be taken in the studies."

"True."

"And it's true in this case, you may depend upon it. Simon Slade is not the man he was, seven years ago. Anybody with half an eye can see that. He's grown selfish, grasping, unscrupulous, and passionate. There could hardly be a greater difference between men than exists between Simon Slade the tavern-keeper, and Simon Slade the miller."

"And intemperate, also?" I suggested.

"He's beginning to take a little too much," was answered.

"In that case, he'll scarcely be as well off five years hence as he is now."

"He's at the top of the wheel, some of us think."

"What has led to this opinion?"

"He's beginning to neglect his house, for one thing."

"A bad sign."

"And there is another sign. Heretofore, he has always been on hand, with the cash, when desirable property went off, under forced sale, at a bargain. In the last three or four months, several great sacrifices have been made, but Simon Slade showed no inclination to buy. Put this fact against another,—week before last, he sold a house and lot in the town for five hundred dollars less than he paid for them, a year ago—and for just that sum less than their true value."

"How came that?" I inquired.

"Ah! there's the question! He wanted money; though for what purpose, he has not intimated to anyone, as far as I can learn."

"What do you think of it?"

"Just this. He and Green have been hunting together in times past; but the professed gambler's instincts are too strong to let him spare even his friend in evil. They have commenced playing one against the other."

"Ah! you think so?"

"I do; and if I conjecture rightly, Simon Slade will be a poorer man, in a year from this time, than he is now."

Here our conversation was interrupted. Some one asked my talkative friend to go and take a drink, and he, nothing loath, left me without ceremony.

Very differently served was the supper I partook of on that evening, from the one set before me on the occasion of my first visit to the "Sickle and Sheaf." The table-cloth was not merely soiled, but offensively dirty; the plates, cups, and saucers, dingy and sticky; the knives and forks unpolished; and the food of a character to satisfy the appetite with a very few mouthfuls. Two greasy-looking Irish girls waited on the table, at which neither landlord nor landlady presided. I was really hungry when the supper-bell rang; but the craving of my stomach soon ceased in the atmosphere of the dining-room, and I was the first to leave the table.

Soon after the lamps were lighted, company began to assembly in the spacious bar-room, where were comfortable seats, with tables, newspapers, backgammon boards, dominos, etc. The first act of nearly every one who came in, was to call for a glass of liquor; and sometimes the same individual drank two or three times in the course of half an hour, on the invitation of newcomers who were convivially inclined.

Most of those who came in were strangers to me. I was looking from face to face to see if any of the old company were present, when one countenance struck me as familiar. I was studying it, in order, if possible, to identify the person, when some one addressed him as "Judge."

Changed as the face was, I now recognised it as that of Judge Lyman. Five years had marred that face terribly. It seemed twice the former size; and all its bright expression was gone. The thickened and protruding eyelids half closed the leaden eyes, and the swollen lips and cheeks gave to his countenance a look of all-predominating sensuality. True manliness had bowed itself in debasing submission to the bestial. He talked loudly, and with a pompous dogmatism—mainly on political subjects—but talked only from memory; for any one could see, that thought came into but feeble activity. And yet, derationalized, so to speak, as he was, through drink, he had been chosen a representative in Congress, at the previous election, on the antitemperance ticket, and by a very handsome majority. He was the rum candidate; and the rum interest, aided by the easily swayed "indifferents," swept aside the claims of law, order, temperance, and good morals; and the district from which he was chosen as a National Legislator sent him up to the National Councils, and said in the act—"Look upon him we have chosen as our representative, and see in him a type of our principles, our quality, and our condition as a community."

Judge Lyman, around whom a little circle soon gathered, was very severe on the temperance party, which, for two years, had opposed his election, and which, at the last struggle, showed itself to be a rapidly growing organization. During the canvass, a paper was publshed by this party, in which his personal habits, character, and moral principles were discussed in the freest manner, and certainly not in a way to elevate him in the estimation of men whose opinion was of any value.

It was not much to be wondered at, that he assumed to think temperance issues at the polls were false issues; and that when temperance men sought to tamper with elections, the liberties of the people were in danger; nor that he pronounced the whole body of temperance men as selfish schemers and canting hypocrites.

"The next thing we will have," he exclaimed, warming with his theme, and speaking so loud that his voice sounded throughout the room, and arrested every one's attention, "will be laws to fine any man who takes a chew of tobacco or lights a cigar. Touch the liberties of the people in the smallest particular, and all guarantees are gone. The Stamp Act, against which our noble forefathers rebelled, was a light measure of oppression to that contemplated by these worse than fanatics."

"You are right there, judge; right for once in your life, if you (hic) were never right before!" exclaimed a battered looking specimen of humanity, who stood near the speaker, slapping Judge Lyman on the shoulder familiarly as he spoke. "There's no telling what they will do. There's (hic) my old uncle Josh Wilson, who's been keeper of the Poor-house these ten years. Well, they're going to turn him out, if ever they get the upper hand in Bolton county."

"If? That word involves a great deal, Harry?" said Lyman. "We mus'n't let them get the upper hand. Every man has a duty to perform to his country in this matter, and every one must do his duty. But what have they got against your Uncle Joshua? What has he been doing to offend this righteous party?"

"They've nothing against him, (hic) I believe. Only, they say, they're not going to have a Poor-house in the county at all."

"What! Going to turn the poor wretches out to starve?" said one.

"Oh no! (hic)," and the fellow grinned, half shrewdly and half maliciously, as he answered—"no, not that. But, when they carry the day, there'll be no need of Poor-houses. At least, that's their talk—and I guess maybe there's something in it, for I never knew a man to go to the Poor-house, who hadn't (hic) rum to blame for his poverty. But, you see, I'm interested in this matter. I go for keeping up the Poor-house (hic); for I guess I'm travelling that road, and I should'nt like to get to the last milestone (hic) and find no snug quarters—no Uncle Josh. You're safe for one vote, anyhow, old chap, on next election day!" And the man's broad hand slapped the member's shoulder again. "Huzza for the rummies! That's (hic) the ticket! Harry Grimes never deserts his friends. True as steel."

"You're a trump!" returned Judge Lyman, with low familiarity. "Never fear about the Poor-house and Uncle Josh. They're all safe."

"But look here, judge," resumed the man. "It isn't only the Poor-house, the jail is to go next."

"Indeed!"

"Yes, that's their talk; and I guess they ain't far out of the way neither. What takes men to jail? You can tell us something about that, judge, for you've jugged a good many in your time. Didn't pretty much all of 'em drink rum? (hic.)"

But the judge answered nothing.

"Silence (hic) gives consent," resumed Grimes. "And they say more; once give 'em the upper hand—and they're confident of beating us—and the Courthouse will be to let. As for judges and lawyers, they'll starve, or go into some better business. So you see, (hic) judge, your liberties are in danger. But fight hard, old fellow; and if you must die, (hic) die game!"

How well Judge Lyman relished this mode of presenting the case, was not very apparent; he was too good a politician and office-seeker, to show any feeling on the subject, and thus endanger a vote. Harry Grimes's vote counted one, and a single vote, sometimes, gained or lost an election.

"One of their gags," he said, laughing. "But I'm too old a stager not to see the flimsiness of such pretensions. Poverty and crime have their origin in the corrupt heart, and their foundations are laid long and long before the first step is taken on the road to inebriety. It is easy to promise results; for only the few look at causes, and trace them to their effects."

"Rum and ruin, (hic). Are they not cause and effect?" asked Grimes.

"Sometimes they are," was the half extorted answer.

"Oh, Green! is that you?" exclaimed the judge, as Harvey Green came in with a soft cat-like step. He was, evidently, glad of a chance to get rid of his familiar friend and elector.

I turned my eyes upon the man, and read his face closely. It was unchanged. The same cold, sinister eye; the same chiselled mouth, so firm now, and now yielding so elastically; the same smile "from the teeth outward"—the same lines that revealed his heart's deep, dark selfishness. If he had indulged in drink during the five intervening years, it had not corrupted his blood, nor added thereto a single degree of heat.

"Have you seen any thing of Hammond this evening?" asked Judge Lyman.

"I saw him an hour or two ago," answered Green.

"How does he like his new horse?"

"He's delighted with him."

"What was the price?"

"Three hundred dollars."

"Indeed!"

The judge had already arisen, and he and Green were now walking side by side across the bar-room floor.

"I want to speak a word with you," I heard Lyman say.

And then the two went out together. I saw no more of them during the evening.

Not long afterward, Willy Hammond came in. Ah! there was a sad change here; a change that in no way belied the words of Matthew the bar-keeper. He went up to the bar, and I heard him ask for Judge Lyman. The answer was in so low a voice, that it did not reach my ear.

With a quick, nervous motion, Hammond threw his hand toward a row of decanters on the shelf behind the bar-keeper, who immediately set one of them containing brandy before him. From this he poured a tumbler half full, and drank it off at a single draught, unmixed with water.

He then asked some further question, which I could not hear, manifesting, as it appeared, considerable excitement of mind. In answering him, Matthew glanced his eyes upward, as if indicating some room in the house. The young man then retired, hurriedly, through the sitting-room.

"What's the matter with Willy Hammond to-night?" asked some one of the bar-keeper. "Who's he after in such a hurry?"

"He wants to see Judge Lyman," replied Matthew.

"Oh!"

"I guess they're after no good," was remarked.

"Not much, I'm afraid."

Two young men, well dressed, and with faces marked by intelligence, came in at the moment, drank at the bar, chatted a little while familiarly with the bar-keeper, and then quietly disappeared through the door leading into the sitting-room. I met the eyes of the man with whom I had talked during the afternoon, and his knowing wink brought to mind his suggestion, that in one of the upper rooms gambling went on nightly, and that some of the most promising young men of the town had been drawn, through the bar attraction, into this vortex of ruin. I felt a shudder creeping along my nerves.

The converstion that now went on among the company was of such an obscene and profane character, that, in disgust, I went out. The night was clear, the air soft, and the moon shining down brightly. I walked for some time in the porch, musing on what I had seen and heard; while a constant stream of visiters came pouring into the bar-room. Only a few of these remained. The larger portion went in quickly, took their glass, and then left, as if to avoid observation as much as possible.

Soon after I commenced walking in the porch I noticed an elderly lady go slowly by, who, in passing, slightly paused, and evidently tried to look through the bar-room door. The pause was but for an instant. In less than ten minutes she came back, again stopped—this time longer—and again moved off slowly, until she passed out of sight. I was yet thinking about her, when, on lifting my eyes from the ground, she was advancing along the road, but a few rods distant. I almost started at seeing her, for there no longer remained a doubt on my mind, that she was some trembling, heart-sick mother, in search of an erring son whose feet were in dangerous paths. Seeing me, she kept on, though lingeringly. She went but a short distance before returning; and this time, she moved in closer to the house, and reached a position that enabled her eyes to range through a large portion of the bar-room. A nearer inspection appeared to satisfy her. She retired with quicker steps; and did not again return during the evening.

Ah! what a commentary upon the uses of an attractive tavern was here! My heart ached, as I thought of all that unknown mother had suffered; and was doomed to suffer. I could not shut out the image of her drooping form as I lay upon my pillow that night; she even haunted me in my dreams.

☞ *Night the Sixth* ☜

MORE CONSEQUENCES

The landlord did not make his appearance on the next morning until nearly ten o'clock; and then he looked like a man who had been on a debauch. It was eleven before Harvey Green came down. Nothing about him indicated the smallest deviation from the most orderly habit. Clean shaved, with fresh linen, and a face every line of which was smoothed into calmness, he looked as if he had slept soundly on a quiet conscience, and now hailed the new day with a tranquil spirit.

The first act of Slade was to go behind the bar and take a stiff glass of brandy and water; the first act of Green, to order beefsteak and coffee for his breakfast. I noticed the meeting between the two men, on the appearance of Green. There was a slight reserve on the part of Green, and an uneasy embarrassment on the part of Slade. Not even the ghost of a smile was visible in either countenance. They spoke a few words together, and then separated as if from a sphere of mutual repulsion. I did not observe them again in company during the day.

"There's trouble over at the mill," was remarked by a gentleman with whom I had some business transactions in the afternoon. He spoke to a person who sat in his office.

"Ah! what's the matter?" said the other.

"All the hands were discharged at noon, and the mill shut down."

"How comes that?"

"They've been losing money from the start."

"Rather bad practice, I should say."

"It involves some bad practices, no doubt."

"On Willy's part?"

"Yes. He is reported to have squandered the means placed in his hands, after a shameless fashion."

"Is the loss heavy?"

"So it is said."

"How much?"

"Reaching to thirty or forty thousand dollars. But this is rumour, and, of course, an exaggeration."

"Of course. No such loss as that could have been made. But what was done with the money? How could Willy have spent it. He dashes about a great deal; buys fast horses, drinks rather freely, and all that;

but thirty or forty thousand dollars couldn't escape in this way."

At the moment a swift trotting horse, bearing a light sulky and a man, went by.

"There goes young Hammond's three hundred dollar animal," said the last speaker.

"It was Willy Hammond's yesterday. But there has been a change of ownership since then; I happen to know."

"Indeed."

"Yes. The man Green, who has been loafing about Cedarville for the last few years—after no good, I can well believe—came into possession to-day."

"Ah? Willy must be very fickle-minded. Does the possession of a coveted object so soon bring satiety?"

"There is something not clearly understood about the transaction. I saw Mr. Hammond during the forenoon, and he looked terribly distressed."

"The embarrassed condition of things at the mill readily accounts for this."

"True; but I think there are causes of trouble beyond the mere embarrassments."

"The dissolute, spendthrift habits of his son," was suggested. "These are sufficient to weigh down the father's spirits,—to bow him to the very dust."

"To speak out plainly," said the other, "I am afraid that the young man adds another vice to that of drinking and idleness."

"What?"

"Gaming."

"No!"

"There is little doubt of it in my mind. And it is further my opinion, that his fine horse, for which he paid three hundred dollars only a few days ago, has passed into the hands of this man Green, in payment of a debt contracted at the gaming table."

"You shock me. Surely, there can be no grounds for such a belief."

"I have, I am sorry to say, the gravest reasons for what I allege. That Green is a professional gambler, who was attracted here by the excellent company that assembled at the 'Sickle and Sheaf' in the beginning of the lazy miller's pauper-making experiment, I do not in the least question. Grant this, and take into account the fact that young Hammond has been much in his company, and you have sufficient cause for the most disastrous effects."

"If this be really so," observed the gentleman, over whose face a shadow of concern darkened, "then Willy Hammond may not be his only victim."

"And is not, you may rest assured. If rumour be true, other of our promising young men are being drawn into the whirling circles that narrow toward a vortex of ruin."

In corroboration of this, I mentioned the conversation I had held with one of the frequenters of Slade's bar-room, on this very subject; and also what I had myself observed on the previous evening.

The man, who had until now been sitting quietly in a chair, started up, exclaiming as he did so—

"Merciful heaven! I never dreamed of this! Whose sons are safe?"

"No man's," was the answer of the gentleman in whose office we were sitting—"No man's—while there are such open doors to ruin as you may find at the 'Sickle and Sheaf.' Did not you vote the anti-temperance ticket at the last election?"

"I did," was the answer; "and from principle."

"On what were your principles based?" was inquired.

"On the broad foundations of civil liberty."

"The liberty to do good or evil, just as the individual may choose?"

"I would not like to say that. There are certain evils against which there can be no legislation that would not do harm. No civil power in this country has the right to say what a citizen shall eat or drink."

"But may not the people, in any community, pass laws, through their delegated law-makers, restraining evil-minded persons from injuring the common good?"

"Oh, certainly—certainly."

"And are you prepared to affirm, that a drinking shop, where young men are corrupted—ay, destroyed, body and soul—does not work an injury to the common good?"

"Ah! but there must be houses of public entertainment."

"No one denies this. But can that be a really Christian community which provides for the moral debasement of strangers, at the same time that it entertains them? Is it necessary that, in giving rest and entertainment to the traveller, we also lead him into temptation?"

"Yes—But—but——it is going too far to legislate on what we are to eat and drink. It is opening too wide a door for fanatical oppression. We must inculcate temperance as a right principal. We must teach our children the evils of intemperance, and send them out into the world as practical teachers of order, virtue, and sobriety. If we do this, the reform becomes radical, and in a few years there will be no bar-rooms, for none will crave the fiery poison."

"Of little value, my friend, will be, in far too many cases, your precepts, if temptation invites our sons at almost every step of their way through life. Thousands have fallen, and thousands are now tottering, soon to fall. Your sons are not safe; nor are mine. We cannot tell the day nor the hour when they may weakly yield to the solicitation of some companion, and enter the wide open door of ruin. And are we wise and good citizens to commission men to do the evil work of enticement? To encourage them to get gain in corrupting and destroying our children? To hesitate over some vague ideal of human liberty, when the sword is among us, slaying our best and dearest? Sir! while you hold back from the work of staying the flood that is desolating our fairest homes, the black waters are approaching your own doors."

There was a startling emphasis in the tones with which this last sentence was uttered; and I did not wonder at the look of anxious alarm that it called to the face of him whose fears it was meant to excite.

"What do you mean, sir?" was inquired.

"Simply, that your sons are in equal danger with others."

"And is that all?"

"They have been seen, of late, in the bar-room of the 'Sickle and Sheaf.' "

"Who says so?"

"Twice within a week I have seen them going in there," was answered.

"Good heavens! No!"

"It is true, my friend. But who is safe? If we dig pits, and conceal them from view, what marvel if our own children fall therein?"

"My sons going to a tavern!" The man seemed utterly confounded. "How *can* I believe it? You must be in error, sir."

"No. What I tell you is the simple truth. And if they go there——"

The man paused not to hear the conclusion of the sentence, but went hastily from the office.

"We are beginning to reap as we have sown," remarked the gentleman, turning to me as his agitated friend left the office. "As I told them in the commencement it would be, so it is happening. The want of a good tavern in Cedarville was over and over again alleged as one of the chief causes of our want of thrift, and when Slade opened the 'Sickle and Sheaf,' the man was almost glorified. The gentleman who has just left us failed not in laudation of the enterprising landlord; the more particularly, as the building of the new tavern advanced the price of ground on the street, and made him a few hundred dollars richer. Really, for a time, one might have thought, from the way people went on, that Simon Slade was going to make every man's fortune in Cedarville. But all that has been gained by a small advance in property, is as a grain of sand to a mountain, compared with the fearful demoralization that has followed."

I readily assented to this, for I had myself seen enough to justify the conclusion.

As I sat in the bar-room of the "Sickle and Sheaf" that evening, I noticed, soon after the lamps were lighted, the gentleman referred to in the above conversation, whose sons were represented as visitors to the bar, come in quietly, and look anxiously about the room. He spoke to no one, and, after satisfying himself that those he sought were not there, went out.

"What sent him here, I wonder?" muttered Slade, speaking partly to himself, and partly aside to Matthew, the bar-keeper.

"After the boys, I suppose," was answered.

"I guess the boys are old enough to take care of themselves."

"They ought to be," returned Matthew.

"And are," said Slade. "Have they been here this evening?"

"No, not yet."

While they yet talked together, two young men whom I had seen on the night before, and noticed particularly as showing signs of intelligence and respectability beyond the ordinary visiters at a bar-room, came in.

"John," I heard Slade say, in a low, confidential voice, to one of them, "your old man was here just now."

"No!" The young man looked startled—almost confounded.

"It's a fact. So you'd better keep shady."

"What did he want?"

"I don't know."

"What did he say?"

"Nothing. He just came in, looked around, and then went out."

"His face was dark as a thunder-cloud," remarked Matthew.

"Is No. 4 vacant?" inquired one of the young men.

"Yes."

"Send us up a bottle of wine and some cigars. And when Bill Harding and Harry Lee come in, tell them where they can find us."

"All right," said Matthew. "And now take a friend's advice and make yourselves scarce."

The young men left the room hastily. Scarcely had they departed, ere I saw the same gentleman come in, whose anxious face had, a little while before, thrown its shadow over the apartment. He was the father in search of his sons. Again he glanced around, nervously; and this time appeared to be disappointed. As he entered, Slade went out.

"Have John and Wilson been here this evening?" he asked, coming up to the bar and addressing Matthew.

"They are not here," replied Matthew, evasively.

"But haven't they been here?"

"They *may* have been here; I only came in from my supper a little while ago."

"I thought I saw them entering, only a moment or two ago."

"They're not here, sir." Matthew shook his head and spoke firmly.

"Where is Mr. Slade?"

"In the house, somewhere."

"I wish you would ask him to step here."

Matthew went out, but in a little while came back with word that the landlord was not to be found.

"You are sure the boys are not here," said the man, with a doubting, dissatisfied manner.

"See for yourself, Mr. Harrison!"

"Perhaps they are in the parlour?"

"Step in, sir," coolly returned Matthew. The man went through the door into the sitting-room, but came back immediately.

"Not there?" said Matthew. The man shook his head. "I don't think you will find them about here," added the bar-keeper.

Mr. Harrison—this was the name by which Matthew had addressed him—stood musing and irresolute for some minutes. He could not be mistaken about the entrance of his sons, and yet they were not there. His manner was much perplexed. At length he took a seat, in a far corner of the bar-room, somewhat beyond the line of observation, evidently with the purpose of waiting to see if those he sought would come in. He had not been there long, before two young men entered, whose appearance at once excited his interest. They went up to the bar and called for liquor. As Matthew set the decanter before them, he leaned over the counter, and said something in a whisper.

"Where?" was instantly ejaculated, in surprise, and both of the young men glanced uneasily about the room. They met the eyes of Mr. Harrison, fixed intently upon them. I do not think, from the way they swallowed their brandy and water, that it was enjoyed very much.

"What the deuce is he doing here?" I heard one of them say, in a low voice.

"After the boys, of course."

"Have they come yet?"

Matthew winked as he answered, "All safe."

"In No. 4!"

"Yes. And the wine and cigars all waiting for you."

"Good."

"You'd better not go through the parlour. Their old man's not at all satisfied. He half suspects they're in the house. Better go off down the street, and come back and enter through the passage."

The young men, acting on this hint, at once retired, the eyes of Harrison following them out.

For nearly an hour Mr. Harrison kept his position, a close observer of all that transpired. I am very much in error, if, before leaving that sink of iniquity, he was not fully satisfied as to the propriety of legislating on the liquor question. Nay, I incline to the opinion, that, if the power of suppression had rested in his hands, there would not have been, in the whole State, at the expiration of an hour, a single dram-selling establishment. The goring of his ox had opened his eyes to the true merits of the question. While he was yet in the bar-room, young Hammond made his appearance. His look was wild and excited. First he called for brandy, and drank with the eagerness of a man long athirst.

"Where is Green?" I heard him inquire, as he set his glass upon the counter.

"Haven't seen any thing since supper," was answered by Matthew.

"Is he in his room?"

"I think it probable."

"Has Judge Lyman been about here to-night?"

"Yes. He spouted here for half an hour against the temperance party, as usual, and then"—Matthew tossed his head toward the door leading to the sitting-room.

Hammond was moving toward this door, when, in glancing around the room, he encountered the fixed gaze of Mr. Harrison—a gaze that instantly checked his progress. Returning to the bar, and leaning over the counter, he said to Matthew,

"What has sent him here?"

Matthew winked knowingly.

"After the boys?" inquired Hammond.

"Yes."

"Where are they?"

"Up-stairs."

"Does he suspect this?"

"I can't tell. If he doesn't think them here now, he is looking for them to come in."

"Do they know he is after them?"

"O yes."

"All safe then?"

"As an iron chest. If you want to see them, just tap at No. 4."

Hammond stood for some minutes leaning on the bar, and then, not once again looking toward that part of the room where Mr. Harrison was seated, passed out through the door leading to the street. Soon afterward Mr. Harrison departed.

Disgusted, as on the night before, with the unceasing flow of vile, obscene, and profane language, I left my place of observation in the bar-room and sought the open air. The sky was unobscured by a single cloud, and the moon, almost at the full, shone abroad with more than common brightness. I had not been sitting long in the porch, when the same lady, whose movements had attracted my attention, came in sight, walking very slowly—the deliberate pace assumed, evidently, for the purpose of better observation. On coming opposite the tavern, she slightly paused, as on the evening before, and then kept on, passing down the street, until she was beyond observation.

"Poor mother!" I was still repeating to myself, when her form again met my eyes. Slowly she advanced, and now came in nearer to the house. The interest excited in my mind was so strong, that I could not repress the desire I felt to address her, and so stepped from the shadow of the porch. She seemed startled, and retreated backward several paces.

"Are you in search of any one?" I inquired, respectfully.

The woman now stood in a position that let the moon shine full upon her face, revealing every feature. She was far past the meridian of life; and there were lines of suffering and sorrow on her fine countenance. I saw that her lips moved, but it was time before I distinguished the words.

"Have you seen my son to-night? They say he comes here."

The manner in which this was said caused a cold thrill to run over me. I perceived that the woman's mind wandered. I answered—

"No, ma'am; I haven't seen any thing of him."

My tone of voice seemed to inspire her with confidence, for she came up close to me, and bent her face toward mine.

"It's a dreadful place," she whispered, huskily. "And they say he comes here. Poor boy! He isn't what he used to be."

"It is a very bad place," said I. "Come"—and I moved a step or two in the direction from which I had seen her approaching—"come, you'd better go away as quickly as possible."

"But if he's here," she answered, not moving from where she stood, "I might save him, you know."

"I am sure you won't find him, ma'am," I urged. "Perhaps he is home, now."

"Oh, no! no!" and she shook her head mournfully. "He never comes home until long after midnight. I wish I could see inside of the bar-room. I'm sure he must be there."

"If you will tell me his name, I will go in and search for him."

After a moment of hesitation, she answered,

"His name is Willy Hammond."

How the name, uttered so sadly, and yet with such moving tenderness by the mother's lips, caused me to start—almost to tremble.

"If he is in the house, ma'am," said I, firmly, "I will see him for you." And I left her and went into the bar.

"In what room do you think I will find young Hammond?" I asked of the bar-keeper.

He looked at me curiously, but did not answer. The question had come upon him unanticipated.

"In Harvey Green's room?" I pursued.

"I don't know, I am sure. He isn't in the house to my knowledge. I saw him go out about half an hour since."

"Green's room is No.——?"

"Eleven," he answered.

"In the front part of the house?"

"Yes."

I asked no further question, but went to No. 11, and tapped on the door. But no one answered the summons. I listened, but could not distinguish the slightest sound within. Again I knocked; but louder. If my ears did not deceive me, the clink of coin was heard. Still there was neither voice nor movement.

I was disappointed. That the room had inmates, I felt sure. Remembering, now, what I had heard about light being seen in this room through a rent in the curtain, I went down-stairs, and out into the street. A short distance beyond the house, I saw, dimly, the woman's form. She had only just passed in her movement to and fro. Glancing up at the window, which I now knew to be the one in Green's room, light through the torn curtain was plainly visible. Back into the house I went, and up to No. 11. This time I knocked imperatively; and this time made myself heard.

"What's wanted?" came from within. I knew the voice to be that of Harvey Green.

I only knocked louder. A hurried movement and the low murmur of voices was heard for some moments; then the door was unlocked and held partly open by Green, whose body so filled the narrow aperture that I could not look into the room. Seeing me, a dark scowl fell upon his countenance.

"What d'ye want?" he inquired, sharply.

"Is Mr. Hammond here? If so, he is wanted down-stairs."

"No, he's not," was the quick answer. "What sent you here for him, hey?"

"The fact that I expected to find him in your room," was my firm answer.

Green was about shutting the door in my face, when some one

placed a hand on his shoulder, and said something to him that I could not hear.

"Who wants to see him?" he inquired of me.

Satisfied, now, that Hammond was in the room, I said, slightly elevating my voice.

"His mother."

The words were an "open sesame" to the room. The door was suddenly jerked open, and with a blanching face, the young man confronted me.

"Who says my mother is down-stairs?" he demanded.

"I come from her in search of you," said I. "You will find her in the road, walking up and down in front of the tavern."

Almost with a bound he swept by me, and descended the stairway at two or three long strides. As the door swung open, I saw, besides Green and Hammond, the landlord and Judge Lyman. It needed not the loose cards on a table near which the latter were sitting to tell me of their business in that room.

As quickly as seemed decorous, I followed Hammond. On the porch I met him, coming in from the road.

"You have deceived me, sir," said he, sternly—almost menacingly.

"No, sir!" I replied. "What I told you was but too true. Look! There she is now."

The young man sprung around, and stood before the woman, a few paces distant.

"Mother! oh, mother! what *has* brought you here?" he exclaimed, in an under tone, as he caught her arm, and moved away. He spoke—not roughly, nor angrily—but with respect—half reproachfulness—and an unmistakable tenderness.

"Oh, Willy! Willy!" I heard her answer. "Somebody said you came here at night, and I couldn't rest. Oh, dear! They'll murder you! I know they will. Don't, oh!—"

My ears took in the sense no further, though her pleading voice still reached my ears. A few moments, and they were out of sight.

Nearly two hours afterward, as I was ascending to my chamber, a man brushed quickly by me. I glanced after him, and recognised the person of young Hammond. He was going to the room of Harvey Green!

☞ *Night the Seventh* ☜

SOWING THE WIND

The state of affairs in Cedarville, it was plain, from the partial glimpses I had received, was rather desperate. Desperate, I mean, as regarded the various parties brought before my observation. An eating cancer was on the community, and so far as the eye could mark its destructive progress, the ravages were fearful. That its roots were striking deep, and penetrating, concealed from view, in many unsuspected directions, there could be no doubt. What appeared on the surface was but a milder form of the disease, compared with its hidden, more vital, and more dangerous advances.

I could not but feel a strong interest in some of these parties. The case of young Hammond, had from the first, awakened concern; and now a new element was added in the unlooked-for appearance of his mother on the stage, in a state that seemed one of partial derangement. The gentleman at whose office I met Mr. Harrison on the day before—the reader will remember Mr. H. as having come to the "Sickle and Sheaf" in search of his sons—was thoroughly conversant with the affairs of the village, and I called upon him early in the day in order to make some inquiries about Mrs. Hammond. My first question, as to whether he knew the lady, was answered by the remark—

"Oh, yes. She is one of my earliest friends."

The allusion to her did not seem to awaken agreeable states of mind. A slight shade obscured his face, and I noticed that he sighed involuntarily.

"Is Willy her only child?"

"Her only living child. She had four; another son, and two daughters; but she lost all but Willy when they were quite young. And," he added, after a pause—"it would have been better for her, and for Willy too, if he had gone to a better land with them."

"His course of life must be to her a terrible affliction," said I.

"It is destroying her reason," he replied, with emphasis. "He was her idol. No mother ever loved a son with more self-devotion than Mrs. Hammond loved her beautiful, fine-spirited, intelligent, affectionate boy. To say that she was proud of him, is but a tame expression. Intense love—almost idolatry—was the strong passion of her heart.

How tender, how watchful was her love! Except when at school, he was scarcely ever separated from her. In order to keep him by her side, she gave up her thoughts to the suggestion and maturing of plans for keeping his mind active and interested in her society—and her success was perfect. Up to the age of sixteen or seventeen, I do not think he had a desire for other companionship than that of his mother. But this, you know, could not last. The boy's maturing thoughts must go beyond the home and social circle. The great world, that he was soon to enter, was before him; and through loopholes that opened here and there, he obtained partial glimpses of what was beyond. To step forth into this world, where he was soon to be a busy actor and worker, and to step forth alone, next came in the natural order of progress. How his mother trembled with anxiety, as she saw him leave her side. Of the danger that would surround his path, she knew too well; and these were magnified by her fears—at least so I often said to her. Alas! how far the sad reality has outrun her most fearful anticipations.

"When Willy was eighteen—he was then reading law—I think I never saw a young man of fairer promise. As I have often heard it remarked of him, he did not appear to have a single fault. But he had a dangerous gift—rare conversational powers, united with great urbanity of manner. Every one who made his acquaintance became charmed with his society; and he soon found himself surrounded by a circle of young men, some of whom were not the best companions he might have chosen. Still, his own pure instincts and honourable principles were his safeguard; and I never have believed that any social allurements would have drawn him away from the right path, if this accursed tavern had not been opened by Slade."

"There was a tavern here before the 'Sickle and Sheaf' was opened," said I.

"Oh, yes. But it was badly kept, and the bar-room visitors were of the lowest class. No respectable young man in Cedarville would have been seen there. It offered no temptations to one moving in Willy's circle. But the opening of the 'Sickle and Sheaf' formed a new era. Judge Hammond—himself not the purest man in the world, I'm afraid —gave his countenance to the establishment, and talked of Simon Slade as an enterprising man who ought to be encouraged. Judge Lyman and other men of position in Cedarville followed his bad example; and the bar-room of the 'Sickle and Sheaf' was at once voted respectable. At all times of the day and evening you could see the flower of our young men going in and out, sitting in front of the bar-room, or talking hand and glove with the landlord, who, from a worthy miller, regarded as well enough in his place, was suddenly elevated into a man of importance, whom the best in the village were delighted to honour.

"In the beginning, Willy went with the tide, and, in an incredibly short period, was acquiring a fondness for drink that startled and alarmed his friends. In going in through Slade's open door, he entered the downward way, and has been moving onward with fleet footsteps ever since. The fiery poison inflamed his mind, at the same time that it dimmed his noble perceptions. Fondness for mere pleasure followed, and this led him into various sensual indulgences, and exciting modes of passing the time. Every one liked him—he was so free, so companionable, and so generous—and almost every one encouraged, rather than repressed, his dangerous proclivities. Even his father, for a time, treated the matter lightly, as only the first flush of young life. 'I commenced sowing my wild oats at quite as early an age,' I have heard him say. 'He'll cool off, and do well enough. Never fear.' But his mother was in a state of painful alarm from the beginning. Her truer instincts, made doubly acute by her yearning love, perceived the imminent danger, and in all possible ways did she seek to lure him from the path in which he was moving at so rapid a pace. Willy was always very much attached to his mother, and her influence over him was strong; but in this case he regarded her fears as chimerical. The way in which he walked was, to him, so pleasant, and the companions of his journey so delightful, that he could not believe in the prophesied evil; and when his mother talked to him in her warning voice, and with a sad countenance, he smiled at her concern, and made light of her fears.

"And so it went on, month after month, and year after year, until the young man's sad declensions were the town talk. In order to throw his mind into a new channel—to awaken, if possible, a new and better interest in life—his father ventured upon the doubtful experiment we spoke of yesterday: that of placing capital in his hands, and making him an equal partner in the business of distilling and cotton-spinning. The disastrous—I might say disgraceful result—you know. The young man squandered his own capital, and heavily embarrassed his father.

"The effect of all this upon Mrs. Hammond has been painful in the extreme. We can only dimly imagine the terrible suffering through which she has passed. Her present aberration was first visible after a long period of sleeplessness, occasioned by distress of mind. During the whole of two weeks, I am told, she did not close her eyes; the most of that time walking the floor of her chamber, and weeping. Powerful anodynes, frequently repeated, at length brought relief. But, when she awoke from a prolonged period of unconsciousness, the brightness of her reason was gone. Since then, she has never been clearly conscious of what was passing around her, and well for her, I have sometimes thought it was, for even obscurity of intellect is a blessing in her case. Ah, me! I always get the heart-ache, when I think of her."

"Did not this event startle the young man from his fatal dream, if I may so call his mad infatuation?" I asked.

"No. He loved his mother, and was deeply afflicted by the calamity; but it seemed as if he could not stop. Some terrible necessity appeared to be impelling him onward. If he formed good resolutions—and I doubt not that he did,—they were blown away like threads of gossamer, the moment he came within the sphere of old associations. His way to the mill was by the 'Sickle and Sheaf;' and it was not easy for him to pass there without being drawn into the bar, either by his own desire for drink or through the invitation of some pleasant companion, who was lounging in front of the tavern."

"There may have been something even more impelling than his love of drink," said I.

"What?"

I related, briefly, the occurrences of the preceding night.

"I feared—nay, I was certain—that he was in the toils of this man! And yet your confirmation of the fact startles and confounds me," said he, moving about his office in a disturbed manner. "If my mind has questioned and doubted in regard to young Hammond, it questions and doubts no longer. The word 'mystery' is not now written over the door of his habitation. Great Father! and is it thus that our young men are led into temptation? Thus that their ruin is premeditated, secured? Thus that the fowler is permitted to spread his net in the open day, and the destroyer licensed to work ruin in darkness? It is awful to contemplate!'

The man was strongly excited.

"Thus it is," he continued; "and we who see the whole extent, origin, and downward rushing force of a widely sweeping desolation, lift our voices of warning almost in vain. Men who have everything at stake—sons to be corrupted, and daughters to become the wives of young men exposed to corrupting influences—stand aloof, questioning and doubting as to the expediency of protecting the innocent from the wolfish designs of bad men, who, to compass their own selfish ends, would destroy them body and soul. We are called fanatics, ultraists, designing, and all that, because we ask our law-makers to stay the fiery ruin. Oh, no! we must not touch the traffic. All the dearest and best interests of society may suffer; but the rum-seller must be protected. He must be allowed to get gain, if the jails and poor-houses are filled, and the graveyards made fat with the bodies of young men stricken down in the flower of their years, and of wives and mothers who have died of broken hearts. Reform, we are told, must commence at home. We must rear temperate children, and then we shall have temperate men. That when there are none to desire liquor, the rum-seller's traffic will cease. And all the while society's true benefactors are engaged in doing this, the weak, the unsuspecting, and the erring must be left an easy prey, even if the work requires for its accomplishment a hundred years. Sir! a human soul destroyed through the rum-seller's infernal agency, is a sacrifice priceless in value. No considerations of worldy gain can, for an instant, be placed in comparison therewith. And yet souls are destroyed by thousands every year; and they will fall by tens of thousands ere society awakens from its fatal indifference, and lays its strong hand of power on the corrupt men who are scattering disease, ruin, and death, broadcast over the land!

"I always get warm on this subject," he added, repressing his enthusiasm. "And who that observes and reflects can help growing excited? The evil is appalling; and the indifference of the community one of the strangest facts of the day."

While he was yet speaking, the elder Mr. Hammond came in. He looked wretched. The redness and humidity of his eyes showed want of sleep, and the relaxed muscles of his face exhaustion from weariness and suffering. He drew the person with whom I had been talking aside, and continued in earnest conversation with him for many minutes—often gesticulating violently. I could see his face, though I heard nothing of what he said. The play of his features was painful to look upon, for every changing muscle showed a new phase of mental suffering.

"Try and see him, will you not?" he said, as he turned, at length, to leave the office.

"I will go there immediately," was answered.

"Bring him home, if possible."

"My very best efforts shall be made."

Judge Hammond bowed, and went out hurriedly.

"Do you know the number of the room occupied by the man Green?" asked the gentleman, as soon as his visitor had retired.

"Yes. It is No. 11."

"Willy has not been home since last night. His father, at this late day, suspects Green to be a gambler! The truth flashed upon him only yesterday; and this, added to his other sources of trouble, is driving him, so he says, almost mad. As a friend, he wishes me to go to the 'Sickle and Sheaf,' and try and find Willy. Have you seen any thing of him this morning?"

I answered in the negative.

"Nor of Green?"

"No."

"Was Slade about when you left the tavern?"

"I saw nothing of him."

"What Judge Hammond fears may be all too true—that, in the present condition of Willy's affairs, which have reached the point of disaster, his tempter means to secure the largest possible share of property yet in his power to pledge or transfer,—to squeeze from his victim the last drop of blood that remains, and then fling him, ruthlessly, from his hands."

"The young man must have been rendered almost desperate, or he would never have returned, as he did, last night. Did you mention this to his father?"

"No. It would have distressed him the more, without effecting any good. He is wretched enough. But time passes, and none is to be lost now. Will you go with me?"

I walked to the tavern with him; and we went into the bar together. Two or three men were at the counter, drinking.

"Is Mr. Green about this morning?" was asked by the person who had come in search of young Hammond.

"Haven't seen any thing of him."

"Is he in his room?"

"I don't know."

"Will you ascertain for me?"

"Certainly. Frank,"—and he spoke to the landlord's son, who was lounging on a settee,—"I wish you would see if Mr. Green is in his room."

"Go and see yourself. I'm not your waiter," was growled back, in an ill-natured voice.

"In a moment I'll ascertain for you," said Matthew, politely.

After waiting on some new customers, who were just entering, Matthew went up-stairs to obtain the desired information. As he left the bar-room, Frank got up and went behind the counter, where he mixed himself a glass of liquor, and drank it off, evidently with real enjoyment.

"Rather a dangerous business for one so young as you are," remarked the gentleman with whom I had come, as Frank stepped out of the bar, and passed near where we were standing. The only answer to this was an ill-natured frown, and an expression of face which said, almost as plainly as words, "It's none of your business."

"Not there," said Matthew, now coming in.

"Are you certain?"

"Yes, sir."

But there was a certain involuntary hesitation in the bar-keeper's manner, which led to a suspicion that his answer was not in accordance with the truth. We walked out together, conferring on the subject, and both concluded that his word was not to be relied upon.

"What is to be done?" was asked.

"Go to Green's room," I replied, "and knock at the door. If he is there, he may answer, not suspecting your errand."

"Show me the room."

I went up with him, and pointed out No. 11. He knocked lightly, but there came no sound from within. He repeated the knock; all was silent. Again and again he knocked, but there came back only a hollow reverberation.

"There's no one there," said he, returning to where I stood, and we walked down-stairs together. On the landing, as we reached the lower passage, we met Mrs. Slade. I had not, during this visit at Cedarville, stood face to face with her before. Oh! what a wreck she presented, with her pale, shrunken countenance, hollow, lustreless eyes, and bent, feeble body. I almost shuddered as I looked at her. What a haunting and sternly rebuking spectre she must have moved, daily, before the eyes of her husband.

"Have you noticed Mr. Green about this morning?" I asked.

"He hasn't come down from his room yet," she replied.

"Are you certain?" said my companion. "I knocked several times at the door just now, but received no answer."

"What do you want with him?" asked Mrs. Slade, fixing her eyes upon us.

"We are in search of Willy Hammond; and it has been suggested that he is with Green."

"Knock twice lightly, and then three times more firmly," said Mrs. Slade; and as she spoke, she glided past us with noiseless tread.

"Shall we go up together?"

I did not object, for, although I had no delegated right of intrusion, my feelings were so much excited in the case, that I went forward, scarcely reflecting on the propriety of so doing.

The signal knock found instant answer. The door was softly opened, and the unshaven face of Simon Slade presented itself.

"Mr. Jacobs!" he said, with surprise in his tones. "Do you wish to see me?"

"No, sir; I wish to see Mr. Green," and with a quick, firm pressure against the door, he pushed it wide open. The same party was there that I had seen on the night before,—Green, young Hammond, Judge Lyman, and Slade. On the table at which the three formerly were sitting, were cards, slips of paper, an inkstand and pens, and a pile of bank-notes. On a side table, or, rather, butler's tray, were bottles, decanters, and glasses.

"Judge Lyman! Is it possible?" exclaimed Mr. Jacobs, the name of my companion: "I did not expect to find you here."

Green instantly swept his hands over the table to secure the money and bills it contained; but, ere he had accomplished his purpose, young Hammond grappled three or four narrow strips of paper, and hastily tore them into shreds.

"You're a cheating scoundrel!" cried Green, fiercely, thrusting his hand into his bosom as if to draw from thence a weapon; but, the words were scarcely uttered, ere Hammond sprung upon him with the fierceness of a tiger, bearing him down upon the floor. Both hands were already about the gambler's neck, and, ere the bewildered spectators could interfere, and drag him off, Green was purple in the face, and nearly strangled.

"Call me a cheating scoundrel!" said Hammond, foaming at the mouth, as he spoke,—"Me! whom you have followed like a thirsty bloodhound. Me! whom you have robbed, and cheated, and debased from the beginning! Oh! for a pistol to rid the earth of the blackest-hearted villain that walks its surface. Let me go, gentlemen! I have nothing left in the world to care for,—there is no consequence I fear. Let me do society one good service before I die!"

And, with one vigorous effort, he swept himself clear of the hands that were pinioning him, and sprung again upon the gambler with the fierce energy of a savage beast. By this time, Green had got his knife free from its sheath, and, as Hammond was closing upon him in his blind rage, plunged it into his side. Quick almost as lightning, the knife was withdrawn, and two more stabs inflicted ere we could seize and disarm the murderer. As we did so, Willy Hammond fell over with a deep groan, the blood flowing from his side.

In the terror and excitement that followed, Green rushed from the room. The doctor, who was instantly summoned, after carefully examining the wound, and the condition of the unhappy young man, gave it as his opinion that he was fatally injured.

Oh! the anguish of the father, who had quickly heard of the dreadful occurrence, when this announcement was made. I never saw such fearful agony in any human countenance. The calmest of all the anxious group was Willy himself. On his father's face his eyes were fixed as if by a kind of fascination.

"Are you in much pain, my poor boy!" sobbed the old man, stooping over him, until his long white hair mingled with the damp locks of the sufferer

"Not much, father," was the whispered reply. "Don't speak of this to mother, yet. I'm afraid it will kill her."

What could the father answer? Nothing! And he was silent.

"Does she know of it?" A shadow went over his face.

Mr. Hammond shook his head.

Yet, even as he spoke, a wild cry of distress was heard below. Some indiscreet person had borne to the ears of the mother the fearful news about her son, and she had come wildly flying toward the tavern, and was just entering.

"It is my poor mother," said Willy, a flush coming into his pale face. "Who could have told her of this?"

Mr. Hammond started for the door, but ere he had reached it, the distracted mother entered.

"Oh! Willy, my boy! my boy!" she exclaimed, in tones of anguish that made the heart shudder. And she crouched down on the floor, the moment she reached the bed whereon he lay, and pressed her lips —oh, so tenderly and lovingly!—to his.

"Dear mother! Sweet mother! Best of mothers!" He even smiled as he said this; and, into the face that now bent over him, looked up with glances of unutterable fondness.

"Oh, Willy! Willy! Willy! my son, my son!" And again her lips were laid closely to his.

Mr. Hammond now interfered, and endeavoured to remove his wife, fearing for the consequence upon his son.

"Don't, father!" said Willy; "let her remain. I am not excited nor disturbed. I am glad that she is here, now. It will be best for us both."

"You must not excite him, dear," said Mr. Hammond—"he is very weak."

"I'll not excite him," answered the mother. "I'll not speak a word. There, love"—and she laid her fingers softly upon the lips of her son— "don't speak a single word."

For only a few moments did she sit with the quiet formality of a nurse, who feels how much depends on the repose of her patient. Then she began, weeping, moaning, and wringing her hands.

"Mother!" The feeble voice of Willy stilled, instantly, the tempest of feeling. "Mother, kiss me!"

She bent down and kissed him.

"Are you there, mother?" His eyes moved about, with a straining motion.

"Yes, love, here I am."

"I don't see you, mother. It's getting so dark. Oh, mother! mother!" he shouted suddenly, starting up and throwing himself forward upon her bosom—"save me! save me!"

How quickly did the mother clasp her arms around him—how eagerly did she strain him to her bosom! The doctor, fearing the worst consequences, now came forward, and endeavoured to release the arms of Mrs. Hammond, but she resisted every attempt to do so.

"I will save you, my son," she murmured in the ears of the young man. "Your mother will protect you. Oh! if you had never left her side, nothing on earth could have done you harm."

"He is dead!" I heard the doctor whisper; and, a thrill of horror went through me. The words reached the ears of Mr. Hammond, and his groan was one of almost mortal agony.

"Who says he is dead?" came sharply from the lips of the mother, as she pressed the form of her child back upon the bed from which he had sprung to her arms, and looked wildly upon his face. One long scream of horror told of her convictions, and she fell, lifeless, across the body of her dead son!

All in the room believed that Mrs. Hammond had only fainted. But the doctor's perplexed, troubled countenance, as he ordered her carried into another apartment, and the ghastliness of her face when it was upturned to the light, suggested to every one what proved to be true. Even to her obscured perceptions, the consciousness that her son was dead came with a terrible vividness—so terrible, that it extinguished her life.

Like fire among dry stubble ran the news of this fearful event through Cedarville. The whole town was wild with excitement. The prominent fact, that Willy Hammond had been murdered by Green, whose real profession was known by many, and now declared to all, was on every tongue; but a hundred different and exaggerated stories as to the cause and the particulars of the event were in circulation. By the time preparations to remove the dead bodies of mother and son from the "Sickle and Sheaf," to the residence of Mr. Hammond, were completed, hundreds of people, men, women, and children, were assembled around the tavern; and many voices were clamorous for Green; while some called out for Judge Lyman, whose name, it thus appeared, had become associated in the minds of the people with the murderous affair. The appearance, in the midst of this excitement, of the two dead bodies, borne forth on settees, did not tend to allay the feverish state of indignation that prevailed. From more than one voice, I heard the words, "Lynch the scoundrel!"

A part of the crowd followed the sad procession, while the greater portion, consisting of men, remained about the tavern. All bodies, no matter for what purpose assembled, quickly finding leading spirits who, feeling the great moving impulse, give it voice and direction. It was so in this case. Intense indignation against Green was firing every bosom; and when a man elevated himself a few feet above the agitated mass of humanity, and cried out—

"The murderer must not escape!"

A wild responding shout, terrible in its fierceness, made the air quiver.

"Let ten men be chosen to search the house and premises," said the leading spirit.

"Ay! ay! Choose them! Name them!" was quickly answered.

Ten men were called by name, who instantly stepped in front of the crowd.

"Search everywhere; from garret to cellar; from hayloft to dog-kennel. Everywhere! everywhere!" cried the man.

And instantly the ten men entered the house. For nearly a quarter of an hour, the crowd waited with increasing signs of impatience. These delegates at length appeared, with the announcement that Green was nowhere about the premises. It was received with a groan.

"Let no man in Cedarville do a stroke of work until the murderer is found," now shouted the individual who still occupied his elevated position.

"Agreed! agreed! No work in Cedarville until the murderer is found," rang out fiercely.

"Let all who have horses, saddle and bridle them as quickly as possible, and assemble, mounted, at the Court House."

About fifty men left the crowd hastily.

"Let the crowd part in the centre, up and down the road, starting from a line in front of me."

This order was obeyed.

"Separate again, taking the centre of the road for a line."

Four distinct bodies of men stood now in front of the tavern.

"Now search for the murderer in every nook and corner, for a distance of three miles from this spot; each party keeping to its own section; the road being one dividing line, and a line through the centre of this tavern the other. The horsemen will pursue the wretch to a greater distance."

More than a hundred acquiescing voices responded to this, as the man sprung down from his elevation and mingled with the crowd, which began instantly to move away on its appointed mission.

As the hours went by, one, and another, and another, of the searching party returned to the village, wearied with their efforts, or confident that the murderer had made good his escape. The horsemen, too, began to come in, during the afternoon, and by sundown, the last of them, worn out and disappointed, made their appearace.

For hours after the exciting events of the forenoon, there were but few visitors at the "Sickle and Sheaf." Slade, who did not show himself among the crowd, came down soon after its dispersion. He had shaved and put on clean linen; but still bore many evidences of a night spent without sleep. His eyes were red and heavy and the eyelids swollen; while his skin was relaxed and colourless. As he descended the stairs, I was walking in the passage. He looked shy at me, and merely nodded. Guilt was written plainly on his countenance; and with it was blended anxiety and alarm. That he might be involved in trouble, he had reason to fear; for, he was one of the party engaged in gambling in Green's room, as both Mr. Jacobs and I had witnessed.

"This is dreadful business," said he, as we met, face to face, half an hour afterward. He did not look me steadily in the eyes.

"It is horrible!" I answered. "To corrupt and ruin a young man, and then murder him! There are few deeds in the catalogue of crime blacker than this."

"It was done in the heat of passion," said the landlord, with something of apology in his manner. "Green never meant to kill him."

"In peaceful intercourse with his fellow men, why did he carry a deadly weapon? There was murder in his heart, sir."

"That is speaking very strongly."

"Not stronger than facts will warrant," I replied. "That Green is a murderer in heart, it needed not this awful consummation to show. With a cool, deliberate purpose, he has sought, from the beginning, to destroy young Hammond."

"It is hardly fair," answered Slade, "in the present feverish excitement against Green, to assume such a questionable position. It may do him a great wrong."

"Did Willy Hammond speak only idle words, when he accused Green of having followed him like a thirsty bloodhound?—of having robbed, and cheated, and debased him from the beginning?"

"He was terribly excited at the moment."

"Yet," said I, "no ear that heard his words could for an instant doubt that they were truthful utterances, wrung from a maddened heart."

My earnest, positive manner had its effect upon Slade. He knew that what I asserted, the whole history of Green's intercourse with young Hammond would prove; and he had, moreover, the guilty consciousness of being a party to the young man's ruin. His eyes cowered beneath the steady gaze I fixed upon him. I thought of him as one implicated in the murder, and my thought must have been visible in my face.

"One murder will not justify another," said he.

"There is no justification for murder on any plea," was my response.

"And yet, if these infuriated men find Green, they will murder him."

"I hope not. Indignation at a horrible crime has fearfully excited the people. But I think their sense of justice is strong enough to prevent the consequences you apprehend."

"I would not like to be in Green's shoes," said the landlord, with an uneasy movement.

I looked him closely in the face. It was the punishment of the man's crime that seemed so fearful in his eyes; not the crime itself. Alas! how the corrupting traffic had debased him.

My words were so little relished by Slade, that he found some ready excuse to leave me. I saw but little more of him during the day.

As evening began to fall, the gambler's unsuccessful pursuers, one after another, found their way to the tavern, and by the time night had fairly closed in, the bar-room was crowded with excited and angry men, chafing over their disappointment, and loud in their threats of vengeance. That Green had made good his escape, was now the general belief; and the stronger this conviction became, the more steadily did the current of passion begin to set in a new direcction. It had become known to every one, that, besides Green and young Hammond, Judge Lyman and Slade were in the room engaged in playing cards. The merest suggestion as to the complicity of these two men with Green in ruining Hammond, and thus driving him mad, was enough to excite strong feeling against them; and now that the mob had been cheated of its victim, its pent up indignation sought eagerly some new channel.

"Where's Slade?" some one asked, in a loud voice, from the centre of the crowded bar-room. "Why does he keep himself out of sight?"

"Yes; where's the landlord?" half a dozen voices responded.

"Did he go on the hunt?" some one inquired.

"No!" "No!" "No!" ran round the room. "Not he."

"And yet, the murder was committed in his own house, and before his own eyes!"

"Yes, before his own eyes!" repeated one and another, indignantly.

"Where's Slade? Where's the landlord? Has anybody seen him to-night? Matthew, where's Simon Slade?"

From lip to lip passed these interrogations; while the crowd of men became agitated, and swayed to and fro.

"I don't think he's home," answered the bar-keeper, in a hesitating manner, and with visible alarm.

"How long since he was here?"

"I haven't seen him for a couple of hours."

"That's a lie!" was sharply said.

"Who says it's a lie?" Matthew affected to be strongly indignant.

"I do!" And a rough, fierce-looking man confronted him.

"What right have you to say so?" asked Matthew, cooling off considerably.

"Because you lie!" said the man, boldly. "You've seen him within a less time than half an hour, and well you know it. Now, if you wish to keep yourself out of this trouble, answer truly. We are in no mood to deal with liars or equivocators. Where is Simon Slade?"

"I do not know," replied Matthew, firmly.

"Is he in the house?"

"He may be, or he may not be. I am just as ignorant of his exact whereabouts as you are."

"Will you look for him?"

Matthew stepped to the door, opening from behind the bar, and called the name of Frank.

"What's wanted?" growled the boy.

"Is your father in the house?"

"I don't know, nor don't care," was responded in the same ungracious manner.

"Some one bring him into the bar-room, and we'll see if we can't make him care a little."

The suggestion was no sooner made, than two men glided behind the bar, and passed into the room from which the voice of Frank had issued. A moment after they reappeared, each grasping an arm of the boy, and bearing him like a weak child between them. He looked thoroughly frightened at this unlooked for invasion of his liberty.

"See here, young man." One of the leading spirits of the crowd addressed him, as soon as he was brought in front of the counter. "If you wish to keep out of trouble, answer our questions at once, and to the point. We are in no mood for trifling. Where's your father?"

"Somewhere about the house, I believe," Frank replied, in an humbled tone. He was no little scared at the summary manner with which he had been treated.

"How long since you saw him?"

"Not long ago."

"Ten minutes?"

"No: nearly half an hour."

"Where was he then?"

"He was going up-stairs."

"Very well, we want him. See him, and tell him so."

Frank went into the house, but came back into the bar-room after an absence of nearly five minutes, and said that he could not find his father anywhere.

"Where is he then?" was angrily demanded.

"Indeed, gentlemen, I don't know." Frank's anxious look and frightened manner showed that he spoke truly.

"There's something wrong about this—something wrong—wrong," said one of the men. "Why should he be absent now? Why has he taken no steps to secure the man who committed a murder in his own house, and before his own eyes?"

"I shouldn't wonder if he aided him to escape," said another, making this serious charge with a restlessness and want of evidence that illustrated the reckless and unjust spirit by which a mob is ever governed.

"No doubt of it in the least!" was the quick and positive response. And at once this erroneous conviction seized upon every one. Not a single fact was presented. The simple, bold assertion, that no doubt existed in the mind of one man as to Slade's having aided Green to escape, was sufficient for the unreflecting mob.

"Where is he? Where is he? Let us find him. He knows where Green is, and he shall reveal the secret."

This was enough. The passions of the crowd were at fever heat again. Two or three men were chosen to search the house and premises, while others dispersed to take a wider range. One of the men who volunteered to go over the house was a person named Lyon, with whom I had formed some acquaintance, and several times conversed with on the state of affairs in Cedarville. He still remained too good a customer at the bar. I left the bar at the same time that he did, and went up to my room. We walked side by side, and parted at my door, I going in, and he continuing on to make his searches. I felt, of course, anxious and much excited, as well in consequence of the events of the day, as the present aspect of things. My head was aching violently, and in the hope of getting relief, I laid myself down. I had already lighted a candle, and turned the key in my door to prevent intrusion. Only for a short time did I lie, listening to the hum of voices that came with a hoarse murmur from below, to the sound of feet moving along the passages, and to the continual opening and shutting of doors, when something like suppressed breathing reached my ears. I started up instantly, and listened; but my quickened pulses were now audible to my own sense, and obscured what was external.

"It is only imagination," I said to myself. Still, I sat upright, listening.

Satisfied, at length, that all was mere fancy, I laid myself back on the pillow, and tried to turn my thoughts away from the suggested idea that some one was in the room. Scarcely had I succeeded in this, when my heart gave a new impulse, as a sound like a movement fell upon my ears.

"Mere fancy!" I said to myself, as some one went past the door at the moment. "My mind is over excited."

Still I raised my head, supporting it with my hand, and listened, directing my attention inside, and not outside of the room. I was about letting my head fall back upon the pillow, when a slight cough, so distinct as not to be mistaken, caused me to spring to the floor, and look under the bed. The mystery was explained. A pair of eyes glittered in the candlelight. The fugitive, Green, was under my bed. For some moments I stood looking at him, so astonished that I had neither utterance nor decision; while he glared at me with a fierce defiance. I saw that he was clutching a revolver.

"Understand!" he said, in a grating whisper, "that I am not to be taken alive."

I let the blanket, which had concealed him from view, fall from my hand, and then tried to collect my thoughts.

"Escape is impossible," said I, again lifting the temporary curtain by which he was hid. "The whole town is armed, and on the search; and should you fall into the hands of the mob, in its present state of exasperation, your life would not be safe an instant. Remain, then, quiet, where you are, until I can see the sheriff, to whom you had better resign yourself, for there's little chance for you except under his protection."

After a brief parley, he consented that things should take this course, and I went out, locking the room door after me, and started in search of the sheriff. On the information I gave, the sheriff acted promptly. With five officers, fully armed for defence, in case an effort were made to get the prisoner out of their hands, he repaired immediately to the "Sickle and Sheaf," I had given the key of my room into his possession.

The appearance of the sheriff, with his posse, was sufficient to start the suggestion that Green was somewhere concealed in the house; and a suggestion was only needed to cause the fact to be assumed, and unhesitatingly declared. Intelligence went through the reassembling crowd like an electric current, and ere the sheriff could manacle and lead forth his prisoner, the stairway down which he had to come was packed with bodies, and echoing with oaths and maledictions.

"Gentlemen, clear the way!" cried the sheriff, as he appeared with the white and trembling culprit at the head of the stairs. "The mur-

derer is now in the hands of the law, and will meet the sure consequences of his crime."

A shout of execration rent the air; but not a single individual
stirred.

"Give way, there! Give way!" And the sheriff took a step or two forward, but the prisoner held back.

"Oh, the murdering villain! The cursed blackleg! Where's Willy
Hammond!" was heard distinctly above the confused mingling of
voices.

"Gentlemen! the law must have its course; and no good citizen will
oppose the law. It is made for your protection—for mine—and for that
of the prisoner."

"Lynch law is good enough for him," shouted a savage voice.
"Hand him over to us, sheriff, and we'll save you the trouble of hanging him, and the county the cost of a gallows. We'll do the business
right."

Five men, each armed with a revolver, now ranged themselves
around the sheriff, and the latter said firmly,

"It is my duty to see this man safely conveyed to prison; and I'm
going to do my duty. If there is any more blood shed here, the blame
will rest with you." And the body of officers pressed forward, the mob
slowly retreating before them.

Green, overwhelmed with terror, held back. I was standing where I
could see his face. It was ghastly with mortal fear. Grasping his pin-
ioned arms, the sheriff forced him onward. After contending with the
crowd for nearly ten minutes, the officers gained the passage below;
but the mob was denser here, and blocking up the door, resolutely
maintained their position.

Again and again the sheriff appealed to the good sense and justice
of the people.

"The prisoner will have to stand a trial; and the law will execute
sure vengeance."

"No, it won't!" was sternly responded.

"Who'll be judge in the case?" was asked.

"Why, Judge Lyman!" was contemptuously answered.

"A blackleg himself!" was shouted by two or three voices.

"Blackleg judge, and blackleg lawyers! Oh, yes! The law will execute sure vengeance! Who was in the room gambling with Green and
Hammond?"

"Judge Lyman!" "Judge Lyman!" was answered back.

"It won't do, sheriff! There's no law in the country to reach the case
but Lynch law; and that the scoundrel must have. Give him to us!"

"Never! On, men, with the prisoner!" cried the sheriff resolutely, and the *posse* made a rush toward the door, bearing back the resisting and now infuriated crowd. Shouts, cries, oaths, and savage imprecations blended in wild discord; in the midst of which my blood was chilled by the sharp crack of a pistol. Another and another shot followed; and then, as a cry of pain thrilled the air, the fierce storm hushed its fury in an instant.

"Who's shot? Is he killed?"

There was a breathless eagerness for the answer.

"It's the gambler!" was replied. "Somebody has shot Green."

A low muttered invective against the victim was heard here and there; but the announcement was not received with a shout of exultation, though there was scarcely a heart that did not feel pleasure at the sacrifice of Harvey Green's life.

It was true as had been declared. Whether the shots were aimed deliberately, or guided by an unseen hand to the heart of the gambler, was never known; nor did the most careful examination, instituted afterward by the county, elicit any information that even directed suspicion toward the individual who became the agent of his death.

At the coroner's inquest, held over the dead body of Harvey Green, Simon Slade was present. Where he had concealed himself while the mob were in search of him, was not known. He looked haggard; and his eyes were anxious and restless. Two murders in his house, occurring in a single day, were quite enough to darken his spirits; and the more so, as his relations with both the victims were not of a character to awaken any thing but self-accusation.

As for the mob, in the death of Green its eager thirst for vengeance was satisfied. Nothing more was said against Slade, as a participator in the ruin and death of young Hammond. The popular feeling was one of pity rather than indignation toward the landlord; for it was seen that he was deeply troubled.

One thing I noticed, and it was that the drinking at the bar was not suspended for a moment. A large proportion of those who made up the crowd of Green's angry pursuers, were excited by drink as well as indignation, and I am very sure that, but for the maddening effects of liquor, the fatal shot would never have been fired. After the fearful catastrophe, and when every mind was sobered, or ought to have been sobered, the crowd returned to the bar-room, where the drinking was renewed. So rapid were the calls for liquor, that both Matthew, and Frank, the landlord's son, were kept busy mixing the various compounds demanded by the thirsty customers.

From the constant stream of human beings that flowed toward the

"Sickle and Sheaf," after the news of Green's discovery and death went forth, it seemed as if every man and boy within a distance of two or three miles had received intelligence of the event. Few, very few of those who came, but went first into the bar-room; and nearly all who entered the bar-room called for liquor. In an hour after the death of Green, the fact that his dead body was laid out in the room immediately adjoining, seemed utterly to pass from the consciousness of every one in the bar. The calls for liquor were incessant; and, as the excitement of drink increased, voices grew louder, and oaths more plentiful, while the sounds of laughter ceased not for an instant.

"They're giving him a regular Irish wake," I heard remarked, with a brutal laugh.

I turned to the speaker, and to my great surprise, saw that it was Judge Lyman, more under the influence of drink than I remembered to have seen him. He was about the last man I expected to find here. If he knew of the strong indignation expressed toward him a little while before, by some of the very men now excited with liquor, his own free drinking had extinguished fear.

"Yes, curse him!" was the answer. "If they have a particularly hot corner 'away down below,' I hope he's made its acquaintance before this."

"Most likely he's smelled brimstone," chuckled the judge.

"Smelled it! If old Clubfoot hasn't treated him with a brimstone-bath long before this, he hasn't done his duty. If I thought as much, I'd vote for sending his majesty a remonstrance forthwith."

"Ha! ha!" laughed the judge. "You're warm on the subject."

"Ain't I? The blackleg scoundrel! Hell's too good for him."

"H-u-s-h! Don't let your indignation run into profanity," said Judge Lyman, trying to assume a serious air; but the muscles of his face but feebly obeyed his will's feeble effort.

"Profanity! Poh! I don't call that profanity. It's only speaking out in meeting, as they say,—it's only calling black, black—and white, white. You believe in a hell, don't you, judge?"

"I suppose there is one; though I don't know very certain."

"You'd better be certain!" said the other, meaningly.

"Why so?"

"Oh! because if there is one, and you don't cut your cards a little differently, you'll be apt to find it at the end of your journey."

"What do you mean by that?" asked the judge, retreating somewhat into himself, and trying to look dignified.

"Just what I say," was unhesitatingly answered.

"Do you mean to insinuate any thing?" asked the judge, whose brows were beginning to knit themselves.

"Nobody thinks you are a saint," replied the man, roughly.

"I never professed to be."

"And it is said,"—the man fixed his gaze almost insultingly upon Judge Lyman's face—"that you'll get about as hot a corner in the lower regions as is to be found there, whenever you make the journey in that direction."

"You are insolent!" exclaimed the judge, his face becoming inflamed.

"Take care what you say, sir!" The man spoke threateningly.

"You'd better take care what *you* say."

"So I will," replied the other. "But——"

"What's to pay here?" inquired a third party, coming up at the moment, and interrupting the speaker.

"The devil will be to pay," said Judge Lyman, "if somebody don't look out sharp."

"Do you mean that for me, ha?" The man, between whom and himself this slight contention had so quickly sprung up, began stripping back his coat sleeves, like one about to commence boxing.

"I mean it for anybody who presumes to offer me an insult."

The raised voices of the two men now drew toward them the attention of every one in the bar-room.

"The devil! There's Judge Lyman!" I heard some one exclaim, in a tone of surprise.

"Wasn't he in the room with Green when Willy Hammond was murdered?" asked another.

"Yes, he was; and what's more, it is said he had been playing against him all night, he and Green sharing the plunder."

This last remark came distinctly to the ears of Lyman, who started to his feet instantly, exclaiming fiercely—

"Whoever says that is a cursed liar!"

The words were scarcely out of his mouth, before a blow staggered him against the wall, near which he was standing. Another blow felled him, and then his assailant sprang over his prostrate body, kicking him, and stamping upon his face and breast in the most brutal, shocking manner.

"Kill him! He's worse than Green!" somebody cried out, in a voice so full of cruelty and murder that it made my blood curdle. "Remember Willy Hammond!"

The terrible scene that followed, in which were heard a confused mingling of blows, cries, yells, and horrible oaths, continued for several minutes, and ceased only when the words—"Don't, don't strike him any more! He's dead!" were repeated several times. Then the wild strife subsided. As the crowd parted from around the body of Judge

Lyman, and gave way, I caught a single glance at his face. It was covered with blood, and every feature seemed to have been literally trampled down, until all was a level surface! Sickened at the sight, I passed hastily from the room into the open air, and caught my breath several times, before respiration again went on freely. As I stood in front of the tavern, the body of Judge Lyman was borne out by three or four men, and carried off in the direction of his dwelling.

"Is he dead?" I inquired of those who had him in charge.

"No," was the answer. "He's not dead, but terribly beaten," and they passed on.

Again the loud voices of men in angry strife arose in the bar-room. I did not return there to learn the cause, or to witness the fiend-like conduct of men, all whose worst passions were stimulated by drink into the wildest fervour. As I was entering my room, the thought flashed through my mind that, as Green was found there, it needed only the bare suggestion that I had aided in his concealment, to direct toward me the insane fury of the drunken mob.

"It is not safe to remain here." I said this to myself, with the emphasis of a strong internal conviction.

Against this, my mind opposed a few feeble arguments; but, the more I thought of the matter, the more clearly did I become satisfied, that to attempt to pass the night in that room was to me a risk it was not prudent to assume.

So I went in search of Mrs. Slade, to ask her to have another room prepared for me. But she was not in the house; and I learned, upon inquiry, that since the murder of young Hammond, she had been suffering from repeated hysterical and fainting fits, and was now, with her daughter, at the house of a relative, whither she had been carried early in the afternoon.

It was on my lips to request the chambermaid to give me another room; but this I felt to be scarcely prudent, for if the popular indignation should happen to turn toward me, the servant would be the one questioned, most likely, as to where I had removed my quarters.

"It isn't safe to stay in the house," said I, speaking to myself. "Two, perhaps three, murders, have been committed already. The tiger's thirst for blood has been stimulated, and who can tell how quickly he may spring again, or in what direction?"

Even while I said this, there came up from the bar-room louder and madder shouts. Then blows were heard, mingled with cries and oaths. A shuddering sense of danger oppressed me, and I went hastily downstairs, and out into the street. As I gained the passage, I looked into the sitting-room, where the body of Green was laid out. Just then, the bar-room door was burst open by a fighting party, who had been thrown, in their fierce contention, against it. I paused only for a moment or two; and even in that brief period of time, saw blows exchanged over the dead body of the gambler!

"This is no place for me," I said, almost aloud, and hurried from the house, and took my way to the residence of a gentleman who had shown me many kindnesses during my visits at Cedarville. There was needed scarcely a word of representation on my part, to secure the cordial tender of a bed.

What a change! It seemed almost like a passage from Pandemonium to a heavenly region, as I seated myself alone in the quiet chamber a cheerful hospitality had assigned me, and mused on the exciting and terrible incidents of the day. They that sow the wind shall reap the whirlwind. How marked had been the realization of this prophecy, couched in such strong but beautiful imagery!

On the next day I was to leave Cedarville. Early in the morning I repaired to the "Sickle and Sheaf." The storm was over, and all was calm and silent as desolation. Hours before, the tempest had subsided; but the evidences left behind of its ravaging fury were fearful to look upon. Doors, chairs, windows, and tables were broken, and even the strong brass rod that ornamented the bar had been partially wrenched from its fastenings by strong hands, under an impulse of murder, that only lacked a weapon to execute its fiendish purpose. Stains of blood, in drops, marks, and even dried-up pools, were to be seen all over the bar-room and passage floors, and in many places on the porch.

In the sitting-room still lay the body of Green. Here, too, were many signs to indicate a fierce struggle. The looking-glass was smashed to a hundred pieces, and the shivered fragments lay yet untouched upon the floor. A chair, which it was plain had been used as a weapon of assault, had two of its legs broken short off, and was thrown into a corner. And even the bearers, on which the dead man lay, were pushed from their true position, showing that even in its mortal sleep, the body of Green had felt the jarring strife of elements he had himself helped to awaken into mad activity. From his face, the sheet had been drawn aside; but no hand ventured to replace it; and there it lay, in its ghastly paleness, exposed to the light, and covered with restless flies, attracted by the first faint odours of putridity. With gaze averted, I approached the body, and drew the covering decently over it.

No person was in the bar. I went out into the stable yard, where I met the hostler with his head bound up. There was a dark blue circle around one of his eyes, and an ugly-looking red scar on his cheek.

"Where is Mr. Slade?" I inquired.

"In bed, and likely to keep it for a week," was answered.

"How comes that?"

"Naturally enough. There was fighting all around last night, and he had to come in for a share. The fool! If he'd just held his tongue, he might have come out of it with a whole skin. But, when the rum is in, the wit is out, with him. It's cost me a black eye and a broken head; for how could I stand by and see him murdered outright?"

"Is he very badly injured?"

"I rather think he is. One eye is clean gone."

"Oh, shocking!"

"It's shocking enough, and no mistake."

"Lost an eye!"

"Too true, sir. The doctor saw him this morning, and says the eye was fairly gouged out, and broken up. In fact, when we carried him up-stairs for dead last night, his eye was lying upon his cheek. I pushed it back with my own hand!"

"Oh, horrible!" The relation made me sick. "Is he otherwise much injured?"

"The doctor thinks there are some bad hurts inside. Why, they kicked and trampled upon him, as if he had been a wild beast! I never saw such a pack of blood thirsty devils in my life."

"So much for rum," said I.

"Yes, sir; so much for rum," was the emphatic response. "It was the rum, and nothing else. Why, some of the very men who acted the most like tigers and devils, are as harmless persons as you will find in Cedarville when sober. Yes, sir; it was the rum, and nothing else. Rum gave me this broken head and black eye."

"So you had been drinking also?"

"Oh, yes. There's no use in denying that."

"Liquor does you harm."

"Nobody knows that better than I do."

"Why do you drink, then?"

"Oh, just because it comes in the way. Liquor is under my eyes and nose all the time, and it's as natural as breathing to take a little now and then. And when I don't think of it myself, somebody will think of it for me, and say—'Come, Sam, let's take something.' So you see, for a body such as I am, there isn't much help for it."

"But ain't you afraid to go on in this way? Don't you know where it will all end?"

"Just as well as anybody. It will make an end of me—or of all that is good in me. Rum and ruin, you know, sir. They go together like twin brothers."

"Why don't you get out of the way of temptation?" said I.

"It's easy enough to ask that question, sir; but how am I to get out of the way of temptation? Where shall I go, and not find a bar in my road, and somebody to say—'Come, Sam, let's take a drink? It can't be done, sir, nohow. I'm a hostler, and don't know how to be anything else."

"Can't you work on a farm?"

"Yes; I can do something in that way. But, when there are taverns and bar-rooms, as many as three or four in every mile all over the country, how are you to keep clear of them? Figure me out that."

"I think you'd better vote on the Maine Law side at next election," said I.

"Faith, and I did it last time!" replied the man, with a brightening face—"and if I'm spared, I'll go the same ticket next year."

"What do you think of the Law?" I asked.

"Think of it! Bless your heart! if I was a praying man, which I'm sorry to say I ain't—my mother was a pious woman, sir"—his voice fell and slightly trembled—"if I was a praying man, sir, I'd pray, night and morning, and twenty times every day of my life, for God to put it into the hearts of the people to give us that Law. I'd have some hope then. But I haven't much as it is. There's no use in trying to let liquor alone."

"Do many drinking men think as you do?"

"I can count up a dozen or two myself. It isn't the drinking men who are so much opposed to the Maine Law, as your politicians. They throw dust in the people's eyes about it, and make a great many who know nothing at all of the evils of drinking in themselves, believe some bugbear story about trampling on the rights of I don't know who, nor they either. As for rum-seller's rights, I never could see any right they had to get rich by ruining poor devils such as I am. I think, though, that we have some right to be protected against them."

The ringing of a bell here announced the arrival of some traveller, and the hostler left me.

I learned, during the morning, that Matthew the bar-keeper, and also the son of Mr. Slade, were both considerably hurt during the affrays in the bar-room, and were confined, temporarily, to their beds. Mrs. Slade still continued in a distressing and dangerous state. Judge Lyman, though shockingly injured, was not thought to be in a critical condition.

A busy day the sheriff had of it, making arrests of various parties engaged in the last night's affairs. Even Slade, unable as he was to lift his head from his pillow, was required to give heavy bail for his appearance at court. Happily, I escaped the inconvenience of being held to appear as a witness, and early in the afternoon had the satisfaction of finding myself rapidly borne away in the stage-coach. It was two years before I entered the pleasant village of Cedarville again.

☞ *Night the Eighth* ☜

REAPING THE WHIRLWIND

I was in Washington City during the succeeding month. It was the short or closing session of a regular Congressional term. The implication of Judge Lyman in the affair of Green and young Hammond had brought him into such bad odour in Cedarville, and the whole district from which he had been chosen, that his party deemed it wise to set him aside, and take up a candidate less likely to meet with so strong, and, it might be, successful an opposition. By so doing, they were able to secure the election, once more, against the growing temperance party, which succeeded, however, in getting a Maine Law man into the State legislature. It was, therefore, Judge Lyman's last winter at the Federal Capital.

While seated in the reading-room at Fuller's Hotel, about noon, on the day after my arrival in Washington, I noticed an individual, whose face looked familiar, come in and glance about, as if in search of some one. While yet questioning in my mind who he could be, I heard a man remark to a person with whom he had been conversing—

"There's that vagabond member away from his place in the House, again."

"Who?" inquired the other.

"Why, Judge Lyman," was answered.

"Oh!" said the other, indifferently; "it isn't of much consequence. Precious little wisdom does he add to that intelligent body."

"His vote is worth something at least, when important questions are at stake."

"What does he charge for it?" was coolly inquired.

There was a shrug of the shoulders, and an arching of the eyebrows, but no answer.

"I'm in earnest, though, in the question," said the last speaker.

"Not in saying that Lyman will sell his vote to the highest bidders?"

"That will depend altogether upon whom the bidders may be. They must be men who have something to lose as well as gain—men, not at all likely to bruit the matter, and in serving whose personal interests no abandonment of party is required. Judge Lyman is always on good terms with the lobby members, and may be found in company with some of them daily. Doubtless, his absence from the House, now, is for the purpose of a special meeting with gentlemen who are ready to pay well for votes in favour of some bill making appropriations of public money for private or corporate benefit."

"You certainly cannot mean all you say to be taken in its broadest sense," was replied to this.

"Yes; in its very broadest. Into just this deep of moral and political degradation has this man fallen, disgracing his constituents, and dishonouring his country."

"His presence at Washington doesn't speak very highly in favour of the community he represents."

"No; still, as things are now, we cannot judge of the moral worth of a community by the men sent from it to Congress. Representatives show merely the strength of parties. The candidate chosen in party primary meetings is not selected because he is the best man they have, and the one fittest to legislate wisely in national affairs; but he who happens to have the strongest personal friends among those who nominate, or who is most likely to poll the highest vote. This is why we find, in Congress, such a large preponderance of tenth-rate men."

"Men, such as you represent Judge Lyman to be, would sell his country like another Arnold."

"Yes, if the bid were high enough."

"Does he gamble?"

"Gambling, I might say, is a part of his profession. Very few nights pass, I am told, without finding him at the gaming table."

I heard no more. At all this, I was not in the least surprised; for my knowledge of the man's antecedents had prepared me for allegations quite as bad as these.

During the week I spent at the Federal Capital, I had several opportunities of seeing Judge Lyman, in the House and out of it,—in the House only when the yeas and nays were called on some important measure, or a vote taken on a bill granting special privileges. In the latter case, his vote, as I noticed, was generally cast on the affirmative side. Several times I saw him staggering on the Avenue, and once brought into the House for the purpose of voting, in so drunken a state, that he had to be supported to his seat. And even worse than this—when his name was called, he was asleep, and had to be shaken several times before he was sufficiently aroused to give his vote!

Happily, for the good of his country, it was his last winter in Washington. At the next session, a better man took his place.

———————

Two years from the period of my last visit to Cedarville, I found myself approaching that quiet village again. As the church-spire came in view, and house after house became visible, here and there, stand-

ing out in pleasant relief against the green background of woods and
fields, all the exciting events which rendered my last visit so memorable came up so fresh in my mind. I was yet thinking of Willy Hammond's dreadful death, and of his broken-hearted mother, whose life
went out with his, when the stage rolled by their old homestead. Oh,
what a change was here! Neglect, decay, and dilapidation were visible,
let the eye fall where it would. The fences were down, here and there;
the hedges, once so green and nicely trimmed, had grown rankly in
some places, but were stunted and dying in others; all the beautiful
walks were weedy and grass-grown, and the box-borders dead; the garden, rainbow-hued in its wealth of choice and beautiful flowers when I
first saw it, was lying waste,—a rooting-ground for hogs. A glance at the
house showed a broken chimney, the bricks unremoved from the spot
where they struck the ground; a moss-grown roof, with a large limb
from a lightning-rent tree lying almost balanced over the eaves, and
threatening to fall at the touch of the first wind-storm that swept over.
Half of the vines that clambered about the portico were dead, and the
rest, untrained, twined themselves in wild disorder, or fell grovelling
to the earth. One of the pillars of the portico was broken, as were,
also, two of the steps that went up to it. The windows of the house
were closed, but the door stood open, and, as the stage went past, my
eyes rested, for a moment, upon an old man seated in the hall. He was
not near enough to the door for me to get a view of his face; but the
white flowing hair left me in no doubt as to his identity. It was Judge
Hammond.

The "Sickle and Sheaf" was yet the stage-house of Cedarville, and
there, a few minutes afterward, I found myself. The hand of change
had been here also. The first object that attracted my attention was
the sign-post, which, at my earlier arrival, some eight or nine years
before, stood up in its new white garment of paint, as straight as a
plummet line, bearing proudly aloft the golden sheaf and gleaming
sickle. Now, the post, dingy and shattered, and worn from the frequent contact of wheels, and gnawing of restless horses, leaned from
its trim perpendicular at an angle of many degrees, as if ashamed of
the faded, weather-worn, lying symbol it bore aloft in the sunshine.
Around the post was a filthy mud-pool, in which a hog lay grunting
out its sense of enjoyment. Two or three old empty whisky barrels
lumbered up the dirty porch, on which a coarse, bloated, vulgar-look-
ing man sat leaning against the wall—his chair tipped back on its hind
legs—squinting at me from one eye, as I left the stage and came forward toward the house.

"Ah! is this you?" said he, as I came near to him, speaking thickly,
and getting up with a heavy motion. I now recognised the altered per-

son of Simon Slade. On looking at him closer, I saw that the eye which I had thought only shut was in fact destroyed. How vividly, now, uprose in imagination the scenes I had witnessed during my last night in his bar-room; the night, when a brutal mob, whom he had inebriated with liquor, came near murdering him.

"Glad to see you once more, my boy! Glad to see you! I—I—I'm not just—you see. How are you? How are you?"

And he shook my hand with a drunken show of cordiality.

I felt shocked and disgusted. Wretched man! down the crumbling sides of the pit he had digged for other feet, he was himself sliding, while not enough strength remained even to struggle with his fate.

I tried for a few minutes to talk with him; but his mind was altogether beclouded, and his questions and answers incoherent; so I left him, and entered the bar-room.

"Can I get accommodations here for a couple of days?" I inquired of a stupid, sleepy-looking man, who was sitting in a chair behind the bar.

"I reckon so," he answered, but did not rise.

I turned, and walked a few paces toward the door, and then walked back again.

"I'd like to get a room," said I.

The man got up slowly, and going to a desk, fumbled about in it for a while. At length he brought out an old, dilapidated blank-book, and throwing it open on the counter, asked me, with an indifferent manner, to write down my name.

"I'll take a pen, if you please."

"Oh, yes!" And he hunted about again in the desk, from which, after a while, he brought forth the blackened stump of a quill, and pushed it toward me across the counter.

"Ink," said I—fixing my eyes upon him with a look of displeasure.

"I don't believe there is any," he muttered. "Frank," and he called the landlord's son, going to the door behind the bar as he did so.

"What d'ye want?" a rough, ill-natured voice answered.

"Where's the ink?"

"Don't know any thing about it."

"You had it last. What did you do with it?"

"Nothing!" was growled back.

"Well, I wish you'd find it."

"Find it yourself, and ——" I cannot repeat the profane language he used.

"Never mind," said I. "A pencil will do just as well." And I drew one from my pocket. The attempt to write with this, on the begrimed and greasy page of the register, was only partially successful. It would have puzzled almost any one to make out the name. From the date of the last entry, it appeared that mine was the first arrival, for over a week, of any person desiring a room.

As I finished writing my name, Frank came stalking in, with a cigar in his mouth, and a cloud of smoke around his head. He had grown into a stout man—though his face presented little that was manly, in the true sense of the word. It was disgustingly sensual. On seeing me, a slight flush tinged his cheeks.

"How do you do?" he said, offering me his hand. "Peter,"—he turned to the lazy-looking bar-keeper—"tell Jane to have No. 11 put in order for a gentleman immediately, and tell her to be sure and change the bed-linen."

"Things look rather dull here," I remarked, as the bar-keeper went out to do as he had been directed.

"Rather; it's a dull place, anyhow."

"How is your mother?" I inquired.

A slight, troubled look came into his face, as he answered—

"No better."

"She's sick, then?"

"Yes; she's been sick a good while; and I'm afraid will never be much better." His manner was not altogether cold and indifferent, but there was a want of feeling in his voice.

"Is she at home?"

"No, sir."

As he showed no inclination to say more on the subject, I asked no further questions, and he soon found occasion to leave me.

The bar-room had undergone no material change, so far as its furniture and arrangements were concerned; but a very great change was apparent in the condition of these. The brass rod around the bar, which, at my last visit, was brightly polished, was now a greenish-black, and there came from it an unpleasant odour of verdigris. The walls were fairly coated with dust, smoke, and fly-specks, and the windows let in the light but feebly, through the dirt-obscured glass. The floor was filthy. Behind the bar, on the shelves designed for a display of liquors, was a confused mingling of empty or half-filled decanters, cigar-boxes, lemons and lemon-peel, old newspapers, glasses, a broken pitcher, a hat, a soiled vest, and a pair of blacking brushes, with other incongruous things, not now remembered. The air of the room was loaded with offensive vapours.

Disgusted with everything about the bar, I went into the sitting-room. Here, there was some order in the arrangement of the dingy furniture; but you might have written your name in dust on the looking-glass and table. The smell of the torpid atmosphere was even worse than that of the bar-room. So I did not linger here, but passed through the hall, and out upon the porch, to get a draught of pure air.

Slade still sat leaning against the wall.

"Fine day this," said he, speaking in a mumbling kind of voice.

"Very fine," I answered.

"Yes, very fine."

"Not doing so well as you were a few years ago," said I.

"No—you see—these—these 'ere blamed temperance people are ruining every thing."

"Ah! Is that so?"

"Yes. Cedarville isn't what it was when you first came to the 'Sickle and Sheaf.' I—I—you see. Curse the temperance people! They've ruined everything, you see. Everything! Ruined—"

And he muttered, and mouthed his words in such a way, that I could understand but little he said; and, in that little, there was scarcely any coherency. So I left him, with a feeling of pity in my heart for the wreck he had become, and went into the town to call upon one or two gentlemen with whom I had business.

In the course of the afternoon, I learned that Mrs. Slade was in an insane asylum, about five miles from Cedarville. The terrible events of the day on which young Hammond was murdered completed the work of mental ruin, begun at the time her husband abandoned the quiet, honourable calling of a miller, and became a tavern-keeper. Reason could hold its position no longer. When word came to her that Willy and his mother were both dead, she uttered a wild shriek and fell down in a fainting fit. From that period the balance of her mind was destroyed. Long before this, her friends saw that reason wavered. Frank had been her idol. A pure, bright, affectionate boy he was, when she removed with him from their pleasant cottage-home, where all the surrounding influences were good, into a tavern, where an angel could scarcely remain without corruption. From the moment this change was decided on by her husband, a shadow fell upon her heart. She saw, before her husband, her children, and herself, a yawning pit, and felt that, in a very few years, all of them must plunge down into its fearful darkness.

Alas! how quickly began the realization of her worst fears in the corruption of her worshipped boy! And how vain proved all effort and remonstrance, looking to his safety, whether made with himself or his father! From the day the tavern was opened, and Frank drew into his lungs full draughts of the changed atmosphere by which he was now surrounded, the work of moral deterioration commenced. The very smell of the liquor exhilarated him unnaturally; while the subjects of conversation, so new to him, that found discussion in the bar-room,

soon came to occupy a prominent place in his imagination, to the ex-
clusion of those humane, childlike, tender, and heavenly thoughts and
impressions it had been the mother's care to impart and awaken.

Ah! with what an eager zest does the heart drink in of evil. And
how almost hopeless is the case of a boy, surrounded, as Frank was,
by the corrupting, debasing associations of a bar-room! Had his father
meditated his ruin, he could not have more surely laid his plans for
the fearful consummation; and he reaped as he had sown. With a
selfish desire to get gain, he embarked in the trade of corruption, ruin,
and death, weakly believing that he and his could pass through the
fire harmless. How sadly a few years demonstrated his error, we have
seen.

Flora, I learned, was with her mother, devoting her life to her. The
dreadful death of Willy Hammond, for whom she had conceived a
strong attachment, came near depriving her of reason also. Since the
day on which that awful tragedy occurred, she had never even looked
upon her old home. She went away with her unconscious mother, and
ever since had remained with her—devoting her life to her comfort.
Long before this, all her own and mother's influence over her brother
had come to an end. It mattered not how she sought to stay his feet,
so swiftly moving along the downward way, whether by gentle entrea-
ty, earnest remonstrance, or tears; in either case, wounds for her own
heart were the sure consequences, while his steps never lingered a
moment. A swift destiny seemed hurrying him on to ruin. The change
in her father—once so tender, so cheerful in his tone, so proud of and
loving toward his daughter—was another source of deep grief to her
pure young spirit. Over him, as well as over her brother, all her power
was lost; and he even avoided her, as though her presence were an
offence to him. And so, when she went out from her unhappy home,
she took with her no desire to return. Even when imagination bore her
back to the "Sickle and Sheaf," she felt an intense, heart-sickening repulsion toward the place where she had first felt the poisoned arrows
of life; and in the depths of her spirit she prayed that her eyes might
never look upon it again. In her almost cloister-like seclusion, she
sought to gather the mantle of oblivion about her heart.

Had not her mother's condition made Flora's duty a plain one, the
true, unselfish instincts of her heart would have doubtless led her back
to the polluted home she had left, there, in a kind of living death, to
minister as best she could to the comfort of a debased father and
brother. But she was spared that trial—that fruitless sacrifice.

Evening found me once more in the bar-room of the "Sickle and
Sheaf." The sleepy, indifferent bar-keeper, was now more in his element—looked brighter, and had quicker motions. Slade, who had partially recovered from the stupefying effects of the heavy draughts of

ale with which he washed down his dinner, was also in a better condition, though not inclined to talk. He was sitting at a table, alone, with
his eyes wandering about the room. Whether his thoughts were agreeable or disagreeable, it was not easy to determine. Frank was there,
the centre of a noisy group of coarse fellows, whose vulgar sayings
and profane expletives continually rung through the room. The nois-
iest, coarsest, and most profane was Frank Slade; yet did not the incessant volume of bad language that flowed from his tongue appear in
the least to disturb his father.

Outraged, at length, by this disgusting exhibition, that had not even
the excuse of an exciting cause, I was leaving the bar-room, when I
heard some one remark to a young man who had just come in—

"What! you here again, Ned? Ain't you afraid your old man will be
after you, as usual?"

"No," answered the person addressed, chuckling inwardly, "he's
gone to a prayer-meeting."

"You'll at least have the benefit of his prayers," was lightly remarked.

I turned to observe the young man more closely. His face I remembered, though I could not identify him at first. But, when I heard him
addressed soon after as Ned Hargrove, I had a vivid recollection of a
little incident that occurred some years before, and which then made
a strong impression. The reader has hardly forgotten the visit of Mr.
Hargrove to the bar-room of the "Sickle and Sheaf," and the conversation among some of its inmates, which his withdrawal, in company
with his son, then occasioned. The father's watchfulness over his boy,
and his efforts to save him from the allurements and temptations of a
bar-room, had proved, as now appeared, unavailing. The son was several years older; but it was sadly evident, from the expression of his
face, that he had been growing older in evil faster than in years.

The few words that I have mentioned as passing between this
young man and another inmate of the bar-room, caused me to turn
back from the door, through which I was about passing, and take a
chair near to where Hargrove had seated himself. As I did so, the eyes
of Simon Slade rested on the last-named individual.

"Ned Hargrove!" he said, speaking roughly—"if you want a drink,
you'd better get it, and make yourself scarce."

"Don't trouble yourself," retorted the young man, "you'll get your
money for the drink in good time."

This irritated the landlord, who swore at Hargrove violently, and
said something about not wanting boys about his place who couldn't
stir from home without having "daddy or mammy running after
them."

"Never fear!" cried out the person who had first addressed Hargrove—"his old man's gone to a prayer meeting. We shan't have the light of his pious countenance here to-night."

I fixed my eyes upon the young man to see what effect this coarse and irreverent allusion to his father would have. A slight tinge of shame was in his face; but I saw that he had not sufficient moral courage to resent the shameful desecration of a parent's name. How should he, when he was himself the first to desecrate that name?

"If he were forty fathoms deep in the infernal regions," answered Slade, "he'd find out that Ned was here, and get half an hour's leave of absence to come after him. The fact is, I'm tired of seeing his solemn, sanctimonious face here every night. If the boy hasn't spirit enough to tell him to mind his own business, as I have done more than fifty times, why, let the boy stay away himself."

"Why don't you send him off with a flea in his ear, Ned?" said one of the company, a young man scarcely his own age. "My old man tried that game with me, but he soon found that I could hold the winning cards."

"Just what I'm going to do the very next time he comes after me."

"Oh, yes! So you've said twenty times," remarked Frank Slade, in a sneering, insolent manner.

Edward Hargrove had not the spirit to resent this; he only answered,

"Just let him show himself here to-night, and you will see."

"No, we won't see," sneered Frank.

"Wouldn't it be fun!" was exclaimed. "I hope to be on hand, should it ever come off."

"He's as 'fraid as death of the old chap," laughed a sottish looking man, whose age ought to have inspired him with some respect for the relation between father and son, and doubtless would, had not a long course of drinking and familiarity with debasing associates blunted his moral sense.

"Now for it!" I heard uttered, in a quick, delighted voice. "Now for fun! Spunk up to him, Ned! Never say die!"

I turned toward the door, and there stood the father of Edward Hargrove. How well I remembered the broad, fine forehead, the steady, yet mild eyes, the firm lips, the elevated superior bearing of the man I had once before seen in that place, and on a like errand. His form was slightly bent now; his hair was whiter; his eyes farther back in his head; his face thinner and marked with deeper lines; and there was in the whole expression of his face a touching sadness. Yet, superior to the marks of time and suffering, an unflinching resolution was visible in his countenance, that gave to it a dignity, and extorted involuntary respect. He stood still, after advancing a few paces, and then, his searching eyes having discovered his son, he said mildly, yet firmly, and with such a strength of parental love in his voice that resistance was scarcely possible.

"Edward! Edward! Come, my son."

"Don't go." The words were spoken in an under tone, and he who uttered them turned his face away from Mr. Hargrove, so that the old man could not see the motion of his lips. A little while before, he had spoken bravely against the father of Edward; now, he could not stand up in his presence.

I looked at Edward. He did not move from where he was sitting, and yet I saw that to resist his father cost him no light struggle.

"Edward." There was nothing imperative—nothing stern—nothing commanding in the father's voice; but its great, its almost irresistible power, lay in its expression of the father's belief that his son would instantly leave the place. And it was this power that prevailed. Edward arose, and, with eyes cast upon the floor, was moving away from his companions, when Frank Slade exclaimed,

"Poor, weak fool!"

It was a lightning flash of indignation, rather than a mere glance from the human eye, that Mr. Hargrove threw instantly upon Frank; while his fine form sprung up erect. He did not speak, but merely transfixed him with a look. Frank curled his lip impotently, as he tried to return the old man's withering glances.

"Now look here!" said Simon Slade, in some wrath, "there's been just about enough of this. I'm getting tired of it. Why don't you keep Ned at home? Nobody wants him here."

"Refuse to sell him liquor," returned Mr. Hargrove.

"It's my trade to sell liquor," answered Slade, boldly.

"I wish you had a more honourable calling," said Hargrove, almost mournfully.

"If you insult my father, I'll strike you down!" exclaimed Frank Slade, starting up and assuming a threatening aspect.

"I respect filial devotion, meet it where I will," calmly replied Mr. Hargrove,—"I only wish it had a better foundation in this case. I only wish the father had merited——"

I will not stain my page with the fearful oath that Frank Slade yelled, rather than uttered, as, with clenched fist, he sprung toward Mr. Hargrove. But ere he had reached the unruffled old man—who stood looking at him as one would look into the eyes of a wild beast, confident that he could not stand the gaze—a firm hand grasped his arm, and a rough voice said—

"Avast there, young man! Touch a hair of that white head, and I'll wring your neck off."

"Lyon!" As Frank uttered the man's name, he raised his fist to strike him. A moment the clenched hand remained poised in the air; then it fell slowly to his side, and he contented himself with an oath and a vile epithet.

"You can swear to your heart's content. It will do nobody any harm but yourself," cooly replied Mr. Lyon, whom I now recognised as the person with whom I had held several conversations during previous visits.

"Thank you, Mr. Lyon," said Mr. Hargrove, "for this manly interference. It is no more than I should have expected from you."

"I never suffer a young man to strike an old man," said Lyon, firmly. "Apart from that, Mr. Hargrove, there are other reasons why your person must be free from violence where I am."

"This is a bad place for you, Lyon," said Mr. Hargrove; "and I've said so to you a good many times." He spoke in rather an under tone. "Why *will* you come here?"

"It's a bad place, I know," replied Lyon, speaking out boldly, "and we all know it. But habit, Mr. Hargrove—habit. That's the cursed thing! If the bar-rooms were all shut up, there would be another story to tell. Get us the Maine law, and there will be some chance for us."

"Why don't you vote the temperance ticket?" asked Mr. Hargrove.

"Why did I? you'd better ask," said Lyon.

"I thought you voted against us."

"Not I. Ain't quite so blind to my own interests as that. And, if the truth were known, I should not at all wonder if every man in this room, except Slade and his son, voted on your side of the house."

"It's a little strange, then," said Mr. Hargrove, "that with the drinking men on our side, we failed to secure the election."

"You must blame that on your moderate men, who see no danger and go blind with their party," answered Lyon. "We have looked the evil in the face, and know its direful quality."

"Come! I would like to talk with you, Mr. Lyon."

Mr. Hargrove, his son, and Mr. Lyon went out together. As they left the room, Frank Slade said—

"What a cursed liar and hypocrite he is!"

"Who?" was asked.

"Why, Lyon," answered Frank, boldly.

"You'd better say that to his face."

"It wouldn't be good for him," remarked one of the company.

At this Frank started to his feet, stalked about the room, and put on all the disgusting airs of a drunken braggart. Even his father saw the ridiculous figure he cut, and growled out—

"There, Frank, that'll do. Don't make a miserable fool of yourself!"

At which Frank retorted, with so much of insolence that his father flew into a towering passion, and ordered him to leave the bar-room.

"You can go out yourself if you don't like the company. I'm very well satisfied," answered Frank.

"Leave this room, you impudent young scoundrel!"

"Can't go, my amiable friend," said Frank, with a cool self-possession that maddened his father, who got up hastily, and moved across the bar-room to the place where he was standing.

"Go out, I tell you!" Slade spoke resolutely.

"Would be happy to oblige you," Frank said, in a taunting voice; "but, 'pon my word, it isn't at all convenient."

Half intoxicated as he was, and already nearly blind with passion, Slade lifted his hand to strike his son. And the blow would have fallen had not some one caught his arm, and held him back from the meditated violence. Even the debased visiters of this bar-room could not stand by and see nature outraged in a bloody strife between father and son; for it was plain from the face and quickly assumed attitude of Frank, that if his father had laid his hand upon him, he would have struck him in return.

I could not remain to hear the awful imprecations that father and son, in their impotent rage, called down from heaven upon each other's heads. It was the most shocking exhibition of depraved human nature that I had ever seen. And so I left the bar-room, glad to escape from its stifling atmosphere and revolting scenes.

☞ *Night the Ninth* ☜

A FEARFUL CONSUMMATION

Neither Slade nor his son was present at the breakfast table on the next morning. As for myself, I did not eat with much appetite. Whether this defect arose from the state of my mind, or the state of the food set before me, I did not stop to inquire; but left the stifling, offensive atmosphere of the dining-room in a very few moments after entering that usually attractive place for a hungry man.

A few early drinkers were already in the bar-room—men with shattered nerves and cadaverous faces, who could not begin the day's work without the stimulus of brandy or whisky. They came in, with gliding foot-steps, asked for what they wanted in low voices, drank in silence, and departed. It was a melancholy sight to look upon.

About nine o'clock the landlord made his appearance. He, too, came gliding into the bar-room, and his first act was to seize upon a brandy decanter, pour out nearly half a pint of the fiery liquid, and drink it off. How badly his hand shook—so badly that he spilled the brandy both in pouring it out, and in lifting the glass to his lips! What a shattered wreck he was! He looked really worse now than he did on the day before when drink gave an artificial vitality to his system, a tension to his muscles, and light to his countenance. The miller of ten years ago, and the tavern-keeper of to-day! Who could have identified them as one?

Slade was turning from the bar, when a man came in. I noticed an instant change in the landlord's countenance. He looked startled; almost frightened. The man drew a small package from his pocket, and after selecting a paper therefrom, presented it to Slade, who received it with a nervous reluctance, opened, and let his eye fall upon the writing within. I was observing him closely at the time, and saw his coutenance flush deeply. In a moment or two it became pale again—paler even than before.

"Very well—all right. I'll attend to it," said the landlord, trying to recover himself, yet swallowing with every sentence.

The man, who was no other than a sheriff's deputy, and who gave him a sober, professional look, then went out with a firm step, and an air of importance. As he passed through the outer door, Slade retired from the bar-room.

"Trouble coming," I heard the bar-keeper remark, speaking partly to himself, and partly with the view, as was evident from his manner, of leading me to question him. But this I did not feel that it was right to do.

"Got the sheriff on him at last," added the bar-keeper.

"What's the matter, Bill?" inquired a man who now came in with a bustling, important air, and leaned familiarly over the bar. "Who was Jenkins after?"

"The old man," replied the bar-keeper, in a voice that showed pleasure rather than regret.

"No!"

"It's a fact." Bill, the bar-keeper, actually smiled.

"What's to pay?" said the man.

"Don't know, and don't care much."

"Did he serve a summons or an execution?"

"Can't tell."

"Judge Lyman's suit went against him."

"Did it?"

"Yes; and I heard Judge Lyman swear, that if he got him on the hip, he'd sell him out, bag and basket. And he's the man to keep his word."

"I never could just make out," said the bar-keeper, "how he ever came to owe Judge Lyman so much. I've never known of any business transactions between them."

"It's been dog eat dog, I rather guess," said the man.

"What do you mean by that?" inquired the bar-keeper.

"You've heard of dogs hunting in pairs?"

"Oh, yes."

"Well, since Harvey Green got his deserts, the business of fleecing our silly young fellows, who happened to have more money than wit or discretion, has been in the hands of Judge Lyman and Slade. They hunted together, Slade holding the game, while the Judge acted as blood-sucker. But that business was interrupted about a year ago; and game got so scarce, that, as I suggested, dog began to eat dog. And here comes the end of the matter, if I'm not mistaken. So mix us a stiff toddy. I want one more good drink at the 'Sickle and Sheaf,' before the colours are struck."

And the man chuckled at his witty effort.

During the day, I learned that affairs stood pretty much as this man had conjectured. Lyman's suits had been on sundry notes, payable on demand; but nobody knew of any property transactions between him and Slade. On the part of Slade, no defence had been made—the suit going by default. The visit of the sheriff's officer was for the purpose of serving an execution.

As I walked through Cedarville on that day, the whole aspect of the place seemed changed. I questioned with myself, often, whether this were really so, or only the effect of imagination. The change was from cheerfulness and thrift, to gloom and neglect. There was, to me, a brooding silence in the air; a pause in the life-movement; a folding of the hands, so to speak, because hope had failed from the heart. The residence of Mr. Harrison, who, some two years before, had suddenly awakened to a lively sense of the evil of rum-selling, because his own sons were discovered to be in danger, had been one of the most tasteful in Cedarville. I had often stopped to admire the beautiful shrubbery and flowers with which it was surrounded; the walks so clear—the borders so fresh and even—the arbours so cool and inviting. There was not a spot upon which the eye could rest, that did not show the hand of taste. When I now came opposite to this house, I was no longer in doubt as to the actuality of a change. There were no marked evidences of neglect; but the high cultivation and nice regard for the small details were lacking. The walks were cleanly swept; but the box borders were not so carefully trimmed. The vines and bushes that in former times were cut and tied so evenly, could hardly have felt the keen touch of the pruning-knife for months.

As I paused to note the change, a lady, somewhat beyond the middle age, came from the house. I was struck by the deep gloom that overshadowed her countenance. Ah! said I to myself, as I passed on, how many dear hopes, that once lived in that heart, must have been scattered to the winds. As I conjectured, this was Mrs. Harrison, and I was not unprepared to hear, as I did a few hours afterward, that her two sons had fallen into drinking habits; and, not only this, had been enticed to the gaming table. Unhappy mother! What a lifetime of wretchedness was compressed for thee into a few short years!

I walked on, noting, here and there, changes even more marked than appeared about the residence of Mr. Harrison. Judge Lyman's beautiful place showed utter neglect; and so did one or two others that, on my first visit to Cedarville, charmed me with their order, neatness, and cultivation. In every instance, I learned, on inquiring that the owners of these, or some members of their families, were, or had been, visitors at the "Sickle and Sheaf;" and that the ruin, in progress or completed, began after the establishment of that point of attraction in the village.

Something of a morbid curiosity, excited by what I saw, led me on to take a closer view of the residence of Judge Hammond than I had obtained on the day before. The first thing that I noticed, on approaching the old, decaying mansion, were handbills, posted on the gate, the front door, and on one of the windows. A nearer inspection revealed their import. The property had been seized, and was now offered at sheriff's sale!

Ten years before, Judge Hammond was known as the richest man in Cedarville: and now, the homestead he had once so loved to beautify—where all that was dearest to him in life once gathered—worn, disfigured, and in ruins, was about being wrested from him. I paused at the gate, and leaning over it, looked in with saddened feelings upon the dreary waste within. No sign of life was visible. The door was shut—the windows closed—not the faintest wreath of smoke was seen above the blackened chimney-tops. How vividly did imagination restore the life, and beauty, and happiness, that made their home there only a few years before,—the mother and her noble boy, one looking with trembling hope, the other with joyous confidence, into the future— the father, proud of his household treasures, but not their wise and jealous guardian.

Ah! that his hands should have unbarred the door, and thrown it wide, for the wolf to enter that precious fold! I saw them all in their sunny life before me; yet, even as I looked upon them, their sky began to darken. I heard the distant mutterings of the storm, and soon the desolating tempest swept down fearfully upon them. I shuddered as it passed away, to look upon the wrecks left scattered around. What a change!

"And all this," said I, "that one man, tired of being useful, and eager to get gain, might gather in accursed gold!"

Pushing open the gate, I entered the yard, and walked around the dwelling, my footsteps echoing in the hushed solitude of the deserted place. Hark! was that a human voice?

I paused to listen.

The sound came, once more, distinctly to my ears. I looked around, above, everywhere, but perceived no living sign. For nearly a minute I stood still, listening. Yes: there it was again—a low, moaning voice, as of one in pain or grief. I stepped onward a few paces; and now saw one of the doors standing ajar. As I pushed this door wide open, the moan was repeated. Following the direction from which the sound came, I entered one of the large drawing-rooms. The atmosphere was stifling, and all as dark as if it were midnight. Groping my way to a window, I drew back the bolt and threw open a shutter. Broadly the light fell across the dusty, uncarpeted floor, and on the dingy furniture of the room. As it did so, the moaning voice which had drawn me thither swelled on the air again; and now I saw, lying upon an old sofa, the form of a man. It needed no second glance to tell me that this was Judge Hammond. I put my hand upon him, and uttered his name: but he answered not. I spoke more firmly, and slightly shook him; but only a piteous moan was returned.

"Judge Hammond!" I now called aloud, and somewhat imperatively.

But it availed nothing. The poor old man aroused not from the stupor in which mind and body were enshrouded.

"He is dying!" thought I; and instantly left the house in search of some friends to take charge of him in his last, sad extremity. The first person to whom I made known the fact shrugged his shoulders, and said it was no affair of his, and that I must find somebody whose business it was to attend to him. My next application was met in the same spirit; and no better success attended my reference of the matter to a third party. No one to whom I spoke seemed to have any sympathy for the broken-down old man. Shocked by this indifference, I went to one of the county officers, who on learning the condition of Judge Hammond, took immediate steps to have him removed to the Almshouse, some miles distant.

"But why to the Alms-house?" I inquired, on learning his purpose. "He has property."

"Everything has been seized for debt," was the reply.

"Will there be nothing left after his creditors are satisfied?"

"Very few, if any, will be satisfied," he answered. "There will not be enough to pay half the judgments against him."

"And is there no friend to take him in—no one, of all who moved by his side in the days of prosperity, to give a few hours' shelter, and soothe the last moments of his unhappy life?"

"Why did you make application here?" was the officer's significant question.

I was silent.

"Your earnest appeals for the poor old man met with no words of sympathy?"

"None."

"He has, indeed, fallen low. In the days of his prosperity, he had many friends, so called. Adversity has shaken them all like dead leaves from sapless branches."

"But why? This is not always so."

"Judge Hammond was a selfish, worldly man. People never liked him much. His favouring, so strongly, the tavern of Slade, and his distillery operations, turned from him some of his best friends. The corruption and terrible fate of his son—and the insanity and death of his wife—all were charged upon him in people's minds; and every one seemed to turn from him instinctively after the fearful tragedy was completed. He never held up his head afterward. Neighbours shunned him as they would a criminal. And here has come the end at last. He will be taken to the Poor-house, to die there—a pauper!"

"And all," said I, partly speaking to myself, "because a man, too lazy to work at an honest calling, must needs go to rum-selling."

"The truth, the whole truth, and nothing but the truth," remarked the officer with emphasis, as he turned from me to see that his directions touching the removal of Mr. Hammond to the Poor-house were promptly executed.

In my wanderings about Cedarville during that day, I noticed a small, but very neat cottage, a little way from the centre of the village. There was not around it a great profusion of flowers and shrubbery; but the few vines, flowers, and bushes that grew green and flourishing about the door, and along the clean walks, added to the air of taste and comfort that so peculiarly marked the dwelling.

"Who lives in that pleasant little spot?" I asked of a man whom I had frequently seen in Slade's bar-room. He happened to be passing the house at the same time that I was.

"Joe Morgan," was answered.

"Indeed!" I spoke in some surprise. "And what of Morgan? How is he doing?"

"Very well."

"Doesn't he drink?"

"No. Since the death of his child, he has never taken a drop. That event sobered him, and he has remained sober ever since."

"What is he doing?"

"Working at his old trade."

"That of a miller?"

"Yes. After Judge Hammond broke down, the distillery apparatus and cotton spinning machinery were all sold and removed from Cedarville. The purchaser of what remained, having something of the fear of God, as well as regard for man, in his heart, set himself to the restoration of the old order of things, and in due time the revolving mill-wheel was at its old and better work of grinding corn and wheat for bread. The only two men in Cedarville competent to take charge of the mill were Simon Slade and Joe Morgan. The first could not be had, and the second came in as a matter of course."

"And he remains sober and industrious?"

"As any man in the village," was the answer.

I saw but little of Slade or his son during the day. But both were in the bar-room at night, and both in a condition sorrowful to look upon. Their presence, together, in the bar-room, half intoxicated as they were, seemed to revive the unhappy temper of the previous evening, as freshly as if the sun had not risen and set upon their anger.

During the early part of the evening, considerable company was present, though not of a very select class. A large proportion were young men. To most of them the fact that Slade had fallen into the sheriff's hands was known; and I gathered from some aside conversation which reached my ears, that Frank's idle, spendthrift habits had hastened the present crisis in his father's affairs. He, too, was in debt to Judge Lyman—on what account, it was not hard to infer.

It was after nine o'clock, and there was not half a dozen persons in the room, when I noticed Frank Slade go behind the bar for the third or fourth time. He was just lifting a decanter of brandy, when his father, who was considerably under the influence of drink, started forward, and laid his hand upon that of his son. Instantly a fierce light gleamed from the eyes of the young man.

"Let go of my hand," he exclaimed.

"No, I won't. Put up that brandy bottle,—you're drunk now."

"Don't meddle with me, old man!" angrily retorted Frank. "I'm not in the mood to bear any thing more from *you*."

"You're drunk as a fool now," returned Slade, who had seized the decanter. "Let go the bottle."

For only an instant did the young man hesitate. Then he drove his half-clenched hand against the breast of his father, who went staggering away several paces from the counter. Recovering himself, and now almost furious, the landlord rushed forward upon his son, his hand raised to strike him.

"Keep off!" cried Frank. "Keep off! If you touch me, I'll strike you down!" At the same time raising the half-filled bottle threateningly.

But his father was in too maddened a state to fear any consequences, and so pressed forward upon his son, striking him in the face the moment he came near enough to do so.

Instantly, the young man, infuriated by drink and evil passions, threw the bottle at his father's head. The dangerous missile fell, crashing upon one of his temples, shivering it into a hundred pieces. A heavy, jarring fall too surely marked the fearful consequences of the blow. When we gathered around the fallen man, and made an effort to lift him from the floor, a thrill of horror went through every heart. A mortal paleness was already on his marred face, and the death-gurgle in his throat! In three minutes from the time the blow was struck, his spirit had gone upward to give an account of the deeds done in the body.

"Frank Slade! you have murdered your father!"

Sternly were these terrible words uttered. It was some time before the young man seemed to comprehend their meaning. But the moment he realized the awful truth, he uttered an exclamation of horror. Almost at the same instant, a pistol-shot came sharply on the ear. But the meditated self-destruction was not accomplished. The aim was not surely taken; and the ball struck harmlessly against the ceiling.

Half an hour afterward, and Frank Slade was a lonely prisoner in the county jail!

Does the reader need a word of comment on this fearful consummation? No: and we will offer none.

☞ *Night the Tenth* ☜

THE CLOSING SCENE AT THE "SICKLE AND SHEAF"

On the day that succeeded the evening of this fearful tragedy, placards were to be seen all over the village, announcing a mass meeting at the "Sickle and Sheaf" that night.

By early twilight, the people commenced assembling. The bar, which had been closed all day, was now thrown open, and lighted; and in this room, where so much of evil had been originated, encouraged, and consummated, a crowd of earnest-looking men were soon gathered. Among them I saw the fine person of Mr. Hargrove. Joe Morgan—or rather Mr. Morgan—was also of the number. The latter I would scarcely have recognised, had not some one near me called him by name. He was well dressed, stood erect, and, though there were many deep lines on his thoughtful countenance, all traces of his former habits were gone. While I was observing him, he arose, and addressing a few words to the assemblage, nominated Mr. Hargrove as chairman of the meeting. To this a unanimous assent was given.

On taking the chair, Mr. Hargrove made a brief address, something to this effect.

"Ten years ago," said he, his voice evincing a light unsteadiness as he began, but growing firmer as he proceeded, "there was not a happier spot in Bolton county than Cedarville. Now, the marks of ruin are everywhere. Ten years ago, there was a kind-hearted, industrious miller in Cedarville, liked by every one, and as harmless as a little child. Now, his bloated, disfigured body lies in that room. His death was violent, and by the hand of his own son!"

Mr. Hargrove's words fell slowly, distinctly, and marked by the most forcible emphasis. There was scarcely one present who did not feel a low shudder run along his nerves, as the last words were spoken in a husky whisper.

"Ten years ago," he proceeded, "the miller had a happy wife, and two innocent, glad-hearted children. Now, his wife, bereft of reason, is in a mad-house, and his son the occupant of a felon's cell, charged with the awful crime of parricide!"

Briefly he paused, while his audience stood gazing upon him with half suspended respiration.

"Ten years ago," he went on, "Judge Hammond was accounted the richest man in Cedarville. Yesterday he was carried, a friendless pauper, to the Almshouse; and to-day he is the unmourned occupant of a pauper's grave! Ten years ago, his wife was the proud, hopeful, loving mother of a most promising son. I need not describe what Willy Hammond was. All here knew him well. Ah! what shattered the fine intellect of that noble-minded woman? Why did her heart break? Where is she? Where is Willy Hammond?"

A low, half repressed groan answered the speaker,

"Ten years ago, you, sir," pointing to a sad-looking old man, and calling him by name, "had two sons—generous, promising, manly-hearted boys. What are they now? You need not answer the question. Too well is their history and your sorrow known. Ten years ago, I had a son—amiable, kind, loving, but weak. Heaven knows how I sought to guard and protect him! But he fell also. The arrows of destruction darkened the very air of our once secure and happy village. And who was safe? Not mine, nor yours!

"Shall I go on? Shall I call up and pass in review before you, one after another, all the wretched victims who have fallen in Cedarville during the last ten years? Time does not permit. It would take hours for the enumeration! No: I will not throw additional darkness into the picture. Heaven knows it is black enough already! But what is the root of this great evil? Where lies the fearful secret? Who understands the disease? A direful pestilence is in the air—it walketh in darkness, and wasteth at noonday. It is slaying the first-born in our houses, and the cry of anguish is swelling on every gale. Is there no remedy?

"Yes! yes! There is a remedy!" was the spontaneous answer from many voices.

"Be it our task, then, to find and apply it this night," answered the chairman, as he took his seat.

"And there is but one remedy," said Morgan, as Mr. Hargrove sat down. "The accursed traffic must cease among us. You must cut off the fountain, if you would dry up the stream. If you would save the young, the weak, and the innocent—on you God has laid the solemn duty of their protection—you must cover them from the tempter. Evil is strong, wily, fierce, and active in the pursuit of its ends. The young, the weak, and the innocent can no more resist its assaults, than the lamb can resist the wolf. They are helpless, if you abandon them to the powerers of evil. Men and brethren! as one who has himself been wellnigh lost—as one who, daily, feels and trembles at the dangers that beset his path—I do conjure you to stay the fiery stream that is bearing every thing good and beautiful among you to destruction. Fathers! for the sake of your young children, be up now and doing. Think of Willy Hammond, Frank Slade, and a dozen more whose names I could repeat, and hesitate no longer! Let us resolve, this night, that from henceforth, the traffic shall cease in Cedarville. Is there not a large majority of citizens in favour of such a measure? And whose rights or interest can be affected by such a restriction? Who, in fact, has any right to sow disease and death in our community? The liberty, under sufferance, to do so, wrongs the individual who uses it, as well as those who become his victims. Do you want proof of this. Look at Simon Slade, the happy, kind-hearted miller; and at Simon Slade, the tavern-keeper. Was he benefited by the liberty to work harm to his neighbour? No! no! In heaven's name, then, let the traffic cease! To this end, I offer these resolutions:—

"Be it resolved by the inhabitants of Cedarville, That from this day henceforth, no more intoxicating drink shall be sold within the limits of the corporation.

"Resolved, further, That all the liquors in the 'Sickle and, Sheaf' be forthwith destroyed, and that a fund be raised to pay the creditors of Simon Slade therefor, should they demand compensation.

"Resolved, That in closing up all other places where liquor is sold, regard shall be had to the right of property which the law secures to every man.

"Resolved, That with the consent of the legal authorities, all the liquor for sale in Cedarville be destroyed; provided the owners thereof be paid its full value out of a fund specially raised for that purpose."

But for the calm, yet resolute opposition of one or two men, these resolutions would have passed by acclamation. A little sober argument showed the excited company that no good end is ever secured by the adoption of wrong means.

There were, in Cedarville, regularly constituted authorities, which alone had the power to determine public measures; or to say what business might or might not be pursued by individuals. And through these authorities they must act in an orderly way.

There was some little chafing at this view of the case. But good sense and reason prevailed. Somewhat modified, the resolution passed, and the more ultra-inclined contented themselves with carrying out the second resolution, to destroy forthwith all the liquor to be found on the premises; which was immediately done. After which the people dispersed to their home, each with a lighter heart, and better hopes for the future of their village.

On the next day, as I entered the stage that was to bear me from Cedarville, I saw a man strike his sharp axe into the worn, faded, and leaning post that had, for so many years, borne aloft the "Sickle and Sheaf;" and just as the driver gave word to his horses, the false emblem which had invited so many to enter the way of destruction, fell crashing to the earth.

IN HIS STEPS

BY CHARLES M. SHELDON

Chapter 1

For hereunto were ye called; because Christ also suffered for you, leaving you an example, that ye should follow his steps.

It was Friday morning and the Rev. Henry Maxwell was trying to finish his Sunday morning sermon. He had been interrupted several times and was growing nervous as the morning wore away, and the sermon grew very slowly toward a satisfactory finish.

"Mary," he called to his wife, as he went upstairs after the last interruption, "if any one comes after this, I wish you would say I am very busy and cannot come down unless it is something very important."

"Yes, Henry. But I am going over to visit the kindergarten and you will have the house all to yourself."

The minister went up into his study and shut the door. In a few minutes he heard his wife go out, and then everything was quiet. He settled himself at his desk with a sigh of relief and began to write. His text was from 1 Peter ii. 21: "For hereunto were ye called; because Christ also suffered for you, leaving you an example that ye should follow his steps."

He had emphasized in the first part of the sermon the Atonement as a personal sacrifice, calling attention to the fact of Jesus' suffering in various ways, in His life as well as in His death. He had then gone on to emphasize the Atonement from the side of example, giving illustrations from the life and teachings of Jesus to show how faith in the Christ helped to save men because of the pattern or character He displayed for their imitation. He was now on the third and last point, the necessity of following Jesus in His sacrifice and example.

He had put down "Three Steps. What are they?" and was about to enumerate them in logical order when the bell rang sharply. It was one of those clock-work bells, and always went off as a clock might go if it tried to strike twelve all at once.

Henry Maxwell sat at his desk and frowned a little. He made no movement to answer the bell. Very soon it rang again; then he rose and walked over to one of his windows which commanded the view of the front door. A man was standing on the steps. He was a young man, very shabbily dressed.

"Looks like a tramp," said the minister. "I suppose I'll have to go down and—"

He did not finish his sentence but he went downstairs and opened the front door. There was a moment's pause as the two men stood facing each other, then the shabby-looking young man said:

"I'm out of a job, sir, and thought maybe you might put me in the way of getting something."

"I don't know of anything. Jobs are scarce—" replied the minister, beginning to shut the door slowly.

"I didn't know but you might perhaps be able to give me a line to the city railway or the superintendent of the shops, or something," continued the young man, shifting his faded hat from one hand to the other nervously.

"I would be of no use. You will have to excuse me. I am very busy this morning. I hope you will find something. Sorry I can't give you something to do here. But I keep only a horse and a cow and do the work myself."

The Rev. Henry Maxwell closed the door and heard the man walk down the steps. As he went up into his study he saw from his hall window that the man was going slowly down the street, still holding his hat between his hands. There was something in the figure so dejected, homeless and forsaken that the minister hesitated a moment as he stood looking at it. Then he turned to his desk and with a sigh began the writing where he had left off. He had no more interruptions, and when his wife came in two hours later the sermon was finished, the loose leaves gathered up and neatly tied together, and laid on his Bible all ready for the Sunday morning service.

"A queer thing happened at the kindergarten this morning, Henry," said his wife while they were eating dinner. "You know I went over with Mrs. Brown to visit the school, and just after the games, while the children were at the tables, the door opened and a young man came in holding a dirty hat in both hands. He sat down near the door and never said a word; only looked at the children. He was evidently a tramp, and Miss Wren and her assistant Miss Kyle were a little frightened at first, but he sat there very quietly and after a few minutes he went out."

"Perhaps he was tired and wanted to rest somewhere. The same man called here, I think. Did you say he looked like a tramp?"

"Yes, very dusty, shabby and generally tramp-like. Not more than thirty or thirty-three years old, I should say."

"The same man," said the Rev. Henry Maxwell thoughtfully.

"Did you finish your sermon, Henry?" his wife asked after a pause.

"Yes, all done. It has been a very busy week with me. The two sermons have cost me a good deal of labor."

"They will be appreciated by a large audience, Sunday, I hope," replied his wife smiling. "What are you going to preach about in the morning?"

"Following Christ. I take up the Atonement under the head of sacrifice and example, and then show the steps needed to follow His sacrifice and example."

"I am sure it is a good sermon. I hope it won't rain Sunday. We have had so many stormy Sundays lately."

"Yes, the audiences have been quite small for some time. People will not come out to church in a storm." The Rev. Henry Maxwell sighed as he said it. He was thinking of the careful, laborious effort he had made in preparing sermons for large audiences that failed to appear.

But Sunday morning dawned on the town of Raymond one of the perfect days that sometimes come after long periods of wind and mud and rain. The air was clear and bracing, the sky was free from all threatening signs, and every one in Mr. Maxwell's parish prepared to go to church. When the service opened at eleven o'clock the large building was filled with an audience of the best-dressed, most comfortable-looking people of Raymond.

The First Church of Raymond believed in having the best music that money could buy, and its quartet choir this morning was a source of great pleasure to the congregation. The anthem was inspiring. All the music was in keeping with the subject of the sermon. And the anthem was an elaborate adaptation to the most modern music of the hymn,

> Jesus, I my cross have taken,
> All to leave and follow Thee.

Just before the sermon the soprano sang a solo, the well-known hymn,

> Where He leads me I will follow,
> I'll go with Him, with Him, all the way.

Rachel Winslow looked very beautiful that morning as she stood up behind the screen of carved oak which was significantly marked with the emblems of the cross and the crown. Her voice was even more beautiful than her face, and that meant a great deal. There was a general rustle of expectation over the audience as she rose. Mr. Maxwell settled himself contentedy behind the pulpit. Rachel Winslow's singing always helped him. He generally arranged for a song before the sermon. It made possible a certain inspiration of feeling that made his delivery more impressive.

People said to themselves they had never heard such singing even

in the First Church. It is certain that if it had not been a church service, her solo would have been vigorously applauded. It even seemed
to the minister when she sat down that something like an attempted
clapping of hands or a striking of feet on the floor swept through the
church. He was startled by it. As he rose, however, and laid his sermon on the Bible, he said to himself he had been deceived. Of course
it could not occur. In a few moments he was absorbed in his sermon
and everything else was forgotten in the pleasure of his delivery.

No one had ever accused Henry Maxwell of being a dull preacher.
On the contrary, he had often been charged with being sensational;
not in what he had said so much as in his way of saying it. But the
First Church people liked that. It gave their preacher and their parish
a pleasant distinction that was agreeable.

It was also true that the pastor of the First Church loved to preach.
He seldom exchanged. He was eager to be in his own pulpit when
Sunday came. There was an exhilarating half hour for him as he faced
a church full of people and knew that he had a hearing. He was peculiarly sensitive to variations in the attendance. He never preached well
before a small audience. The weather also affected him decidedly. He
was at his best before just such an audience as faced him now, on just
such a morning. He felt a glow of satisfaction as he went on. The
church was the first in the city. It had the best choir. It had a membership composed of the leading people, representatives of the wealth,
society and intelligence of Raymond. He was going abroad on a three
months vacation in the summer, and the circumstances of his pastorate, his influence and his position as pastor of the First Church of the
city—

It is not certain that the Rev. Henry Maxwell knew just how he
could carry on that thought in connection with his sermon, but as he
drew near the end of it he knew that he had at some point in his delivery had all those feelings. They had entered into the very substance
of his thought; it might have been all in a few seconds of time, but he
had been conscious of defining his position and his emotions as well as
if he took a soliloquy, and his delivery partook of the thrill of deep
personal satisfaction.

The sermon was interesting. It was full of striking sentences. They
would have commanded attention printed. Spoken with the passion of
a dramatic utterance that had the good taste never to offend with a
suspicion of ranting or declamation, they were very effective. If the
Rev. Henry Maxwell that morning felt satisfied with the conditions of
his pastorate, the First Church also had a similar feeling as it congrat-
ulated itself on the presence in the pulpit of this scholarly, refined,
somewhat striking face and figure, preaching with such animation and
freedom from all vulgar, noisy or disagreeable mannerism.

Suddenly, into the midst of this perfect accord and concord between preacher and audience, there came a very remarkable interruption. It would be difficult to indicate the extent of the shock which this interruption measured. It was so unexpected, so entirely contrary to any thought of any person present that it offered no room for argument or, for the time being, of resistance.

The sermon had come to a close. Mr. Maxwell had just turned the half of the big Bible over upon his manuscript and was about to sit down as the quartet prepared to arise to sing the closing selection,

> All for Jesus, all for Jesus,
> All my being's ransomed powers,

when the entire congregation was startled by the sound of a man's voice. It came from the rear of the church, from one of the seats under the gallery. The next moment the figure of a man came out of the shadow there and walked down the middle aisle. Before the startled congregation fairly realized what was going on the man had reached the open space in front of the pulpit and had turned about facing the people.

"I've been wondering since I came in here"—they were the words he used under the gallery, and he repeated them—"if it would be just the thing to say a word at the close of the service. I'm not drunk and I'm not crazy, and I am perfectly harmless, but if I die, as there is every likelihood I shall in a few days, I want the satisfaction of thinking that I said my say in a place like this, and before this sort of a crowd."

Mr. Maxwell had not taken his seat, and he now remained standing, leaning on his pulpit, looking down at the stranger. It was the man who had come to his house the Friday before, the same dusty, worn, shabby-looking young man. He held his faded hat in his two hands. It seemed to be a favorite gesture. He had not been shaved and his hair was rough and tangled. It is doubtful if any one like this had ever confronted the First Church within the sanctuary. It was tolerably familiar with this sort of humanity out on the street, around the railroad shops, wandering up and down the avenue, but it had never dreamed of such an incident as this so near.

There was nothing offensive in the man's manner or tone. He was not excited and he spoke in a low but distinct voice. Mr. Maxwell was conscious, even as he stood there smitten into dumb astonishment at the event, that somehow the man's action reminded him of a person he had once seen walking and talking in his sleep.

No one in the house made any motion to stop the stranger or in any way interrupt him. Perhaps the first shock of his sudden appearance deepened into a genuine perplexity concerning what was best to do.

However that may be, he went on as if he had no thought of interruption and no thought of the unusual element which he had introduced into the decorum of the First Church service. And all the while he was speaking, the minister leaned over the pulpit, his face growing more white and sad every moment. But he made no movement to stop him, and the people sat smitten into breathless silence. One other face, that of Rachel Winslow from the choir, stared white and intent down at the shabby figure with the faded hat. Her face was striking at any time. Under the pressure of the present unheard-of incident it was as personally distinct as if it had been framed in fire.

"I'm not an ordinary tramp, though I don't know of any teaching of Jesus that makes one kind of a tramp less worth saving than another. Do you?" He put the question as naturally as if the whole congregation had been a small Bible class. He paused just a moment and coughed painfully. Then he went on.

"I lost my job ten months ago. I am a printer by trade. The new linotype machines are beautiful specimens of invention, but I know six men who have killed themselves inside of the year just on account of those machines. Of course I don't blame the newspapers for getting the machines. Meanwhile, what can a man do? I know I never learned but the one trade, and that's all I can do. I've tramped all over the country trying to find something. There are a good many others like me. I'm not complaining, am I? Just stating facts. But I was wondering as I sat there under the gallery, if what you call following Jesus is the same thing as what He taught. What did He mean when He said: 'follow me!' The minister said," here the man turned about and looked up at the pulpit, "that it is necessary for the disciple of Jesus to follow His steps, and he said the steps are 'obedience, faith, love and imitation.' But I did not hear tell you just what he meant that to mean, especially the last step. What do you Christians mean by following the steps of Jesus?

"I've tramped through this city for three days trying to find a job; and in all that time I've not had a word of sympathy or comfort except from your minister here, who said he was sorry for me and hoped I would find a job somewhere. I suppose it is because you get so imposed on by the professional tramp that you have lost your interest in any other sort. I'm not blaming anybody, am I? Just stating facts. Of course, I understand you can't all go out of your way to hunt up jobs for other people like me. I'm not asking you to; but what I feel puzzled about is, what is meant by following Jesus. What do you mean when you sing 'I'll go with Him, with Him, all the way?' Do you mean that you are suffering and denying yourselves and trying to save lost, suffering humanity just as I understand Jesus did? What do you mean by it? I see the ragged edge of things a good deal. I understand

there are more than five hundred men in this city in my case. Most of
them have families. My wife died four months ago. I'm glad she is out
of trouble. My little girl is staying with a printer's family until I find a
job. Somehow I get puzzled when I see so many Christians living in
luxury and singing 'Jesus, I my cross have taken, all to leave and follow Thee,' and remember how my wife died in a tenement in New
York City, gasping for air and asking God to take the little girl too. Of
course I don't expect you people can prevent every one from dying of
starvation, lack of proper nourishment and tenement air, but what
does following Jesus mean? I understand that Christian people own a
good many of the tenements. A member of a church was the owner of
the one where my wife died, and I have wondered if following Jesus
all the way was true in his case. I heard some people singing at a
church prayer meeting the other night,

> All for Jesus, all for Jesus,
> All my being's ransomed powers,
> All my thoughts, and all my doings,
> All my days, and all my hours,

and I kept wondering as I sat on the steps outside just what they
meant by it. It seems to me there's an awful lot of trouble in the world
that somehow wouldn't exist if all the people who sing such songs
went and lived them out. I suppose I don't understand. But what
would Jesus do? Is that what you mean by following His steps? It
seems to me sometimes as if the people in the big churches had good
clothes and nice houses to live in, and money to spend for luxuries,
and could go away on summer vacations and all that, while the people
outside the churches, thousands of them, I mean, die in tenements,
and walk the streets for jobs, and never have a piano or a picture in
the house, and grow up in misery and drunkenness and sin."

The man suddenly gave a queer lurch over in the direction of the
communion table and laid one grimy hand on it. His hat fell upon the
carpet at his feet. A stir went through the congregation. Dr. West half
rose from his pew, but as yet the silence was unbroken by any voice
or movement worth mentioning in the audience. The man passed his
other hand across his eyes, and then, without any warning, fell heavily
forward on his face, full length up the aisle. Henry Maxwell spoke:

"We will consider the service closed."

He was down the pulpit stairs and kneeling by the prostrate form
before any one else. The audience instantly rose and the aisles were
crowded. Dr. West pronounced the man alive. He had fainted away.
"Some heart trouble," the doctor also muttered as he helped carry him
out into the pastor's study.

Chapter 2

Henry Maxwell and a group of his church members remained some time in the study. The man lay on the couch there and breathed heavily. When the question of what to do with him came up, the minister insisted on taking the man to his own house; he lived near by and had an extra room. Rachel Winslow said:

"Mother has no company at present. I am sure we would be glad to give him a place with us."

She looked strongly agitated. No one noticed it particularly. They were all excited over the strange event, the strangest that First Church people could remember. But the minister insisted on taking charge of the man, and when a carriage came the unconscious but living form was carried to his house; and with the entrance of that humanity into the minister's spare room a new chapter in Henry Maxwell's life began, and yet no one, himself least of all, dreamed of the remarkable change it was destined to make in all his after definition of the Christian discipleship.

The event created a great sensation in the First Church parish. People talked of nothing else for a week. It was the general impression that the man had wandered into the church in a condition of mental disturbance caused by his troubles, and that all the time he was talking he was in a strange delirium of fever and really ignorant of his surroundings. That was the most charitable construction to put upon his action. It was the general agreement also that there was a singular absence of anything bitter or complaining in what the man had said. He had, throughout, spoken in a mild, apologetic tone, almost as if he were one of the congregation seeking for light on a very difficult subject.

The third day after his removal to the minister's house there was a marked change in his condition. The doctor spoke of it but offered no hope. Saturday morning he still lingered, although he had rapidly failed as the week drew near its close. Sunday morning, just before the clock struck one, he rallied and asked if his child had come. The minister had sent for her at once as soon as he had been able to secure her address from some letters found in the man's pocket. He had been conscious and able to talk coherently only a few moments since his attack.

"The child is coming. She will be here," Mr. Maxwell said as he sat there, his face showing marks of the strain of the week's vigil; for he had insisted on sitting up nearly every night.

"I shall never see her in this world," the man whispered. Then he uttered with great difficulty the words, "You have been good to me. Somehow I feel as if it was what Jesus would do."

After a few minutes he turned his head slightly, and before Mr. Maxwell could realize the fact, the doctor said quietly, "He is gone."

The Sunday morning that dawned on the city of Raymond was exactly like the Sunday of a week before. Mr. Maxwell entered his pulpit to face one of the largest congregations that had ever crowded the First Church. He was haggard and looked as if he had just risen from a long illness. His wife was at home with the little girl, who had come on the morning train an hour after her father had died. He lay in that spare room, his troubles over, and the minister could see the face as he opened the Bible and arranged his different notices on the side of the desk as he had been in the habit of doing for ten years.

The service that morning contained a new element. No one could remember when Henry Maxwell had preached in the morning without notes. As a matter of fact he had done so occasionally when he first entered the ministry, but for a long time he had carefully written every word of his morning sermon, and nearly always his evening discourses as well. It cannot be said that his sermon this morning was striking or impressive. He talked with considerable hesitation. It was evident that some great idea struggled in his thought for utterance, but it was not expressed in the theme he had chosen for his preaching. It was near the close of his sermon that he began to gather a certain strength that had been painfully lacking at the beginning.

He closed the Bible and, stepping out at the side of the desk, faced his people and began to talk to them about the remarkable scene of the week before.

"Our brother," somehow the words sounded a little strange coming from his lips, "passed away this morning. I have not yet had time to learn all his history. He had one sister living in Chicago. I have written her and have not yet received an answer. His little girl is with us and will remain for the time."

He paused and looked over the house. He thought he had never seen so many earnest faces during his entire pastorate. He was not able yet to tell his people his experiences, the crisis through which he was even now moving. But something of his feeling passed from him to them, and it did not seem to him that he was acting under a careless impulse at all to go on and break to them this morning something of the message he bore in his heart.

So he went on:

"The appearance and words of this stranger in the church last Sunday made a very powerful impression on me. I am not able to conceal from you or myself the fact that what he said, followed as it has been by his death in my house, has compelled me to ask as I never asked before, 'What does following Jesus mean?' I am not in a position yet to utter any condemnation of this people or, to a certain extent, of myself, either in our Christ-like relations to this man or the numbers that he represents in the world. But all that does not prevent me from feeling that much that the man said was so vitally true that we must face it in an attempt to answer it or else stand condemned as Christian disciples. A good deal that was said here last Sunday was in the nature of a challenge to Christianity as it is seen and felt in our churches. I have felt this with increasing emphasis every day since.

"And I do not know that any time is more appropriate than the present for me to propose a plan, or a purpose, which has been forming in my mind as a satisfactory reply to much that was said here last Sunday."

Again Henry Maxwell paused and looked into the faces of his people. There were some strong, earnest men and women in the First Church.

He could see Edward Norman, editor of the Raymond *Daily News*. He had been a member of the First Church for ten years. No man was more honored in the community. There was Alexander Powers, superintendent of the great railroad shops in Raymond, a typical railroad man, one who had been born into the business. There sat Donald Marsh, president of Lincoln College, situated in the suburbs of Raymond. There was Milton Wright, one of the great merchants of Raymond, having in his employ at least one hundred men in various shops. There was Dr. West, who, although still comparatively young, was quoted as authority in special surgical cases. There was young Jasper Chase the author, who had written one successful book and was said to be at work on a new novel. There was Miss Virginia Page the heiress, who through the recent death of her father had inherited a million at least, and was gifted with unusual attractions of person and intellect. And not least of all, Rachel Winslow, from her seat in the choir, glowed with her peculiar beauty of light this morning because she was so intensely interested in the whole scene.

There was some reason, perhaps, in view of such material in the First Church, for Henry Maxwell's feeling of satisfaction whenever he considered his parish as he had the previous Sunday. There was an unusually large number of strong, individual characters who claimed membership there. But as he noted their faces this morning he was simply wondering how many of them would respond to the strange proposition he was about to make. He continued slowly, taking time to choose his words carefully, and giving the people an impression they had never felt before, even when he was at his best with his most dramatic delivery.

"What I am going to propose now is something which ought not to appear unusual or at all impossible of execution. Yet I am aware that it will be so regarded by a large number, perhaps, of the members of this church. But in order that we may have a thorough understanding of what we are considering, I will put my proposition very plainly, perhaps bluntly. I want volunteers from the First Church who will pledge themselves, earnestly and honestly for an entire year, not to do anything without first asking the question, 'What would Jesus do?' And after asking that question, each one will follow Jesus as exactly as he knows how, no matter what the result may be. I will of course include myself in this company of volunteers, and shall take for granted that my church here will not be surprised at my future conduct, as based upon this standard of action, and will not oppose whatever is done if they think Christ would do it. Have I made my meaning clear? At the close of the service I want all those members who are willing to join such a company to remain and we will talk over the details of the plan. Our motto will be, 'What would Jesus do?' Our aim will be to act just as He would if He was in our places, regardless of immediate results. In other words, we propose to follow Jesus' steps as closely and as literally as we believe He taught His disciples to do. And those who volunteer to do this will pledge themselves for an entire year, beginning with today, so to act."

Henry Maxwell paused again and looked out over his people. It is not easy to describe the sensation that such a simple proposition apparently made. Men glanced at one another in astonishment. It was not like Henry Maxwell to define Christian discipleship in this way. There was evident confusion of thought over his proposition. It was understood well enough, but there was, apparently, a great difference of opinion as to the application of Jesus' teaching and example.

He calmly closed the service with a brief prayer. The organist began his postlude immediately after the benediction and the people began to go out. There was a great deal of conversation. Animated groups stood all over the church discussing the minister's proposition. It was evidently provoking great discussion. After several minutes he asked all who expected to remain to pass into the lecture-room which joined the large room on the side. He was himself detained at the front of the church talking with several persons there, and when he finally turned around, the church was empty. He walked over to the lecture-room entrance and went in. He was almost startled to see the people who were there. He had not made up his mind about any of his members, but he had hardly expected that so many were ready to enter into such a literal testing of their Christian discipleship as now awaited him. There were perhaps fifty present, among them Rachel Winslow and Virginia Page, Mr. Norman, President Marsh, Alexander Powers the railroad superintendent, Milton Wright, Dr. West and Jasper Chase.

He closed the door of the lecture-room and went and stood before the little group. His face was pale and his lips trembled with genuine emotion. It was to him a genuine crisis in his own life and that of his parish. No man can tell until he is moved by the Divine Spirit what he may do, or how he may change the current of a lifetime of fixed habits of thought and speech and action. Henry Maxwell did not, as we have said, yet know himself all that he was passing through, but he was conscious of a great upheaval in his definition of Christian discipleship, and he was moved with a depth of feeling he could not measure as he looked into the faces of those men and women on this occasion.

It seemed to him that the most fitting word to be spoken first was that of prayer. He asked them all to pray with him. And almost with the first syllable he uttered there was a distinct presence of the Spirit felt by them all. As the prayer went on, this presence grew in power. They all felt it. The room was filled with it as plainly as if it had been visible. When the prayer closed there was a silence that lasted several moments. All the heads were bowed. Henry Maxwell's face was wet with tears. If an audible voice from heaven had sanctioned their pledge to follow the Master's steps, not one person present could have felt more certain of the divine blessing. And so the most serious movement ever started in the First Church of Raymond was begun.

"We all understand," said he, speaking very quietly, "what we have undertaken to do. We pledge ourselves to do everything in our daily lives after asking the question, 'What would Jesus do?' regardless of what may be the result to us. Some time I shall be able to tell you what a marvelous change has come over my life within a week's time. I cannot now. But the experience I have been through since last Sunday has left me so dissatisfied with my previous definition of Christian discipleship that I have been compelled to take this action. I did not dare begin it alone. I know that I am being led by the hand of divine love in all this. The same divine impulse must have led you also.

"Do we understand fully what we have undertaken?"

"I want to ask a question," said Rachel Winslow. Everyone turned towards her. Her face glowed with a beauty that no physical loveliness could ever create.

"I am a little in doubt as to the source of our knowledge concerning what Jesus would do. Who is to decide for me just what He would do in my case? It is a different age. There are many perplexing questions in our civilization that are not mentioned in the teachings of Jesus. How am I going to tell what He would do?"

"There is no way that I know of," replied the pastor, "except as we study Jesus Christ through the medium of the Holy Spirit. You remember what Christ said speaking to His disciples about the Holy Spirit: 'Howbeit when He the spirit of truth is come, He shall guide you into all the truth; for he shall not speak for Himself; but what things soever He shall hear, there shall He speak; and He shall declare unto you the things that are to come. He shall glorify me; for He shall take of mine and declare it unto you. All things whatsoever the Father hath are mine; therefore said I, that he taketh of mine and shall declare it unto you.' There is no other test that I know of. We shall all have to decide what Jesus would do after going to that source of knowledge."

"What if others say of us, when we do certain things, that Jesus would not do so?" asked the superintendent of railroads.

"We cannot prevent that. But we must be absolutely honest with ourselves. The standard of Christian action cannot vary in most of our acts."

"And yet what one church member thinks Jesus would do, another refuses to accept as His probable course of action. What is to render our conduct uniformly Christ-like? Will it be possible to reach the same conclusions always in all cases?" asked President Marsh.

Mr. Maxwell was silent some time. Then he answered, "No; I don't know that we can expect that. But when it comes to a genuine, honest, enlightened following of Jesus' steps, I cannot believe there will be any confusion either in our own minds or in the judgment of others. We must be free from fanaticism on one hand and too much caution on the other. If Jesus' example is the example for the world to follow, it certainly must be feasible to follow it. But we need to remember this great fact. After we have asked the Spirit to tell us what Jesus would do and have received an answer to it, we are to act regardless of the results to ourselves. Is that understood?"

All the faces in the room were raised towards the minister in solemn assent. There was no misunderstanding that proposition. Henry Maxwell's face quivered again as he noted the president of the Endeavor Society with several members seated back of the older men and women.

They remained a little longer talking over the details and asking questions, and agreed to report to one another every week at a regular meeting the result of their experiences in following Jesus this way.

Henry Maxwell prayed again. And again as before the Spirit made Himself manifest. Every head remained bowed a long time. They went away finally in silence. There was a feeling that prevented speech. The pastor shook hands with them all as they went out. Then he went into his own study room back of the pulpit and kneeled. He remained there alone nearly half an hour. When he went home he went into the room where the dead body lay. As he looked at the face he cried in his heart again for strength and wisdom. But not even yet did he realize that a movement had begun which would lead to the most remarkable series of events that the city of Raymond had ever known.

Chapter 3

He that saith he abideth in Him ought himself also to walk even as He walked.

Edward Norman, editor of the Raymond *Daily News,* sat in his office room Monday morning and faced a new world of action. He had made his pledge in good faith to do everything after asking "What would Jesus do?" and, as he supposed, with his eyes open to all the possible results. But as the regular life of the paper started on another week's rush and whirl of activity, he confronted it with a degree of hesitation and a feeling nearly akin to fear.

He had come down to the office very early, and for a few minutes was by himself. He sat at his desk in a growing thoughtfulness that finally became a desire which he knew was as great as it was unusual. He had yet to learn, with all the others in that little company pledged to do the Christlike thing, that the Spirit of Life was moving in power through his own life as never before. He rose and shut his door, and then did what he had not done for years. He kneeled down by his desk and prayed for the Divine Presence and wisdom to direct him.

He rose with the day before him, and his promise distinct and clear in his mind. "Now for action," he seemed to say. But he would be led by events as fast as they came on.

He opened his door and began the routine of the office work. The managing editor had just come in and was at his desk in the adjoining room. One of the reporters there was pounding out something on a typewriter. Edward Norman began to write an editorial. The *Daily News* was an evening paper, and Norman usually completed his leading editorial before nine o'clock.

He had been writing for fifteen minutes when the managing editor called out:

"Here's this press report of yesterday's prize fight at the Resort. It will make up three columns and a half. I suppose it all goes in?"

Norman was one of those newspaper men who keep an eye on every detail of the paper. The managing editor always consulted his chief in matters of both small and large importance. Sometimes, as in this case, it was merely a nominal inquiry.

"Yes—No. Let me see it."

He took the type-written matter just as it came from the telegraph editor and ran over it carefully. Then he laid the sheets down on his desk and did some very hard thinking.

"We won't run this today," he said finally.

The managing editor was standing in the doorway between the two rooms. He was astounded at his chief's remark, and thought he had perhaps misunderstood him.

"What did you say?"

"Leave it out. We won't use it."

"But—" The managing editor was simply dumbfounded. He stared at Norman as if the man was out of his mind.

"I don't think, Clark, that it ought to be printed, and that's the end of it," said Norman, looking up from his desk.

Clark seldom had any words with the chief. His word had always been law in the office and he had seldom been known to change his mind. The circumstances now, however, seemed to be so extraordinary that Clark could not help expressing himself.

"Do you mean that the paper is to go to press without a word of the prize fight in it?"

"Yes. That's what I mean."

"But it's unheard of. All the other papers will print it. What will our subscribers say? Why, it is simply—" Clark paused, unable to find words to say what he thought.

Norman looked at Clark thoughtfully. The managing editor was a member of a church of a different denomination from that of Norman's. The two men had never talked together on religious matters although they had been associated on the paper for several years.

"Come in here a minute, Clark, and shut the door," said Norman.

Clark came in and the two men faced each other alone. Norman did not speak for a minute Then he said abruptly:

"Clark, if Christ was editor of a daily paper, do you honestly think

He would print three columns and a half of prize fight in it?"

"No, I don't suppose He would."

"Well, that's my only reason for shutting this account out of the *News*. I have decided not to do a thing in connection with the paper for a whole year that I honestly believe Jesus would not do."

Clark could not have looked more amazed if the chief had suddenly gone crazy. In fact, he did think something was wrong, though Mr. Norman was one of the last men in the world, in his judgment, to lose his mind.

"What effect will that have on the paper?" he finally managed to ask in a faint voice.

"What do you think?" asked Norman with a keen glance.

"I think it will simply ruin the paper," replied Clark promptly. He was gathering up his bewildered senses, and began to remonstrate, "Why, it isn't feasible to run a paper nowadays on any such basis. It's too ideal. The world isn't ready for it. You can't make it pay. Just as sure as you live, if you shut out this prize fight report you will lose hundreds of subscribers. It doesn't take a prophet to see that. The very best people in town are eager to read it. They know it has taken place, and when they get the paper this evening they will expect half a page at least. Surely, you can't afford to disregard the wishes of the public to such an extent. It will be a great mistake if you do, in my opinion."

Norman sat silent a minute. Then he spoke gently but firmly.

"Clark, what in your honest opinion is the right standard for determining conduct? Is the only right standard for every one, the probable action of Jesus Christ? Would you say that the highest, best law for a man to live by was contained in asking the question, 'What would Jesus do?' And then doing it regardless of results? In other words, do you think men everywhere ought to follow Jesus' example as closely as they can in their daily lives?" Clark turned red, and moved uneasily in his chair before he answered the editor's question.

"Why—yes—I suppose if you put it on the ground of what men ought to do there is no other standard of conduct. But the question is, What is feasible? Is it possible to make it pay? To succeed in the newspaper business we have got to conform to custom and the recognized methods of society. We can't do as we would in an ideal world."

"Do you mean that we can't run the paper strictly on Christian principles and make it succeed?"

"Yes, that's just what I mean. It can't be done. We'll go bankrupt in thirty days."

Norman did not reply at once. He was very thoughtful.

"We shall have occasion to talk this over again, Clark. Meanwhile, I think we ought to understand each other frankly. I have pledged myself for a year to do everything connected with the paper after answering the question, 'What would Jesus do?' as honestly as possible. I shall continue to do this in the belief that not only can we succeed but that we can succeed better than we ever did."

Clark rose. "The report does not go in?"

"It does not. There is plenty of good material to take its place, and you know what it is."

Clark hesitated. "Are you going to say anything about the absence of the report?"

"No, let the paper go to press as if there had been no such thing as a prize fight yesterday."

Clark walked out of the room to his own desk feeling as if the bottom had dropped out of everything. He was astonished, bewildered, excited and considerably angered. His great respect for Norman checked his rising indignation and disgust, but with it all was a feeling of growing wonder at the sudden change of motive which had entered the office of the *Daily News* and threatened, as he firmly believed, to destroy it.

Before noon every reporter, pressman and employee on *Daily News* was informed of the remarkable fact that the paper was going to press without a word in it about the famous prize fight of Sunday. The reporters were simply astonished beyond measure at the announcement of the fact. Every one in the stereotyping and composing rooms had something to say about the unheard-of omission. Two or three times during the day when Mr. Norman had occasion to visit the composing rooms the men stopped their work or glanced around their cases looking at him curiously. He knew that he was being observed, but said nothing and did not appear to note it.

There had been several minor changes in the paper, suggested by the editor, but nothing marked. He was waiting and thinking deeply.

He felt as if he needed time and considerable opportunity for the exercise of his best judgment in several matters before he answered his ever present question in the right way. It was not because there were not a great many things in the life of the paper that were contrary to the spirit of Christ that he did not act at once, but because he was yet honestly in doubt concerning what action Jesus would take.

When the *Daily News* came out that evening it carried to its subscribers a distinct sensation.

The presence of the report of the prize fight could not have produced anything equal to the effect of its omission. Hundreds of men in the hotels and stores down town, as well as regular subscribers, eagerly opened the paper and searched it through for the account of the great fight; not finding it, they rushed to the news stands and bought other papers. Even the newsboys had not all understood the fact of omission. One of them was calling out *"Daily News!* Full 'count great prize fight 't Resort. *News,* sir?"

A man on the corner of the avenue close by the *News* office bought the paper, looked over its front page hurriedly and then angrily called the boy back.

"Here, boy! What's the matter with your paper? There's no prize fight here! What do you mean by selling old papers?"

"Old papers nuthin'!" replied the boy indignantly. "Dat's today's paper. What's de matter wid you?"

"But there is no account of the prize fight here! Look!"

The man handed back the paper and the boy glanced at it hurriedly. Then he whistled, while a bewildered look crept over his face. Seeing another boy running by with papers he called out "Say, Sam, lemme see your pile!" A hasty examination revealed the remarkable fact that all the copies of the *News* were silent on the subject of the prize fight.

"Here, give me another paper!" shouted the customer; "one with the prize fight account."

He received it and walked off, while the two boys remained comparing notes and lost in wonder at the result. "Sump'n slipped a cog in the *Newsy,* sure," said the first boy. But he couldn't tell why, and ran over to the *News* office to find out.

There were several other boys at the delivery room and they were all excited and disgusted. The amount of slangy remonstrance hurled at the clerk back of the long counter would have driven any one else to despair.

He was used to more or less of it all the time, and consequently hardened to it. Mr. Norman was just coming down-stairs on his way home, and he paused as he went by the door of the delivery room and looked in.

"What's the matter here, George?" he asked the clerk as he noted the unusual confusion.

"The boys say they can't sell any copies of the *News* tonight because the prize fight isn't in it," replied George, looking curiously at the editor as so many of the employees had done during the day. Mr. Norman hesitated a moment, then walked into the room and confronted the boys.

"How many papers are there here? Boys, count them out, and I'll buy them tonight."

There was a combined stare and a wild counting of papers on the part of the boys.

"Give them their money, George, and if any of the other boys come in with the same complaint buy their unsold copies. Is that fair?" he

asked the boys who were smitten into unusual silence by the unheard-
of action on the part of the editor.

"Fair! Well, I should—But will you keep this up? Will dis be a continual performance for de benefit of de fraternity?"

Mr. Norman smiled slightly but he did not think it was necessary to
answer the question.

He walked out of the office and went home. On the way he could
not avoid that constant query, "Would Jesus have done it?" It was not
so much with reference to this last transaction as to the entire motive
that had urged him on since he had made the promise.

The newsboys were necessarily sufferers through the action he had
taken. Why should they lose money by it? They were not to blame.
He was a rich man and could afford to put a little brightness into their
lives if he chose to do it. He believed, as he went on his way home,
that Jesus would have done either what he did or something similar in
order to be free from any possible feeling of injustice.

He was not deciding these questions for any one else but for his
own conduct. He was not in a position to dogmatize, and he felt that
he could answer only with his own judgment and conscience as to his
interpretation of his Master's probable action. The falling off in sales of
the paper he had in a measure foreseen. But he was yet to realize the full
extent of the loss to the paper, if such a policy should be continued.

Chapter 4

During the week he was in receipt of numerous letters commenting
on the absence from the *News* of the account of the prize fight. Two
or three of these letters may be of interest.

Editor of the News:

Dear Sir—I have been thinking for some time of changing my
paper. I want a journal that is up to the times, progressive and
enterprising, supplying the public demand at all points. The recent freak of your paper in refusing to print the account of the
famous contest at the Resort has decided me finally to change my
paper. Please discontinue it.

Very truly yours,

Here followed the name of a business man who had been a subscriber for many years.

Edward Norman,
      Editor of the Daily News, Raymond:
    Dear Ed.—What is this sensation you have given the people of your burg? What new policy have you taken up? Hope you don't intend to try the "Reform Business" through the avenue of the press. It's dangerous to experiment much along that line. Take my advice and stick to the enterprising modern methods you have made so successful for the News. The public wants prize fights and such. Give it what it wants, and let some one else do the Reforming business.
                          Yours,
                                      _____

Here followed the name of one of Norman's old friends, the editor of a daily in an adjoining town.

My Dear Mr. Norman:
    I hasten to write you a note of appreciation for the evident carrying out of your promise. It is a splendid beginning and no one feels the value of it more than I do. I know something of what it will cost you, but not all. Your pastor,
                                HENRY MAXWELL.

One other letter which he opened immediately after reading this from Maxwell revealed to him something of the loss to his business that possibly awaited him.

Mr. Edward Norman,
      Editor of the Daily News:
    Dear Sir—At the expiration of my advertising limit, you will do me the favor not to continue it as you have done heretofore. I enclose check for payment in full and shall consider my account with your paper closed after date.
                      Very truly yours,
                                      _____

Here followed the name of one of the largest dealers in tobacco in the city. He had been in the habit of inserting a column of conspicuous advertising and paying for it a very large price.

Norman laid this letter down thoughtfully, and then after a moment he took up a copy of his paper and looked through the advertising columns. There was no connection implied in the tobacco merchant's letter between the omission of the prize fight and the withdrawal of the advertisement, but he could not avoid putting the two together. In point of fact, he afterward learned that the tobacco dealer withdrew his advertisement because he had heard that the editor of the *News* was about to enter upon some queer reform policy that would be certain to reduce its subscription list.

But the letter directed Norman's attention to the advertising phase of his paper. He had not considered this before.

As he glanced over the columns he could not escape the conviction that his Master could not permit some of them in his paper.

What would He do with that other long advertisement of choice liquors and cigars? As a member of a church and a respected citizen, he had incurred no special censure because the saloon men advertised in his columns. No one thought anything about it. It was all legitimate business. Why not? Raymond enjoyed a system of high license, and the saloon and the billiard hall and the beer garden were a part of the city's Christian civilization. He was simply doing what every other business man in Raymond did. And it was one of the best paying sources of revenue. What would the paper do if it cut these out? Could it live? That was the question. But—was that the question after all? "What would Jesus do?" That was the question he was answering, or trying to answer, this week. Would Jesus advertise whiskey and tobacco in his paper?

Edward Norman asked it honestly, and after a prayer for help and wisdom he asked Clark to come into the office.

Clark came in, feeling that the paper was at a crisis, and prepared for almost anything after his Monday morning experience. This was Thursday.

"Clark," said Norman, speaking slowly and carefully, "I have been looking at our advertising columns and have decided to dispense with some of the matter as soon as the contracts run out. I wish you would notify the advertising agent not to solicit or renew the ads that I have marked here."

He handed the paper with the marked places over to Clark, who took it and looked over the columns with a very serious air.

"This will mean a great loss to the *News*. How long do you think you can keep this sort of thing up?" Clark was astounded at the editor's action and could not understand it.

"Clark, do you think if Jesus was the editor and proprietor of a daily paper in Raymond He would permit advertisements of whiskey and tobacco in it?"

"Well—no—I don't suppose He would. But what has that to do with us? We can't do as He would. Newspapers can't be run on any such basis."

"Why not?" asked Norman quietly.

"Why not? Because they will lose more money than they make, that's all!" Clark spoke out with an irritation that he really felt. "We shall certainly bankrupt the paper with this sort of business policy."

"Do you think so?" Norman asked the question not as if he expected an answer, but simply as if he were talking with himself. After a pause he said:

"You may direct Marks to do as I have said. I believe it is what Christ would do, and as I told you, Clark, that is what I have promised to try to do for a year, regardless of what the results may be to me. I cannot believe that by any kind of reasoning we could reach a conclusion justifying our Lord in the advertisement, in this age, of whiskey and tobacco in a newspaper. There are some other advertisements of a doubtful character I shall study into. Meanwhile, I feel a conviction in regard to these that cannot be silenced."

Clark went back to his desk feeling as if he had been in the presence of a very peculiar person. He could not grasp the meaning of it all. He felt enraged and alarmed. He was sure any such policy would ruin the paper as soon as it became generally known that the editor was trying to do everything by such an absurd moral standard. What would become of business if this standard was adopted? It would upset every custom and introduce endless confusion. It was simply foolishness. It was downright idiocy. So Clark said to himself, and when Marks was informed of the action he seconded the managing editor with some very forcible ejaculations. What was the matter with the chief? Was he insane? Was he going to bankrupt the whole business?

But Edward Norman had not yet faced his most serious problem. When he came down to the office Friday morning he was confronted with the usual program for the Sunday morning edition. The *News* was one of the few evening papers in Raymond to issue a Sunday edition, and it had always been remarkably successful financially. There was an average of one page of literary and religious items to thirty or forty pages of sport, theatre, gossip, fashion, society and political material. This made a very interesting magazine of all sorts of reading matter, and had always been welcomed by all the subscribers, church members and all, as a Sunday morning necessity.

Edward Norman now faced this fact and put to himself the question: "What would Jesus do?" If He was the editor of a paper, would He deliberately plan to put into the homes of all the church people and Christians of Raymond such a collection of reading matter on the one day in the week which ought to be given up to something better and holier? He was of course familiar with the regular arguments of the Sunday paper, that the public needed something of the sort; and the working man especially, who would not go to church anyway, ought to have something entertaining and instructive on Sunday, his only day of rest. But suppose the Sunday morning paper did not pay? Suppose there was no money in it? How eager would the editor or publisher be then to supply this crying need of the poor workman? Edward Norman communed honestly with himself over the subject.

Taking everything into accout, would Jesus probably edit a Sunday morning paper? No matter whether it paid. That was not the question. As a matter of fact, the Sunday *News* paid so well that it would be a direct loss of thousands of dollars to discontinue it. Besides, the regular subscribers had paid for a seven-day paper. Had he any right now to give them less than they supposed they had paid for?

He was honestly perplexed by the question. So much was involved in the discontinuance of the Sunday edition that for the first time he almost decided to refuse to be guided by the standard of Jesus' probable action. He was the sole proprietor of the paper; it was his to shape as he chose. He had no board of directors to consult as to policy. But as he sat there surrounded by the usual quantity of material for the Sunday edition he reached some definite conclusions. And among them was a determination to call in the force of the paper and frankly state his motive and purpose. He sent word for Clark and the other men in the office, including the few reporters who were in the building and the foreman, with what men were in the composing room (it was early in the morning and they were not all in) to come into the mailing room. This was a large room, and the men came in curiously and perched around on the tables and counters. It was a very unusual proceeding, but they all agreed that the paper was being run on new principles anyhow, and they all watched Mr. Norman carefully as he spoke.

"I called you in here to let you know my further plans for the *News*. I propose certain changes which I believe are necessary. I understand very well that some things I have already done are regarded by the men as very strange. I wish to state my motive in doing what I have done."

Here he told the men what he had already told Clark, and they stared as Clark had done, and looked as painfully conscious.

"Now, in acting on this standard of conduct I have reached a conclusion which will, no doubt, cause some surprise.

"I have decided that the Sunday morning edition of the *News* shall be discontinued after next Sunday's issue. I shall state in that issue my reasons for discontinuing. In order to make up to the subscribers the amount of reading matter they may suppose themselves entitled to, we can issue a double number on Saturday, as is done by many evening papers that make no attempt at a Sunday edition. I am convinced that from a Christian point of view more harm than good has been done by our Sunday morning paper. I do not believe that Jesus would be responsible for it if He were in my place today. It will occasion some

trouble to arrange the details caused by this change with the adver-
tisers and subscribers. That is for me to look after. The change itself is
one that will take place. So far as I can see, the loss will fall on myself. Neither the reporters nor the pressmen need make any particular
changes in their plans."

He looked around the room and no one spoke. He was struck for
the first time in his life with the fact that in all the years of his newspaper life he had never had the force of the paper together in this
way. Would Jesus do that? That is, would He probably run a newspaper on some loving family plan, where editors, reporters, pressmen
and all meet to discuss and devise and plan for the making of a paper
that should have in view—

He caught himself drawing almost away from the facts of typo-
graphical unions and office rules and reporters' enterprise and all the
cold, businesslike methods that make a great daily successful. But still
the vague picture that came up in the mailing room would not fade
away when he had gone into his office and the men had gone back to
their places with wonder in their looks and questions of all sorts on
their tongues as they talked over the editor's remarkable actions.

Clark came in and had a long, serious talk with his chief. He was
thoroughly roused, and his protest almost reached the point of resigning his place. Norman guarded himself carefully. Every minute of the
interview was painful to him, but he felt more than ever the necessity
of doing the Christ-like thing. Clark was a very valuable man. It would
be difficult to fill his place. But he was not able to give any reasons for
continuing the Sunday paper that answered the question, "What
would Jesus do?" by letting Jesus print that edition.

"It comes to this, then," said Clark frankly, "you will bankrupt the
paper in thirty days. We might as well face that future fact."

"I don't think we shall. Will you stay by the *News* until it is bankrupt?" asked Norman with a strange smile.

"Mr. Norman, I don't understand you. You are not the same man
this week that I always knew before."

"I don't know myself either, Clark. Something remarkable has
caught me up and borne me on. But I was never more convinced of
final success and power for the paper. You have not answered my
question. Will you stay with me?"

Clark hesitated a moment and finally said yes. Norman shook hands
with him and turned to his desk. Clark went back into his room,
stirred by a number of conflicting emotions. He had never before
known such an exciting and mentally disturbing week, and he felt
now as if he was connected with an enterprise that might at any moment collapse and ruin him and all connected with it.

Chapter 5

Sunday morning dawned again on Raymond, and Henry Maxwell's church was again crowded. Before the service began Edward Norman attracted great attention. He sat quietly in his usual place about three seats from the pulpit. The Sunday morning issue of the *News* containing the statement of its discontinuance had been expressed in such remarkable language that every reader was struck by it. No such series of distinct sensations had ever disturbed the usual business custom of Raymond. The events connected with the *News* were not all. People were eagerly talking about strange things done during the week by Alexander Powers at the railroad shops, and Milton Wright in his stores on the avenue. The service progressed upon a distinct wave of excitement in the pews. Henry Maxwell faced it all with a calmness which indicated a strength and purpose more than usual. His prayers were very helpful. His sermon was not so easy to describe. How would a minister be apt to preach to his people if he came before them after an entire week of eagerly asking, "How would Jesus preach? What would He probably say?" It is very certain that he did not preach as he had done two Sundays before. Tuesday of the past week he had stood by the grave of the dead stranger and said the words, "Earth to earth, ashes to ashes, dust to dust," and still he was moved by the spirit of a deeper impulse than he could measure as he thought of his people and yearned for the Christ message when he should be in his pulpit again.

Now that Sunday had come and the people were there to hear, what would the Master tell them? He agonized over his preparation for them, and yet he knew he had not been able to fit his message into his ideal of the Christ. Nevertheless no one in the First Church could remember ever hearing such a sermon before. There was in it rebuke for sin, especially hypocrisy, there was definite rebuke of the greed of wealth and the selfishness of fashion, two things that First Church never heard rebuked this way before, and there was a love of his people that gathered new force as the sermon went on. When it was finished there were those who were saying in their hearts, "The Spirit moved that sermon." And they were right.

Then Rachel Winslow rose to sing, this time after the sermon, by

Mr. Maxwell's request. Rachel's singing did not provoke applause this time. What deeper feeling carried the people's hearts into a reverent silence and tenderness of thought? Rachel was beautiful. But her consciousness of her remarkable loveliness had always marred her singing with those who had the deepest spiritual feeling. It had also marred her rendering of certain kinds of music with herself. Today this was all gone. There was no lack of power in her grand voice. But there was an actual added element of humility and purity which the audience distinctly felt and bowed to.

Before service closed Mr. Maxwell asked those who had remained the week before to stay again for a few moments of consultation, and any others who were willing to make the pledge taken at that time. When he was at liberty he went into the lecture-room. To his astonishment it was almost filled. This time a large proportion of young people had come, but among them were a few business men and officers of the church.

As before, he, Maxwell, asked them to pray with him. And, as before, a distinct answer came from the presence of the divine Spirit. There was no doubt in the minds of any present that what they purposed to do was so clearly in line with the divine will, that a blessing rested upon it in a very special manner.

They remained some time to ask questions and consult together. There was a feeling of fellowship such as they had never known in their church membership. Mr. Norman's action was well understood by them all, and he answered several questions.

"What will be the probable result of your discontinuance of the Sunday paper?" asked Alexander Powers, who sat next to him.

"I don't know yet. I presume it will result in the falling off of subscriptions and advertisements. I anticipate that."

"Do you have any doubts about your action? I mean, do you regret it, or fear it is not what Jesus would do?" asked Mr. Maxwell.

"Not in the least. But I would like to ask, for my own satisfaction, if any of you here think Jesus would issue a Sunday morning paper?"

No one spoke for a minute. Then Jasper Chase said, "We seem to think alike on that, but I have been puzzled several times during the week to know just what He would do. It is not always an easy question to answer."

"I find that trouble," said Virginia Page. She sat by Rachel Winslow. Every one who knew Virginia Page was wondering how she would succeed in keeping her promise. "I think perhaps I find it specially difficult to answer that question on account of my money. Our Lord never owned any property, and there is nothing in His example to guide me in the use of mine. I am studying and praying. I think I see clearly a part of what He would do, but not all. What would He do with a million dollars? is my question really. I confess I am not yet able to answer it to my satisfaction."

"I could tell you what you could do with a part of it," said Rachel, turning her face toward Virginia.

"That does not trouble me," replied Virginia with a slight smile. "What I am trying to discover is a principle that will enable me to come to the nearest possible to His action as it ought to influence the entire course of my life so far as my wealth and its use are concerned."

"That will take time," said the minister slowly. All the rest of the room were thinking hard of the same thing. Milton Wright told something of his experience. He was gradually working out a plan for his business relations with his employees, and it was opening up a new world to him and to them. A few of the young men told of special attempts to answer the question. There was almost general consent over the fact that the application of the Christ spirit and practice to the everyday life was the serious thing. It required a knowledge of Him and an insight into His motives that most of them did not yet possess.

When they finally adjourned after a silent prayer that marked with growing power the Divine Presence, they went away discussing earnestly their difficulties and seeking light from one another.

Rachel Winslow and Virginia Page went out together. Edward Norman and Milton Wright became so interested in their mutual conference that they walked on past Norman's house and came back together. Jasper Chase and the president of the Endeavor Society stood talking earnestly in one corner of the room. Alexander Powers and Henry Maxwell remained, even after the others had gone.

"I want you to come down to the shops tomorrow and see my plan and talk to the men. Somehow I feel as if you could get nearer to them than any one else just now."

"I don't know about that, but I will come," replied Mr. Maxwell a little sadly. How was he fitted to stand before two or three hundred working men and give them a message? Yet in the moment of his weakness, as he asked the question, he rebuked himself for it. What would Jesus do? That was an end to the discussion.

He went down the next day and found Mr. Powers in his office. It lacked a few minutes of twelve and the superintendent said, "Come upstairs, and I'll show you what I've been trying to do."

They went through the machine shop, climbed a long flight of stairs and entered a very large, empty room. It had once been used by the company for a store room.

"Since making that promise a week ago I have had a good many things to think of," said the superintendent, "and among them is this: The company gives me the use of this room, and I am going to fit it up with tables and a coffee plant in the corner there where those steam pipes are. My plan is to provide a good place where the men can come up and eat their noon lunch, and give them, two or three times a week, the privilege of a fifteen minutes' talk on some subject that will be a real help to them in their lives."

Maxwell looked surprised and asked if the men would come for any such purpose.

"Yes, they'll come. After all, I know the men pretty well. They are among the most intelligent working men in the country today. But they are, as a whole, entirely removed from church influence. I asked, 'What would Jesus do?' and among other things it seemed to me He would begin to act in some way to add to the lives of these men more physical and spiritual comfort. It is a very little thing, this room and what it represents, but I acted on the first impulse, to do the first thing that appealed to my good sense, and I want to work out this idea. I want you to speak to the men when they come up at noon. I have asked them to come up and see the place and I'll tell them something about it."

Maxwell was ashamed to say how uneasy he felt at being asked to speak a few words to a company of working men. How could he speak without notes, or to such a crowd? He was honestly in a condition of genuine fright over the prospect. He actually felt afraid of facing those men. He shrank from the ordeal of confronting such a crowd, so different from the Sunday audiences he was familiar with.

There were a dozen rude benches and tables in the room, and when the noon whistle sounded the men poured upstairs from the machine shops below and, seating themselves at the tables, began to eat their lunch. There were present about three hundred of them. They had read the superintendent's notice which he had posted up in various places, and came largely out of curiosity.

They were favorably impressed. The room was large and airy, free from smoke and dust, and well warmed from the steam pipes. At about twenty minutes to one Mr. Powers told the men what he had in mind. He spoke very simply, like one who understands thoroughly the character of his audience, and then introduced the Rev. Henry Maxwell of the First Church, his pastor, who had consented to speak a few minutes.

Maxwell will never forget the feeling with which for the first time he stood before the grimy-faced audience of working men. Like hundreds of other ministers, he had never spoken to any gatherings except those made up of people of his own class in the sense that they were familiar in their dress and education and habits. This was a new world to him, and nothing but his new rule of conduct could have made possible his message and its effect. He spoke on the subject of satisfaction with life; what caused it, what its real sources were. He had the great good sense on this his first appearance not to recognize the men as a class distinct from himself. He did not use the term working man, and did not say a word to suggest any difference between their lives and his own.

The men were pleased. A good many of them shook hands with him before going down to their work, and the minister telling it all to his wife when he reached home, said that never in all his life had he known the delight he then felt in having the handshake from a man of physical labor. The day marked an important one in his Christian experience, more important than he knew. It was the beginning of a fellowship between him and the working world. It was the first plank laid down to help bridge the chasm between the church and labor in Raymond.

Alexander Powers went back to his desk that afternoon much pleased with his plan and seeing much help in it for the men. He knew where he could get some good tables from an abandoned eating house at one of the stations down the road, and he saw how the coffee arrangement could be made a very attractive feature. The men had responded even better than he anticipated, and the whole thing could not help being a great benefit to them.

He took up the routine of his work with a glow of satisfaction. After all, he wanted to do as Jesus would, he said to himself.

It was nearly four o'clock when he opened one of the company's long envelopes which he supposed contained orders for the purchasing of stores. He ran over the first page of type-written matter in his usual quick, business-like manner, before he saw that what he was reading was not intended for his office but for the superintendent of the freight department.

He turned over a page mechanically, not meaning to read what was not addressed to him, but before he knew it, he was in possession of evidence which conclusively proved that the company was engaged in a systematic violation of the Interstate Commerce Laws of the United States. It was as distinct and unequivocal a breaking of law as if a private citizen should enter a house and rob the inmates. The discrimination shown in rebates was in total contempt of all the statutes. Under the laws of the state it was also a distinct violation of certain provisions recently passed by the legislature to prevent railroad trusts. There was no question that he had in his hands evidence sufficient to convict the company of willful, intelligent violation of the law of the commission and the law of the state also.

He dropped the papers on his desk as if they were poison, and instantly the question flashed across his mind, "What would Jesus do?" He tried to shut the question out. He tried to reason with himself by saying it was none of his business. He had known in a more or less definite way, as did nearly all the officers of the company, that this had been going on right along on nearly all the roads. He was not in a position, owing to his place in the shops, to prove anything direct, and he had regarded it as a matter which did not concern him at all. The papers now before him revealed the entire affair. They had through some carelessness been addressed to him. What business of his was it? If he saw a man entering his neighbor's house to steal, would it not be his duty to inform the officers of the law? Was a railroad company such a different thing? Was it under a different rule of conduct, so that it could rob the public and defy law and be undisturbed because it was such a great organization? What would Jesus do? Then there was his family. Of course, if he took any steps to inform the commission it would mean the loss of his position. His wife and daughter had always enjoyed luxury and a good place in society. If he came out against this lawlessness as a witness it would drag him into courts, his motives would be misunderstood, and the whole thing would end in his disgrace and the loss of his position. Surely it was none of his business. He could easily get the papers back to the freight department and no one be the wiser. Let the iniquity go on. Let the law be defied. What was it to him? He would work out his plans for bettering the condition just before him. What more could a man do in this railroad business when there was so much going on anyway that made it impossible to live by the Christian standard? But what would Jesus do if He knew the facts? That was the question that confronted Alexander Powers as the day wore into evening.

The lights in the office had been turned on. The whirr of the great engine and the clash of the planers in the big shop continued until six o'clock. Then the whistle blew, the engine slowed up, the men dropped their tools and ran for the block house.

Powers heard the familiar click, click, of the clocks as the men filed past the window of the block house just outside. He said to his clerks, "I'm not going just yet. I have something extra tonight." He waited until he heard the last man deposit his block. The men behind the block case went out. The engineer and his assistants had work for half an hour but they went out by another door.

At seven o'clock any one who had looked into the superintendent's office would have seen an unusual sight. He was kneeling, and his face was buried in his hands as he bowed his head upon the papers on his desk.

Chapter 6

If any man cometh unto me and hateth not his own father and mother and wife and children and brethren and sisters, yea, and his own life also, he cannot be my disciple.
And whosoever forsaketh not all that he hath, he cannot be my disciple.

When Rachel Winslow and Virginia Page separated after the meeting at the First Church on Sunday they agreed to continue their conversation the next day. Virginia asked Rachel to come and lunch with her at noon, and Rachel accordingly rang the bell at the Page mansion about half-past eleven. Virginia herself met her and the two were soon talking earnestly.

"The fact is," Rachel was saying, after they had been talking a few moments, "I cannot reconcile it with my judgment of what Christ would do. I cannot tell another person what to do, but I feel that I ought not to accept this offer."

"What will you do then?" asked Virginia with great interest.

"I don't know yet, but I have decided to refuse this offer."

Rachel picked up a letter that had been lying in her lap and ran over its contents again. It was a letter from the manager of a comic opera offering her a place with a large traveling company of the season. The salary was a very large figure, and the prospect held out by the manager was flattering. He had heard Rachel sing that Sunday morning when the stranger had interrupted the service. He had been much impressed. There was money in that voice and it ought to be used in comic opera, so said the letter, and the manager wanted a reply as soon as possible.

"There's no great virtue in saying 'No' to this offer when I have the other one," Rachel went on thoughtfully. "That's harder to decide. But I've about made up my mind. To tell the truth, Virginia, I'm completely convinced in the first case that Jesus would never use any talent like a good voice just to make money. But now, take this concert offer. Here is a reputable company, to travel with an impersonator and a violinist and a male quartet, all people of good reputation. I'm asked to go as one of the company and sing leading soprano. The salary—I mentioned it, didn't I?—is guaranteed to be $200 a month for the season. But I don't feel satisfied that Jesus would go. What do you think?"

"You mustn't ask me to decide for you," replied Virginia with a sad smile. "I believe Mr. Maxwell was right when he said we must each one of us decide according to the judgment we feel for ourselves to be Christ-like. I am having a harder time than you are, dear, to decide what He would do."

"Are you?" Rachel asked. She rose and walked over to the window and looked out. Virginia came and stood by her. The street was crowded with life and the two young women looked at it silently for a moment. Suddenly Virginia broke out as Rachel had never heard her before:

"Rachel, what does all this contrast in conditions mean to you as you ask this question of what Jesus would do? It maddens me to think that the society in which I have been brought up, the same to which we are both said to belong, is satisfied year after year to go on dressing and eating and having a good time, giving and receiving entertainments, spending its money on houses and luxuries and, occasionally, to ease its conscience, donating, without any personal sacrifice, a little money to charity. I have been educated, as you have, in one of the most expensive schools in America; launched into society as an heiress; supposed to be in a very enviable position. I'm perfectly well; I can travel or stay at home. I can do as I please. I can gratify almost any want or desire; and yet when I honestly try to imagine Jesus living the life I have lived and am expected to live, and doing for the rest of my life what thousands of other rich people do, I am under condemnation for being one of the most wicked, selfish, useless creatures in all the world. I have not looked out of this window for weeks without a feeling of horror toward myself as I see the humanity that passes by this house."

Virginia turned away and walked up and down the room. Rachel watched her and could not repress the rising tide of her own growing definition of discipleship. Of what Christian use was her own talent of song? Was the best she could do to sell her talent for so much a month, go on a concert company's tour, dress beautifully, enjoy the excitement of public applause and gain a reputation as a great singer? Was that what Jesus would do?

She was not morbid. She was in sound health, was conscious of her great powers as a singer, and knew that if she went out into public life she could make a great deal of money and become well known. It is doubtful if she overestimated her ability to accomplish all she thought herself capable of. And Virginia—what she had just said smote Rachel with great force because of the similar position in which the two friends found themselves.

Lunch was announced and they went out and were joined by Virginia's grandmother, Madam Page, a handsome, stately woman of sixty-five, and Virginia's brother Rollin, a young man who spent most of his time at one of the clubs and had no ambition for anything but a growing admiration for Rachel Winslow, and whenever she dined or lunched at the Pages', if he knew of it he always planned to be at home.

These three made up the Page family. Virginia's father had been a banker and grain speculator. Her mother had died ten years before, her father within the past year. The grandmother, a Southern woman in birth and training, had all the traditions and feelings that accompany the possession of wealth and social standing that have never been disturbed. She was a shrewd, careful business woman of more than average ability. The family property and wealth were invested, in large measure, under her personal care. Virginia's portion was, without any restriction, her own. She had been trained by her father to understand the ways of the business world, and even the grandmother had been compelled to acknowledge the girl's capacity for taking care of her own money.

Perhaps two persons could not be found anywhere less capable of understanding a girl like Virginia than Madam Page and Rollin. Rachel, who had known the family since she was a girl playmate of Virginia's, could not help thinking of what confronted Virginia in her own home when she once decided on the course which she honestly believed Jesus would take. Today at lunch, as she recalled Virginia's outbreak in the front room, she tried to picture the scene that would at some time occur between Madam Page and her granddaughter.

"I understand that you are going on the stage, Miss Winslow. We shall all be delighted, I'm sure," said Rollin during the conversation, which had not been very animated.

Rachel colored and felt annoyed. "Who told you?" she asked, while Virginia, who had been very silent and reserved, suddenly roused herself and appeared ready to join in the talk.

"Oh! we hear a thing or two on the street. Besides, every one saw Crandall the manager at church two weeks ago. He doesn't go to church to hear the preaching. In fact, I know other people who don't either, not when there's something better to hear."

Rachel did not color this time, but she answered quietly, "You're mistaken. I'm not going on the stage."

"It's a great pity. You'd make a hit. Everybody is talking about your singing."

This time Rachel flushed with genuine anger. Before she could say anything, Virginia broke in:

"Whom do you mean by 'everybody'?"

"Whom? I mean all the people who hear Miss Winslow on Sundays. What other time do they hear her? It's a great pity, I say, that the general public outside of Raymond cannot hear her voice."

"Let us talk about something else," said Rachel a little sharply. Madam Page glanced at her and spoke with a gentle courtesy.

"My dear, Rollin never could pay an indirect compliment. He is like his father in that. But we are all curious to know something of your plans. We claim the right from old acquaintance, you know; and Virginia has already told us of your concert company offer."

"I supposed of course that was public property," said Virginia, smiling across the table. "I was in the News office day before yesterday."

"Yes, yes," replied Rachel hastily. "I understand that, Madam Page. Well, Virginia and I have been talking about it. I have decided not to accept, and that is as far as I have gone at present."

Rachel was conscious of the fact that the conversation had, up to this point, been narrowing her hesitation concerning the concert company's offer down to a decision that would absolutely satisfy her own judgment of Jesus' probable action. It had been the last thing in the world, however, that she had desired, to have her decision made in any way so public as this. Somehow what Rollin Page had said and his manner in saying it had hastened her decision in the matter.

"Would you mind telling us, Rachel, your reasons for refusing the offer? It looks like a great opportunity for a young girl like you. Don't you think the general public ought to hear you? I feel like Rollin about that. A voice like yours belongs to a larger audience than Raymond and the First Church."

Rachel Winslow was naturally a girl of great reserve. She shrank from making her plans or her thoughts public. But with all her repression there was possible in her an occasional sudden breaking out that was simply an impulsive, thoroughly frank, truthful expression of her most inner personal feeling. She spoke now in reply to Madam Page in one of those rare moments of unreserve that added to the attractiveness of her whole character.

"I have no other reason than a conviction that Jesus Christ would do the same thing," she said, looking into Madam Page's eyes with a clear, earnest gaze.

Madam Page turned red and Rollin stared. Before her grandmother could say anthing, Virginia spoke. Her rising color showed how she was stirred. Virginia's pale, clear complexion was that of health, but it was generally in marked contrast with Rachel's tropical type of beauty.

"Grandmother, you know we promised to make that the standard of our conduct for a year. Mr. Maxwell's proposition was plain to all who heard it. We have not been able to arrive at our decisions very rapidly. The difficulty in knowing what Jesus would do has perplexed Rachel and me a good deal."

Madam Page looked sharply at Virginia before she said anything.

"Of course I understand Mr. Maxwell's statement. It is perfectly impracticable to put it into practice. I felt confident at the time that those who promised would find it out after a trial and abandon it as visionary and absurd. I have nothing to say about Miss Winslow's affairs, but," she paused and continued with a sharpness that was new to Rachel, "I hope you have no foolish notions in this matter, Virginia."

"I have a great many notions," replied Virginia quietly. "Whether they are foolish or not depends upon my right understanding of what He would do. As soon as I find out I shall do it."

"Excuse me, ladies," said Rollin, rising from the table. "The conversation is getting beyond my depth. I shall retire to the library for a cigar."

He went out of the dining-room and there was silence for a moment. Madam Page waited until the servant had brought in something and then asked her to go out. She was angry and her anger was formidable, although checked in some measure by the presence of Rachel.

"I am older by several years than you, young ladies," she said, and her traditional type of bearing seemed to Rachel to rise up like a great frozen wall between her and every conception of Jesus as a sacrifice. "What you have promised, in a spirit of false emotion I presume, is impossible of performance."

"Do you mean, grandmother, that we cannot possibly act as our Lord would? or do you mean that, if we try to, we shall offend the customs and prejudices of society?" asked Virginia.

"It is not required! It is not necessary! Besides, how can you act with any—" Madam Page paused, broke off her sentence, and then turned to Rachel. "What will your mother say to your decision? My dear, is it not foolish? What do you expect to do with your voice anyway?"

"I don't know what mother will say yet," Rachel answered, with a great shrinking from trying to give her mother's probable answer. If there was a woman in all Raymond with great ambitions for her daughter's success as a singer, Mrs. Winslow was that woman.

"Oh! you will see it in a different light after wiser thought of it. My dear," continued Madam Page rising from the table, "you will live to regret it if you do not accept the concert company's offer or something like it."

Rachel said something that contained a hint of the struggle she was

still having. And after a little she went away, feeling that her depar-
ture was to be followed by a very painful conversation between Virginia and her grandmother. As she afterward learned, Virginia passed
through a crisis of feeling during that scene with her grandmother that
hastened her final decision as to the use of her money and her social
position.

Chapter 7

Rachel was glad to escape and be by herself. A plan was slowly
forming in her mind, and she wanted to be alone and think it out
carefully. But before she had walked two blocks she was annoyed to
find Rollin Page walking beside her.

"Sorry to disturb your thoughts, Miss Winslow, but I happened to
be going your way and had an idea you might not object. In fact, I've
been walking here for a whole block and you haven't objected."

"I did not see you," said Rachel briefly.

"I wouldn't mind that if you only thought of me once in a while,"
said Rollin suddenly. He took one last nervous puff on his cigar, tossed
it into the street and walked along with a pale look on his face.

Rachel was surprised, but not startled. She had known Rollin as a
boy, and there had been a time when they had used each other's first
name familiarly. Lately, however, something in Rachel's manner had
put an end to that. She was used to his direct attempts at compliments
and was sometimes amused by them. Today she honestly wished him
anywhere else.

"Do you ever think of me, Miss Winslow?" asked Rollin after a pause.

"Oh, yes, quite often!" said Rachel with a smile.

"Are you thinking of me now?"

"Yes. That is—yes—I am."

"What?"

"Do you want me to be absolutely truthful?"

"Of course."

"Then I was thinking that I wished you were not here."

Rollin bit his lip and looked gloomy.

"Now look here, Rachel—oh, I know that's forbidden, but I've got to

speak some time!—you know how I feel. What makes you treat me so?
You used to like me a little, you know."

"Did I? Of course we used to get on very well as boy and girl. But
we are older now."

Rachel still spoke in the light, easy way she had used since her first
annoyance at seeing him. She was still somewhat preoccupied with
her plan which had been disturbed by Rollin's sudden appearance.

They walked along in silence a little way. The avenue was full of
people. Among the persons passing was Jasper Chase. He saw Rachel
and Rollin and bowed as they went by. Rollin was watching Rachel
closely.

"I wish I was Jasper Chase. Maybe I would stand some chance
then," he said moodily.

Rachel colored in spite of herself. She did not say anything and
quickened her pace a little. Rollin seemed determined to say something, and Rachel seemed helpless to prevent him. After all, she
thought, he might as well know the truth one time as another.

"You know well enough, Rachel, how I feel toward you. Isn't there
any hope? I could make you happy. I've loved you a good many years
—"

"Why, how old do you think I am?" broke in Rachel with a nervous
laugh. She was shaken out of her usual poise of manner.

"You know what I mean," went on Rollin doggedly. "And you have
no right to laugh at me just because I want you to marry me."

"I'm not! But it is useless for you to speak, Rollin," said Rachel after
a little hesitation, and then using his name in such a frank, simple way
that he could attach no meaning to it beyond the familiarity of the old
family acquaintance. "It is impossible." She was still a little agitated
by the fact of receiving a proposal of marriage on the avenue. But the
noise on the street and sidewalk made the conversation as private as if
they were in the house.

"Would—that is—do you think—if you gave me time I would—"

"No!" said Rachel. She spoke firmly; perhaps, she thought afterward, although she did not mean to, she spoke harshly.

They walked on for some time without a word. They were nearing
Rachel's home and she was anxious to end the scene.

As they turned off the avenue into one of the quieter streets Rollin
spoke suddenly and with more manliness than he had yet shown.
There was a distinct note of dignity in his voice that was new to Rachel.

"Miss Winslow, I ask you to be my wife. Is there any hope for me
that you will ever consent?"

"None in the least." Rachel spoke decidedly.

"Will you tell me why?" He asked the question as if he had a right to a truthful answer.

"Because I do not feel toward you as a woman ought to feel toward the man she marries."

"In other words, you do not love me?"

"I do not and I cannot."

"Why?" That was another question, and Rachel was a little surprised that he should ask it.

"Because—" she hesitated for fear she might say too much in an attempt to speak the exact truth.

"Tell me just why. You can't hurt me more than you have already."

"Well, I do not and I cannot love you because you have no purpose in life. What do you ever do to make the world better? You spend your time in club life, in amusements, in travel, in luxury. What is there in such a life to attract a woman?"

"Not much, I guess," said Rollin with a bitter laugh. "Still, I don't know that I'm any worse than the rest of the men around me. I'm not so bad as some. I'm glad to know your reasons."

He suddenly stopped, took off his hat, bowed gravely and turned back. Rachel went on home and hurried into her room, disturbed in many ways by the event which had so unexpectedly thrust itself into her experience.

When she had time to think it all over she found herself condemned by the very judgment she had passed on Rollin Page. What purpose had she in life? She had been abroad and studied music with one of the famous teachers of Europe. She had come home to Raymond and had been singing in the First Church choir now for a year. She was well paid. Up to that Sunday two weeks ago she had been quite satisfied with herself and with her position. She had shared her mother's ambition, and anticipated growing triumphs in the musical world. What possible career was before her except the regular career of every singer?

She asked the question again and, in the light of her recent reply to Rollin, asked again, if she had any very great purpose in life herself. What would Jesus do? There was a fortune in her voice. She knew it, not necessarily as a matter of personal pride or professional egotism, but simply as a fact. And she was obliged to acknowledge that until two weeks ago she had purposed to use her voice to make money and win admiration and applause. Was that a much higher purpose, after all, than Rollin Page lived for?

She sat in her room a long time and finally went downstairs, resolved to have a frank talk with her mother about the concert company's offer and the new plan which was gradually shaping in her mind.

She had already had one talk with her mother and knew that she expected Rachel to accept the offer and enter on a successful career as a public singer.

"Mother," Rachel said, coming at once to the point, much as she dreaded the interview, "I have decided not to go out with the company. I have a good reason for it."

Mrs. Winslow was a large, handsome woman, fond of much company, ambitious for distinction in society and devoted, according to her definitions of success, to the success of her children. Her youngest boy, Louis, two years younger than Rachel, was ready to graduate from a military academy in the summer. Meanwhile she and Rachel were at home together. Rachel's father, like Virginia's, had died while the family was abroad. Like Virginia she found herself, under her present rule of conduct, in complete antagonism with her own immediate home circle. Mrs. Winslow waited for Rachel to go on.

"You know the promise I made two weeks ago, mother?"

"Mr. Maxwell's promise?"

"No, mine. You know what it was, do you not, mother?"

"I suppose I do. Of course all the church members mean to imitate Christ and follow Him, as far as is consistent with our present day surroundings. But what has that to do with our decision in the concert company matter?"

"It has everything to do with it. After asking, 'What would Jesus do?' and going to the source of authority for wisdom, I have been obliged to say that I do not believe He would, in my case, make that use of my voice."

"Why? Is there anything wrong about such a career?"

"No, I don't know that I can say there is."

"Do you presume to sit in judgment on other people who go out to sing in this way? Do you presume to say they are doing what Christ would not do?"

"Mother, I wish you to understand me. I judge no one else; I condemn no other professional singer. I simply decide my own course. As I look at it, I have a conviction that Jesus would do something else."

"What else?" Mrs. Winslow had not yet lost her temper. She did not understand the situation nor Rachel in the midst of it, but she was anxious that her daughter's course should be as distinguished as her natural gifts promised. And she felt confident that when the present unusual religious excitement in the First Church had passed away, Rachel would go on with her public life according to the wishes of the family. She was totally unprepared for Rachel's next remark.

"What? Something that will serve mankind where it most needs the service of song. Mother, I have made up my mind to use my voice in some way so as to satisfy my own soul that I am doing something better than pleasing fashionable audiences, or making money, or even gratifying my own love of singing. I am going to do something that will satisfy me when I ask: 'What would Jesus do?' I am not satisfied, and cannot be, when I think of myself as singing myself into the career of a concert company performer."

Rachel spoke with a vigor and earnestness that surprised her mother. But Mrs. Winslow was angry now; and she never tried to conceal her feelings.

"It is simply absurd! Rachel, you are a fanatic! What can you do?"

"The world has been served by men and women who have given it other things that were gifts. Why should I, because I am blessed with a natural gift, at once proceed to put a market price on it and make all the money I can out of it? You know, mother, that you have taught me to think of a musical career always in the light of financial and social success. I have been unable, since I made my promise two weeks ago, to imagine Jesus joining a concert company to do what I should do and live the life I should have to live if I joined it."

Mrs. Winslow rose and then sat down again. With a great effort she composed herself.

"What do you intend to do then? You have not answered my question."

"I shall continue to sing for the time being in the church. I am pledged to sing there through the spring. During the week I am going to sing at the White Cross meetings, down in the Rectangle."

"What! Rachel Winslow! Do you know what you are saying? Do you know what sort of people those are down there?"

Rachel almost quailed before her mother. For a moment she shrank back and was silent. Then she spoke firmly:

"I know very well. That is the reason I am going. Mr. and Mrs. Gray have been working there several weeks. I learned only this morning that they want singers from the churches to help them in their meetings, They use a tent. It is in a part of the city where Christian work is most needed. I shall offer them my help. Mother!" Rachel cried out with the first passionate utterance she had yet used, "I want to do something that will cost me something in the way of sacrifice. I know you will not understand me. But I am hungry to suffer for something. What have we done all our lives for the suffering, sinning side of Raymond? How much have we denied ourselves or given of our personal ease and pleasure to bless the place in which we live or imitate the life of the Saviour of the world? Are we always to go on doing as society selfishly dictates, moving on its little narrow round of pleasures and entertainments, and never knowing the pain of things that cost?"

"Are you preaching at me?" asked Mrs. Winslow slowly. Rachel rose, and understood her mother's words.

"No. I am preaching at myself," she replied gently. She paused a moment as if she thought her mother would say something more, and then went out of the room. When she reached her own room she felt that so far as her own mother was concerned she could expect no sympathy, nor even a fair understanding from her.

She kneeled. It is safe to say that within the two weeks since Henry Maxwell's church had faced that shabby figure with the faded hat, more members of his parish had been driven to their knees in prayer than during all the previous term of his pastorate.

She rose, and her face was wet with tears. She sat thoughtfully a little while and then wrote a note to Virginia Page. She sent it to her by a messenger and then went downstairs and told her mother that she and Virginia were going down to the Rectangle that evening to see Mr. and Mrs. Gray, the evangelists.

"Virginia's uncle, Dr. West, will go with us, if she goes. I have asked her to call him up by telephone and go with us. The Doctor is a friend of the Grays, and attended some of their meetings last winter."

Mrs. Winslow did not say anthing. Her manner showed her complete disapproval of Rachel's course, and Rachel felt her unspoken bitterness.

About seven o'clock the Doctor and Virginia appeared, and together the three started for the scene of the White Cross meetings.

The Rectangle was the most notorious district in Raymond. It was on the territory close by the railroad shops and the packing houses. The great slum and tenement district of Raymond congested its worst and most wretched elements about the Rectangle. This was a barren field used in the summer by circus companies and wandering showmen. It was shut in by rows of saloons, gambling hells and cheap, dirty boarding and lodging houses.

The First Church of Raymond had never touched the Rectangle problem. It was too dirty, too coarse, too sinful, too awful for close contact. Let us be honest. There had been an attempt to cleanse this sore spot by sending down an occasional committee of singers or Sunday-school teachers or gospel visitors from various churches. But the First Church of Raymond, as an institution, had never really done anything to make the Rectangle any less a stronghold of the devil as the years went by.

Into this heart of the coarse part of the sin of Raymond the traveling evangelist and his brave little wife had pitched a good-sized tent and begun meetings. It was the spring of the year and the evenings were beginning to be pleasant. The evangelists had asked for the help of Christian people, and had received more than the usual amount of encouragement. But they felt a great need of more and better music. During the meetings on the Sunday just gone, the assistant at the organ had been taken ill. The volunteers from the city were few and the voices were of ordinary quality.

"There will be a small meeting tonight, John," said his wife, as they entered the tent a little after seven o'clock and began to arrange the chairs and light up.

"Yes, I fear so." Mr. Gray was a small, energetic man, with a pleasant voice and the courage of a high-born fighter. He had already made friends in the neighborhood and one of his converts, a heavy-faced man who had just come in, began to help in the arranging of seats.

It was after eight o'clock when Alexander Powers opened the door of his office and started for home. He was going to take a car at the corner of the Rectangle. But he was roused by a voice coming from the tent.

It was the voice of Rachel Winslow. It struck through his consciousness of struggle over his own question that had sent him into the Divine Presence for an answer. He had not yet reached a conclusion. He was tortured with uncertainty. His whole previous course of action as a railroad man was the poorest possible preparation for anything sacrificial. And he could not yet say what he would do in the matter.

Hark! What was she singing? How did Rachel Winslow happen to be down here? Several windows nearby went up. Some men quarreling near a saloon stopped and listened. Other figures were walking rapidly in the direction of the Rectangle and the tent. Surely Rachel Winslow had never sung like that in the First Church. It was a marvelous voice. What was it she was singing? Again Alexander Powers, Superintendent of the machine shops, paused and listened.

> Where He leads me I will follow,
> Where He leads me I will follow,
> Where He leads me I will follow,
> I'll go with Him, with Him
> All the way!

The brutal, coarse, impure life of the Rectangle stirred itself into new life as the song, as pure as the surroundings were vile, floated out and into saloon and den and foul lodging. Someone stumbling hastily by Alexander Powers said in answer to a question:

"De tent's beginning to run over tonight. That's what the talent calls music, eh?"

The Superintendent turned toward the tent. Then he stopped. After a minute of indecision he went on to the corner and took the car for his home. But before he was out of the sound of Rachel's voice he knew he had settled for himself the question of what Jesus would do.

Chapter 8

If any man would come after me, let him deny himself and take up his cross daily and follow me.

Henry Maxwell paced his study back and forth. It was Wednesday and he had started to think out the subject of his evening service which fell upon that night. Out of one of his study windows he could see the tall chimney of the railroad shops. The top of the evangelist's tent just showed over the buildings around the Rectangle. He looked out of his window every time he turned in his walk. After a while he sat down at his desk and drew a large piece of paper toward him. After thinking several moments he wrote in large letters the following:

A NUMBER OF THINGS THAT JESUS WOULD PROBABLY DO
IN THIS PARISH

1. Live in a simple, plain manner, without needless luxury on the one hand or undue asceticism on the other.

2. Preach fearlessly to the hypocrites in the church, no matter what their social importance or wealth.

3. Show in some practical form His sympathy and love for the common people as well as for the well-to-do, educated, refined people who make up the majority of the parish.

4. Identify Himself with the great causes of humanity in some personal way that would call for self-denial and suffering.

5. Preach against the saloon in Raymond.

6. Become known as a friend and companion of the sinful people in the Rectangle.

7. Give up the summer trip to Europe this year. (I have been abroad twice and cannot claim any special need of rest. I am well, and could forego this pleasure, using the money for some

one who needs a vacation more than I do. There are probably plenty of such people in the city.)

He was conscious, with a humility that was once a stranger to him, that his outline of Jesus' probable action was painfully lacking in depth and power, but he was seeking carefully for concrete shapes into which he might cast his thought of Jesus' conduct. Nearly every point he had put down, meant, for him, a complete overturning of the custom and habit of years in the ministry. In spite of that, he still searched deeper for sources of the Christ-like spirit. He did not attempt to write any more, but sat at his desk absorbed in his effort to catch more and more the spirit of Jesus in his own life. He had forgotten the particular subject for his prayer meeting with which he had begun his morning study.

He was so absorbed over his thought that he did not hear the bell ring; he was roused by the servant who announced a caller. He had sent up his name, Mr. Gray.

Maxwell stepped to the head of the stairs and asked Gray to come up. So Gray came up and stated the reason for his call.

"I want your help, Mr. Maxwell. Of course you have heard what a wonderful meeting we had Monday night and last night. Miss Winslow has done more with her voice than I could do, and the tent won't hold the people."

"I've heard of that. It is the first time the people there have heard her. It is no wonder they are attracted."

"It has been a wonderful revelation to us, and a most encouraging event in our work. But I came to ask if you could not come down tonight and preach. I am suffering from a severe cold. I do not dare trust my voice again. I know it is asking a good deal from such a busy man. But, if you can't come, say so frankly, and I'll try somewhere else."

"I'm sorry, but it's my regular prayer meeting night," began Henry Maxwell. Then he flushed and added, "I shall be able to arrange it in some way so as to come down. You can count on me."

Gray thanked him earnestly and rose to go.

"Won't you stay a minute, Gray, and let us have a prayer together?"

"Yes," said Gray simply.

So the two men kneeled together in the study. Henry Maxwell prayed like a child. Gray was touched to tears as he knelt there. There was something almost pitiful in the way this man who had lived his ministerial life in such a narrow limit of exercise now begged for wisdom and strength to speak a message to the people in the Rectangle.

Gray rose and held out his hand. "God bless you, Mr. Maxwell. I'm sure the Spirit will give you power tonight."

Henry Maxwell made no answer. He did not even trust himself to say that he hoped so. But he thought of his promise and it brought him a certain peace that was refreshing to his heart and mind alike.

So that is how it came about that when the First Church audience came into the lecture-room that evening it met with another surprise. There was an unusually large number present. The prayer meetings ever since that remarkable Sunday morning had been attended as never before in the history of the First Church. Mr. Maxwell came at once to the point.

"I feel that I am called to go down to the Rectangle tonight, and I will leave it with you to say whether you will go on with this meeting here. I think perhaps the best plan would be for a few volunteers to go down to the Rectangle with me prepared to help in the after-meeting, if necessary, and the rest to remain here and pray that the Spirit power may go with us."

So half a dozen of the men went with the pastor, and the rest of the audience stayed in the lecture-room. Maxwell could not escape the thought as he left the room that probably in his entire church membership there might not be found a score of disciples who were capable of doing work that would successfully lead needy, sinful men into the knowledge of Christ. The thought did not linger in his mind to vex him as he went his way, but it was simply a part of his whole new conception of the meaning of Christian discipleship.

When he and his little company of volunteers reached the Rectangle, the tent was already crowded. They had difficulty in getting to the platform. Rachel was there with Virginia and Jasper Chase who had come instead of the Doctor tonight.

When the meeting began with a song in which Rachel sang the solo and the people were asked to join in the chorus, not a foot of standing room was left in the tent. The night was mild and the sides of the tent were up and a great border of faces stretched around, looking in and forming part of the audience. After the singing, and a prayer by one of the city pastors who was present, Gray stated the reason for his inability to speak, and in his simple manner turned the service over to "Brother Maxwell, of the First Church."

"Who's de bloke?" asked a hoarse voice near the outside of the tent.

"De Fust Church parson. We've got de whole hightone swell outfit tonight."

"Did you say Fust Church? I know him. My landlord's got a front pew up there," said another voice, and there was a laugh, for the speaker was a saloon keeper.

"Trow out de life line 'cross de dark wave!" began a drunken man near by, singing in such an unconscious imitation of a local traveling singer's nasal tone that roars of laughter and jeers of approval rose around him. The people in the tent turned in the direction of the disturbance. There were shouts of "Put him out!" "Give the Fust Church a chance!" "Song! Song! Give us another song!"

Henry Maxwell stood up, and a great wave of actual terror went over him. This was not like preaching to the well-dressed, respectable, good-mannered people up on the boulevard. He began to speak, but the confusion increased. Gray went down into the crowd, but did not seem able to quiet it. Maxwell raised his arm and his voice. The crowd in the tent began to pay attention, but the noise on the outside increased. In a few minutes the audience was beyond his control. He turned to Rachel with a sad smile.

"Sing something, Miss Winslow. They will listen to you," he said, and then sat down and covered his face with his hands.

It was Rachel's opportunity, and she was fully equal to it. Virginia was at the organ and Rachel asked her to play a few notes of the hymn.

> Saviour, I follow on,
>   Guided by Thee,
> Seeing not yet the hand
>   That leadeth me.
> Hushed be my heart and still
> Fear I no farther ill,
> Only to meet Thy will,
>   My will shall be.

Rachel had not sung the first line before the people in the tent were all turned toward her, hushed and reverent. Before she had finished the verse the Rectangle was subdued and tamed. It lay like some wild beast at her feet, and she sang it into harmlessness. Ah! What were the flippant, perfumed, critical audiences in concert halls compared with this dirty, drunken, impure, besotted mass of humanity that trembled and wept and grew strangely, sadly thoughtful under the touch of this divine ministry of this beautiful young woman! Mr. Maxwell, as he raised his head and saw the transformed mob, had a glimpse of something that Jesus would probably do with a voice like Rachel Winslow's. Jasper Chase sat with his eyes on the singer, and his greatest longing as an ambitious author was swallowed up in his thought of what Rachel Winslow's love might sometimes mean to him. And over in the shadow outside stood the last person any one might have expected to see at a gospel tent service—Rollin Page, who, jostled on every side by rough men and women who stared at the swell in fine clothes, seemed careless of his surroundings and at the same time evidently swayed by the power that Rachel possessed. He had just come over from the club. Neither Rachel nor Virginia saw him that night.

The song was over. Maxwell rose again. This time he felt calmer. What would Jesus do? He spoke as he thought once he never could speak. Who were these people? They were immortal souls. What was Christianity? A calling of sinners, not the righteous, to repentance. How would Jesus speak? What would He say? He could not tell all that His massage would include, but he felt sure of a part of it. And in that certainty he spoke on. Never before had he felt "compassion for the multitude." What had the multitude been to him during his ten years in the First Church but a vague, dangerous, dirty, troublesome factor in society, outside of the church and of his reach, an element that caused him occasionally an unpleasant twinge of conscience, a factor in Raymond that was talked about at associations as the "masses," in papers written by the brethren in attempts to show why the "masses" were not being reached. But tonight as he faced the masses he asked himself whether, after all, this was not just about such a multitude as Jesus faced oftenest, and he felt the genuine emotion of love for a crowd which is one of the best indications a preacher ever has that he is living close to the heart of the world's eternal Life. It is easy to love an individual sinner, especially if he is personally picturesque or interesting. To love a multitude of sinners is distinctively a Christ-like quality.

When the meeting closed, there was no special interest shown. No one stayed to the after-meeting. The people rapidly melted away from the tent, and the saloons, which had been experiencing a dull season while the meetings progressed, again drove a thriving trade. The Rectangle, as if to make up for lost time, started in with vigor on its usual night debauch. Maxwell and his little party, including Virginia, Rachel and Jasper Chase, walked down past the row of saloons and dens until they reached the corner where the cars passed.

"This is a terrible spot," said the minister as he stood waiting for their car. "I never realized that Raymond had such a festering sore. It does not seem possible that this is a city full of Christian disciples."

"Do you think anyone can ever remove this great curse of drink?" asked Jasper Chase.

"I have thought lately as never before of what Christian people might do to remove the curse of the saloon. Why don't we all act together against it? Why don't the Christian pastors and the church members of Raymond move as one man against the traffic? What would Jesus do? Would He keep silent? Would He vote to license these causes of crime and death?"

He was talking to himself more than to the others. He remembered that he had always voted for license, and so had nearly all his church members. What would Jesus do? Could he answer that question? Would the Master preach and act against the saloon if He lived today? How would He preach and act? Suppose it was not popular to preach against license? Suppose the Christian people thought it was all that could be done to license the evil and so get revenue from the necessary sin? Or suppose the church members themselves owned the property where the saloons stood—what then? He knew that those were the facts in Raymond. What would Jesus do?

He went up into his study the next morning with that question only partly answered. He thought of it all day. He was still thinking of it and reaching certain real conclusions when the *Evening News* came. His wife brought it up and sat down a few minutes while he read to her.

The *Evening News* was at present the most sensational paper in Raymond. That is to say, it was being edited in such a remarkable fashion that its subscribers had never been so excited over a newspaper before. First they had noticed the absence of the prize fight, and gradually it began to dawn upon them that the *News* no longer printed accounts of crime with detailed descriptions, or scandals in private life. Then they noticed that the advertisements of liquor and tobacco were dropped, together with certain others of a questionable character. The discontinuance of the Sunday paper caused the greatest comment of all, and now the character of the editorials was creating the greatest excitement. A quotation from the Monday paper of this week will show what Edward Norman was doing to keep his promise. The editorial was headed:

THE MORAL SIDE OF POLITICAL QUESTIONS

The editor of the News has always advocated the principles of the great political party at present in power, and has heretofore discussed all political questions from the standpoint of expediency, or of belief in the party as opposed to other political organizations. Hereafter, to be perfectly honest with all our readers, the editor will present and discuss all political questions from the standpoint of right and wrong. In other words, the first question asked in this office about any political question will not be, "Is it in the interests of our party?" or, "Is it according to the principles laid down by our party in its platform?" but the question first asked will be, "Is this measure in accordance with the spirit and teachings of Jesus as the author of the greatest standard of life known to men?" That is, to be perfectly plain, the moral side of every political question will be considered its most important side, and the ground will be distinctly taken that nations as well as

individuals are under the same law to do all things to the glory
of God as the first rule of action.

The same principle will be observed in this office toward candi-
dates for places of responsibility and trust in the republic. Regardless of party politics the editor of the News will do all in his
power to bring the best men into power, and will not knowingly
help to support for office any candidate who is unworthy, no matter how much he may be endorsed by the party. The first question asked about the man and about the measures will be, "Is he
the right man for the place?" "Is he a good man with ability?"
"Is the measure right?"

There had been more of this, but we have quoted enough to show
the character of the editorial. Hundreds of men in Raymond had read
it and rubbed their eyes in amazement. A good many of them had
promptly written to the *News*, telling the editor to stop their paper.
The paper still came out, however, and was eagerly read all over the
city. At the end of a week Edward Norman knew very well that he
was fast losing a large number of subscribers. He faced the conditions
calmly, although Clark, the managing editor, grimly anticipated ulti-
mate bankruptcy, especially since Monday's editorial.

Tonight, as Maxwell read to his wife, he could see in almost every
column evidences of Norman's conscientious obedience to his promise.
There was an absence of slangy, sensational scare heads. The reading
matter under the headlines was in perfect keeping with them. He noticed in two columns that the reporters' names appeared signed at the
bottom. And there was a distinct advance in the dignity and style of
their contributions.

"So Norman is beginning to get his reporters to sign their work. He
has talked with me about that. It is a good thing. It fixes responsibility
for items where it belongs and raises the standard of work done. A
good thing all around for the public and the writers."

Maxwell suddenly paused. His wife looked up from some work she
was doing. He was reading something with the utmost interest. "Listen to this, Mary," he said, after a moment while his lip trembled:

This morning Alexander Powers, Superintendent of the L. and
T. R. R. shops in this city, handed in his resignation to the road,
and gave as his reason the fact that certain proofs had fallen
into his hands of the violation of the Interstate Commerce Law,
and also of the state law which has recently been framed to prevent and punish railroad pooling for the benefit of certain favored
shippers. Mr. Powers states in his resignation that he can no
longer consistently withhold the information he possesses against
the road. He will be a witness against it. He has placed his

evidence against the company in the hands of the Commission
and it is now for them to take action upon it.

The News wishes to express itself on this action of Mr. Powers.
In the first place he has nothing to gain by it. He has lost a very
valuable place voluntarily, when by keeping silent he might have
retained it. In the second place, we believe his action ought to receive the approval of all thoughtful, honest, citizens who believe
in seeing law obeyed and lawbreakers brought to justice. In a
case like this, where evidence against a railroad company is generally understood to be almost impossible to obtain, it is the general belief that the officers of the road are often in possession of
incriminating facts but do not consider it to be any of their business to inform the authorities that the law is being defied. The
entire result of this evasion of responsibility on the part of those
who are responsible is demoralizing to every young man connected with the road. The editor of the News recalls the statement made by a prominent railroad official in this city a little
while ago, that nearly every clerk in a certain department of the
road understood that large sums of money were made by shrewd
violations of the Interstate Commerce Law, was ready to admire
the shrewdness with which it was done, and declared that they
would all do the same thing if they were high enough in railroad
circles to attempt it.*

It is not necessary to say that such a condition of business is
destructive to all the nobler and higher standards of conduct, and
no young man can live in such an atmosphere of unpunished dis-
honesty and lawlessness without wrecking his character.

In our judgment, Mr. Powers did the only thing that a Christian
man could do. He has rendered brave and useful service to the
state and the general public. It is not always an easy matter to
determine the relations that exist between the individual citizen
and his fixed duty to the public. In this case there is no doubt in
our minds that the step which Mr. Powers has taken commends
itself to every man who believes in law and its enforcement.
There are times when the individual must act for the people in
ways that will mean sacrifice and loss to him of the gravest
character. Mr. Powers will be misunderstood and misrepresented,
but there is no question that his course will be approved by every
citizen who wishes to see the greatest corporations as well as the
weakest individual subject to the same law. Mr. Powers has done
all that a loyal, patriotic citizen could do. It now remains for the
Commission to act upon his evidence which, we understand, is
overwhelming proof of the lawlessness of the L. and T. Let the
law be enforced, no matter who the persons may be who have
been guilty.

* This was actually said in one of the General Offices of a great Western
railroad, to the author's knowledge. [Sheldon's note.]

‖‖‖‖‖‖

Chapter 9

Henry Maxwell finished reading and dropped the paper.

"I must go and see Powers. This is the result of his promise."

He rose, and as he was going out, his wife said:

"Do you think, Henry, that Jesus would have done that?"

Maxwell paused a moment. Then he answered slowly, "Yes, I think He would. At any rate, Powers has decided so and each one of us who made the promise understands that he is not deciding Jesus' conduct for anyone else, only for himself."

"How about his family? How will Mrs. Powers and Celia be likely to take it?"

"Very hard, I've no doubt. That will be Powers' cross in this matter. They will not understand his motive."

Maxwell went out and walked over to the next block where Superintendent Powers lived. To his relief, Powers himself came to the door.

The two men shook hands silently. They instantly understood each other without words. There had never before been such a bond of union between the minister and his parishioner.

"What are you going to do?" Henry Maxwell asked after they had talked over the facts in the case.

"You mean another position? I have no plans yet. I can go back to my old work as a telegraph operator. My family will not suffer, except in a social way."

Powers spoke calmly and sadly. Henry Maxwell did not need to ask him how the wife and daughter felt. He knew well enough that the superintendent had suffered deepest at that point.

"There is one matter I wish you would see to," said Powers after awhile, "and that is, the work begun at the shops. So far as I know, the company will not object to that going on. It is one of the contradictions of the railroad world that Y. M. C. A.'s and other Christian influences are encouraged by the roads, while all the time the most un-Christian and lawless acts may be committed in the official management of the roads themselves. Of course it is well understood that it pays a railroad to have in its employ men who are temperate, honest and Christian. So I have no doubt the master mechanic will have the same courtesy shown him in the use of the room. But what I want you to do, Mr. Maxwell, is to see that my plan is carried out. Will you? You understand what it was in general. You made a very favorable impression on the men. Go down there as often as you can. Get Milton Wright interested to provide something for the furnishing and expense of the coffee plant and reading tables. Will you do it?"

"Yes," replied Henry Maxwell. He stayed a little longer. Before he went away, he and the superintendent had a prayer together, and they parted with that silent hand grasp that seemed to them like a new token of their Christian discipleship and fellowship.

The pastor of the First Church went home stirred deeply by the events of the week. Gradually the truth was growing upon him that the pledge to do as Jesus would was working out a revolution in his parish and throughout the city. Every day added to the serious results of obedience to that pledge. Maxwell did not pretend to see the end. He was, in fact, only now at the very beginning of events that were destined to change the history of hundreds of families not only in Raymond but throughout the entire country. As he thought of Edward Norman and Rachel and Mr. Powers, and of the results that had already come from their actions, he could not help a feeling of intense interest in the probable effect if all the persons in the First Church who had made the pledge, faithfully kept it. Would they all keep it, or would some of them turn back when the cross became too heavy?

He was asking this question the next morning as he sat in his study when the President of the Endeavor Society of his church called to see him.

"I suppose I ought not to trouble you with my case," said young Morris, coming at once to his errand, "but I thought, Mr. Maxwell, that you might advise me a little."

"I'm glad you came. Go on, Fred." He had known the young man ever since his first year in the pastorate, and loved and honored him for his consistent, faithful service in the church.

"Well, the fact is, I am out of a job. You know I've been doing reporter work on the morning *Sentinel* since I graduated last year. Well, last Saturday Mr. Burr asked me to go down the road Sunday morning and get the details of that train robbery at the Junction, and write the thing up for the extra edition that came out Monday morning, just to get the start of the *News*. I refused to go, and Burr gave me my dismissal. He was in a bad temper, or I think perhaps he would not have done it. He has always treated me well before. Now, do you think Jesus would have done as I did? I ask because the other fellows say I was a fool not to do the work. I want to feel that a Christian acts from motives that may seem strange to others sometimes, but not foolish. What do you think?"

"I think you kept your promise, Fred. I cannot believe Jesus would do newspaper reporting on Sunday as you were asked to do it."

"Thank you, Mr. Maxwell. I felt a little troubled over it, but the longer I think it over the better I feel."

Morris rose to go, and his pastor rose and laid a loving hand on the young man's shoulder.

"What are you going to do, Fred?"

"I don't know yet. I have thought some of going to Chicago or some large city."

"Why don't you try the *News?*"

"They are all supplied. I have not thought of applying there."

Maxwell thought a moment. "Come down to the *News* office with me, and let us see Norman about it."

So a few minutes later Edward Norman received into his room the minister and young Morris, and Maxwell briefly told the cause of the errand.

"I can give you a place on the *News*," said Norman with his keen look softened by a smile that made it winsome. "I want reporters who won't work Sundays. And what is more, I am making plans for a special kind of reporting which I believe you can develop because you are in sympathy with what Jesus would do."

He assigned Morris a definite task, and Maxwell started back to his study, feeling that kind of satisfaction (and it is a very deep kind) which a man feels when he has been even partly instrumental in finding an unemployed person a remunerative position.

He had intended to go right to his study, but on his way home he passed by one of Milton Wright's stores. He thought he would simply step in and shake hands with his parishioner and bid him God-speed in what he had heard he was doing to put Christ into his business. But when he went into the office, Wright insisted on detaining him to talk over some of his new plans. Maxwell asked himself if this was the Milton Wright he used to know, eminently practical, business-like, according to the regular code of the business world, and viewing every thing first and foremost from the standpoint of, "Will it pay?"

"There is no use to disguise the fact, Mr. Maxwell, that I have been compelled to revolutionize the entire method of my business since I made that promise. I have been doing a great many things during the last twenty years in this store that I know Jesus would not do. But that is a small item compared with the number of things I begin to believe Jesus would do. My sins of commission have not been as many as those of omission in business relations."

"What was the first change you made?" He felt as if his sermon could wait for him in his study. As the interview with Milton Wright continued, he was not so sure but that he had found material for a sermon without going back to his study.

"I think the first change I had to make was in my thought of my employees. I came down here Monday morning after that Sunday and asked myself, 'What would Jesus do in His relation to these clerks, bookkeepers, office-boys, draymen, salesmen? Would He try to establish some sort of personal relation to them different from that which I have sustained all these years?' I soon answered this by saying, 'Yes.' Then came the question of what that relation would be and what it would lead me to do. I did not see how I could answer it to my satisfaction without getting all my employees together and having a talk with them. So I sent invitations to all of them, and we had a meeting out there in the warehouse Tuesday night. A good many things came out of that meeting. I can't tell you all. I tried to talk with the men as I imagined Jesus might. It was hard work, for I have not been in the habit of it, and must have made some mistakes. But I can hardly make you believe, Mr. Maxwell, the effect of that meeting on some of the men. Before it closed I saw more than a dozen of them with tears on their faces. I kept asking, 'What would Jesus do?' and the more I asked it the farther along it pushed me into the most intimate and loving relations with the men who have worked for me all these years. Every day something new is coming up and I am right now in the midst of a reconstruction of the entire business so far as its motive for being conducted is concerned. I am so practically ignorant of all plans for co-operation and its application to business that I am trying to get information from every possible source. I have lately made a special study of the life of Titus Salt, the great mill-owner of Bradford, England, who afterward built that model town on the banks of the Aire. There is a good deal in his plans that will help me. But I have not yet reached definite conclusions in regard to all the details. I am not enough used to Jesus' methods. But see here."

Wright eagerly reached up into one of the pigeon holes of his desk and took out a paper.

"I have sketched out what seems to me like a program such as Jesus might go by in a business like mine. I want you to tell me what you think of it:

WHAT JESUS WOULD PROBABLY DO IN MILTON WRIGHT'S PLACE
AS A BUSINESS MAN

1. He would engage in the business first of all for the purpose of glorifying God, and not for the primary purpose of making money.

2. All money that might be made he would never regard as his own, but as trust funds to be used for the good of humanity.

3. His relations with all the persons in his employ would be the most loving and helpful. He could not help thinking of all of them in the light of souls to be saved. This thought would always be greater than his thought of making money in the business.

4. He would never do a single dishonest or questionable thing or try in any remotest way to get the advantage of any one else in the same business.

5. The principle of unselfishness and helpfulness in the business would direct all its details.

6. Upon this principle he would shape the entire plan of his relations to his employees, to the people who were his customers and to the general business world with which he was connected.

Henry Maxwell read this over slowly. It reminded him of his own attempts the day before to put into a concrete form his thought of Jesus' probable action. He was very thoughtful as he looked up and met Wright's eager gaze.

"Do you believe you can continue to make your business pay on these lines?"

"I do. Intelligent unselfishness ought to be wiser than intelligent selfishness, don't you think? If the men who work as employees begin to feel a personal share in the profits of the business and, more than that, a personal love for themselves on the part of the firm, won't the result be more care, less waste, more diligence, more faithfulness?"

"Yes, I think so. A good many other business men don't, do they? I mean as a general thing. How about your relations to the selfish world that is not trying to make money on Christian principles?"

"That complicates my action, of course."

"Does your plan contemplate what is coming to be known as co-operation?"

"Yes, as far as I have gone, it does. As I told you, I am studying out my details carefully. I am absolutely convinced that Jesus in my place would be absolutely unselfish. He would love all these men in His employ. He would consider the main purpose of all the business to be a mutual helpfulness, and would conduct it all so that God's kingdom would be evidently the first object sought. On those general principles, as I say, I am working. I must have time to complete the details."

When Maxwell finally left he was profoundly impressed with the revolution that was being wrought already in the business. As he passed out of the store he caught something of the new spirit of the place. There was no mistaking the fact that Milton Wright's new relations to his employees were beginning even so soon, after less than two weeks, to transform the entire business. This was apparent in the conduct and faces of the clerks.

"If he keeps on he will be one of the most influential preachers in Raymond," said Maxwell to himself when he reached his study. The question rose as to this continuance in this course when he began to lose money by it, as was possible. He prayed that the Holy Spirit, who had shown Himself with growing power in the company of First Church disciples, might abide long with them all. And with that prayer on his lips and in his heart he began the preparation of a sermon in which he was going to present to his people on Sunday the subject of the saloon in Raymond, as he now believed Jesus would do. He had never preached against the saloon in this way before. He knew that the things he should say would lead to serious results. Nevertheless, he went on with his work, and every sentence he wrote or shaped was preceded with the question, "Would Jesus say that?" Once in the course of his study, he went down on his knees. No one except himself could know what that meant to him. When had he done that in his preparation of sermons, before the change that had come into his thought of discipleship? As he viewed his ministry now, he did not dare preach without praying long for wisdom. He no longer thought of his dramatic delivery and its effect on his audience. The great question with him now was, "What would Jesus do?"

Saturday night at the Rectangle witnessed some of the most remarkable scenes that Mr. Gray and his wife had ever known. The meetings had intensified with each night of Rachel's singing. A stranger passing through the Rectangle in the day-time might have heard a good deal about the meetings in one way and another. It cannot be said that up to that Saturday night there was any appreciable lack of oaths and impurity and heavy drinking. The Rectangle would not have acknowledged that it was growing any better or that even the singing had softened its outward manner. It had too much local pride in being "tough." But in spite of itself there was a yielding to a power it had never measured and did not know well enough to resist beforehand.

Gray had recovered his voice so that by Saturday he was able to speak. The fact that he was obliged to use his voice carefully made it necessary for the people to be very quiet if they wanted to hear. Gradually they had come to understand that this man was talking these many weeks and giving his time and strength to give them a knowledge of a Saviour, all out of a perfectly unselfish love for them. Tonight the great crowd was as quiet as Henry Maxwell's decorous audience ever was. The fringe around the tent was deeper and the saloons were practically empty. The Holy Spirit had come at last, and Gray knew that one of the great prayers of his life was going to be answered.

And Rachel—her singing was the best, most wonderful, that Virginia or Jasper Chase had ever known. They came together again tonight, this time with Dr. West, who had spent all his spare time that week in the Rectangle with some charity cases. Virginia was at the organ, Jasper sat on a front seat looking up at Rachel, and the Rectangle swayed as one man towards the platform as she sang:

> Just as I am, without one plea,
> But that Thy blood was shed for me,
> And that Thou bidst me come to Thee,
> O Lamb of God, I come, I come.

Gray hardly said a word. He stretched out his hand with a gesture of invitation. And down the two aisles of the tent, broken, sinful creatures, men and women, stumbled towards the platform. One woman out of the street was near the organ. Virginia caught the look of her face, and for the first time in the life of the rich girl the thought of what Jesus was to the sinful woman came with a suddenness and power that was like nothing but a new birth. Virginia left the organ, went to her, looked into her face and caught her hands in her own. The other girl trembled, then fell on her knees sobbing, with her head down upon the back of the rude bench in front of her, still clinging to Virginia. And Virginia, after a moment's hesitation, kneeled down by her and the two heads were bowed close together.

But when the people had crowded in a double row all about the platform, most of them kneeling and crying, a man in evening dress, different from the others, pushed through the seats and came and kneeled down by the side of the drunken man who had disturbed the meeting when Maxwell spoke. He kneeled within a few feet of Rachel Winslow, who was still singing softly. And as she turned for a moment and looked in his direction, she was amazed to see the face of Rollin Page! For a moment her voice faltered. Then she went on.

> Just as I am, thou wilt receive,
> Wilt welcome, pardon, cleanse, relieve,
> Because Thy promise I believe,
> O Lamb of God, I come, I come.

The voice was as the voice of divine longing, and the Rectangle for the time being was swept into the harbor of redemptive grace.

Chapter 10

If any man serve me, let him follow me.

It was nearly midnight before the services at the Rectangle closed. Gray stayed up long into Sunday morning, praying and talking with a little group of converts who in the great experiences of their new life, clung to the evangelist with a personal helplessness that made it as impossible for him to leave them as if they had been depending upon him to save them from physical death. Among these converts was Rollin Page.

Virginia and her uncle had gone home about eleven o'clock, and Rachel and Jasper Chase had gone with them as far as the avenue where Virginia lived. Dr. West had walked on a little way with them to his own home, and Rachel and Jasper had then gone on together to her mother's.

That was a little after eleven. It was now striking midnight, and Jasper Chase sat in his room staring at the papers on his desk and going over the last half hour with painful persistence.

He had told Rachel Winslow of his love for her, and she had not given him her love in return. It would be difficult to know what was most powerful in the impulse that had moved him to speak to her tonight. He had yielded to his feelings without any special thought of results to himself, because he had felt so certain that Rachel would respond to his love. He tried to recall the impression she made on him when he first spoke to her.

Never had her beauty and her strength influenced him as tonight. While she was singing he saw and heard no one else. The tent swarmed with a confused crowd of faces and he knew he was sitting there hemmed in by a mob of people, but they had no meaning to him. He felt powerless to avoid speaking to her. He knew he should speak when they were alone.

Now that he had spoken, he felt that he had misjudged either Rachel or the opportunity. He knew, or thought he knew, that she had begun to care something for him. It was no secret between them that the heroine of Jasper's first novel had been his own ideal of Rachel, and the hero in the story was himself and they had loved each other in the book, and Rachel had not objected. No one else knew. The names and characters had been drawn with a subtle skill that revealed to Rachel, when she received a copy of the book from Jasper, the fact of his love for her, and she had not been offended. That was nearly a year ago.

Tonight he recalled the scene between them with every inflection and movement unerased from his memory. He even recalled the fact that he began to speak just at that point on the avenue where, a few days before, he had met Rachel walking with Rollin Page. He had wondered at the time what Rollin was saying.

"Rachel," Jasper had said, and it was the first time he had ever spoken her first name, "I never knew till tonight how much I loved you. Why should I try to conceal any longer what you have seen me look? You know I love you as my life. I can no longer hide it from you if I would."

The first intimation he had of a repulse was the trembling of Rachel's arm in his. She had allowed him to speak and had neither turned her face toward him nor away from him. She had looked straight on and her voice was sad but firm and quiet when she spoke.

"Why do you speak to me now? I cannot bear it—after what we have seen tonight."

"Why—what—" he had stammered and then was silent.

Rachel withdrew her arm from his but still walked near him. Then he had cried out with the anguish of one who begins to see a great loss facing him where he expected a great joy.

"Rachel! Do you not love me? Is not my love for you as sacred as anything in all of life itself?"

She had walked silent for a few steps after that. They passed a street lamp. Her face was pale and beautiful. He had made a movement to clutch her arm and she had moved a little farther from him.

"No," she had replied. "There was a time—I cannot answer for that —you should not have spoken to me—now."

He had seen in these words his answer. He was extremely sensitive. Nothing short of a joyous response to his own love would ever have satisfied him. He could not think of pleading with her.

"Some time—when I am more worthy?" he had asked in a low voice, but she did not seem to hear, and they had parted at her home, and he recalled vividly the fact that no good-night had been said.

Now as he went over the brief but significant scene he lashed himself for his foolish precipitancy. He had not reckoned on Rachel's tense, passionate absorption of all her feeling in the scenes at the tent which were so new in her mind. But he did not know her well enough even yet to understand the meaning of her refusal. When the clock in the First Church struck one he was still sitting at his desk staring at the last page of manuscript of his unfinished novel.

Rachel went up to her room and faced her evening's experience with conflicting emotions. Had she ever loved Jasper Chase? Yes. No. One moment she felt that her life's happiness was at stake over the result of her action. Another, she had a strange feeling of relief that she had spoken as she had. There was one great, overmastering feeling in her. The response of the wretched creatures in the tent to her singing, the swift, powerful, awesome presence of the Holy Spirit had affected her as never in all her life before. The moment Jasper had spoken her name and she realized that he was telling her of his love she had felt a sudden revulsion for him, as if he should have respected the supernatural events they had just witnessed. She felt as if it was not the time to be absorbed in anything less than the divine glory of those conversions. The thought that all the time she was singing, with the one passion of her soul to touch the conscience of that tent full of sin, Jasper Chase had been unmoved by it except to love her for herself, gave her a shock as of irreverence on her part as well as on his. She could not tell why she felt as she did, only she knew that if he had not told her tonight she would still have felt the same toward him as she always had. What was that feeling? What had he been to her? Had she made a mistake? She went to her book case and took out the novel which Jasper had given her. Her face deepened in color as she turned to certain passages which she had read often and which she knew Jasper had written for her. She read them again. Somehow they failed to touch her strongly. She closed the book and let it lie on the table. She gradually felt that her thought was busy with the sights she had witnessed in the tent. Those faces, men and women, touched for the first time with the Spirit's glory—what a wonderful thing life was after all! The complete regeneration revealed in the sight of drunken, vile, debauched humanity kneeling down to give itself to a life of purity and Christlikeness—oh, it was surely a witness to the superhuman in the world! And the face of Rollin Page by the side of that miserable wreck out of the gutter! She could recall as if she now saw it, Virginia crying with her arms about her brother just before she left the tent, and Mr. Gray kneeling close by, and the girl Virginia had taken into her heart while she whispered something to her before she went out. All these pictures drawn by the Holy Spirit in the human tragedies brought to a climax there in the most abandoned spot in all Raymond, stood out in Rachel's memory now, a memory so recent that her room seemed for the time being to contain all the actors and their movements.

"No! No!" she said aloud. "He had no right to speak after all that!

He should have respected the place where our thoughts should have been. I am sure I do not love him—not enough to give him my life!"

And after she had thus spoken, the evening's experience at the tent came crowding in again, thrusting out all other things. It is perhaps the most striking evidence of the tremendous spiritual factor which had now entered the Rectangle that Rachel felt, even when the great love of a strong man had come very near to her, that the spiritual manifestation moved her with an agitation far greater than anything Jasper had felt for her personally or she for him.

The people of Raymond awoke Sunday morning to a growing knowledge of events which were beginning to revolutionize many of the regular, customary habits of the town. Alexander Powers' action in the matter of the railroad frauds had created a sensation not only in Raymond but throughout the country. Edward Norman's daily changes of policy in the conduct of his paper had startled the community and caused more comment than any recent political event. Rachel Winslow's singing at the Rectangle meeting had made a stir in society and excited the wonder of all her friends.

Virginia's conduct, her presence every night with Rachel, her absence from the usual circle of her wealthy, fashionable acquaintances, had furnished a great deal of material for gossip and question. In addition to these events which centered about these persons who were so well known, there had been all through the city, in very many homes and in business and social circles, strange happenings. Nearly one hundred persons in Henry Maxwell's church had made the pledge to do everything after asking: "What would Jesus do?" and the result had been, in many cases, unheard-of actions. The city was stirred as it had never been before. As a climax to the week's events had come the spiritual manifestation at the Rectangle, and the announcement which came to most people before church time of the actual conversion at the tent of nearly fifty of the worst characters in that neighborhood, together with the conversion of Rollin Page, the well-known society and club man.

It is no wonder that under the pressure of all this the First Church of Raymond came to the morning service in a condition that made it quickly sensitive to any large truth. Perhaps nothing had astonished the people more than the great change that had come over the minister, since he had proposed to them the imitation of Jesus in conduct. The dramatic delivery of his sermons no longer impressed them. The self-satisfied, contented, easy attitude of the fine figure and refined face in the pulpit had been displaced by a manner that could not be compared with the old style of his delivery. The sermon had become a message. It was no longer delivered. It was brought to them with a

love, an earnestness, a passion, a desire, a humility that poured its enthusiasm about the truth and made the speaker no more prominent
than he had to be as the living voice of God. His prayers were unlike
any the people had heard before. They were often broken, even once
or twice they had been actually ungrammatical in a phrase or two.
When had Henry Maxwell so far forgotten himself in a prayer as to
make a mistake of that sort? He knew that he had often taken as
much pride in the diction and delivery of his prayers as of his sermons. Was it possible he now so abhorred the elegant refinement of a
formal public petition that he purposely chose to rebuke himself for
his previous precise manner of prayer? It is more likely that he had no
thought of all that. His great longing to voice the needs and wants of
his people made him unmindful of an occasional mistake. It is certain
that he had never prayed so effectively as he did now.

There are times when a sermon has a value and power due to conditions in the audience rather than to anything new or startling or eloquent in the words said or arguments presented. Such conditions
faced Henry Maxwell this morning as he preached against the saloon,
according to his purpose determined on the week before. He had no
new statements to make about the evil influence of the saloon in Raymond. What new facts were there? He had no startling illustrations of
the power of the saloon in business or politics. What could he say that
had not been said by temperance orators a great many times? The
effect of his message this morning owed its power to the unusual fact
of his preaching about the saloon at all, together with the events that
had stirred the people. He had never in the course of his ten years'
pastorate mentioned the saloon as something to be regarded in the
light of an enemy, not only to the poor and tempted, but to the business life of the place and the church itself. He spoke now with a freedom that seemed to measure his complete sense of conviction that
Jesus would speak so. At the close he pleaded with the people to remember the new life that had begun at the Rectangle. The regular
election of city officers was near at hand. The question of license
would be an issue in the election. What of the poor creatures surrounded by the hell of drink, while just beginning to feel the joy of
deliverance from sin? Who could tell what depended on their environment? Was there one word to be said by the Christian disciple, business man, citizen, in favor of continuing the license to crime and
shame-producing institutions? Was not the most Christian thing they
could do to act as citizens in the matter, fight the saloon at the polls,
elect good men to the city offices, and clean the municipality? How
much had prayers helped to make Raymond better while votes and
actions had really been on the side of the enemies of Jesus? Would not

Jesus do this? What disciple could imagine Him refusing to suffer or to take up His cross in this matter? How much had the members of the First Church ever suffered in an attempt to imitate Jesus? Was Christian discipleship a thing of conscience simply, of custom, of tradition? Where did the suffering come in? Was it necessary in order to follow Jesus' steps to go up Calvary as well as the Mount of Transfiguration?

His appeal was stronger at this point than he knew. It is not too much to say that the spiritual tension of the people reached this highest point right there. The imitation of Jesus which had begun with the volunteers in the church was working like leaven in the organization, and Henry Maxwell would even thus early in his life have been amazed if he could have measured the extent of desire on the part of his people to take up the cross. While he was speaking this morning, before he closed with a loving appeal to the discipleship of two thousand years' knowledge of the Master, many a man and woman in the church was saying as Rachel had said so passionately to her mother: "I want to do something that will cost me something in the way of sacrifice. I am hungry to suffer something." Truly, Mazzini was right when he said that no appeal is quite so powerful in the end as the call: "Come and suffer."

The service was over, the great audience had gone, and Maxwell again faced the company gathered in the lecture-room as on the two previous Sundays. He had asked all to remain who had made the pledge of discipleship, and any others who wished to be included. The after-service seemed now to be a necessity. As he went in and faced the people there his heart trembled. There were at least one hundred present. The Holy Spirit was never before so manifest. He missed Jasper Chase. But all the others were present. He asked Milton Wright to pray. The very air was charged with divine possibilities. What could resist such a baptism of power? How had they lived all these years without it?

They counseled together and there were many prayers. Henry Maxwell dated from that meeting some of the serious events that afterward became a part of the history of the First Church and of Raymond. When finally they went home, all of them were impressed with the glory of the Spirit's power.

Chapter 11

Donald Marsh, President of Lincoln College, walked home with Mr. Maxwell.

"I have reached one conclusion, Maxwell," said Marsh, speaking slowly. "I have found my cross and it is a heavy one, but I shall never be satisfied until I take it up and carry it." Maxwell was silent and the President went on.

"Your sermon today made clear to me what I have long been feeling I ought to do. 'What would Jesus do in my place?' I have asked the question repeatedly since I made my promise. I have tried to satisfy myself that He would simply go on as I have done, attending to the duties of my college work, teaching the classes in Ethics and Philosophy. But I have not been able to avoid the feeling that He would do something more. That something is what I do not want to do. It will cause me genuine suffering to do it. I dread it with all my soul. You may be able to guess what it is."

"Yes, I think I know. It is my cross too. I would almost rather do anything else."

Donald Marsh looked surprised, then relieved. Then he spoke sadly but with great conviction:

"Maxwell, you and I belong to a class of professional men who have always avoided the duties of citizenship. We have lived in a little world of literature and scholarly seclusion, doing work we have enjoyed and shrinking from the disagreeable duties that belong to the life of the citizen. I confess with shame that I have purposely avoided the responsibility that I owe to this city personally. I understand that our city officials are a corrupt, unprincipled set of men, controlled in large part by the whiskey element and thoroughly selfish so far as the affairs of city government are concerned. Yet all these years I, with nearly every teacher in the college, have been satisfied to let other men run the municipality and have lived in a little world of my own, out of touch and sympathy with the real world of the people. 'What would Jesus do?' I have even tried to avoid an honest answer. I can no longer do so. My plain duty is to take a personal part in this coming election, go to the primaries, throw the weight of my influence, whatever it is, toward the nomination and election of good men, and plunge into the very depths of the entire horrible whirlpool of deceit, bribery, political trickery and saloonism as it exists in Raymond today. I would sooner walk up to the mouth of a cannon any time than do this. I dread it because I hate the touch of the whole matter. I would give almost anything to be able to say, 'I do not believe Jesus would do anything of the sort.' But I am more and more persuaded that He would. This is where the suffering comes for me. It would not hurt me half so much to lose my position or my home. I loathe the contact with this municipal problem. I would so much prefer to remain quietly in my scholastic life with my classes in Ethics and Philosophy. But the call has come to me so plainly that I cannot escape. 'Donald Marsh, follow me. Do your duty as a citizen of Raymond at the point where your citizenship will cost you something. Help to cleanse this municipal stable, even if you do have to soil your aristocratic feelings a little.' Maxwell, this is my cross, I must take it up or deny my Lord."

"You have spoken for me also," replied Maxwell with a sad smile. "Why should I, simply because I am a minister, shelter myself behind my refined, sensitive feelings, and like a coward refuse to touch, except in a sermon possibly, the duty of citizenship? I am unused to the ways of the political life of the city. I have never taken an active part in any nomination of good men. There are hundreds of ministers like me. As a class we do not practice in the municipal life the duties and privileges we preach from the pulpit. 'What would Jesus do?' I am now at a point where, like you, I am driven to answer the question one way. My duty is plain. I must suffer. All my parish work, all my little trials or self-sacrifices are as nothing to me compared with the breaking into my scholarly, intellectual, self-contained habits, of this open, coarse, public fight for a clean city life. I could go and live at the Rectangle the rest of my life and work in the slums for a bare living, and I could enjoy it more than the thought of plunging into a fight for the reform of this whiskey-ridden city. It would cost me less. But, like you, I have been unable to shake off my responsibility. The answer to the question 'What would Jesus do?' in this case leaves me no peace except when I say, Jesus would have me act the part of a Christian citizen. Marsh, as you say, we professional men, ministers, professors, artists, literary men, scholars, have almost invariably been political cowards. We have avoided the sacred duties of citizenship either ignorantly or selfishly. Certainly Jesus in our age would not do that. We can do no less than take up this cross, and follow Him."

The two men walked on in silence for a while. Finally President Marsh said:

"We do not need to act alone in this matter. With all the men who have made the promise we certainly can have companionship, and strength even, of numbers. Let us organize the Christian forces of Raymond for the battle against rum and corruption. We certainly ought to enter the primaries with a force that will be able to do more than enter a protest. It is a fact that the saloon element is cowardly and easily frightened in spite of its lawlessness and corruption. Let us plan a campaign that will mean something because it is organized righteousness. Jesus would use great wisdom in this matter. He would employ means. He would make large plans. Let us do so. If we bear this cross let us do it bravely, like men."

They talked over the matter a long time and met again the next day in Maxwell's study to develop plans. The city primaries were called for Friday. Rumors of strange and unknown events to the average citizen were current that week in political circles throughout Raymond. The Crawford system of balloting for nominations was not in use in the state, and the primary was called for a public meeting at the court house.

The citizens of Raymond will never forget that meeting. It was so unlike any political meeting ever held in Raymond before, that there was no attempt at comparison. The special officers to be nominated were mayor, city council, chief of police, city clerk and city treasurer.

The evening *News* in its Saturday edition gave a full acccount of the primaries, and in the editorial columns Edward Norman spoke with a directness and conviction that the Christian people of Raymond were learning to respect deeply, because it was so evidently sincere and unselfish. A part of that editorial is also a part of this history. We quote the following:

"It is safe to say that never before in the history of Raymond was there a primary like the one in the court house last night. It was, first of all, a complete surprise to the city politicians who have been in the habit of carrying on the affairs of the city as if they owned them, and every one else was simply a tool or a cipher. The overwhelming surprise of the wire-pullers last night consisted in the fact that a large number of the citizens of Raymond who have heretofore taken no part in the city's affairs, entered the primary and controlled it, nominating some of the best men for all the offices to be filled at the coming election.

"It was a tremendous lesson in good citizenship. President Marsh of Lincoln College, who never before entered a city primary, and whose face was not even known to the ward politicians, made one of the best speeches ever made in Raymond. It was almost ludicrous to see the faces of the men who for years have done as they pleased, when President Marsh rose to speak. Many of them asked, 'Who is he?' The consternation deepened as the primary proceeded and it became evident that the old time ring of city rulers was outnumbered. Rev. Henry Maxwell of the First Church, Milton Wright, Alexander Powers, Professors Brown, Willard and Park of Lincoln College, Dr. West, Rev. George Main of the Pilgrim Church, Dean Ward of the Holy Trinity, and scores of well-known business men and professional men, most of them church members, were present, and it did not take long to see that they had all come with the one direct and definite purpose of nominating the best men possible. Most of those men had never before been seen in a primary. They were complete strangers to the politicians. But they had evidently profited by the politician's methods and were able by organized and united effort to nominate the entire ticket.

"As soon as it became plain that the primary was out of their control the regular ring withdrew in disgust and nominated another ticket. The *News* simply calls the attention of all decent citizens to the fact that this last ticket contains the names of whiskey men, and the line is sharply and distinctly drawn between the saloon and corrupt management such as we have known for years, and a clean, honest, capable, business-like city administration, such as every good citizen ought to want. It is not necessary to remind the people of Raymond that the question of local option comes up at the election. That will be the most important question on the ticket. The crisis of our city affairs has been reached. The issue is squarely before us. Shall we continue the rule of rum and boodle and shameless incompetency, or shall we, as President Marsh said in his noble speech, rise as good citizens and begin a new order of things, cleansing our city of the worst enemy known to municipal honesty, and doing what lies in our power to do with the ballot to purify our civic life?

"The *News* is positively and without reservation on the side of the new movement. We shall henceforth do all in our power to drive out the saloon and destroy its political strength. We shall advocate the election of the men nominated by the majority of citizens met in the first primary and we call upon all Christians, church members, lovers of right, purity, temperance, and the home, to stand by President Marsh and the rest of the citizens who have thus begun a long-needed reform in our city."

President Marsh read this editorial and thanked God for Edward Norman. At the same time he understood well enough that every other paper in Raymond was on the other side. He did not underestimate the importance and seriousness of the fight which was only just begun. It was no secret that the *News* had lost enormously since it had been governed by the standard of "What would Jesus do?" And the question was, Would the Christian people of Raymond stand by it? Would they make it possible for Norman to conduct a daily Christian paper? Or would the desire for what is called news in the way of crime, scandal, political partisanship of the regular sort, and a dislike to champion so remarkable a reform in journalism, influence them to drop the paper and refuse to give it their financial support? That was, in fact, the question Edward Norman was asking even while he wrote that Saturday editorial. He knew well enough that his action expressed in that editorial would cost him very heavily from the hands of many business men in Raymond. And still, as he drove his pen over the paper, he asked another question, "What would Jesus do?" That question had become a part of his whole life now. It was greater than any other.

But for the first time in its history Raymond had seen the professional men, the teachers, the college professors, the doctors, the ministers, take political action and put themselves definitely and sharply in public antagonism to the evil forces that had so long controlled the machine of the municipal government. The fact itself was astounding. President Marsh acknowledged to himself with a feeling of humiliation, that never before had he known what civic righteousness could accomplish. From that Friday night's work he dated for himself and his college a new definition of the worn phrase, "the scholar in politics." Education for him and those who were under his influence ever after meant some element of suffering. Sacrifice must now enter into the factor of development.

At the Rectangle that week the tide of spiritual life rose high, and as yet showed no signs of flowing back. Rachel and Virginia went every night. Virginia was rapidly reaching a conclusion with respect to a large part of her money. She had talked it over with Rachel and they had been able to agree that if Jesus had a vast amount of money at His disposal He might do with some of it as Virginia planned. At any rate they felt that whatever He might do in such case would have as large an element of variety in it as the differences in persons and circumstances. There could be no one fixed Christian way of using money. The rule that regulated its use was unselfish utility.

But meanwhile the glory of the Spirit's power possessed all their best thought. Night after night that week witnessed miracles as great as walking on the sea or feeding the multitude with a few loaves and fishes. For what greater miracle is there than a regenerate humanity? The transformation of these coarse, brutal, sottish lives into praying, rapturous lovers of Christ, struck Rachel and Virginia every time with the feeling that people may have had when they saw Lazarus walk out of the tomb. It was an experience full of profound excitement for them.

Rollin Page came to all the meetings. There was no doubt of the change that had come over him. Rachel had not yet spoken much with him. He was wonderfully quiet. It seemed as if he was thinking all the time. Certainly he was not the same person. He talked more with Gray than with any one else. He did not avoid Rachel, but he seemed to shrink from any appearance of seeming to wish to renew the acquaintance with her. Rachel found it even difficult to express to him her pleasure at the new life he had begun to know. He seemed to be waiting to adjust himself to his previous relations before this new life began. He had not forgotten those relations. But he was not yet able to fit his consciousness into new ones.

The end of the week found the Rectangle struggling hard between two mighty opposing forces. The Holy Spirit was battling with all His supernatural strength against the saloon devil which had so long held a jealous grasp on its slaves. If the Christian people of Raymond once could realize what the contest meant to the souls newly awakened to a purer life it did not seem possible that the election could result in the old system of license. But that remained yet to be seen. The horror of the daily surroundings of many of the converts was slowly burning its way into the knowledge of Virginia and Rachel, and every night as they went up town to their luxurious homes they carried heavy hearts.

"A good many of these poor creatures will go back again," Gray would say with sadness too deep for tears. "The environment does have a good deal to do with the character. It does not stand to reason that these people can always resist the sight and smell of the devilish drink about them. O Lord, how long shall Christian people continue to support by their silence and their ballots the greatest form of slavery known in America?"

He asked the question, and did not have much hope of an immediate answer. There was a ray of hope in the action of Friday night's primary, but what the result would be he did not dare to anticipate. The whiskey forces were organized, alert, aggressive, roused into unusual hatred by the events of the last week at the tent and in the city. Would the Christian forces act as a unit against the saloon? Or would they be divided on account of their business interests or because they were not in the habit of acting all together as the whiskey power always did? That remained to be seen. Meanwhile the saloon reared itself about the Rectangle like some deadly viper hissing and coiling, ready to strike its poison into any unguarded part.

Saturday afternoon as Virginia was just stepping out of her house to go and see Rachel to talk over her new plans, a carriage drove up containing three of her fashionable friends. Virginia went out to the drive-way and stood there talking with them. They had not come to make a formal call but wanted Virginia to go driving with them up on the boulevard. There was a band concert in the park. The day was too pleasant to be spent indoors.

"Where have you been all this time, Virginia?" asked one of the girls, tapping her playfully on the shoulder with a red silk parasol. "We hear that you have gone into the show business. Tell us about it."

Virginia colored, but after a moment's hesitation she frankly told something of her experience at the Rectangle. The girls in the carriage began to be really interested.

"I tell you, girls, let's go 'slumming' with Virginia this afternoon instead of going to the band concert. I've never been down to the Rectangle. I've heard it's an awful wicked place and lots to see. Virginia will act as a guide, and it would be"—"real fun" she was going to say, but Virginia's look made her substitute the word "interesting."

Virginia was angry. At first thought she said to herself she would never go under such circumstances. The other girls seemed to be of the same mind with the speaker. They chimed in with earnestness and asked Virginia to take them down there.

Suddenly she saw in the idle curiosity of the girls an opportunity. They had never seen the sin and misery of Raymond. Why should they not see it, even if their motive in going down there was simply to pass away an afternoon.

"Very well, I'll go with you. You must obey my orders and let me take you where you can see the most," she said, as she entered the carriage and took the seat beside the girl who had first suggested the trip to the Rectangle.

Chapter 12

For I come to set a man at variance against his father, and the daughter against her mother, and the daughter-in-law against her mother-in-law; and a man's foes shall be they of his own household.

Be ye therefore imitators of God, as beloved children; and walk in love, even as Christ also loved you.

"Hadn't we better take a policeman along?" said one of the girls with a nervous laugh. "It really isn't safe down there, you know."

"There's no danger," said Virginia briefly.

"Is it true that your brother Rollin has been converted?" asked the first speaker, looking at Virginia curiously. It impressed her during the drive to the Rectangle that all three of her friends were regarding her with close attention as if she were peculiar.

"Yes, he certainly is."

"I understand he is going around to the clubs talking with his old friends there, trying to preach to them. Doesn't that seem funny?" said the girl with the red silk parasol.

Virginia did not answer, and the other girls were beginning to feel sober as the carriage turned into a street leading to the Rectangle. As they neared the district they grew more and more nervous. The sights and smells and sounds which had become familiar to Virginia struck the senses of these refined, delicate society girls as something horrible. As they entered farther into the district, the Rectangle seemed to stare as with one great, bleary, beer-soaked countenance at this fine carriage with its load of fashionably dressed young women. "Slumming" had never been a fad with Raymond society, and this was perhaps the first time that the two had come together in this way. The girls felt that instead of seeing the Rectangle they were being made the objects of curiosity. They were frightened and disgusted.

"Let's go back. I've seen enough," said the girl who was sitting with Virginia.

They were at that moment just opposite a notorious saloon and gambling house. The street was narrow and the sidewalk crowded. Suddenly, out of the door of this saolon a young woman reeled. She was singing in a broken, drunken sob that seemed to indicate that she partly realized her awful condition, "Just as I am, without one plea"— and as the carriage rolled past she leered at it, raising her face so that Virginia saw it very close to her own. It was the face of the girl who had kneeled sobbing, that night with Virginia kneeling beside her and praying for her.

"Stop!" cried Virginia, motioning to the driver who was looking around. The carriage stopped, and in a moment she was out and had gone up to the girl and taken her by the arm. "Loreen!" she said, and that was all. The girl looked into her face, and her own changed into a look of utter horror. The girls in the carriage were smitten into helpless astonishment. The saloon-keeper had come to the door of the saloon and was standing there looking on with his hands on his hips. And the Rectangle from its windows, its saloon steps, its filthy sidewalk, gutter and roadway, paused and with undisguised wonder stared at the two girls. Over the scene the warm sun of spring poured its mellow light. A faint breath of music from the band-stand in the park floated into the Rectangle. The concert had begun, and the fashion and wealth of Raymond were displaying themselves up town on the boulevard.

When Virginia left the carriage and went up to Loreen she had no definite idea as to what she would do or what the result of her action would be. She simply saw a soul that had tasted of the joy of a better life slipping back again into its old hell of shame and death. And before she had touched the drunken girl's arm she had asked only one question, "What would Jesus do?" That question was becoming with her, as with many others, a habit of life.

She looked around now as she stood close by Loreen, and the whole scene was cruelly vivid to her. She thought first of the girls in the carriage.

"Drive on; don't wait for me. I am going to see my friend home," she said calmly enough.

The girl with the red parasol seemed to gasp at the word "friend," when Virginia spoke it. She did not say anything. The other girls seemed speechless.

"Go on. I cannot go back with you," said Virginia. The driver started the horses slowly. One of the girls leaned a little out of the carriage.

"Can't we—that is—do you want our help? Couldn't you—"

"No, no!" exclaimed Virginia. "You cannot be of any help to me."

The carriage moved on and Virginia was alone with her charge. She looked up and around. Many faces in the crowd were sympathetic.

They were not all cruel or brutal. The Holy Spirit had softened a good deal of the Rectangle.

"Where does she live?" asked Virginia.

No one answered. It occurred to Virginia afterward when she had time to think it over, that the Rectangle showed a delicacy in its sad silence that would have done credit to the boulevard. For the first time it flashed across her that the immortal being who was flung like wreckage upon the shore of this early hell called the saloon, had no place that could be called home. The girl suddenly wrenched her arm from Virginia's grasp. In doing so she nearly threw Virginia down.

"You shall not touch me! Leave me! Let me go to hell! That's where I belong! The devil is waiting for me. See him!" she exclaimed hoarse-ly. She turned and pointed with a shaking finger at the saloon-keeper. The crowd laughed. Virginia stepped up to her and put her arm about her.

"Loreen," she said firmly, "come with me. You do not belong to hell. You belong to Jesus and He will save you. Come."

The girl suddenly burst into tears. She was only partly sobered by the shock of meeting Virginia.

Virginia looked around again. "Where does Mr. Gray live?" she asked. She knew that the evangelist boarded somewhere near the tent. A number of voices gave the direction.

"Come, Loreen, I want you to go with me to Mr. Gray's," she said, still keeping her hold of the swaying, trembling creature who moaned and sobbed and now clung to her as firmly as before she had repulsed her.

So the two moved on through the Rectangle toward the evangelist's lodging place. The sight seemed to impress the Rectangle seriously. It never took itself seriously when it was drunk, but this was different. The fact that one of the richest, most beautifully-dressed girls in all Raymond was taking care of one of the Rectangle's most noted char-acters, who reeled along under the influence of liquor, was a fact as-tounding enough to throw more or less dignity and importance about Loreen herself. The event of Loreen's stumbling through the gutter dead-drunk always made the Rectangle laugh and jest. But Loreen staggering along with a young lady from the society circles up town supporting her, was another thing. The Rectangle viewed it with soberness and more or less wondering admiration.

When they finally reached Mr. Gray's lodging place the woman who answered Virginia's knock said that both Mr. and Mrs. Gray were out somewhere and would not be back until six o'clock.

Virginia had not planned anything farther than a possible appeal to the Grays, either to take charge of Loreen for a while or find some safe place for her until she was sober. She stood now at the door after the woman had spoken, and she was really at a loss to know what to do. Loreen sank down stupidly on the steps and buried her face in her arms. Virginia eyed the miserable figure of the girl with a feeling that she was afraid would grow into disgust.

Finally a thought possessed her that she could not escape. What was to hinder her from taking Loreen home with her? Why should not this homeless, wretched creature, reeking with the fumes of liquor, be cared for in Virginia's own home instead of being consigned to strangers in some hospital or house of charity? Virginia really knew very little about any such places of refuge. As a matter of fact, there were two or three such institutions in Raymond, but it is doubtful if any of them would have taken a person like Loreen in her present condition. But that was not the question with Virginia just now. "What would Jesus do with Loreen?" That was what Virginia faced, and she finally answered it by touching the girl again.

"Loreen, come. You are going home with me. We will take the car here at the corner."

Loreen staggered to her feet and, to Virginia's surprise, made no trouble. She had expected resistance or a stubborn refusal to move. When they reached the corner and took the car it was nearly full of people going up town. Virginia was painfully conscious of the stare that greeted her and her companion as they entered. But her thought was directed more and more to the approaching scene with her grandmother. What would Madam Page say?

Loreen was nearly sober now. But she was lapsing into a state of stupor. Virginia was obliged to hold fast to her arm. Several times the girl lurched heavily against her, and as the two went up the avenue a curious crowd of so-called civilized people turned and gazed at them. When she mounted the steps of her handsome house Virginia breathed a sigh of relief, even in the face of the interview with the grandmother, and when the door shut and she was in the wide hall with her homeless outcast, she felt equal to anything that might now come.

Madam Page was in the library. Hearing Virginia come in, she came into the hall. Virginia stood there supporting Loreen, who stared stupidly at the rich magnificence of the furnishings around her.

"Grandmother," Virginia spoke without hesitation and very clearly, "I have brought one of my friends from the Rectangle. She is in trouble and has no home. I am going to care for her here a little while."

Madam Page glanced from her granddaughter to Loreen in astonishment.

"Did you say she is one of your friends?" she asked in a cold, sneering voice that hurt Virginia more than anything she had yet felt.

"Yes, I said so." Virginia's face flushed, but she seemed to recall a verse that Mr. Gray had used for one of his recent sermons, "A friend of publicans and sinners." Surely, Jesus would do this that she was doing.

"Do you know what this girl is?" asked Madam Page, in an angry whisper, stepping near Virginia.

"I know very well. She is an outcast. You need not tell me, grandmother. I know it even better than you do. She is drunk at this minute. But she is also a child of God. I have seen her on her knees, repentant. And I have seen hell reach out its horrible fingers after her again. And by the grace of Christ I feel that the least that I can do is to rescue her from such peril. Grandmother, we call ourselves Christians. Here is a poor, lost human creature without a home, slipping back into a life of misery and possibly eternal loss, and we have more than enough. I have brought her here, and I shall keep her."

Madam Page glared at Virginia and clenched her hands. All this was contrary to her social code of conduct. How could society excuse familiarity with the scum of the streets? What would Virginia's action cost the family in the way of criticism and loss of standing, and all that long list of necessary relations which people of wealth and position must sustain to the leaders of society? To Madam Page society represented more than the church or any other institution. It was a power to be feared and obeyed. The loss of its good-will was a loss more to be dreaded than anything except the loss of wealth itself.

She stood erect and stern and confronted Virginia, fully aroused and determined. Virginia placed her arm about Loreen and calmly looked her grandmother in the face.

"You shall not do this, Virginia! You can send her to the asylum for helpless women. We can pay all the expenses. We cannot afford for the sake of our reputations to shelter such a person."

"Grandmother, I do not wish to do anything that is displeasing to you, but I must keep Loreen here tonight, and longer if it seems best."

"Then you can answer for the consequences! I do not stay in the same house with a miserable—" Madam Page lost her self-control. Virginia stopped her before she could speak the next word.

"Grandmother, this house is mine. It is your home with me as long as you choose to remain. But in this matter I must act as I fully believe Jesus would in my place. I am willing to bear all that society may say or do. Society is not my God. By the side of this poor soul I do not count the verdict of society as of any value."

"I shall not stay here, then!" said Madam Page. She turned suddenly and walked to the end of the hall. She then came back, and going up to Virginia said, with an emphasis that revealed her intense excitement of passion:

"You can always remember that you have driven your grandmother out of your house in favor of a drunken woman;" then, without waiting for Virginia to reply, she turned again and went upstairs. Virginia called a servant and soon had Loreen cared for. She was fast lapsing into a wretched condition. During the brief scene in the hall she had clung to Virginia so hard that her arm was sore from the clutch of the girl's fingers.

Virginia did not know whether her grandmother would leave the house or not. She had abundant means of her own, was perfectly well and vigorous and capable of caring for herself. She had sisters and brothers living in the South and was in the habit of spending several weeks in the year with them. Virginia was not anxious about her welfare as far as that went. But the interview had been a painful one. Going over it, as she did in her room before she went down to tea, she found little cause for regret. "What would Jesus do?" There was no question in her mind that she had done the right thing. If she had made a mistake, it was one of judgment, not of heart.

Chapter 13

When the bell rang for tea she went down and her grandmother did not appear. She sent a servant to her room who brought back word that Madam Page was not there. A few minutes later Rollin came in. He brought word that his grandmother had taken the evening train for the South. He had been at the station to see some friends off, and had by chance met his grandmother as he was coming out. She had told him her reason for going.

Virginia and Rollin comforted each other at the tea table, looking at each other with earnest, sad faces.

"Rollin," said Virginia, and for the first time, almost, since his conversion she realized what a wonderful thing her brother's changed life meant to her, "do you blame me? Am I wrong?"

"No, dear, I cannot believe you are. This is very painful for us. But if you think this poor creature owes her safety and salvation to your personal care, it was the only thing for you to do. Oh Virginia, to think that we have all these years enjoyed our beautiful home and all these luxuries selfishly, forgetful of the multitudes like this woman! Surely Jesus in our places would do what you have done."

And so Rollin comforted Virginia and counseled with her that evening. And of all the wonderful changes that she henceforth was to know on account of her great pledge, nothing affected her so powerfully as the thought of Rollin's change of life. Truly, this man in Christ was a new creature. Old things were passed away. Behold, all things in him had become new.

Dr. West came that evening at Virginia's summons and did everything necessary for the outcast. She had drunk herself almost into delirium. The best that could be done for her now was quiet nursing and careful watching and personal love. So, in a beautiful room, with a picture of Christ walking by the Sea hanging on the wall, where her bewildered eyes caught daily something more of its hidden meaning, Loreen lay, tossed she hardly knew how into this haven, and Virginia crept nearer the Master than she had ever been, as her heart went out towards this wreck which had thus been flung torn and beaten at her feet.

Meanwhile the Rectangle awaited the issue of the election with more than usual interest; and Mr. Gray and his wife wept over the poor, pitiful creatures who, after a struggle with surroundings that daily tempted them, too often wearied of the struggle and, like Loreen, threw up their arms and went whirling over the cataract into the boiling abyss of their previous condition.

The after-meeting at the First Church was now eagerly established. Henry Maxwell went into the lecture-room on the Sunday succeeding the week of the primary, and was greeted with an enthusiasm that made him tremble at first for its reality. He noted again the absence of Jasper Chase, but all the others were present, and they seemed drawn very close together by a bond of common fellowship that demanded and enjoyed mutual confidences. It was the general feeling that the spirit of Jesus was the spirit of very open, frank confession of experience. It seemed the most natural thing in the world, therefore, for Edward Norman to be telling all the rest of the company about the details of his newspaper.

"The fact is, I have lost a great deal of money during the last three weeks. I cannot tell just how much. I am losing a great many subscribers every day."

"What do the subscribers give as their reason for dropping the paper?" asked Mr. Maxwell. All the rest were listening eagerly.

"There are a good many different reasons. Some say they want a paper that prints all the news; meaning, by that, the crime details, sensations like prize fights, scandals and horrors of various kinds. Others object to the discontinuance of the Sunday edition. I have lost hundreds of subscribers by that action, although I have made satisfactory arrangements with many of the old subscribers by giving them even more in the extra Saturday edition than they formerly had in the Sunday issue. My greatest loss has come from a falling off in advertisements, and from the attitude I have felt obliged to take on political questions. The last action has really cost me more than any other. The bulk of my subscribers are intensely partisan. I may as well tell you all frankly that if I continue to pursue the plan which I honestly believe Jesus would pursue in the matter of political issues and their treatment from a non-partisan and moral standpoint, the *News* will not be able to pay its operating expenses unless one factor in Raymond can be depended on."

He paused a moment and the room was very quiet. Virginia seemed specially interested. Her face glowed with interest. It was like the interest of a person who had been thinking hard of the same thing which Norman went on to mention.

"That one factor is the Christian element in Raymond. Say the *News* has lost heavily from the dropping off of people who do not care for a Christian daily, and from others who simply look upon a newspaper as a purveyor of all sorts of material to amuse or interest them, are there enough genuine Christian people in Raymond who will rally to the support of a paper such as Jesus would probably edit? Or are the habits of the church people so firmly established in their demand for the regular type of journalism that they will not take a paper unless it is stripped largely of the Christian and moral purpose? I may say in this fellowship gathering that owing to recent complications in my business affairs outside of my paper I have been obliged to lose a large part of my fortune. I had to apply the same rule of Jesus' probable conduct to certain transactions with other men who did not apply it to their conduct, and the result has been the loss of a great deal of money. As I understand the promise we made, we were not to ask any question about 'Will it pay?' but all our action was to be based on the one question, 'What would Jesus do?' Acting on that rule of conduct, I have been obliged to lose nearly all the money I have accumulated in my paper. It is not necessary for me to go into details. There is no question with me now, after the three weeks' experience I have had, that a great many men would lose vast sums of money under the present system of business if this rule of Jesus was honestly applied. I mention my loss here because I have the fullest faith in the final success of a daily paper conducted on the lines I have recently laid down, and I had planned to put into it my entire fortune in order to win final success. As it is now, unless, as I said, the Christian people of Raymond, the church members and professing disciples, will support the paper with subscriptions and advertisements, I cannot continue its publication on the present basis."

Virginia asked a question. She had followed Mr. Norman's confession with the most intense eagerness.

"Do you mean that a Christian daily ought to be endowed with a large sum like a Christian college in order to make it pay?"

"That is exactly what I mean. I had laid out plans for putting into the *News* such a variety of material in such a strong and truly interesting way that it would more than make up for whatever was absent from its columns in the way of un-Christian matter. But my plans called for a very large output of money. I am very confident that a Christian daily such as Jesus would approve, containing only what He would print, can be made to succeed financially if it is planned on the right lines. But it will take a large sum of money to work out the plans."

"How much, do you think?" asked Virginia quietly.

Edward Norman looked at her keenly, and his face flushed a moment as an idea of her purpose crossed his mind. He had known her when she was a little girl in the Sunday-school, and he had been on intimate business relations with her father.

"I should say half a million dollars in a town like Raymond could be well spent in the establishment of a paper such as we have in mind," he answered. His voice trembled a little. The keen look on his grizzled face flashed out with a stern but thoroughly Christian anticipation of great achievements in the world of newspaper life, as it had opened up to him within the last few seconds.

"Then," said Virginia, speaking as if the thought was fully considered, "I am ready to put that amount of money into the paper on the one condition, of course, that it be carried on as it has been begun."

"Thank God!" exclaimed Mr. Maxwell softly. Norman was pale. The rest were looking at Virginia. She had more to say.

"Dear friends," she went on, and there was a sadness in her voice that made an impression on the rest that deepened when they thought it over afterwards, "I do not want any of you to credit me with an act of great generosity. I have come to know lately that the money which

I have called my own is not mine, but God's. If I, as steward of His, see some wise way to invest His money, it is not an occasion for vainglory or thanks from any one simply because I have proved honest in my administration of the funds He has asked me to use for His glory. I have been thinking of this very plan for some time. The fact is, dear friends, that in our coming fight with the whiskey power in Raymond —and it has only just begun—we shall need the *News* to champion the Christian side. You all know that all the other papers are for the saloon. As long as the saloon exists, the work of rescuing dying souls at the Rectangle is carried on at a terrible disadvantage. What can Mr. Gray do with his gospel meetings, when half his converts are drinking people, daily tempted and enticed by the saloon on every corner? It would be giving up to the enemy to allow the *News* to fail. I have great confidence in Mr. Norman's ability. I have not seen his plans, but I have the same confidence that he has in making the paper succeed if it is carried forward on a large enough scale. I cannot believe that Christian intelligence in journalism will be inferior to un-Christian intelligence, even when it comes to making the paper pay financially. So that is my reason for putting this money—God's, not mine—into this powerful agent for doing as Jesus would do. If we can keep such a paper going for one year, I shall be willing to see that amount of money used in that experiment. Do not thank me. Do not consider my doing it a wonderful thing. What have I done with God's money all these years but gratify my own selfish personal desires? What can I do with the rest of it but try to make some reparation for what I have stolen from God? That is the way I look at it now. I believe it is what Jesus would do."

Over the lecture-room swept that unseen yet distinctly felt wave of Divine Presence. No one spoke for a while. Mr. Maxwell standing there, where the faces lifted their intense gaze into his, felt what he had already felt—a strange setting back out of the nineteenth century into the first, when the disciples had all things in common, and a spirit of fellowship must have flowed freely between them such as the First Church of Raymond had never before known. How much had his church membership known of this fellowship in daily interests before this little company had begun to do as they believed Jesus would do? It was with difficulty that he thought of his present age and surroundings. The same thought was present with all the rest, also. There was an unspoken comradeship such as they had never known. It was present with them while Virginia was speaking, and during the silence that followed. If it had been defined by any of them it would perhaps have taken some such shape as this: "If I shall, in the course of my obedience to my promise, meet with loss or trouble in the world, I can de-

pend upon the genuine, practical sympathy and fellowship of any
other Christian in this room who has, with me, made the pledge to do
all things by the rule, 'What would Jesus do?' "

All this, the distinct wave of spiritual power emphasized. It had the
effect that a physical miracle may have had on the early disciples in
giving them a feeling of confidence in the Lord that helped them to
face loss and martyrdom with courage and even joy.

Before they went away this time there were several confidences like
those of Edward Norman's. Some of the young men told of loss of
places owing to their honest obedience to their promise. Alexander
Powers spoke briefly of the fact that the Commission had promised to
take action on his evidence at the earliest date possible.

He was engaged at his old work of telegraphy. It was a significant
fact that, since his action in resigning his position, neither his wife nor
daughter had appeared in public. No one but himself knew the bitterness of that family estrangement and misunderstanding of the higher
motive. Yet many of the disciples present in the meeting carried
similar burdens. These were things which they could not talk about.
Henry Maxwell, from his knowledge of his people, could almost certainly know that obedience to their pledge had produced in the heart
of families separation of sympathy and even the introduction of enmi-
ty and hatred. Truly, a man's foes are they of his own household
when the rule of Jesus is obeyed by some and disobeyed by others.
Jesus is a great divider of life. One must walk parallel with Him or
directly across His way.

Chapter 14

But more than any other feeling at this meeting rose the tide of fellowship for one another. Maxwell watched it, trembling for its climax
which he knew was not yet reached. When it was, where would it
lead them? He did not know, but he was not unduly alarmed about it.
Only he watched with growing wonder the results of that simple
promise as it was being obeyed in these various lives. Those results
were already being felt all over the city. Who could measure their
influence at the end of a year?

One practical form of this fellowship showed itself in the assurances which Edward Norman received of support for his paper. There was a general flocking toward him when the meeting closed, and the response to his appeal for help from the Christian disciples in Raymond was fully understood by this little company. The value of such a paper in the homes and in behalf of good citizenship, especially at the present crisis in the city, could not be measured. It remained to be seen what could be done now that the paper was endowed so liberally. But it still was true, as Norman insisted, that money alone could not make the paper a power. It must receive the support and sympathy of the Christians in Raymond before it could be counted as one of the great forces of the city.

The week that followed this Sunday meeting was one of great excitement in Raymond. It was the week of the election. President Marsh, true to his promise, took up his cross and bore it manfully, but with shuddering, with groans and even tears, for his deepest conviction was touched, and he tore himself out of the scholarly seclusion of years with a pain and anguish that cost him more than anything he had ever done as a follower of Christ. With him were a few of the college professors who had made the pledge in the First Church. Their experience and suffering were the same as his; for their isolation from all the duties of citizenship had been the same. The same was also true of Henry Maxwell, who plunged into the horror of this fight against whiskey and its allies with a sickening dread of each day's new encounter with it. For never before had he borne such a cross. He staggered under it, and in the brief intervals when he came in from the work and sought the quiet of his study for rest, the sweat broke out on his forehead, and he felt the actual terror of one who marches into unseen, unknown horrors. Looking back on it afterwards he was amazed at his experience. He was not a coward, but he felt the dread that any man of his habits feels when confronted suddenly with a duty which carries with it the doing of certain things so unfamiliar that the actual details connected with it betray his ignorance and fill him with the shame of humiliation.

When Saturday, the election day, came, the excitement rose to its height. An attempt was made to close all the saloons. It was only partly successful. There was a great deal of drinking going on all day. The Rectangle boiled and heaved and cursed and turned its worst side out to the gaze of the city. Gray had continued his meetings during the week, and the results had been even greater than he had dared to hope. When Saturday came, it seemed to him that the crisis in his work had been reached. The Holy Spirit and the Satan of rum seemed to rouse up to a desperate conflict. The more interest in the meetings, the more ferocity and vileness outside. The saloon men no longer concealed their feelings. Open threats of violence were made. Once during the week Gray and his little company of helpers were assailed with missiles of various kinds as they left the tent late at night. The police sent down a special force, and Virginia and Rachel were always under the protection of either Rollin or Dr. West. Rachel's power in song had not diminished. Rather, with each night, it seemed to add to the intensity and reality of the Spirit's presence.

Gray had at first hesitated about having a meeting that night. But he had a simple rule of action, and was always guided by it. The Spirit seemed to lead him to continue the meeting, and so Saturday night he went on as usual.

The excitement all over the city had reached its climax when the polls closed at six o'clock. Never before had there been such a contest in Raymond. The issue of license or no-license had never been an issue under such circumstances. Never before had such elements in the city been arrayed against each other. It was an unheard-of-thing that the President of Lincoln College, the pastor of the First Church, the Dean of the Cathedral, the professional men living in fine houses on the boulevard, should come personally into the wards, and by their presence and their example represent the Christian conscience of the place. The ward politicians were astonished at the sight. However, their astonishment did not prevent their activity. The fight grew hotter every hour, and when six o'clock came neither side could have guessed at the result with any certainty. Every one agreed that never before had there been such an election in Raymond, and both sides awaited the announcement of the result with the greatest interest.

It was after ten o'clock when the meeting at the tent was closed. It had been a strange and, in some respects, a remarkable meeting. Maxwell had come down again at Gray's request. He was completely worn out by the day's work, but the appeal from Gray came to him in such a form that he did not feel able to resist it. President Marsh was also present. He had never been to the Rectangle, and his curiosity was aroused from what he had noticed of the influence of the evangelist in the worst part of the city. Dr. West and Rollin had come with Rachel and Virginia; and Loreen, who still stayed with Virginia, was present near the organ, in her right mind, sober, with a humility and dread of herself that kept her as close to Virginia as a faithful dog. All through the service she sat with bowed head, weeping a part of the time, sobbing when Rachel sang the song, "I was a wandering sheep," clinging with almost visible, tangible yearning to the one hope she had found, listening to prayer and appeal and confession all about her like one who was a part of a new creation, yet fearful of her right to share in it fully.

The tent had been crowded. As on some other occasions, there was more or less disturbance on the outside. This had increased as the night advanced, and Gray thought it wise not to prolong the service.

Once in a while a shout as from a large crowd swept into the tent. The returns from the election were beginning to come in, and the Rectangle had emptied every lodging house, den and hovel into the streets.

In spite of these distractions Rachel's singing kept the crowd in the tent from dissolving. There were a dozen or more conversions. Finally the people became restless and Gray closed the service, remaining a little while with the converts.

Rachel, Virginia, Loreen, Rollin and the Doctor, President Marsh, Mr. Maxwell and Dr. West went out together, intending to go down to the usual waiting place for their car. As they came out of the tent they were at once aware that the Rectangle was trembling on the verge of a drunken riot, and as they pushed through the gathering mobs in the narrow streets they began to realize that they themselves were objects of great attention.

"There he is—the bloke in the tall hat! He's the leader!" shouted a rough voice. President Marsh, with his erect, commanding figure, was conspicuous in the little company.

"How has the election gone? It is too early to know the result yet, isn't it?" He asked the question aloud, and a man answered:

"They say second and third wards have gone almost solid for no-license. If that is so, the whiskey men have been beaten."

"Thank God! I hope it is true!" exclaimed Maxwell. "Marsh, we are in danger here. Do you realize our situation? We ought to get the ladies to a place of safety."

"That is true," said Marsh gravely. At that moment a shower of stones and other missiles fell over them. The narrow street and sidewalk in front of them was completely choked with the worst elements of the Rectangle.

"This looks serious," said Maxwell. With Marsh and Rollin and Dr. West he started to go forward through a small opening, Virginia, Rachel, and Loreen following close and sheltered by the men, who now realized something of their danger. The Rectangle was drunk and enraged. It saw in Marsh and Maxwell two of the leaders in the election contest which had perhaps robbed them of their beloved saloon.

"Down with the aristocrats!" shouted a shrill voice, more like a woman's than a man's. A shower of mud and stones followed. Rachel remembered afterwards that Rollin jumped directly in front of her and received on his head and chest a number of blows that would probably have struck her if he had not shielded her from them.

And just then, before the police reached them, Loreen darted forward in front of Virginia and pushed her aside, looking up and screaming. It was so sudden that no one had time to catch the face of the one who did it. But out of the upper window of a room, over the very saloon where Loreen had come out a week before, some one had thrown a heavy bottle. It struck Loreen on the head and she fell to the ground. Virginia turned and instantly kneeled down by her. The police officers by that time had reached the little company.

President Marsh raised his arm and shouted over the howl that was beginning to rise from the wild beast in the mob.

"Stop! You've killed a woman!" The announcement partly sobered the crowd.

"Is it true?" Maxwell asked it, as Dr. West kneeled on the other side of Loreen, supporting her.

"She's dying!" said Dr. West briefly.

Loreen opened her eyes and smiled at Virginia, who wiped the blood from her face and then bent over and kissed her. Loreen smiled again, and the next minute her soul was in Paradise.

And yet this is only one woman out of thousands killed by this drink evil. Crowd back, now, ye sinful men and women in this filthy street! Let this august dead form be borne through your stupefied, sobered ranks! She was one of your own children. The Rectangle had stamped the image of the beast on her. Thank Him who died for sinners that the other image of a new soul now shines out of her pale clay. Crowd back! Give them room! Let her pass reverently, followed and surrounded by the weeping, awestruck company of Christians. Ye killed her, ye drunken murderers! And yet—and yet—O Christian America, who killed this woman? Stand back! Silence, there! A woman has been killed. Who? Loreen. Child of the streets. Poor, drunken, vile sinner. O Lord God, how long, how long? Yes. The saloon killed her; that is, the Christians of America, who license the saloon. And the Judgment Day only shall declare who was the murderer of Loreen.

⸙⸙⸙⸙⸙⸙

Chapter 15

He that followeth me shall not walk in darkness.

The body of Loreen lay in state at the Page mansion on the avenue. It was Sunday morning and the clear sweet spring air, just beginning to breathe over the city the perfume of early blossoms in the woods and fields, swept over the casket from one of the open windows at the end of the grand hall. The church bells were ringing and people on the avenue going by to service turned curious, inquiring looks up at the great house and then went on, talking of the recent events which had so strangely entered into and made history in the city.

At the First Church, Mr. Maxwell, bearing on his face marks of the scene he had been through, confronted an immense congregation, and spoke to it with a passion and a power that came so naturally out of the profound experiences of the day before that his people felt for him something of the old feeling of pride they once had in his dramatic delivery. Only this was with a different attitude. And all through his impassioned appeal this morning, there was a note of sadness and rebuke and stern condemnation that made many of the members pale with self-accusation or with inward anger.

For Raymond had awakened that morning to the fact that the city had gone for license after all. The rumor at the Rectangle that the second and third wards had gone no-license proved to be false. It was true that the victory was won by a very meager majority. But the result was the same as if it had been overwhelming. Raymond had voted to continue for another year the saloon. The Christians of Raymond stood condemned by the result. More than a hundred professing Christian disciples had failed to go to the polls, and many more than that number had voted with the whiskey men. If all the church members of Raymond had voted against the saloon, it would today be outlawed instead of crowned king of the municipality. For that had been the fact in Raymond for years. The saloon ruled. No one denied that. What would Jesus do? And this woman who had been brutally struck down by the very hand that had assisted so eagerly to work her earthly ruin—what of her? Was it anything more than the logical sequence of the whole horrible system of license, that for another year the very saloon that received her so often and compassed her degradation, from whose very spot the weapon had been hurled that struck her dead, would, by the law which the Christian people of Raymond voted to support, perhaps open its doors tomorrow and damn a hundred Loreens before the year had drawn to its bloody close?

All this, with a voice that rang and trembled and broke in sobs of anguish for the result, did Henry Maxwell pour out upon his people that Sunday morning. And men and women wept as he spoke. President Marsh sat there, his usual erect, handsome, firm, bright self-confident bearing all gone; his head bowed upon his breast, the great tears rolling down his cheeks, unmindful of the fact that never before had he shown outward emotion in a public service. Edward Norman sat near by with his clear-cut, keen face erect, but his lip trembled and he clutched the end of the pew with a feeling of emotion that struck deep into his knowledge of the truth as Maxwell spoke it. No man had given or suffered more to influence public opinion that week than Norman. The thought that the Christian conscience had been aroused too late or too feebly, lay with a weight of accusation upon the heart of the editor. What if he had begun to do as Jesus would have done, long ago? Who could tell what might have been accomplished by this time! And up in the choir, Rachel Winslow, with her face bowed on the railing of the oak screen, gave way to a feeling which she had not allowed yet to master her, but it so unfitted her for her part that when Mr. Maxwell finished and she tried to sing the closing solo after the prayer, her voice broke, and for the first time in her life she was obliged to sit down, sobbing, and unable to go on.

Over the church, in the silence that followed this strange scene, sobs and the noise of weeping arose. When had the First Church yielded to such a baptism of tears? What had become of its regular, precise, conventional order of service, undisturbed by any vulgar emotion and unmoved by any foolish excitement? But the people had lately had their deepest convictions touched. They had been living so long on their surface feelings that they had almost forgotten the deeper wells of life. Now that they had broken the surface, the people were convicted of the meaning of their discipleship.

Mr. Maxwell did not ask, this morning, for volunteers to join those who had already pledged to do as Jesus would. But when the congregation had finally gone, and he had entered the lecture-room, it needed but a glance to show him that the original company of followers had been largely increased. The meeting was tender; it glowed with the Spirit's presence; it was alive with strong and lasting resolve to begin a war on the whiskey power in Raymond that would break its reign forever. Since the first Sunday when the first company of volunteers had pledged themselves to do as Jesus would do, the different meetings had been characterized by distinct impulses or impressions.

Today, the entire force of the gathering seemed to be directed to this one large purpose. It was a meeting full of broken prayers of contrition, of confession, of strong yearning for a new and better city life. And all through it ran one general cry for deliverance from the saloon and its awful curse.

But if the First Church was deeply stirred by the events of the last week, the Rectangle also felt moved strangely in its own way. The death of Loreen was not in itself so remarkable a fact. It was her recent acquaintance with the people from the city that lifted her into special prominence and surrounded her death with more than ordinary importance. Every one in the Rectangle knew that Loreen was at this moment lying in the Page mansion up on the avenue. Exaggerated reports of the magnificence of the casket had already furnished material for eager gossip. The Rectangle was excited to know the details of the funeral. Would it be public? What did Miss Page intend to do? The Rectangle had never before mingled even in this distant personal manner with the aristocracy on the boulevard. The opportunities for doing so were not frequent. Gray and his wife were besieged by inquirers who wanted to know what Loreen's friends and acquaintances were expected to do in paying their last respects to her. For her acquaintance was large and many of the recent converts were among her friends.

So that is how it happened that Monday afternoon, at the tent, the funeral service of Loreen was held before an immense audience that choked the tent and overflowed beyond all previous bounds. Gray had gone up to Virginia's and, after talking it over with her and Maxwell, the arrangements had been made.

"I am and always have been opposed to large public funerals," said Gray, whose complete wholesome simplicity of character was one of its great sources of strength; "but the cry of the poor creatures who knew Loreen is so earnest that I do not know how to refuse this desire to see her and pay her poor body some last little honor. What do you think, Mr. Maxwell? I will be guided by your judgment in the matter. I am sure that whatever you and Miss Page think best, will be right."

"I feel as you do," replied Mr. Maxwell. "Under the circumstances I have a great distaste for what seems like display at such times. But this seems different. The people at the Rectangle will not come here to service. I think the most Christian thing will be to let them have the service at the tent. Do you think so, Miss Virginia?"

"Yes," said Virginia. "Poor soul! I do not know but that sometime I shall know she gave her life for mine. We certainly cannot and will not use the occasion for vulgar display. Let her friends be allowed the gratification of their wishes. I see no harm in it."

So the arrangements were made, with some difficulty, for the service at the tent; and Virginia with her uncle and Rollin, accompanied by Maxwell, Rachel and President Marsh, and the quartet from the First Church, went down and witnessed one of the strange things of their lives.

It happened that that afternoon a somewhat noted newspaper correspondent was passing through Raymond on his way to an editorial convention in a neighboring city. He heard of the contemplated service at the tent and went down. His description of it was written in a graphic style that caught the attention of very many readers the next day. A fragment of his account belongs to this part of the history of Raymond:

"There was a very unique and unusual funeral service held here this afternoon at the tent of an evangelist, Rev. John Gray, down in the slum district known as the Rectangle. The occasion was caused by the killing of a woman during an election riot last Saturday night. It seems she had been recently converted during the evangelist's meetings, and was killed while returning from one of the meetings in company with other converts and some of her friends. She was a common street drunkard, and yet the services at the tent were as impressive as any I ever witnessed in a metropolitan church over the most distinguished citizen.

"In the first place, a most exquisite anthem was sung by a trained choir. It struck me, of course—being a stranger in the place—with considerable astonishment to hear voices like those one naturally expects to hear only in great churches or concerts, at such a meeting as this. But the most remarkable part of the music was a solo sung by a strikingly beautiful young woman, a Miss Winslow who, if I remember right, is the young singer who was sought for by Crandall the manager of National Opera, and who for some reason refused to accept his offer to go on the stage. She had a most wonderful manner in singing, and everybody was weeping before she had sung a dozen words. That, of course, is not so strange an effect to be produced at a funeral service, but the voice itself was one of thousands. I understand Miss Winslow sings in the First Church of Raymond and could probably command almost any salary as a public singer. She will probably be heard from soon. Such a voice could win its way anywhere.

"The service aside from the singing was peculiar. The evangelist, a man of apparently very simple, unassuming style, spoke a few words, and he was followed by a fine-looking man, the Rev. Henry Maxwell, pastor of the First Church of Raymond. Mr. Maxwell spoke of the fact that the dead woman had been fully prepared to go, but he spoke in a peculiarly sensitive manner of the effect of the liquor business on the lives of men and women like this one. Raymond, of course, being a railroad town and the centre of the great packing interests for this region, is full of saloons. I caught from the minister's remarks that he had only recently changed his views in regard to license. He certainly made a very striking address, and yet it was in no sense inappropriate for a funeral.

"Then followed what was perhaps the queer part of this strange service. The women in the tent, at least a large part of them up near the coffin, began to sing in a soft, tearful way, 'I was a wandering sheep.' Then while the singing was going on, one row of women stood up and walked slowly past the casket, and as they went by, each one placed a flower of some kind upon it. Then they sat down and another row filed past, leaving their flowers. All the time the singing continued softly like rain on a tent cover when the wind is gentle. It was one of the simplest and at the same time one of the most impressive sights I ever witnessed. The sides of the tent were up, and hundreds of people who could not get in, stood outside, all as still as death itself, with wonderful sadness and solemnity for such rough looking people. There must have been a hundred of these women, and I was told many of them had been converted at the meetings just recently. I cannot describe the effect of that singing. Not a man sang a note. All women's voices, and so soft, and yet so distinct, that the effect was startling.

"The service closed with another solo by Miss Winslow, who sang, 'There were ninety and nine.' And then the evangelist asked them all to bow their heads while he prayed. I was obliged in order to catch my train to leave during the prayer, and the last view I caught of the service as the train went by the shops was a sight of the great crowd pouring out of the tent and forming in open ranks while the coffin was borne out by six of the women. It is a long time since I have seen such a picture in this unpoetic Republic."

If Loreen's funeral impressed a passing stranger like this, it is not difficult to imagine the profound feelings of those who had been so intimately connected with her life and death. Nothing had ever entered the Rectangle that had moved it so deeply as Loreen's body in that coffin. And the Holy Spirit seemed to bless with special power the use of this senseless clay. For that night He swept more than a score of lost souls, mostly women, into the fold of the Good Shepherd.

It should be said here that Mr. Maxwell's statements concerning the opening of the saloon from whose windows Loreen had been killed, proved nearly exactly true. It was formally closed Monday and Tuesday while the authorities made arrests of the proprietors charged with the murder. But nothing could be proved against any one, and before Saturday of that week the saloon was running as regularly as ever. No one on the earth was ever punished by earthly courts for the murder of Loreen.

Chapter 16

No one in all Raymond, including the Rectangle, felt Loreen's death more keenly than Virginia. It came like a distinct personal loss to her. That short week while the girl had been in her home had opened Virginia's heart to a new life. She was talking it over with Rachel the day after the funeral. They were sitting in the hall of the Page mansion.

"I am going to do something with my money to help those women to a better life." Virginia looked over to the end of the hall where, the day before, Loreen's body had lain. "I have decided on a good plan, as it seems to me. I have talked it over with Rollin. He will devote a large part of his money also to the same plan."

"How much money have you, Virginia, to give in this way?" asked Rachel. Once, she would never have asked such a personal question. Now, it seemed as natural to talk frankly about money as about anything else that belonged to God.

"I have available for use at least four hundred and fifty thousand dollars. Rollin has as much more. It is one of his bitter regrets now that his extravagant habits of life before his conversion practically threw away half that father left him. We are both eager to make all the reparation in our power. 'What would Jesus do with this money?' We want to answer that question honestly and wisely. The money I shall put into the *News* is, I am confident, in a line with His probable action. It is as necessary that we have a Christian daily paper in Raymond, especially now that we have the saloon influence to meet, as it is to have a church or a college. So I am satisfied that the five hundred thousand dollars that Mr. Norman will know how to use so well will be a powerful factor in Raymond to do as Jesus would.

"About my other plan, Rachel, I want you to work with me. Rollin and I are going to buy up a large part of the property in the Rectangle. The field where the tent now is, has been in litigation for years. We mean to secure the entire tract as soon as the courts have settled the title. For some time I have been making a special study of the various forms of college settlements and residence methods of Christian work and Institutional church work in the heart of great city slums. I do not know that I have yet been able to tell just what is the wisest and most effective kind of work that can be done in Raymond. But I do know this much. My money—I mean God's, which he wants me to use—can build wholesome lodging-houses, refuges for poor women, asylums for shop girls, safety for many and many a lost girl like Loreen. And I do not want to be simply a dispenser of this money. God help me! I do want to put myself into the problem. But you know, Rachel, I have a feeling all the time that all that limitless money and limitless personal sacrifice can possibly do, will not really lessen very much the awful condition at the Rectangle as long as the saloon is legally established there. I think that is true of any Christian work now being carried on in any great city. The saloon furnishes material to be saved faster than the settlement or residence or rescue mission work can save it."

Virginia suddenly rose and paced the hall. Rachel answered sadly, and yet with a note of hope in her voice:

"It is true. But, Virginia, what a wonderful amount of good can be done with this money! And the saloon cannot always remain here. The time must come when the Christian forces in the city will triumph."

Virginia paused near Rachel, and her pale, earnest face lighted up.

"I believe that too. The number of those who have promised to do as Jesus would is increasing. If we once have, say, five hundred such disciples in Raymond, the saloon is doomed. But now, dear. I want you to look at your part in this plan for capturing and saving the Rectangle. Your voice is a power. I have had many ideas lately. Here is one of them. You could organize among the girls a Musical Institute; give them the benefit of your training. There are some splendid voices in the rough there. Did any one ever hear such singing as that yesterday by those women? Rachel, what a beautiful opportunity! You shall have the best of material in the way of organs and orchestras that money can provide, and what cannot be done with music to win souls there into higher and purer and better living?"

Before Virginia had ceased speaking, Rachel's face was perfectly transformed with the thought of her life work. It flowed into her heart and mind like a flood, and the torrent of her feeling overflowed in tears that could not be restrained. It was what she had dreamed of doing herself. It represented to her something that she felt was in keeping with a right use of her talent.

"Yes," she said, as she rose and put her arm about Virginia, while both girls in the excitement of their enthusiasm paced the hall. "Yes, I will gladly put my life into that kind of service. I do believe that Jesus would have me use my life in this way. Virginia, what miracles can we not accomplish in humanity if we have such a lever as consecrated money to move things with!"

"Add to it consecrated personal enthusiasm like yours, and it certainly can accomplish great things," said Virginia smiling. And before Rachel could reply, Rollin came in.

He hesitated a moment, and then was passing out of the hall into the library when Virginia called him back and asked some questions about his work.

Rollin came back and sat down, and together the three discussed their future plans. Rollin was apparently entirely free from embarrassment in Rachel's presence while Virginia was with them, only his manner with her was almost precise, if not cold. The past seemed to have been entirely absorbed in his wonderful conversion. He had not forgotten it, but he seemed to be completely caught up for this present time in the purpose of his new life. After a while Rollin was called out, and Rachel and Virginia began to talk of other things.

"By the way, what has become of Jasper Chase?" Virginia asked the question innocently, but Rachel flushed and Virginia added with a smile, "I suppose he is writing another book. Is he going to put you into this one, Rachel? You know I always suspected Jasper Chase of doing that very thing in his first story."

"Virginia," Rachel spoke with the frankness that had always existed between the two friends, "Jasper Chase told me the other night that he—in fact—he proposed to me—or he would, if—"

Rachel stopped and sat with her hands clasped on her lap, and there were tears in her eyes.

"Virginia, I thought a little while ago I loved him, as he said he loved me. But when he spoke, my heart felt repelled, and I said what I ought to say. I told him no. I have not seen him since. That was the night of the first conversions at the Rectangle."

"I am glad for you," said Virginia quietly.

"Why?" asked Rachel a little startled.

"Because, I have never really liked Jasper Chase. He is too cold and —I do not like to judge him, but I have always distrusted his sincerity in taking the pledge at the church with the rest."

Rachel looked at Virginia thoughtfully.

"I have never given my heart to him, I am sure. He touched my emotions, and I admired his skill as a writer. I have thought at times that I cared a good deal for him. I think perhaps if he had spoken to me at any other time than the one he chose, I could easily have persuaded myself that I loved him. But not now."

Again Rachel paused suddenly, and when she looked up at Virginia again there were tears on her face. Virginia came to her and put her arm about her tenderly.

When Rachel had left the house, Virginia sat in the hall thinking over the confidence her friend had just shown her. There was something still to be told, Virginia felt sure from Rachel's manner, but she did not feel hurt that Rachel had kept back something. She was simply conscious of more on Rachel's mind than she had revealed.

Very soon Rollin came back, and he and Virginia, arm in arm as they had lately been in the habit of doing, walked up and down the long hall. It was easy for their talk to settle finally upon Rachel because of the place she was to occupy in the plans which were being made for the purchase of property at the Rectangle.

"Did you ever know of a girl of such really gifted powers in vocal music who was willing to give her life to the people as Rachel is going to do? She is going to give music lessons in the city, have private pupils to make her living, and then give the people in the Rectangle the benefit of her culture and her voice."

"It is certainly a very good example of self-sacrifice," replied Rollin a little stiffly.

Virginia looked at him a little sharply. "But don't you think it is a very unusual example? Can you imagine—" here Virginia named half a dozen famous opera singers—"doing anything of this sort?"

"No, I cannot," Rollin answered briefly. "Neither can I imagine Miss—" he spoke the name of the girl with the red parasol who had begged Virginia to take the girls to the Rectangle—"doing what you are doing, Virginia."

"Any more than I can imagine Mr.—" Virginia spoke the name of a young society leader—"going about to the clubs doing your work, Rollin." The two walked on in silence for the length of the hall.

"Coming back to Rachel," began Virginia, "Rollin, why do you treat her with such a distinct, precise manner? I think, Rollin—pardon me if I hurt you—that she is annoyed by it. You need to be on easy terms. I don't think Rachel likes this change."

Rollin suddenly stopped. He seemed deeply agitated. He took his arm from Virginia's and walked alone to the end of the hall. Then he returned, with his hands behind him, and stopped near his sister and said, "Virginia, have you not learned my secret?"

Virginia looked bewildered, then over her face the unusual color crept, showing that she understood.

"I have never loved any one but Rachel Winslow." Rollin spoke calmly enough now. "That day she was here when you talked about her refusal to join the concert company, I asked her to be my wife; out there on the avenue. She refused me, as I knew she would. And she gave as her reason the fact that I had no purpose in life, which was true enough. Now that I have a purpose, now that I am a new man, don't you see, Virginia, how impossible it is for me to say anything? I owe my very conversion to Rachel's singing. And yet that night while she sang I can honestly say that, for the time being, I never thought of her voice except as God's message. I believe that all my personal love for her was for the time merged into a personal love to my God and my Saviour." Rollin was silent, then he went on with more emotion. "I still love her, Virginia. But I do not think she ever could love me." He stopped and looked his sister in the face with a sad smile.

"I don't know about that," said Virginia to herself. She was noting Rollin's handsome face, his marks of dissipation nearly all gone now, the firm lips showing manhood and courage, the clear eyes looking into hers frankly, the form strong and graceful. Rollin was a man now. Why should not Rachel come to love him in time? Surely the two were well fitted for each other, especially now that their purpose in life was moved by the same Christian force.

She said something of all this to Rollin, but he did not find much comfort. When they closed the interview, Virginia carried away the impression that Rollin meant to go his way with his chosen work, trying to reach the fashionable men at the clubs, and while not avoiding Rachel, seeking no occasions for meeting her. He was distrustful of his power to control his feeling. And Virginia could see that he dreaded even the thought of a second refusal in case he did let Rachel know that his love was still the same.

Chapter 17

The next day she went down to the *News* office to see Edward Norman and arrange the details of her part in the establishment of the paper on its new foundation. Mr. Maxwell was present at this conference, and the three agreed that whatever Jesus would do in detail as editor of a daily paper, He would be guided by the same general principles that directed His conduct as the Saviour of the world.

"I have tried to put down here in concrete form some of the things that it has seemed to me Jesus would do," said Edward Norman. He read from a paper lying on his desk, and Maxwell was reminded again of his own effort to put into written form his own conception of Jesus' probable action, and also of Milton Wright's same attempt in his business.

"I have headed this, 'What would Jesus do as Edward Norman, editor of a daily newspaper in Raymond?'

"1. He would never allow a sentence or a picture in his paper that could be called bad or coarse or impure in any way.

"2. He would probably conduct the political part of the paper from the standpoint of non-partisan patriotism, always looking upon all political questions in the light of their relation to the Kingdom of God, and advocating measures from the standpoint of their relation to the welfare of the people, always on the basis of 'What is right?' never on the basis of 'What is for the best interest of this or that party?' In other words, He would treat all political questions as He would treat every other subject, from the standpoint of the advancement of the Kingdom of God on earth."

Edward Norman looked up from the reading a moment. "You understand that is my opinion of Jesus' probable action on political matters in a daily paper. I am not passing judgment on other newspaper men who may have a different conception of Jesus' probable action from mine. I am simply trying to answer honestly, 'What would Jesus do as Edward Norman?' And the answer I find is what I have put down.

"3. The end and aim of a daily paper conducted by Jesus would be to do the will of God. That is, His main purpose in carrying on a newspaper would not be to make money, or gain political influence; but His first and ruling purpose would be to so conduct his paper that it would be evident to all his subscribers that He was trying to seek first the Kingdom of God by means of His paper. This purpose would be as distinct and unquestioned as the purpose of a minister or a missionary or any unselfish martyr in Christian work anywhere.

"4. All questionable advertisements would be impossible.

"5. The relations of Jesus to the employees on the paper would be of the most loving character.

"So far as I have gone," said Norman again looking up, "I am of the opinion that Jesus would employ practically some form of co-operation that would represent the idea of a mutual interest in a business where all were to move together for the same great end. I am working out such a plan, and I am confident it will be successful. At any rate, once introduce the element of personal love into a business like this, take out the selfish principle of doing it for personal profits to a man or company, and I do not see any way except the most loving personal interest between editors, reporters, pressmen, and all who contribute anything to the life of the paper. And that interest would be expressed not only in the personal love and sympathy but in a sharing with the profits of the business.

"6. As editor of a daily paper today, Jesus would give large space to the work of the Christian world. He would devote a page possibly to the facts of Reform, of sociological problems, of institutional church work and similar movements.

"7. He would do all in His power in His paper to fight the saloon as an enemy of the human race and an unnecessary part of our civilization. He would do this regardless of public sentiment in the matter and, of course, always regardless of its effect upon His subscription list."

Again Edward Norman looked up. "I state my honest conviction on this point. Of course, I do not pass judgment on the Christian men who are editing other kinds of papers today. But as I interpret Jesus, I believe He would use the influence of His paper to remove the saloon entirely from the political and social life of the nation.

"8. Jesus would not issue a Sunday edition.

"9. He would print the news of the world that people ought to know. Among the things they do not need to know, and which would not be published, would be accounts of brutal prize fights, long accounts of crimes, scandals in private families, or any other human events which in any way would conflict with the first point mentioned in this outline.

"10. If Jesus had the amount of money to use on a paper which we have, He would probably secure the best and strongest Christian men and women to co-operate with him in the matter of contributions. That will be my purpose, as I shall be able to show you in a few days.

"11. Whatever the details of the paper might demand as the paper developed along its definite plan, the main principle that guided it would always be the establishment of the Kingdom of God in the world. This large general principle would necessarily shape all the detail."

Edward Norman finished reading the plan. He was very thoughtful.

"I have merely sketched a faint outline. I have a hundred ideas for making the paper powerful that I have not thought out fully as yet. This is simply suggestive. I have talked it over with other newspaper men. Some of them say I will have a weak, namby-pamby Sunday-school sheet. If I get out something as good as a Sunday-school it will be pretty good. Why do men, when they want to characterize something as particularly feeble, always use a Sunday-school as a comparison, when they ought to know that the Sunday-school is one of the strongest, most powerful influences in our civilization in this country today? But the paper will not necessarily be weak because it is good. Good things are more powerful than bad. The question with me is largely one of support from the Christian people of Raymond. There are over twenty thousand church members here in this city. If half of them will stand by the *News* its life is assured. What do you think, Maxwell, of the probability of such support?"

"I don't know enough about it to give an intelligent answer. I believe in the paper with all my heart. If it lives a year, as Miss Virginia said, there is no telling what it can do. The great thing will be to issue such a paper, as near as we can judge, as Jesus probably would, and put into it all the elements of Christian brains, strength, intelligence and sense; and command respect for freedom from bigotry, fanaticism, narrowness in anything else that is contrary to the spirit of Jesus. Such a paper will call for the best that human thought and action is capable of giving. The greatest minds in the world would have their powers taxed to the utmost to issue a Christian daily."

"Yes," Edward Norman spoke humbly. "I shall make a great many mistakes, no doubt. I need a great deal of wisdom. But I want to do as Jesus would. 'What would He do?' I have asked it, and shall continue to do so, and abide by the results."

"I think we are beginning to understand," said Virginia, "the meaning of that command, 'Grow in the grace and knowledge of our Lord and Saviour Jesus Christ.' I am sure I do not know all that He would do in detail until I know Him better."

"That is very true," said Henry Maxwell. "I am beginning to understand that I cannot interpret the probable action of Jesus until I know better what His spirit is. The greatest question in all of human life is summed up when we ask, 'What would Jesus do?' if, as we ask it, we also try to answer it from a growth in knowledge of Jesus Himself. We must know Jesus before we can imitate Him."

When the arrangement had been made between Virginia and Edward Norman, he found himself in possession of the sum of five hundred thousand dollars to use for the establishment of a Christian daily paper. When Virginia and Maxwell had gone, Norman closed his door and, alone with the Divine Presence, asked like a child for help from his all-powerful Father. All through his prayer as he knelt before his desk ran the promise, "If any man lack wisdom, let him ask of God who giveth to all men liberally and upbraideth not, and it shall be given him." Surely his prayer would be answered, and the kingdom advanced through this instrument of God's power, this mighty press, which had become so largely degraded to the base uses of man's avarice and ambition.

Two months went by. They were full of action and of results in the city of Raymond and especially in the First Church. In spite of the approaching heat of the summer season, the after-meeting of the disciples who had made the pledge to do as Jesus would do, continued with enthusiasm and power. Gray had finished his work at the Rectangle, and an outward observer going through the place could not have seen any difference in the old conditions, although there was an actual change in hundreds of lives. But the saloons, dens, hovels, gambling houses, still ran, overflowing their vileness into the lives of fresh victims to take the place of those rescued by the evangelist. And the devil recruited his ranks very fast.

Henry Maxwell did not go abroad. Instead of that, he took the money he had been saving for the trip and quietly arranged for a summer vacation for a whole family living down in the Rectangle, who had never gone outside of the fowl district of the tenements. The pastor of the First Church will never forget the week he spent with this family making the arrangements. He went down into the Rectangle one hot day when something of the terrible heat in the horrible tenements was beginning to be felt, and helped the family to the station, and then went with them to a beautiful spot on the coast where, in the home of a Christian woman, the bewildered city tenants breathed for the first time in years the cool salt air, and felt blow about them the pine-scented fragrance of a new lease of life.

There was a sickly babe with the mother, and three other children, one a cripple. The father, who had been out of work until he had been, as he afterwards confessed to Maxwell, several times on the edge of suicide, sat with the baby in his arms during the journey, and when Maxwell started back to Raymond, after seeing the family settled, the man held his hand at parting, and choked with his utterance, and finally broke down, to Maxwell's great confusion. The mother, a wearied, worn-out woman who had lost three children the year before from a fever scourge in the Rectangle, sat by the car window all the way and drank in the delights of sea and sky and field. It all seemed a miracle to her. And Maxwell, coming back into Raymond at the end of that week, feeling the scorching, sickening heat all the more because of his little taste of the ocean breezes, thanked God for the joy he had witnessed, and entered upon his discipleship with a humble heart, knowing for almost the first time in his life this special kind of sacrifice. For never before had he denied himself his regular summer trip away from the heat of Raymond, whether he felt in any great need of rest or not.

"It is a fact," he said in reply to several inquiries on the part of his church, "I do not feel in need of a vacation this year. I am very well and prefer to stay here." It was with a feeling of relief that he succeeded in concealing from every one but his wife what he had done with this other family. He felt the need of doing anything of that sort without display or approval from others.

So the summer came on, and Maxwell grew into a large knowledge of his Lord. The First Church was still swayed by the power of the Spirit. Maxwell marveled at the continuance of His stay. He knew very well that from the beginning nothing but the Spirit's presence had kept the church from being torn asunder by the remarkable testing it had received of its discipleship. Even now there were many of the members among those who had not taken the pledge, who regarded the whole movement as Mrs. Winslow did, in the nature of a fanatical interpretation of Christian duty, and looked for the return of the old normal condition. Meanwhile the whole body of disciples was under the influence of the Spirit, and the pastor went his way that summer, doing his parish work in great joy, keeping up his meetings with the railroad men as he had promised Alexander Powers, and daily growing into a better knowledge of the Master.

Early one afternoon in August, after a day of refreshing coolness following a long period of heat, Jasper Chase walked to his window in the apartment house on the avenue and looked out.

On his desk lay a pile of manuscript. Since that evening when he had spoken to Rachel Winslow he had not met her. His singularly sensitive nature—sensitive to the point of extreme irritability when he was thwarted—served to thrust him into an isolation that was intensified by his habits as an author.

All through the heat of summer he had been writing. His book was nearly done now. He had thrown himself into its construction with a feverish strength that threatened at any moment to desert him and leave him helpless. He had not forgotten his pledge made with the other church members at the First Church. It had forced itself upon his notice all through his writing, and ever since Rachel had said no to him, he had asked a thousand times, "Would Jesus do this? Would He write this story?" It was a social novel, written in a style that had proved popular. It had no purpose except to amuse. Its moral teaching was not bad, but neither was it Christian in any positive way. Jasper Chase knew that such a story would probably sell. He was conscious of powers in this way that the social world petted and admired. "What would Jesus do?" He felt that Jesus would never write such a book. The question obtruded on him at the most inopportune times. He became irascible over it. The standard of Jesus for an author was too ideal. Of course, Jesus would use His powers to produce something useful or helpful, or with a purpose. What was he, Jasper Chase, writing this novel for? Why, what nearly every writer wrote for—money, money, and fame as a writer. There was no secret with him that he was writing this new story with that object. He was not poor, and so had no great temptation to write for money. But he was urged on by his desire for fame as much as anything. He must write this kind of matter. But what would Jesus do? The question plagued him even more than Rachel's refusal.

Was he going to break his promise? "Did the promise mean much after all?" he asked.

As he stood at the window, Rollin Page came out of the club house just opposite. Jasper noted his handsome face and noble figure as he started down the street. He went back to his desk and turned over some papers there. Then he came back to the window. Rollin was walking down past the block and Rachel Winslow was walking beside him. Rollin must have overtaken her as she was coming from Virginia's that afternoon.

Jasper watched the two figures until they disappeared in the crowd on the walk. Then he turned to his desk and began to write. When he had finished the last page of the last chapter of his book it was nearly dark. "What would Jesus do?" He had finally answered the question by denying his Lord. It grew darker in his room. He had deliberately chosen his course, urged on by his disappointment and loss.

"But Jesus said unto him, no man having put his hand to the plow, and looking back, is fit for the Kingdom of God."

Chapter 18

What is that to thee? Follow thou Me.

When Rollin started down the street the afternoon that Jasper stood looking out of his window he was not thinking of Rachel Winslow and did not expect to see her anywhere. He had come suddenly upon her as he turned into the avenue and his heart had leaped up at the sight of her. He walked along by her now, rejoicing after all in a little moment of this earthly love he could not drive out of his life.

"I have just been over to see Virginia," said Rachel. "She tells me the arrangements are nearly completed for the transfer of the Rectangle property."

"Yes. It has been a tedious case in the courts. Did Virginia show you all the plans and specifications for building?"

"We looked over a good many. It is astonishing to me where Virginia has managed to get all her ideas about this work."

"Virginia knows more now about Arnold Toynbee and East End London and Institutional Church work in America than a good many professional slum workers. She has been spending nearly all summer in getting information." Rollin was beginning to feel more at ease as they talked over this coming work of humanity. It was safe, common ground.

"What have you been doing all summer? I have not seen much of you," Rachel suddenly asked, and then her face warmed with its quick flush of tropical color as if she might have implied too much interest in Rollin or too much regret at not seeing him oftener.

"I have been busy," replied Rollin briefly.

"Tell me something about it," persisted Rachel. "You say so little. Have I a right to ask?"

She put the question very frankly, turning toward Rollin in real earnest.

"Yes, certainly," he replied, with a graceful smile. "I am not so certain that I can tell you much. I have been trying to find some way to reach the men I once knew and win them into more useful lives."

He stopped suddenly as if he were almost afraid to go on. Rachel did not venture to suggest anything.

"I have been a member of the same company to which you and Virginia belong," continued Rollin, beginning again. "I have made the pledge to do as I believe Jesus would do, and it is in trying to answer this question that I have been doing my work."

"That is what I do not understand. Virginia told me about the other. It seems wonderful to think that you are trying to keep that pledge with us. But what can you do with the club men?"

"You have asked me a direct question and I shall have to answer it now," replied Rollin, smiling again. "You see, I asked myself after that night at the tent, you remember" (he spoke hurriedly and his voice trembled a little), "what purpose I could now have in my life to redeem it, to satisfy my thought of Christian discipleship? And the more I thought of it, the more I was driven to a place where I knew I must take up the cross. Did you ever think that of all the neglected beings in our social system none are quite so completely left alone as the fast young men who fill the clubs and waste their time and money as I used to? The churches look after the poor, miserable creatures like those in the Rectangle; they make some effort to reach the working man, they have a large constituency among the average salary-earning people, they send money and missionaries to the foreign heathen, but the fashionable, dissipated young men around town, the club men, are left out of all plans for reaching and Christianizing. And yet no class of people need it more. I said to myself: 'I know these men, their good and their bad qualities. I have been one of them. I am not fitted to reach the Rectangle people. I do not know how. But I think I could possibly reach some of the young men and boys who have money and time to spend.' So that is what I have been trying to do. When I asked as you did, 'What would Jesus do?' that was my answer. It has been also my cross."

Rollin's voice was so low on this last sentence that Rachel had difficulty in hearing him above the noise around them. But she knew what he had said. She wanted to ask what his methods were. But she did not know how to ask him. Her interest in his plan was larger than mere curiosity. Rollin Page was so different now from the fashionable young man who had asked her to be his wife that she could not help thinking of him and talking with him as if he were an entirely new acquaintance.

They had turned off the avenue and were going up the street to Rachel's home. It was the same street where Rollin had asked Rachel why she could not love him. They were both stricken with a sudden shyness as they went on. Rachel had not forgotten that day and Rollin could not. She finally broke a long silence by asking what she had not found words for before.

"In your work with the club men, with your old acquaintances, what sort of reception do they give you? How do you approach them? What do they say?"

Rollin was relieved when Rachel spoke. He answered quickly:

"Oh, it depends on the man. A good many of them think I am a crank. I have kept my membership up and am in good standing in that way. I try to be wise and not provoke any unnecessary criticism. But you would be surprised to know how many of the men have responded to my appeal. I could hardly make you believe that only a few nights ago a dozen men became honestly and earnestly engaged in a conversation over religious matters. I have had the great joy of seeing some of the men give up bad habits and begin a new life. 'What would Jesus do?' I keep asking it. The answer comes slowly, for I am feeling my way slowly. One thing I have found out. The men are not fighting shy of me. I think that is a good sign. Another thing: I have actually interested some of them in the Rectangle work, and when it is started up they will give something to help make it more powerful. And in addition to all the rest, I have found a way to save several of the young fellows from going to the bad in gambling."

Rollin spoke with enthusiasm. His face was transformed by his interest in the subject which had now become a part of his real life. Rachel again noted the strong, manly tone of his speech. With it all she knew there was a deep, underlying seriousness which felt the burden of the cross even while carrying it with joy. The next time she spoke it was with a swift feeling of justice due to Rollin and his new life.

"Do you remember I reproached you once for not having any purpose worth living for?" she asked, while her beautiful face seemed to Rollin more beautiful than ever when he had won sufficient self-control to look up. "I want to say, I feel the need of saying, in justice to you now, that I honor you for your courage and your obedience to the promise you have made as you interpret the promise. The life you are living is a noble one."

Rollin trembled. His agitation was greater than he could control. Rachel could not help seeing it. They walked along in silence. At last Rollin said:

"I thank you. It has been worth more to me than I can tell you to hear you say that." He looked into her face for one moment. She read his love for her in that look, but he did not speak.

When they separated Rachel went into the house and, sitting down in her room, she put her face in her hands and said to herself: "I am beginning to know what it means to be loved by a noble man. I shall love Rollin Page after all. What am I saying! Rachel Winslow, have you forgotten—"

She rose and walked back and forth. She was deeply moved. Nevertheless, it was evident to herself that her emotion was not that of regret or sorrow. Somehow a glad new joy had come to her. She had entered another circle of experience, and later in the day she rejoiced with a very strong and sincere gladness that her Christian discipleship found room in this crisis for her feeling. It was indeed a part of it, for if she was beginning to love Rollin Page it was the Christian man she had begun to love; the other never would have moved her to this great change.

And Rollin, as he went back, treasured a hope that had been a stranger to him since Rachel had said no that day. In that hope he went on with his work as the days sped on, and at no time was he more successful in reaching and saving his old acquaintances than in the time that followed that chance meeting with Rachel Winslow.

The summer had gone and Raymond was once more facing the rigor of her winter season. Virginia had been able to accomplish a part of her plan for "capturing the Rectangle," as she called it. But the building of houses in the field, the transforming of its bleak, bare aspect into an attractive park, all of which was included in her plan, was a work too large to be completed that fall after she had secured the property. But a million dollars in the hands of a person who truly wants to do with it as Jesus would, ought to accomplish wonders for humanity in a short time, and Henry Maxwell, going over to the scene of the new work one day after a noon hour with the shop men, was amazed to see how much had been done outwardly.

Yet he walked home thoughtfully, and on his way he could not avoid the question of the continual problem thrust upon his notice by the saloon. How much had been done for the Rectangle after all? Even counting Virginia's and Rachel's work and Mr. Gray's, where had it actually counted in any visible quantity? Of course, he said to himself, the redemptive work begun and carried on by the Holy Spirit in His wonderful displays of power in the First Church and in the tent meetings had had its effect upon the life of Raymond. But as he walked past saloon after saloon and noted the crowds going in and coming out of them, as he saw the wretched dens, as many as ever apparently, as he caught the brutality and squalor and open misery and degradation on countless faces of men and women and children, he sickened at the sight. He found himself asking how much cleansing could a million dollars poured into this cesspool accomplish? Was not the living source of nearly all the human misery they sought to relieve untouched as long as the saloons did their deadly but legitimate work? What could even such unselfish Christian discipleship as Virginia's and Rachel's do to lessen the stream of vice and crime so long as the great spring of vice and crime flowed as deep and strong as ever? Was it not a practical waste of beautiful lives for these young women to throw themselves into this earthy hell, when for every soul rescued by their sacrifice the saloon made two more that needed rescue?

He could not escape the question. It was the same that Virginia had put to Rachel in her statement that, in her opinion, nothing really permanent would ever be done until the saloon was taken out of the Rectangle. Henry Maxwell went back to his parish work that afternoon with added convictions on the license business.

But if the saloon was a factor in the problem of the life of Raymond, no less was the First Church and its little company of disciples who had pledged to do as Jesus would do. Henry Maxwell, standing at the very centre of the movement, was not in a position to judge of its power as some one from the outside might have done. But Raymond itself felt the touch in very many ways, not knowing all the reasons for the change.

The winter was gone and the year was ended, the year which Henry Maxwell had fixed as the time during which the pledge should be kept to do as Jesus would do. Sunday, the anniversary of that one a year ago, was in many ways the most remarkable day that the First Church ever knew. It was more important than the disciples in the First Church realized. The year had made history so fast and so seriously that the people were not yet able to grasp its significance. And the day itself which marked the completion of a whole year of such discipleship was characterized by such revelations and confessions that the immediate actors in the events themselves could not understand the value of what had been done, or the relation of their trial to the rest of the churches and cities of the country.

It happened that the week before that anniversary Sunday the Rev. Calvin Bruce, D.D., of the Nazareth Avenue Church, Chicago, was in Raymond, where he had come on a visit to some old friends, and incidentally to see his old seminary classmate, Henry Maxwell. He was present at the First Church and was an exceedingly attentive and interested spectator. His account of the events in Raymond, and especially of that Sunday, may throw more light on the entire situation than any description or record from other sources.

Chapter 19

[Letter from Rev. Calvin Bruce, D.D., of the Nazareth Avenue Church, Chicago, to Rev. Philip A. Caxton, D.D., New York City.]

"My Dear Caxton:

"It is late Sunday night, but I am so intensely awake and so overflowing with what I have seen and heard that I feel driven to write you now some account of the situation in Raymond as I have been studying it, and as it has apparently come to a climax today. So this is my only excuse for writing so extended a letter at this time.

"You remember Henry Maxwell in the Seminary. I think you said the last time I visited you in New York that you had not seen him since we graduated. He was a refined, scholarly fellow, you remember, and when he was called to the First Church of Raymond within a year after leaving the Seminary, I said to my wife, 'Raymond has made a good choice. Maxwell will satisfy them as a sermonizer.' He has been here eleven years, and I understand that up to a year ago he had gone on in the regular course of the ministry, giving good satisfaction and drawing good congregations. His church was counted the largest and wealthiest church in Raymond. All the best people attended it, and most of them belonged. The quartet choir was famous for its music, especially for its soprano, Miss Winslow, of whom I shall have more to say; and, on the whole, as I understand the facts, Maxwell was in a comfortable berth, with a very good salary, pleasant surroundings, a not very exacting parish of refined, rich, respectable people—such a church and parish as nearly all the young men of the seminary in our time looked forward to as very desirable.

"But a year ago today Maxwell came into his church on Sunday morning, and at the close of the service made the astounding proposition that the members of his church volunteer for a year not to do anything without first asking the question, 'What would Jesus do?' and, after answering it, to do what in their honest judgment He would do, regardless of what the result might be to them.

"The effect of this proposition, as it has been met and obeyed by a number of members of the church, has been so remarkable that, as you know, the attention of the whole country has been directed to the movement. I call it a 'movement' because from the action taken today, it seems probable that what has been tried here will reach out into the other churches and cause a revolution in methods, but more especially in a new definition of Christian discipleship.

"In the first place, Maxwell tells me he was astonished at the response to his proposition. Some of the most prominent members in the church made the promise to do as Jesus would. Among them were Edward Norman, editor of the *Daily News*, which has made such a sensation in the newspaper world; Milton Wright, one of the leading merchants in Raymond; Alexander Powers, whose action in the matter of the railroads against the interstate commerce laws made such a stir about a year ago; Miss Page, one of Raymond's leading society heiresses, who has lately dedicated her entire fortune, as I understand, to the Christian daily paper and the work of reform in the slum district known as the Rectangle; and Miss Winslow, whose reputation as a singer is now national, but who in obedience to what she has decided to be Jesus' probable action, has devoted her talent to volunteer work among the girls and women who make up a large part of the city's worst and most abandoned population.

"In addition to these well-known people has been a gradually increasing number of Christians from the First Church and lately from other churches of Raymond. A large proportion of these volunteers who pledged themselves to do as Jesus would do comes from the Endeavor Societies. The young people say that they have already embodied in their society pledge the same principle in the words, 'I promise Him that I will strive to do whatever He would have me do.' This is not exactly what is included in Maxwell's proposition, which is that the disciple shall try to do what Jesus would probably do in the disciple's place. But the result of an honest obedience to either pledge, he claims, will be practically the same, and he is not surprised that the largest numbers have joined the new discipleship from the Endeavor Society.

"I am sure the first question you will ask is, 'What has been the result of this attempt? What has it accomplished or how has it changed in any way the regular life of the church or the community?'

"You already know something, from reports of Raymond that have gone over the country, what the events have been. But one needs to come here and learn something of the changes in individual lives, and especially the change in the church life, to realize all that is meant by this following of Jesus' steps so literally. To tell all that would be to write a long story or series of stories. I am not in a position to do that, but I can give you some idea perhaps of what has been done as told me by friends here and by Maxwell himself.

"The result of the pledge upon the First Church has been two-fold. It has brought about a spirit of Christian fellowship which Maxwell tells me never before existed, and which now impresses him as being very nearly what the Christian fellowship of the apostolic churches must have been; and it has divided the church into two distinct groups of members. Those who have not taken the pledge regard the others as foolishly literal in their attempt to imitate the example of Jesus. Some of them have drawn out of the church and no longer attend, or they have removed their membership entirely to other churches. Some are an element of internal strife, and I heard rumors of an attempt on their part to force Maxwell's resignation. I do not know that this element is very strong in the church. It has been held in check by a wonderful continuance of spiritual power, which dates from the first Sunday the pledge was taken a year ago, and also by the fact that so many of the most prominent members have been identified with the movement.

"The effect on Maxwell is very marked. I heard him preach in our State Association four years ago. He impressed me at the time as having considerable power in dramatic delivery, of which he himself was somewhat conscious. His sermon was well-written and abounded in what the Seminary students used to call 'fine passages.' The effect of it was what an average congregation would call 'pleasing.' This morning I heard Maxwell preach again, for the first time since then. I shall speak of that farther on. He is not the same man. He gives me the impression of one who has passed through a crisis of revolution. He tells me this revolution is simply a new definition of Christian discipleship. He certainly has changed many of his old habits and many of his old views. His attitude on the saloon question is radically opposite to the one he entertained a year ago. And in his entire thought of the ministry, his pulpit and parish work, I find he has made a complete change. So far as I can understand, the idea that is moving him on now is the idea that the Christianity of our times must represent a more literal imitation of Jesus, and especially in the element of suffering. He quoted to me in the course of our conversation several times the verses in Peter: 'For even hereunto were ye called, because Christ also suffered for you, leaving you an example, that ye would follow His steps'; and he seems filled with the conviction that what our churches need today more than anything else is this factor of joyful suffering for Jesus in some form. I do not know as I agree with him, altogether; but, my dear Caxton, it is certainly astonishing to note the results of this idea as they have impressed themselves upon this city and this church.

"You ask how about the results on the individuals who have made this pledge and honestly tried to be true to it. Those results are, as I have said, a part of individual history and cannot be told in detail. Some of them I can give you so that you may see that this form of discipleship is not merely sentiment or fine posing for effect.

"For instance, take the case of Mr. Powers, who was superintendent of the machine shops of the L. and T. R. R. here. When he acted upon the evidence which incriminated the road he lost his position, and more than that, I learn from my friends here, his family and social relations have become so changed that he and his family no longer appear in public. They have dropped out of the social circle where once they were so prominent. By the way, Caxton, I understand in this connection that the Commission, for one reason or another, postponed action on this case, and it is now rumored that the L. and T. R. R. will pass into a receiver's hands very soon. The president of the road who, according to the evidence submitted by Powers, was the principal offender, has resigned, and complications which have risen since point to the receivership. Meanwhile, the superintendent has gone back to his old work as a telegraph operator. I met him at the church yesterday. He impressed me as a man who had, like Maxwell, gone through a crisis in character. I could not help thinking of him as being good material for the church of the first century when the disciples had all things in common.

"Or take the case of Mr. Norman, editor of the *Daily News*. He risked his entire fortune in obedience to what he believed was Jesus' action, and revolutionized his entire conduct of the paper at the risk of a failure. I send you a copy of yesterday's paper. I want you to read it carefully. To my mind it is one of the most interesting and remarkable papers ever printed in the United States. It is open to criticism, but what could any mere man attempt in this line that would be free from criticism. Take it all in all, it is so far above the ordinary conception of a daily paper that I am amazed at the result. He tells me that the paper is beginning to be read more and more by the Christian people of the city. He was very confident of its final success. Read his editorial on the money questions, also the one on the coming election in Raymond when the question of license will again be an issue. Both articles are of the best from his point of view. He says he never begins an editorial or, in fact, any part of his newspaper work, without first asking, 'What would Jesus do?' The result is certainly apparent.

"Then there is Milton Wright, the merchant. He has, I am told, so revolutionized his business that no man is more beloved today in Raymond. His own clerks and employees have an affection for him that is very touching. During the winter, while he was lying dangerously ill at his home, scores of clerks volunteered to watch and help in any way possible, and his return to his store was greeted with marked demonstrations. All this has been brought about by the element of personal love introduced into the business. This love is not mere words, but the business itself is carried on under a system of co-operation that is not a patronizing recognition of inferiors, but a real sharing in the whole business. Other men on the street look upon Milton Wright as odd. It is a fact, however, that while he has lost heavily in some directions, he has increased his business, and is today respected and honored as one of the best and most successful merchants in Raymond.

"And there is Miss Winslow. She has chosen to give her great talent to the poor of the city. Her plans include a Musical Institute where choruses and classes in vocal music shall be a feature. She is enthusiastic over her life work. In connection with her friend Miss Page she has planned a course in music which, if carried out, will certainly do much to lift up the lives of the people down there. I am not too old, dear Caxton, to be interested in the romantic side of much that has also been tragic here in Raymond, and I must tell you that it is well understood here that Miss Winslow expects to be married this spring to a brother of Miss Page who was once a society leader and club man, and who was converted in a tent where his wife-that-is-to-be took an active part in the service. I don't know all the details of this little romance, but I imagine there is a story wrapped up in it, and it would make interesting reading if we only knew it all.

"These are only a few illustrations of results in individual lives owing to obedience to the pledge. I meant to have spoken of President Marsh of Lincoln College. He is a graduate of my alma mater and I knew him slightly when I was in the senior year. He has taken an active part in the recent municipal campaign, and his influence in the city is regarded as a very large factor in the coming election. He impressed me, as did all the other disciples in this movement, as having fought out some hard questions, and as having taken up some real burdens that have caused and still do cause that suffering of which Henry Maxwell speaks, a suffering that does not eliminate, but does appear to intensity, a positive and practical joy.

Chapter 20

"But I am prolonging this letter, possibly to your weariness. I am unable to avoid the feeling of fascination which my entire stay here has increased. I want to tell you something of the meeting in the First Church today.

"As I said, I heard Maxwell preach. At his earnest request I had preached for him the Sunday before, and this was the first time I had heard him since the Association meeting four years ago. His sermon this morning was as different from his sermon then as if it had been thought out and preached by some one living on another planet. I was profoundly touched. I believe I actually shed tears once. Others in the congregation were moved like myself. His text was: 'What is that to thee? Follow thou Me.' It was a most unusually impressive appeal to the Christians of Raymond to obey Jesus' teachings and follow in His steps regardless of what others might do. I cannot give you even the plan of the sermon. It would take too long. At the close of the service there was the usual after-meeting that has become a regular feature of the First Church. Into this meeting have come all those who made the pledge to do as Jesus would do, and the time is spent in mutual fellowship, confession, question as to what Jesus would do in special cases, and prayer that the one great guide of every disciple's conduct may be the Holy Spirit.

"Maxwell asked me to come into the meeting. Nothing in all my ministerial life, Caxton, has so moved me as that meeting. I never felt the Spirit's presence so powerfully. It was a meeting of reminiscences and of the most loving fellowship. I was irresistibly driven in thought back to the first years of Christianity. There was something about all this that was apostolic in its simplicity and Christ imitation.

"I asked questions. One that seemed to arouse more interest than any other was in regard to the extent of the Christian disciple's sacrifice of personal property. Maxwell tells me that so far no one has interpreted the spirit of Jesus in such a way as to abandon his earthly possessions, give away of his wealth, or in any literal way imitate the Christians of the order, for example, of St. Francis of Assisi. It was the unanimous consent, however, that if any disciple should feel that Jesus in his own particular case would do that, there could be only one answer to the question. Maxwell admitted that he was still to a certain degree uncertain as to Jesus' probable action when it came to the details of household living, the possession of wealth, the holding of certain luxuries. It is, however, very evident that many of these disciples have repeatedly carried their obedience to Jesus to the extreme limit, regardless of financial loss. There is no lack of courage or consistency at this point.

"It is also true that some of the business men who took the pledge have lost great sums of money in this imitation of Jesus, and many have, like Alexander Powers, lost valuable positions owing to the impossibility of doing what they had been accustomed to do and at the same time what they felt Jesus would do in the same place. In connection with these cases it is pleasant to record the fact that many who have suffered in this way have been at once helped financially by those who still have means. In this respect I think it is true that these disciples have all things in common. Certainly such scenes as I witnessed at the First Church at that after-service this morning I never saw in my church or in any other. I never dreamed that such Christian fellowship could exist in this age of the world. I was almost incredulous as to the witness of my own senses. I still seem to be asking myself if this is the close of the nineteenth century in America.

"But now, dear friend, I come to the real cause of this letter, the real heart of the whole question as the First Church of Raymond has forced it upon me. Before the meeting closed today steps were taken to secure the co-operation of all other Christian disciples in this country. I think Maxwell took this step after long deliberation. He said as much to me one day when we were discussing the effect of this movement upon the church in general.

" 'Why,' he said, 'suppose that the church membership generally in this country made this pledge and lived up to it! What a revolution it would cause in Christendom! But why not? Is it any more than the disciple ought to do? Has he followed Jesus, unless he is willing to do this? Is the test of discipleship any less today than it was in Jesus' time?'

"I do not know all that preceded or followed his thought of what ought to be done outside of Raymond, but the idea crystallized today in a plan to secure the fellowship of all the Christians in America. The churches, through their pastors, will be asked to form disciple gatherings like the one in the First Church. Volunteers will be called for in the great body of church members in the United States, who will promise to do as Jesus would do. Maxwell spoke particularly of the result of such general action on the saloon question. He is terribly in earnest over this. He told me that there was no question in his mind that the saloon would be beaten in Raymond at the election now near at hand. If so, they could go on with some courage to do the redemptive work begun by the evangelist and now taken up by the disciples in his own church. If the saloon triumphs again there will be a terrible and, as he thinks, unnecessary waste of Christian sacrifice. But, however we differ on that point, he convinced his church that the time had come for a fellowship with other Christians. Surely, if the First Church could work such changes in society and its surroundings, the church in general if combining such a fellowship, not of creed but of conduct, ought to stir the entire nation to a higher life and a new conception of Christian following.

"This is a grand idea, Caxton, but right here is where I find myself hesitating. I do not deny that the Christian disciple ought to follow Christ's steps as closely as these here in Raymond have tried to do. But I cannot avoid asking what the result would be if I ask my church in Chicago to do it. I am writing this after feeling the solemn, profound touch of the Spirit's presence, and I confess to you, old friend, that I cannot call up in my church a dozen prominent business or professional men who would make this trial at the risk of all they hold dear. Can you do any better in your church? What are we to say? That the churches would not respond to the call: 'Come and suffer?' Is our standard of Christian discipleship a wrong one? Or are we possibly deceiving ourselves, and would we be agreeably disappointed if we once asked our people to take such a pledge faithfully? The actual results of the pledge as obeyed here in Raymond are enough to make any pastor tremble, and at the same time long with yearning that they might occur in his own parish. Certainly never have I seen a church so signally blessed by the Spirit as this one. But—am I myself ready to take this pledge? I ask the question honestly, and I dread to face an honest answer. I know well enough that I should have to change very much in my life if I undertook to follow His steps so closely. I have called myself a Christian for many years. For the past ten years I have enjoyed a life that has had comparatively little suffering in it. I am, honestly I say it, living at a long distance from municipal problems and the life of the poor, the degraded and the abandoned. What would the obedience to this pledge demand of me? I hesitate to answer. My church is wealthy, full of well-to-do, satisfied people. The standard of their discipleship is, I am aware, not of a nature to respond to the call of suffering or personal loss. I say: 'I am aware.' I may be mistaken. I may have erred in not stirring their deeper life. Caxton, my friend, I have spoken my inmost thought to you. Shall I go back to my people next Sunday and stand up before them in my large city church and say: 'Let us follow Jesus closer; let us walk in His steps where it will cost us something more than it is costing us now; let us pledge not to do anything without first asking: What would Jesus do?' If I should go before them with that message, it would be a strange and startling one to them. But why? Are we not ready to follow Him all the way? What is it to be a follower of Jesus? What does it mean to imitate Him? What does it mean to walk in His steps?"

The Rev. Calvin Bruce, D. D., of the Nazareth Avenue Church, Chicago, let his pen fall on the table. He had come to the parting of the ways, and his question, he felt sure, was the question of many and many a man in the ministry and in the church. He went to his window and opened it. He was oppressed with the weight of his convictions and he felt almost suffocated with the air in the room. He wanted to see the stars and feel the breath of the world.

The night was very still. The clock in the First Church was just striking midnight. As it finished a clear, strong voice down in the direction of the Rectangle came floating up to him as if borne on radiant pinions.

It was a voice of one of Gray's old converts, a night watchman at the packing houses, who sometimes solaced his lonesome hours by a verse or two of some familiar hymn:

> Must Jesus bear the cross alone
> And all the world go free?
> No, there's a cross for every one,
> And there's a cross for me.

The Rev. Calvin Bruce turned away from the window and, after a little hesitation, he kneeled. "What would Jesus do?" That was the burden of his prayer. Never had he yielded himself so completely to the Spirit's searching revealing of Jesus. He was on his knees a long time. He retired and slept fitfully with many awakenings. He rose before it was clear dawn, and threw open his window again. As the light in the east grew stronger he repeated to himself: "What would Jesus do? Shall I follow His steps?"

The sun rose and flooded the city with its power. When shall the dawn of a new discipleship usher in the conquering triumph of a closer walk with Jesus? When shall Christendom tread more closely the path He made?

> It is the way the Master trod;
> Shall not the servant tread it still?

With this question throbbing through his whole being, the Rev. Calvin Bruce, D. D., went back to Chicago, and the great crisis in his Christian life in the ministry suddenly broke irresistibly upon him.

Chapter 21

Master, I will follow Thee whithersoever Thou goest.

The Saturday afternoon matinee at the Auditorium in Chicago was just over and the usual crowd was struggling to get to its carriage before any one else. The Auditorium attendant was shouting out the numbers of different carriages and the carriage doors were slamming as the horses were driven rapidly up to the curb, held there impatiently by the drivers who had shivered long in the raw east wind, and then let go to plunge for a few minutes into the river of vehicles that tossed under the elevated railway and finally went whirling off up the avenue.

"Now then, 624," shouted the Auditorium attendant; "624!" he repeated, and there dashed up to the curb a splendid span of black horses attached to a carriage having the monogram, "C. R. S." in gilt letters on the panel of the door.

Two girls stepped out of the crowd towards the carriage. The older one had entered and taken her seat and the attendant was still holding the door open for the younger, who stood hesitating on the curb.

"Come, Felicia! What are you waiting for! I shall freeze to death!" called the voice from the carriage.

The girl outside of the carriage hastily unpinned a bunch of English violets from her dress and handed them to a small boy who was standing shivering on the edge of the sidewalk almost under the horses' feet. He took them, with a look of astonishment and a "Thank ye, lady!" and instantly buried a very grimy face in the bunch of perfume.

The girl stepped into the carriage, the door shut with the incisive bang peculiar to well-made carriages of this sort, and in a few moments the coachman was speeding the horses rapidly up one of the boulevards.

"You are always doing some queer thing or other, Felicia," said the older girl as the carriage whirled on past the great residences already brilliantly lighted.

"Am I? What have I done that is queer now, Rose?" asked the other, looking up suddenly and turning her head towards her sister.

"Oh, giving those violets to that boy! He looked as if he needed a good hot supper more than a bunch of violets. It's a wonder you didn't invite him home with us. I shouldn't have been surprised if you had. You are always doing such queer things."

"Would it be queer to invite a boy like that to come to the house and get a hot supper?" Felicia asked the question softly and almost as if she were alone.

"'Queer' isn't just the word, of course," replied Rose indifferently. "It would be what Madam Blanc calls 'outre.' Decidedly. Therefore you will please not invite him or others like him to hot suppers because I suggested it. Oh, dear! I'm awfully tired."

She yawned, and Felicia silently looked out of the window in the door.

"The concert was stupid and the violinist was simply a bore. I don't see how you could sit so still through it all," Rose exclaimed a little impatiently.

"I liked the music," answered Felicia quietly.

"You like anything. I never saw a girl with so little critical taste."

Felicia colored slightly, but would not answer. Rose yawned again, and then hummed a fragment of a popular song. Then she exclaimed abruptly:

"I'm sick of 'most everything. I hope the 'Shadows of London' will be exciting tonight."

"The 'Shadows of Chicago,'" murmured Felicia.

"The 'Shadows of Chicago!' The 'Shadows of London,' the play, the great drama with its wonderful scenery, the sensation of New York for two months. You know we have a box with the Delanos tonight."

Felicia turned her face towards her sister. Her great brown eyes were very expressive and not altogether free from a sparkle of luminous heat.

"And yet we never weep over the real thing on the actual stage of life. What are the 'Shadows of London' on the stage to the shadows of London or Chicago as they really exist? Why don't we get excited over the facts as they are?"

"Because the actual people are dirty and disagreeable and it's too much bother, I suppose," replied Rose carelessly. "Felicia, you can never reform the world. What's the use? We're not to blame for the poverty and misery. There have always been rich and poor; and there always will be. We ought to be thankful we're rich."

"Suppose Christ had gone on that principle," replied Felicia, with unusual persistence. "Do you remember Dr. Bruce's sermon on that verse a few Sundays ago: 'For ye know the grace of our Lord Jesus Christ, that though he was rich yet for our sakes he became poor, that ye through his poverty might become rich'?"

"I remember it well enough," said Rose with some petulance, "and didn't Dr. Bruce go on to say that there is no blame attached to people who have wealth if they are kind and give to the needs of the poor? And I am sure that he himself is pretty comfortably settled. He never gives up his luxuries just because some people go hungry. What good would it do if he did? I tell you, Felicia, there will always be poor and rich in spite of all we can do. Ever since Rachel Winslow has written about those queer doings in Raymond you have upset the whole family. People can't live at that concert pitch all the time. You see if Rachel doesn't give it up soon. It's a great pity she doesn't come to Chicago and sing in the Auditorium concerts. I heard today that she had received an offer. I'm going to write and urge her to come. I'm just dying to hear her sing."

Felicia looked out of the window and was silent. The carriage rolled on past two blocks of magnificent private residences and turned into a wide driveway under a covered passage, and the sisters hurried into the house. It was an elegant mansion of gray stone furnished like a palace, every corner of it warm with the luxury of paintings, sculpture, art and modern refinement.

The owner of it all, Mr. Charles R. Sterling, stood before an open grate fire smoking a cigar. He had made his money in grain speculation and railroad ventures, and was reputed to be worth something over two millions. His wife was a sister of Mrs. Winslow of Raymond. She had been an invalid for several years. The two girls, Rose and Felicia, were the only children. Rose was twenty-one years old, fair, vivacious, educated in a fashionable college, just entering society and already somewhat cynical and indifferent. A very hard young lady to please, her father said, sometimes playfully, sometimes sternly. Felicia was nineteen, with a tropical beauty somewhat like her cousin, Rachel Winslow, with warm, generous impulses just waking into Christian feeling, capable of all sorts of expression, a puzzle to her father, a source of irritation to her mother and with a great unsurveyed territory of thought and action in herself, of which she was more than dimly conscious. There was that in Felicia that would easily endure any condition in life if only the liberty to act fully on her conscientious convictions were granted her.

"Here's a letter for you, Felicia," said Mr. Sterling, handing it to her.

Felicia sat down and instantly opened the letter, saying as she did so: "It's from Rachel."

"Well, what's the latest news from Raymond?" asked Mr. Sterling, taking his cigar out of his mouth and looking at Felicia as he often did with half-shut eyes, as if he were studying her.

"Rachel says Dr. Bruce has been staying in Raymond for two Sundays and has seemed very much interested in Mr. Maxwell's pledge in the First Chruch."

"What does Rachel say about herself?" asked Rose, who was lying on a couch almost buried under a half dozen elegant cushions.

"She is still singing at the Rectangle. Since the tent meeings closed she sings in an old hall until the new buildings which her friend, Virginia Page, is putting up are completed."

"I must write Rachel to come to Chicago and visit us. She ought not to throw away her voice in that railroad town upon all those people who don't appreciate her."

Mr. Sterling lighted a new cigar and Rose exclaimed:

"Rachel is so queer. She might set Chicago wild with her voice if she sang in the Auditorium. And there she goes on throwing it away on people who don't know what they are hearing."

"Rachel won't come here unless she can do it and keep her pledge at the same time," said Felicia, after a pause.

"What pledge?" Mr. Sterling asked the question and then added hastily: "Oh, I know, yes! A very peculiar thing that. Alexander Powers used to be a friend of mine. We learned telegraphy in the same office. Made a great sensation when he resigned and handed over that evidence to the Interstate Commerce Commission. And he's back at his telegraph again. There have been queer doings in Raymond during the past year. I wonder what Dr. Bruce thinks of it on the whole. I must have a talk with him about it."

"He is at home and will preach tomorrow," said Felicia. "Perhaps he will tell us something about it."

There was silence for a minute. Then Felicia said abruptly, as if she had gone on with a spoken thought to some invisible hearer: "And what if he should propose the same pledge to the Nazareth Avenue Church?"

"Who? What are you talking about?" asked her father a little sharply.

"About Dr. Bruce. I say, what if he should propose to our church what Mr. Maxwell proposed to his, and ask for volunteers who would pledge themselves to do everything after asking the question, 'What would Jesus do?' "

"There's no danger of it," said Rose, rising suddenly from the couch as the tea-bell rang.

"It's a very impracticable movement, to my mind," said Mr. Sterling shortly.

"I understand from Rachel's letter that the Raymond church is going to make an attempt to extend the idea of the pledge to other churches. If it succeeds it will certainly make great changes in the churches and in people's lives," said Felicia.

"Oh, well, let's have some tea first!" said Rose, walking into the dining-room. Her father and Felicia followed, and the meal proceeded in silence. Mrs. Sterling had her meals served in her room. Mr. Sterling was preoccupied. He ate very little and excused himself early, and although it was Saturday night, he remarked as he went out that he should be down town late on some special business.

"Don't you think father looks very much disturbed lately?" asked Felicia a little while after he had gone out.

"Oh, I don't know! I hadn't noticed anything unusual," replied Rose. After a silence she said: "Are you going to the play tonight, Felicia? Mrs. Delano will be here at half past seven. I think you ought to go. She will feel hurt if you refuse."

"I'll go. I don't care about it. I can see shadows enough without going to the play."

"That's a doleful remark for a girl nineteen years old to make," replied Rose. "But then you're queer in your ideas anyhow, Felicia. If you are going up to see mother, tell her I'll run in after the play if she is still awake."

Felicia went up to see her mother and remained with her until the Delano carriage came. Mrs. Sterling was worried about her husband. She talked incessantly, and was irritated by every remark Felicia made. She would not listen to Felicia's attempts to read even a part of Rachel's letter, and when Felicia offered to stay with her for the evening, she refused the offer with a good deal of positive sharpness.

Chapter 22

Felicia started off to the play not very happy, but she was familiar with that feeling, only sometimes she was more unhappy than at others. Her feeling expressed itself tonight by a withdrawal into herself. When the company was seated in the box and the curtain had gone up Felicia was back of the others and remained for the evening by herself. Mrs. Delano, as chaperon for half a dozen young ladies, understood Felicia well enough to know that she was "queer," as Rose so often said, and she made no attempt to draw her out of her corner. And so the girl really experienced that night by herself one of the feelings that added to the momentum that was increasing the coming on of her great crisis.

The play was an English melodrama, full of startling situations, realistic scenery and unexpected climaxes. There was one scene in the third act that impressed even Rose Sterling.

It was midnight on Blackfriars Bridge. The Thames flowed dark and forbidding below. St. Paul's rose through the dim light imposing, its dome seeming to float above the buildings surrounding it. The figure of a child came upon the bridge and stood there for a moment peering about as if looking for some one. Several persons were crossing the bridge, but in one of the recesses about midway of the river a woman stood, leaning out over the parapet, with a strained agony of face and figure that told plainly of her intention. Just as she was stealthily mounting the parapet to throw herself into the river, the child caught sight of her, ran forward with a shrill cry more animal than human, and seizing the woman's dress dragged back upon it with all her little strength. Then there came suddenly upon the scene two other characters who had already figured in the play, a tall, handsome, athletic gentleman dressed in the fashion, attended by a slim-figured lad who was as refined in dress and appearance as the little girl clinging to her mother was mournfully hideous in her rags and repulsive poverty. These two, the gentleman and the lad, prevented the attempted suicide, and after a tableau on the bridge where the audience learned that the man and woman were brother and sister, the scene was transferred to the interior of one of the slum tenements in the East Side of London. Here the scene painter and carpenter had done their utmost to produce an exact copy of a famous court and alley well known to the poor creatures who make up a part of the outcast London humanity. The rags, the crowding, the vileness, the broken furniture, the horrible animal existence forced upon creatures made in God's image were so skilfully shown in this scene that more than one elegant woman in the theatre, seated like Rose Sterling in a sumptuous box surrounded with silk hangings and velvet covered railing, caught herself shrinking back a little as if contamination were possible from the nearness of this piece of scenery. It was almost too realistic, and yet it had a horrible fascination for Felicia as she sat there alone, buried back in a cushioned seat and absorbed in thoughts that went far beyond the dialogue on the stage.

From the tenement scene the play shifted to the interior of a nobleman's palace, and almost a sigh of relief went up all over the house at the sight of the accustomed luxury of the upper classes. The contrast was startling. It was brought about by a clever piece of staging that allowed only a few moments to elapse between the slum and the palace scene. The dialogue went on, the actors came and went in their various roles, but upon Felicia the play made but one distinct impression. In reality the scenes on the bridge and in the slums were only incidents in the story of the play, but Felicia found herself living those scenes over and over. She had never philosophized about the causes of human misery, she was not old enough, she had not the temperament that philosophizes. But she felt intensely, and this was not the first time she had felt the contrast thrust into her feeling between the upper and the lower conditions of human life. It had been growing upon her until it had made her what Rose called "queer," and other people in her circle of wealthy acquaintances called very unusual. It was simply the human problem in its extreme of riches and poverty, its refinement and its vileness, that was, in spite of her unconscious attempts to struggle against the facts, burning into her life the impression that would in the end either transform her into a woman of rare love and self-sacrifice for the world, or a miserable enigma to herself and all who knew her.

"Come, Felicia, aren't you going home?" said Rose. The play was over, the curtain down, and people were going noisily out, laughing and gossiping as if "The Shadows of London" were simply good diversion, as they were, put on the stage so effectively.

Felicia rose and went out with the rest quietly, and with the absorbed feeling that had actually left her in her seat oblivious of the play's ending. She was never absentminded, but often thought herself into a condition that left her alone in the midst of a crowd.

"Well, what did you think of it?" asked Rose when the sisters had reached home and were in the drawing-room. Rose really had considerable respect for Felicia's judgment of a play.

"I thought it was a pretty fair picture of real life."

"I mean the acting," said Rose, annoyed.

"The bridge scene was well acted, especially the woman's part. I thought the man overdid the sentiment a little."

"Did you? I enjoyed that. And wasn't the scene between the two cousins funny when they first learned they were related? But the slum scene was horrible. I think they ought not to show such things in a play. They are too painful."

"They must be painful in real life, too," replied Felicia.

"Yes, but we don't have to look at the real thing. It's bad enough at the theatre where we pay for it."

Rose went into the dining-room and began to eat from a plate of fruit and cakes on the sideboard.

"Are you going up to see mother?" asked Felicia after a while. She had remained in front of the drawing-room fire.

"No," replied Rose from the other room. "I won't trouble her tonight. If you go in tell her I am too tired to be agreeable."

So Felicia turned into her mother's room, as she went up the great staircase and down the upper hall. The light was burning there, and the servant who always waited on Mrs. Sterling was beckoning Felicia to come in.

"Tell Clara to go out," exclaimed Mrs. Sterling as Felicia came up to the bed.

Felicia was surprised, but she did as her mother bade her, and then inquired how she was feeling.

"Felicia," said her mother, "can you pray?"

The question was so unlike any her mother had ever asked before that she was startled. But she answered:

"Why, yes, mother. Why do you ask such a question?"

"Felicia, I am frightened. Your father—I have had such strange fears about him all day. Something is wrong with him. I want you to pray."

"Now, here, mother?"

"Yes. Pray, Felicia."

Felicia reached out her hand and took mother's. It was trembling. Mrs. Sterling had never shown such tenderness for her younger daughter, and her strange demand now was the first real sign of any confidence in Felicia's character.

The girl kneeled, still holding her mother's trembling hand, and prayed. It is doubtful if she had ever prayed aloud before. She must have said in her prayer the words that her mother needed, for when it was silent in the room the invalid was weeping softly and her nervous tension was over.

Felicia stayed some time. When she was assured that her mother would not need her any longer she rose to go.

"Good night, mother. You must let Clara call me if you feel badly in the night."

"I feel better now." Then as Felicia was moving away, Mrs. Sterling said: "Won't you kiss me, Felicia?"

Felicia went back and bent over her mother. The kiss was almost as strange to her as the prayer had been. When Felicia went out of the room her cheeks were wet with tears. She had not often cried since she was a little child.

Sunday morning at the Sterling mansion was generally very quiet. The girls usually went to church at eleven o'clock service. Mr. Sterling was not a member but a heavy contributor, and he generally went to church in the morning. This time he did not come down to breakfast, and finally sent word by a servant that he did not feel well enough to go out. So Rose and Felicia drove up to the door of the Nazareth Avenue Church and entered the family pew alone.

When Dr. Bruce walked out of the room at the rear of the platform and went up to the pulpit to open the Bible as his custom was, those who knew him best did not detect anything unusual in his manner or his expression. He proceeded with the service as usual. He was calm and his voice was steady and firm. His prayer was the first intimation the people had of anything new or strange in the service. It is safe to say that the Nazareth Avenue Church had not heard Dr. Bruce offer such a prayer before during the twelve years he had been pastor there. How would a minister be likely to pray who had come out of a revolution in Christian feeling that had completely changed his definition of what was meant by following Jesus? No one in Nazareth Avenue Church had any idea that the Rev. Calvin Bruce, D. D., the dignified, cultured, refined Doctor of Divinity, had within a few days been crying like a little child on his knees, asking for strength and courage and Christlikeness to speak his Sunday message; and yet the prayer was an unconscious involuntary disclosure of his soul's experience such as the Nazareth Avenue people had seldom heard, and never before from that pulpit.

In the hush that succeeded the prayer a distinct wave of spiritual power moved over the congregation. The most careless persons in the church felt it. Felicia, whose sensitive religious nature responded swiftly to every touch of emotion, quivered under the passing of that supernatural pressure, and when she lifted her head and looked up at the minister there was a look in her eyes that announced her intense,

eager anticipation of the scene that was to follow. And she was not
alone in her attitude. There was something in the prayer and the result of it that stirred many and many a disciple in that church. All
over the house men and women leaned forward, and when Dr. Bruce
began to speak of his visit to Raymond, in the opening sentence of his
address which this morning preceded his sermon, there was an answering response in the people that came back to him as he spoke,
and thrilled him with the hope of a spiritual baptism such as he had
never during all his ministry experienced.

Chapter 23

"I am just back from a visit to Raymond," Dr. Bruce began, "and I
want to tell you something of my impressions of the movement there."
He paused and his look went out over his people with yearning for
them and at the same time with a great uncertainty at his heart. How
many of his rich, fashionable, refined, luxury-loving members would
understand the nature of the appeal he was soon to make to them? He
was altogether in the dark as to that. Nevertheless he had been
through his desert, and had come out of it ready to suffer. He went on
now after that brief pause and told them the story of his stay in Raymond. The people already knew something of that experiment in the
First Church. The whole country had watched the progress of the
pledge as it had become history in so many lives. Mr. Maxwell had at
last decided that the time had come to seek the fellowship of other
churches throughout the country. The new discipleship in Raymond
had proved to be so valuable in its results that he wished the churches
in general to share with the disciples in Raymond. Already there had
begun a volunteer movement in many churches throughout the country, acting on their own desire to walk closer in the steps of Jesus. The
Christian Endeavor Society had, with enthusiasm, in many churches
taken the pledge to do as Jesus would do, and the result was already
marked in a deeper spiritual life and a power in church influence that
was like a new birth for the members.

All this Dr. Bruce told his people simply and with a personal interest that evidently led the way to the announcement which now fol-

lowed. Felicia had listened to every word with strained attention. She
sat there by the side of Rose, in contrast like fire beside snow, although even Rose was alert and as excited as she could be.

"Dear friends," he said, and for the first time since his prayer the
emotion of the occasion was revealed in his voice and gesture, "I am
going to ask that Nazareth Avenue Church take the same pledge that
Raymond Church has taken. I know what this will mean to you and
me. It will mean the complete change of very many habits. It will
mean, possibly, social loss. It will mean very probably, in many cases,
loss of money. It will mean suffering. It will mean what following
Jesus meant in the first century, and then it meant suffering, loss,
hardship, separation from everthing un-Christian. But what does following Jesus mean? The test of discipleship is the same now as then.
Those of us who volunteer in this church to do as Jesus would do,
simply promise to walk in his steps as He gave us commandment."

Again he paused, and now the result of his announcement was
plainly visible in the stir that went up over the congregation. He
added in a quiet voice that all who volunteered to make the pledge to
do as Jesus would do, were asked to remain after the morning service.

Instantly he proceeded with his sermon. His text was, "Master, I
will follow Thee whithersoever Thou goest." It was a sermon that
touched the deep springs of conduct; it was a revelation to the people
of the definition their pastor had been learning; it took them back to
the first century of Christianity; above all, it stirred them below the
conventional thought of years as to the meaning and purpose of
church membership. It was such a sermon as a man can preach once
in a lifetime, and with enough in it for people to live on all through
the rest of their lifetime.

The service closed in a hush that was slowly broken. People rose
here and there, a few at a time. There was a reluctance in the movements of some that was very striking. Rose, however, walked straight
out of the pew, and as she reached the aisle she turned her head and
beckoned to Felicia. By that time the congregation was rising all over
the church. "I am going to stay," she said, and Rose had heard her
speak in the same manner on other occasions, and knew that her resolve could not be changed. Nevertheless she went back into the pew
two or three steps and faced her.

"Felicia," she whispered, and there was a flush of anger on her
cheeks, "this is folly. What can you do? You will bring some disgrace
on the family. What will father say? Come!"

Felicia looked at her but did not answer at once. Her lips were
moving with a petition that came from the depth of feeling that measured a new life for her. She shook her head.

"No, I am going to stay. I shall take the pledge. I am ready to obey it. You do not know why I am doing this."

Rose gave her one look and then turned and went out of the pew, and down the aisle. She did not even stop to talk with her acquaintances. Mrs. Delano was going out of the church just as Rose stepped into the vestibule.

"So you are not going to join Dr. Bruce's volunteer company?" Mrs. Delano asked, in a queer tone that made Rose redden.

"No, are you? It is simply absurd. I have always regarded that Raymond movement as fanatical. You know cousin Rachel keeps us posted about it."

"Yes, I understand it is resulting in a great deal of hardship in many cases. For my part, I believe Dr. Bruce has simply provoked disturbance here. It will result in splitting our church. You see if it isn't so. There are scores of people in the church who are so situated that they can't take such a pledge and keep it. I am one of them," added Mrs. Delano as she went out with Rose.

When Rose reached home, her father was standing in his usual attitude before the open fireplace, smoking a cigar.

"Where is Felicia?" he asked as Rose came in.

"She stayed to an after-meeting," replied Rose shortly. She threw off her wraps and was going upstairs when Mr. Sterling called after her.

"An after-meeting? What do you mean?"

"Dr. Bruce asked the church to take the Raymond pledge."

Mr. Sterling took his cigar out of his mouth and twirled it nervously between his fingers.

"I didn't expect that of Dr. Bruce. Did many of the members stay?"

"I don't know. I didn't," replied Rose, and she went upstairs leaving her father standing in the drawing-room.

After a few moments he went to the window and stood there looking out at the people driving on the boulevard. His cigar had gone out, but he still fingered it nervously. Then he turned from the window and walked up and down the room. A servant stepped across the hall and announced dinner and he told her to wait for Felicia. Rose came downstairs and went into the library. And still Mr. Sterling paced the drawing-room restlessly.

He had finally wearied of the walking apparently, and throwing himself into a chair was brooding over something deeply when Felicia came in.

He rose and faced her. Felicia was evidently very much moved by the meeting from which she had just come. At the same time she did not wish to talk too much about it. Just as she entered the drawing-room, Rose came in from the library.

"How many stayed?" she asked. Rose was curious. At the same time she was skeptical of the whole movement in Raymond.

"About a hundred," replied Felicia gravely. Mr. Sterling looked surprised. Felicia was going out of the room, but he called to her:

"Do you really mean to keep the pledge?" he asked.

Felicia colored. Over her face and neck the warm blood flowed and she answered, "You would not ask such a question, father, if you had been at the meeting." She lingered a moment in the room, then asked to be excused from dinner for a while and went up to see her mother.

No one but they two ever knew what that interview between Felicia and her mother was. It is certain that she must have told her mother something of the spiritual power that had awed every person present in the company of disciples who faced Dr. Bruce in that meeting after the morning service. It is also certain that Felicia had never before known such an experience, and would never have thought of sharing it with her mother if it had not been for the prayer the evening before. Another fact is also known of Felicia's experience at this time. When she finally joined her father and Rose at the table she seemed unable to tell them much about the meeting. There was a reluctance to speak of it as one might hesitate to attempt a description of a wonderful sunset to a person who never talked about anything but the weather.

When that Sunday in the Sterling mansion was drawing to a close and the soft, warm lights throughout the dwelling were glowing through the great windows, in a corner of her room, where the light was obscure, Felicia kneeled, and when she raised her face and turned it towards the light, it was the face of a woman who had already defined for herself the greatest issues of earthly life.

That same evening, after the Sunday evening service, Dr. Bruce was talking over the events of the day with his wife. They were of one heart and mind in the matter, and faced their new future with all the faith and courage of new disciples. Neither was deceived as to the probable results of the pledge to themselves or to the church.

They had been talking but a little while when the bell rang and Dr. Bruce going to the door exclaimed, as he opened it:

"It is you, Edward! Come in."

There came into the hall a commanding figure. The Bishop was of extraordinary height and breadth of shoulder, but of such good proportions that there was no thought of ungainly or even of unusual size. The impression the Bishop made on strangers was, first, that of great health, and then of great affection.

He came into the parlor and greeted Mrs. Bruce, who after a few moments was called out of the room, leaving the two men together. The Bishop sat in a deep, easy chair before the open fire. There was

just enough dampness in the early spring of the year to make an open
fire pleasant.

"Calvin, you have taken a very serious step today," he finally said,
lifting his large dark eyes to his old college classmate's face. "I heard
of it this afternoon. I could not resist the desire to see you about it tonight."

"I'm glad you came." Dr. Bruce laid a hand on the Bishop's shoulder. "You understand what this means, Edward?"

"I think I do. Yes, I am sure." The Bishop spoke very slowly and
thoughtfully. He sat with his hands clasped together. Over his face,
marked with lines of consecration and service and the love of men, a
shadow crept, a shadow not caused by the firelight. Again he lifted his
eyes toward his old friend.

"Calvin, we have always understood each other. Ever since our
paths led us in different ways in church life we have walked together
in Christian fellowship."

"It is true," replied Dr. Bruce with an emotion he made no attempt
to conceal or subdue. "Thank God for it. I prize your fellowship more
than any other man's. I have always known what it meant, though it
has always been more than I deserve."

The Bishop looked affectionately at his friend. But the shadow still
rested on his face. After a pause he spoke again:

"The new discipleship means a crisis for you in your work. If you
keep this pledge to do all things as Jesus would do—as I know you will
—it requires no prophet to predict some remarkable changes in your
parish." The Bishop looked wistfully at his friend and then continued:
"In fact, I do not see how a perfect upheaval of Christianity, as we
now know it, can be prevented if the ministers and churches generally
take the Raymond pledge and live it out." He paused as if he were
waiting for his friend to say something, to ask some question. But
Bruce did not know of the fire that was burning in the Bishop's heart
over the very question that Maxwell and himself had fought out.

"Now, in my church, for instance," continued the Bishop, "it would
be rather a difficult matter, I fear, to find very many people who
would take a pledge like that and live up to it. Martyrdom is a lost art
with us. Our Christianity loves its ease and comfort too well to take
up anything so rough and heavy as a cross. And yet what does following Jesus mean? What is it to walk in His steps?"

The Bishop was soliloquizing now and it is doubtful if he thought,
for the moment, of his friend's presence. For the first time there
flashed into Dr. Bruce's mind a suspicion of the truth. What if the
Bishop would throw the weight of his great influence on the side of
the Raymond movement? He had the following of the most aristo-

cratic, wealthy, fashionable people, not only in Chicago, but in several large cities. What if the Bishop should join this new discipleship!

The thought was about to be followed by the word. Dr. Bruce had reached out his hand and with the familiarity of lifelong friendship had placed it on the Bishop's shoulder and was about to ask a very important question, when they were both startled by the violent ringing of the bell. Mr. Bruce had gone to the door and was talking with some one in the hall. There was a loud exclamation and then, as the Bishop rose and Bruce was stepping toward the curtain that hung before the entrance to the parlor, Mrs. Bruce pushed it aside. Her face was white and she was trembling.

"O Calvin! Such terrible news! Mr. Sterling—oh, I cannot tell it! What a blow to those girls!"

"What is it?" Mr. Bruce advanced with the Bishop into the hall and confronted the messenger, a servant from the Sterlings'. The man was without his hat and had evidently run over with the news, as Dr. Bruce lived nearest of any intimate friends of the family.

"Mr. Sterling shot himself, sir, a few minutes ago. He killed himself in his bed-room. Mrs. Sterling—"

"I will go right over, Edward. Will you go with me? The Sterlings are old friends of yours."

The Bishop was very pale, but calm as always. He looked his friend in the face and answered:

"Aye, Calvin, I will go with you not only to this house of death, but also the whole way of human sin and sorrow, please God."

And even in that moment of horror at the unexpected news, Dr. Bruce understood what the Bishop had promised to do.

Chapter 24

These are they which follow the Lamb whithersoever He goeth.

When Dr. Bruce and the Bishop entered the Sterling mansion everything in the usually well-appointed household was in the greatest confusion and terror. The great rooms downstairs were empty, but overhead were hurried footsteps and confused noises. One of the servants ran down the grand staircase with a look of horror on her face just as the Bishop and Dr. Bruce were starting to go up.

"Miss Felicia is with Mrs. Sterling," the servant stammered in answer to a question, and then burst into a hysterical cry and ran through the drawing-room and out of doors.

At the top of the staircase the two men were met by Felicia. She walked up to Dr. Bruce at once and put both hands in his. The Bishop then laid his hand on her head and the three stood there a moment in perfect silence. The Bishop had known Felicia since she was a little child. He was the first to break the silence.

"The God of all mercy be with you, Felicia, in this dark hour. Your mother—"

The Bishop hesitated. Out of the buried past he had, during his hurried passage from his friend's to this house of death, irresistibly drawn the one tender romance of his young manhood. Not even Bruce knew that. But there had been a time when the Bishop had offered the incense of a singularly undivided affection upon the altar of his youth to the beautiful Camilla Rolfe, and she had chosen between him and the millionaire. The Bishop carried no bitterness with his memory; but it was still a memory.

For answer to the Bishop's unfinished query, Felicia turned and went back into her mother's room. She had not said a word yet, but both men were struck with her wonderful calm. She returned to the hall door and beckoned to them, and the two ministers, with a feeling that they were about to behold something very unusual, entered.

Rose lay with her arms outstretched upon the bed. Clara, the nurse, sat with her head covered, sobbing in spasms of terror. And Mrs. Sterling with "the light that never was on sea or land" luminous on her face, lay there so still that even the Bishop was deceived at first. Then, as the great truth broke upon him and Dr. Bruce, he staggered, and the sharp agony of the old wound shot through him. It passed, and left him standing there in that chamber of death with the eternal calmness and strength that the children of God have a right to possess. And right well he used that calmness and strength in the days that followed.

The next moment the house below was in a tumult. Almost at the same time the doctor who had been sent for at once, but lived some distance away, came in, together with police officers, who had been summoned by frightened servants. With them were four or five newspaper correspondents and several neighbors. Dr. Bruce and the Bishop met this miscellaneous crowd at the head of the stairs and succeeded in excluding all except those whose presence was necessary. With these the two friends learned all the facts ever known about the "Sterling tragedy," as the papers in their sensational accounts next day called it.

Mr. Sterling had gone into his room that evening about nine o'clock and that was the last seen of him until, in half an hour, a shot was heard in the room, and a servant who was in the hall ran into the room and found him dead on the floor, killed by his own hand. Felicia at the time was sitting by her mother. Rose was reading in the library. She ran upstairs, saw her father as he was being lifted upon the couch by the servants, and then ran screaming into her mother's room, where she flung herself down at the foot of the bed in a swoon. Mrs. Sterling had at first fainted at the shock, then rallied with a wonderful swiftness and sent for Dr. Bruce. She had then insisted on seeing her husband. In spite of Felicia's efforts, she had compelled Clara to support her while she crossed the hall and entered the room where her husband lay. She had looked upon him with a tearless face, and gone back to her own room, was laid on her bed, and as Dr. Bruce and the Bishop entered the house she, with a prayer of forgiveness for herself and for her husband on her quivering lips, had died, with Felicia bending over her and Rose still lying senseless at her feet.

So great and swift had been the entrance of grim Death into that palace of luxury that Sunday night! But the full cause of his coming was not learned until the facts in regard to Mr. Sterling's business affairs were finally disclosed.

Then it was learned that for some time he had been facing financial ruin owing to certain speculations that had in a month's time swept his supposed wealth into complete destruction. With the cunning and desperation of a man who battles for his very life when he saw his money, which was all the life he ever valued, slipping from him, he had put off the evil day to the last moment. Sunday afternoon, however, he had received news that proved to him beyond a doubt the fact of his utter ruin. The very house that he called his, the chairs in which he sat, his carriage, the dishes from which he ate, had all been bought with money for which he himself had never really done an honest stroke of pure labor.

It had all rested on a tissue of deceit and speculation that had no foundation in real values. He knew that fact better than any one else, but he had hoped, with the hope such men always have, that the same methods that brought him the money would also prevent the loss. He had been deceived in this as many others have been. As soon as the truth that he was practically a beggar had dawned upon him, he saw no escape from suicide. It was the irresistible result of such a life as he had lived. He had made money his god. As soon as that god was gone out of his little world there was nothing more to worship;

and when a man's object of worship is gone he has no more to live for. Thus died the great millionaire, Charles R. Sterling. And, verily, he died as the fool dieth, for what is the gain or the loss of money compared with the unsearchable riches of eternal life which are beyond the reach of speculation, loss or change?

Mrs. Sterling's death was the result of the shock. She had not been taken into her husband's confidence for years, but she knew that the source of his wealth was precarious. Her life for several years had been a death in life. The Rolfes always gave an impression that they could endure more disaster unmoved than any one else. Mrs. Sterling illustrated the old family tradition when she was carried into the room where her husband lay. But the feeble tenement could not hold the spirit and it gave up the ghost, torn and weakened by long years of suffering and disappointment.

The effect of this triple blow, the death of father and mother, and the loss of property, was instantly apparent in the sisters. The horror of events stupefied Rose for weeks. She lay unmoved by sympathy or any effort to rally. She did not seem yet to realize that the money which had been so large a part of her very existence was gone. Even when she was told that she and Felicia must leave the house and be dependent on relatives and friends, she did not seem to understand what it meant.

Felicia, however, was fully conscious of the facts. She knew just what had happened and why. She was talking over her future plans with her cousin Rachel a few days after the funerals. Mrs. Winslow and Rachel had left Raymond and come to Chicago at once as soon as the terrible news had reached them, and with other friends of the family were planning for the future of Rose and Felicia.

"Felicia, you and Rose must come to Raymond with us. That is settled. Mother will not hear to any other plan at present," Rachel had said, while her beautiful face glowed with love for her cousin, a love that had deepened day by day, and was intensified by the knowledge that they both belonged to the new discipleship.

"Unless I can find something to do here," answered Felicia. She looked wistfully at Rachel, and Rachel said gently:

"What could you do, dear?"

"Nothing. I was never taught to do anything except a little music, and I do not know enough about it to teach it or earn my living at it. I have learned to cook a little," Felicia added with a slight smile.

"Then you can cook for us. Mother is always having trouble with her kitchen," said Rachel, understanding well enough she was now dependent for her very food and shelter upon the kindness of family friends. It is true the girls received a little something out of the wreck of their father's fortune, but with a speculator's mad folly he had managed to involve both his wife's and his children's portion in the common ruin.

"Can I? Can I?" Felicia responded to Rachel's proposition as if it were to be considered seriously. "I am ready to do any thing honorable to make my living and that of Rose. Poor Rose! She will never be able to get over the shock of our trouble."

"We will arrange the details when we get to Raymond," Rachel said, smiling through her tears at Felicia's eager willingness to care for herself.

So in a few weeks Rose and Felicia found themselves a part of the Winslow family in Raymond. It was a bitter experience for Rose, but there was nothing else for her to do and she accepted the inevitable, brooding over the great change in her life and in many ways adding to the burden of Felicia and her cousin Rachel.

Felicia at once found herself in an atmosphere of discipleship that was like heaven to her in its revelation of companionship. It is true that Mrs. Winslow was not in sympathy with the course that Rachel was taking, but the remarkable events in Raymond since the pledge was taken were too powerful in their results not to impress even such a woman as Mrs. Winslow. With Rachel, Felicia found a perfect fellowship. She at once found a part to take in the new work at the Rectangle. In the spirit of her new life she insisted upon helping in the housework at her aunt's, and in a short time demonstrated her ability as a cook so clearly that Virginia suggested that she take charge of the cooking at the Rectangle.

Felicia entered upon this work with the keenest pleasure. For the first time in her life she had the delight of doing something of value for the happiness of others. Her resolve to do everything after asking, "What would Jesus do?" touched her deepest nature. She began to develop and strengthen wonderfully. Even Mrs. Winslow was obliged to acknowledge the great usefulness and beauty of Felicia's character. The aunt looked with astonishment upon her niece, this city-bred girl, reared in the greatest luxury, the daughter of a millionaire, now walking around in her kitchen, her arms covered with flour and occasionally a streak of it on her nose, for Felicia at first had a habit of rubbing her nose forgetfully when she was trying to remember some recipe, mixing various dishes with the greatest interest in their result, washing up pans and kettles and doing the ordinary work of a servant in the Winslow kitchen and at the rooms at the Rectangle Settlement. At first Mrs. Winslow remonstrated.

"Felicia, it is not your place to be out here doing this common work. I cannot allow it."

"Why, Aunt? Don't you like the muffins I made this morning?" Felicia would ask meekly, but with a hidden smile, knowing her aunt's weakness for that kind of muffin.

"They were beautiful, Felicia. But it does not seem right for you to be doing such work for us."

"Why not? What else can I do?"

Her aunt looked at her thoughtfully, noting her remarkable beauty of face and expression.

"You do not always intend to do this kind of work, Felicia?"

"Maybe I shall. I have had a dream of opening an ideal cook shop in Chicago or some large city and going around to the poor families in some slum district like the Rectangle, teaching the mothers how to prepare food properly. I remember hearing Dr. Bruce say once that he believed one of the great miseries of comparative poverty consisted in poor food. He even went so far as to say that he thought some kinds of crime could be traced to soggy biscuit and tough beefsteak. I'm sure I would be able to make a living for Rose and myself and at the same time help others."

Felicia brooded over this dream until it became a reality. Meanwhile she grew into the affections of the Raymond people and the Rectangle folks, among whom she was known as the "angel cook." Underneath the structure of the beautiful character she was growing, always rested her promise made in Nazareth Avenue Church. "What would Jesus do?" She prayed and hoped and worked and regulated her life by the answer to that question. It was the inspiration of her conduct and the answer to all her ambition.

Chapter 25

Three months had gone by since the Sunday morning when Dr. Bruce came into his pulpit with the message of the new discipleship. They were three months of great excitement in Nazareth Avenue Church. Never before had Rev. Calvin Bruce realized how deep the feeling of his members flowed. He humbly confessed that the appeal he had made met with an unexpected response from men and women who, like Felicia, were hungry for something in their lives that the conventional type of church membership and fellowship had failed to give them.

But Dr. Bruce was not yet satisfied for himself. I cannot tell what his feeling was or what led to the movement he finally made, to the great astonishment of all who knew him, better than by relating a conversation between him and the Bishop at this time in the history of the pledge in Nazareth Avenue Church. The two friends were as before in Dr. Bruce's house, seated in his study.

"You know what I have come in this evening for?" the Bishop was saying after the friends had been talking some time about the results of the pledge with the Nazareth Avenue people.

Dr. Bruce looked over at the Bishop and shook his head.

"I have come to confess that I have not yet kept my promise to walk in His steps in the way that I believe I shall be obliged to if I satisfy my thought of what it means to walk in His steps."

Dr. Bruce had risen and was pacing his study. The Bishop remained in the deep easy chair with his hands clasped, but his eye burned with the glow that belonged to him before he made some great resolve.

"Edward," Dr. Bruce spoke abruptly, "I have not yet been able to satisfy myself, either, in obeying my promise. But I have at last decided on my course. In order to follow it I shall be obliged to resign from Nazareth Avenue Church."

"I knew you would," replied the Bishop quietly. "And I came in this evening to say that I shall be obliged to do the same thing with my charge."

Dr. Bruce turned and walked up to his friend. They were both laboring under a repressed excitement.

"Is it necessary in your case?" asked Bruce.

"Yes. Let me state my reasons. Probably they are the same as yours. In fact, I am sure they are." The Bishop paused a moment, then went on with increasing feeling:

"Calvin, you know how many years I have been doing the work of my position, and you know something of the responsibility and care of it. I do not mean to say that my life has been free from burden-bearing or sorrow. But I have certainly led what the poor and desperate of this sinful city would call a very comfortable, yes, a very luxurious life. I have had a beautiful house to live in, the most expensive food, clothing and physical pleasures. I have been able to go abroad at least a dozen times, and have enjoyed for years the beautiful companionship of art and letters and music and all the rest, of the very best. I have never known what it meant to be without money or its equivalent. And I have been unable to silence the question of late: 'What have I suffered for the sake of Christ?' Paul was told what great things he must suffer for the sake of his Lord. Maxwell's position at Raymond is well taken when he insists that to walk in the steps of Christ means to suffer. Where has my suffering come in? The petty trials and annoyances of my clerical life are **not** worth mentioning as sorrows or sufferings. Compared with Paul or any of the Christian martyrs or early disciples I have lived a luxurious, sinful life, full of ease and pleasure. I cannot endure this any longer. I have that within me which of late rises in overwhelming condemnation of such a following of Jesus. I have not been walking in His steps. Under the present system of church and social life I see no escape from this condemnation except to give the most of my life personally to the actual physical and soul needs of the wretched people in the worst part of the city."

The Bishop had risen now and walked over to the window. The street in front of the house was as light as day, and he looked out at the crowds passing, then turned and with a passionate utterance that showed how deep the volcanic fire in him burned, he exclaimed:

"Calvin, this is a terrible city in which we live! Its misery, its sin, its selfishness, appall my heart. And I have struggled for years with the sickening dread of the time when I should be forced to leave the pleasant luxury of my official position to put my life into contact with the modern paganism of this century. The awful condition of the girls in some great business places, the brutal selfishness of the insolent society fashion and wealth that ignores all the sorrow of the city, the fearful curse of the drink and gambling hell, the wail of the unemployed, the hatred of the church by countless men who see in it only great piles of costly stone and upholstered furniture and the minister as a luxurious idler, all the vast tumult of this vast torrent of humanity with its false and its true ideas, its exaggeration of evils in the church and its bitterness and shame that are the result of many complex causes, all this as a total fact in its contrast with the easy, comfortable life I have lived, fills me more and more with a sense of mingled terror and self accusation. I have heard the words of Jesus many times lately: 'Inasmuch as ye did it not unto one of these least My brethren, ye did it not unto Me.' and when have I personally visited the prisoner or the desperate or the sinful in any way that has actually caused me suffering? Rather, I have followed the conventional soft habits of my position and have lived in the society of the rich, refined, aristocratic members of my congregations. Where has the suffering come in? What have I suffered for Jesus' sake? Do you know, Calvin," he turned abruptly toward his friend, "I have been tempted of late to lash myself with a scourge. If I had lived in Martin Luther's time I should have bared my back to a self-inflicted torture."

Dr. Bruce was very pale. Never had he seen the Bishop **or heard** him when under the influence of such a passion. There was a sudden silence in the room. The Bishop sat down again and bowed his head.

Dr. Bruce spoke at last:

"Edward, I do not need to say that you have expressed my feelings also. I have been in a similar position for years. My life has been one of comparative luxury. I do not, of course, mean to say that I have not had trials and discouragements and burdens in my church ministry. But I cannot say that I have suffered any for Jesus. That verse in Peter constantly haunts me: 'Christ also suffered for you, leaving you an example that ye should follow His steps.' I have lived in luxury. I do not know what it means to want. I also have had my leisure for travel and beautiful companionship. I have been surrounded by the soft, easy comforts of civilization. The sin and misery of this great city have beaten like waves against the stone walls of my church and of this house in which I live, and I have hardly heeded them, the walls have been so thick. I have reached a point where I cannot endure this any longer. I'm not condemning the Church. I love her. I am not forsaking the Church. I believe in her mission and have no desire to destroy. Least of all, in the step I am about to take do I desire to be charged with abandoning the Christian fellowship. But I feel that I must resign my place as pastor of Nazareth Church in order to satisfy myself that I am walking as I ought to walk in His steps. In this action I judge no other minister and pass no criticism on others' discipleship. But I feel as you do. Into a close contact with the sin and shame and degradation of this great city I must come personally. And I know that to do that I must sever my immediate connection with Nazareth Avenue Church. I do not see any other way for myself to suffer for His sake as I feel that I ought to suffer."

Again that sudden silence fell over those two men. It was no ordinary action they were deciding. They had both reached the same conclusion by the same reasoning, and they were too thoughtful, too well accustomed to the measuring of conduct, to underestimate the seriousness of their position.

"What is your plan?" The Bishop at last spoke gently, looking with the smile that always beautified his face. The Bishop's face grew in glory now every day.

"My plan," replied Dr. Bruce slowly, "is, in brief, the putting of myself into the centre of the greatest human need I can find in this city and living there. My wife is fully in accord with me. We have already decided to find a residence in that part of the city where we can make our personal lives count for the most."

"Let me suggest a place." The Bishop was on fire now. His fine face actually glowed with the enthusiasm of the movement in which he and his friend were inevitably embarked. He went on and unfolded a plan of such far-reaching power and possibility that Dr. Bruce, capable and experienced as he was, felt amazed at the vision of a greater soul than his own.

They sat up late, and were as eager and even glad as if they were planning for a trip together to some rare land of unexplored travel. Indeed, the Bishop said many times afterward that the moment his decision was reached to live the life of personal sacrifice he had chosen he suddenly felt an uplifting as if a great burden were taken from him. He was exultant. So was Dr. Bruce from the same cause.

Their plan as it finally grew into a workable fact was in reality nothing more than the renting of a large building formerly used as a warehouse for a brewery, reconstructing it and living in it themselves in the very heart of a territory where the saloon ruled with power, where the tenement was its filthiest, where vice and ignorance and shame and poverty were congested into hideous forms. It was not a new idea. It was an idea started by Jesus Christ when He left His Father's house and forsook the riches that were His in order to get nearer humanity and, by becoming a part of its sin, helping to draw humanity apart from its sin. The University Settlement idea is not modern. It is as old as Bethlehem and Nazareth. And in this particular case it was the nearest approach to anything that would satisfy the hunger of these two men to suffer for Christ.

There had sprung up in them at the same time a longing that amounted to a passion, to get nearer the great physical poverty and spiritual destitution of the mighty city that throbbed around them. How could they do this except as they became a part of it as nearly as one man can become a part of another's misery? Where was the suffering to come in unless there was an actual self-denial of some sort? And what was to make that self-denial apparent to themselves or any one else, unless it took this concrete, actual, personal form of trying to share the deepest suffering and sin of the city?

So they reasoned for themselves, not judging others. They were simply keeping their own pledge to do as Jesus would do, as they honestly judged He would do. That was what they had promised. How could they quarrel with the result if they were irresistibly compelled to do what they were planning to do?

The Bishop had money of his own. Every one in Chicago knew that he had a handsome fortune. Dr. Bruce had acquired and saved by literary work carried on in connection with his parish duties more than a comfortable competence. This money, a large part of it, the two friends agreed to put at once into the work, most of it into the furnishing of the Settlement House.

Chapter 26

Meanwhile, Nazareth Avenue Church was experiencing something never known before in all its history. The simple appeal on the part of its pastor to his members to do as Jesus would do had created a sensation that still continued. The result of that appeal was very much the same as in Henry Maxwell's church in Raymond, only this church was far more aristocratic, wealthy and conventional. Nevertheless when, one Sunday morning in early summer, Dr. Bruce came into his pulpit and announced his resignation, the sensation deepened all over the city, although he had advised with his board of trustees, and the movement he intended was not a matter of surprise to them. But when it became publicly known that the Bishop had also announced his resignation and retirement from the position he had held so long, in order to go and live himself in the centre of the worst part of Chicago, the public astonishment reached its height.

"But why?" the Bishop replied to one valued friend who had almost with tears tried to dissuade him from his purpose. "Why should what Dr. Bruce and I propose to do seem so remarkable a thing, as if it were unheard of that a Doctor of Divinity and a Bishop should want to save lost souls in this particular manner? If we were to resign our charge for the purpose of going to Bombay or Hong Kong or any place in Africa, the churches and the people would exclaim at the heroism of missions. Why should it seem so great a thing if we have been led to give our lives to help rescue the heathen and the lost of our own city in the way we are going to try it? Is it then such a tremendous event that two Christian ministers should be not only willing but eager to live close to the misery of the world in order to know it and realize it? Is it such a rare thing that love of humanity should find this particular form of expression in the rescue of souls?"

And however the Bishop may have satisfied himself that there ought to be nothing so remarkable about it at all, the public continued to talk and the churches to record their astonishment that two such men, so prominent in the ministry, should leave their comfortable homes, voluntarily resign their pleasant social positions and enter upon a life of hardship, of self-denial and actual suffering. Christian America! Is it a reproach on the form of our discipleship that the exhibition of actual suffering for Jesus on the part of those who walk in His steps always provokes astonishment as at the sight of something very unusual?

Nazareth Avenue Church parted from its pastor with regret for the most part, although the regret was modified with a feeling of relief on the part of those who had refused to take the pledge. Dr. Bruce carried with him the respect of men who, entangled in business in such a way that obedience to the pledge would have ruined them, still, held in their deeper, better natures a genuine admiration for courage and consistency. They had known Dr. Bruce many years as a kindly, conservative, safe man, but the thought of him in the light of sacrifice of this sort was not familiar to them. As fast as they understood it, they gave their pastor the credit of being absolutely true to his recent convictions as to what following Jesus meant. Nazareth Avenue Church never lost the impulse of that movement started by Dr. Bruce. Those who went with him in making the promise breathed into the church the very breath of divine life, and are continuing that life-giving work at this present time.

• • • • •

It was fall again, and the city faced another hard winter. The Bishop one afternoon came out of the Settlement and walked around the block, intending to go on a visit to one of his new friends in the district. He had walked about four blocks when he was attracted by a shop that looked different from the others. The neighborhood was still quite new to him, and every day he discovered some strange spot or stumbled upon some unexpected humanity.

The place that attracted his notice was a small house close by a Chinese laundry. There were two windows in the front, very clean, and that was remarkable to begin with. Then, inside the window, was a tempting display of cookery, with prices attached to the various articles that made him wonder somewhat, for he was familiar by this time with many facts in the life of the people once unknown to him. As he stood looking at the windows, the door between them opened and Felicia Sterling came out.

"Felicia!" exclaimed the Bishop. "When did you move into my parish without my knowledge?"

"How did you find me so soon?" inquired Felicia.

"Why, don't you know? These are the only clean windows in the block."

"I believe they are," replied Felicia with a laugh that did the Bishop good to hear.

"But why have you dared to come to Chicago without telling me, and how have you entered my diocese without my knowledge?" asked the Bishop. And Felicia looked so like that beautiful, clean, educated, refined world he once knew, that he might be pardoned for seeing in her something of the old Paradise. Although, to speak truth for him, he had no desire to go back to it.

"Well, dear Bishop," said Felicia, who had always called him so, "I knew how overwhelmed you were with your work. I did not want to burden you with my plans. And besides, I am going to offer you my services. Indeed, I was just on my way to see you and ask your advice. I am settled here for the present with Mrs. Bascom, a saleswoman who rents out three rooms, and with one of Rachel's music pupils who is being helped to a course in violin by Virginia Page. She is from the people," continued Felicia, using the words "from the people" so grave and unconsciously that her hearer smiled, "and I am keeping house for her and at the same time beginning an experiment in pure food for the masses. I am an expert and I have a plan I want you to admire and develop. Will you, dear Bishop?"

"Indeed I will," he replied. The sight of Felicia and her remarkable vitality, enthusiasm and evident purpose almost bewildered him.

"Martha can help at the Settlement with her violin and I will help with my messes. You see, I thought I would get settled first and work out something, and then come with some real thing to offer. I'm able to earn my own living now."

"You are?" the Bishop said a little incredulously. "How? Making those things?"

"Those things!" said Felicia with a show of indignation. "I would have you know, sir, that 'those things' are the best-cooked, purest food products in this whole city."

"I don't doubt it," he replied hastily, while his eyes twinkled. "Still, 'the proof of the pudding'—you know the rest."

"Come in and try some!" she exclaimed. "You poor Bishop! You look as if you hadn't had a good meal for a month."

She insisted on his entering the little front room where Martha, a wide-awake girl with short, curly hair, and an unmistakable air of music about her, was busy with practice.

"Go right on, Martha. This is the Bishop. You have heard me speak of him so often. Sit down there and let me give you a taste of the fleshpots of Egypt, for I believe you have been actually fasting."

So they had an improvised lunch, and the Bishop who, to tell the truth, had not taken time for weeks to enjoy his meals, feasted on the delight of his unexpected discovery and was able to express his astonishment and gratification at the quality of the cookery.

"I thought you would at least say it is as good as the meals you used to get at the Auditorium at the big banquets," said Felicia slyly.

"As good as! The Auditorium banquets were simply husks compared with this one, Felicia. But you must come to the Settlement. I want you to see what we are doing. And I am simply astonished to find you here earning your living this way. I begin to see what your plan is. You can be of infinite help to us. You don't really mean that you will live here and help these people to know the value of good food?"

"Indeed I do," she answered gravely. "That is my gospel. Shall I not follow it?"

"Aye, Aye! You're right. Bless God for sense like yours! When I left the world," the Bishop smiled at the phrase, "they were talking a good deal about the 'new woman.' If you are one of them, I am a convert right now and here."

"Flattery! Still is there no escape from it, even in the slums of Chicago?" Felicia laughed again. And the man's heart, heavy though it had grown during several months of vast sin-bearing, rejoiced to hear it! It sounded good. It was good. It belonged to God.

Felicia wanted to visit the Settlement, and went back with him. She was amazed at the results of what considerable money and a good deal of consecrated brains had done. As they walked through the building they talked incessantly. She was the incarnation of vital enthusiasm, and he wondered at the exhibition of it as it bubbled up and sparkled over.

They went down into the basement and the Bishop pushed open a door from behind which came the sound of a carpenter's plane. It was a small but well-equipped carpenter's shop. A young man with a paper cap on his head and clad in blouse and overalls was whistling and driving the plane as he whistled. He looked up as the two entered, and took off his cap. As he did so, his little finger carried a small curling shaving up to his hair and it caught there.

"Miss Sterling, Mr. Stephen Clyde," said the Bishop. "Clyde is one of our helpers here two afternoons in the week."

Just then the bishop was called upstairs and he excused himself a moment, leaving Felicia and the young carpenter together.

"We have met before," said Felicia looking at Clyde frankly.

"Yes, 'back in the world,' as the Bishop says," replied the young man, and his fingers trembled a little as they lay on the board he had been planning.

"Yes." Felicia hesitated. "I am very glad to see you."

"Are you?" The flush of pleasure mounted to the young carpenter's forehead. "You have had a great deal of trouble since—since—then," he said and then he was afraid he had wounded her, or called up painful memories. But she had lived over all that.

"Yes, and you also. How is it that you're working here?"

"It is a long story, Miss Sterling. My father lost his money and I was obliged to go to work. A very good thing for me. The Bishop says I ought to be very grateful. I am. I am very happy now. I learned the trade, hoping some time to be of use. I am night clerk at one of the hotels. That Sunday morning when you took the pledge at Nazareth Avenue Church, I took it with the others."

"Did you?" said Felicia slowly. "I am glad."

Just then the Bishop came back, and very soon he and Felicia went away leaving the young carpenter at his work. Some one noticed that he whistled louder than ever as he planed.

"Felicia," said the Bishop, "did you know Stephen Clyde before?"

"Yes, 'back in the world,' dear Bishop. He was one of my acquaintances in Nazareth Avenue Church."

"Ah!" said the Bishop.

"We were very good friends," added Felicia.

"But nothing more?" the Bishop ventured to ask.

Felicia's face glowed for an instant. Then she looked her companion in the eyes frankly and answered:

"Truly and truly, nothing more."

"It would be just the way of the world for those two people to come to like each other, though," thought the man to himself, and somehow the thought made him grave. It was almost like the old pang over Camilla. But it passed, leaving him afterwards, when Felicia had gone back, with tears in his eyes and a feeling that was almost hope that Felicia and Stephen would like each other. "After all," he said, like the sensible, good man that he was, "is not romance a part of humanity? Love is older than I am, and wiser."

The week following, the Bishop had an experience that belongs to this part of the Settlement history. He was coming back to the Settlement very late from some gathering of the striking tailors, and was walking along with his hands behind him, when two men jumped out from behind an old fence that shut off an abandoned factory from the street, and faced him. One of the men thrust a pistol in his face, and the other threatened him with a ragged stake that had evidently been torn from the fence.

"Hold up your hands, and be quick about it!" said the man with the pistol.

The place was solitary and the Bishop had no thought of resistance. He did as he was commanded, and the man with the stake began to go through his pockets. He was calm. His nerves did not quiver. As he stood there with his hands uplifted, an ignorant spectator might have thought that he was praying for the souls of these two men. And he was. And his prayer was singularly answered that very night.

Chapter 27

Righteousness shall go before him and shall set us in the way of his steps.

The Bishop was not in the habit of carrying much money with him, and the man with the stake who was searching him uttered an oath at the small amount of change he found. As he uttered it, the man with the pistol savagely said, "Jerk out his watch! We might as well get all we can out of the job!"

The man with the stake was on the point of laying hold of the chain when there was a sound of footsteps coming towards him.

"Get behind the fence! We haven't half searched him yet! Mind you keep shut now, if you don't want—"

The man with the pistol made a significant gesture with it and, with his companion, pulled and pushed the Bishop down the alley and through a ragged, broken opening in the fence. The three stood still there in the shadow until the footsteps passed.

"Now, then, have you got the watch?" asked the man with the pistol.

"No, the chain is caught somewhere!" and the other man swore again.

"Break it then!"

"No, don't break it," the Bishop said, and it was the first time he had spoken. "The chain is the gift of a very dear friend. I should be sorry to have it broken."

At the sound of the Bishop's voice the man with the pistol started as if he had been suddenly shot by his own weapon. With a quick movement of his other hand he turned the Bishop's head towards what little light was shining from the alleyway, at the same time taking a step nearer. Then, to the amazement of his companion, he said roughly:

"Leave the watch alone! We've got the money. That's enough!"

"Enough! Fifty cents! You don't reckon—"

Before the man with the stake could say another word he was confronted with the muzzle of the pistol turned from the Bishop's head
towards his own.

"Leave that watch be! And put back the money too. This is the
Bishop we've held up—the Bishop—do you hear?"

"And what of it! The President of the United States wouldn't be too
good to hold up, if—"

"I say, you put the money back, or in five seconds I'll blow a hole
through your head that'll let in more sense than you have to spare
now!" said the other.

For a second the man with the stake seemed to hesitate at this
strange turn in events, as if measuring his companion's intention. Then
he hastily dropped the money back into the rifled pocket.

"You can take your hands down, sir." The man lowered his weapon
slowly, still keeping an eye on the other man, and speaking with
rough respect. The Bishop slowly brought his arms to his side, and
looked earnestly at the two men. In the dim light it was difficult to
distinguish features. He was evidently free to go his way now, but he
stood there making no movement.

"You can go on. You needn't stay any longer on our account." The
man who had acted as spokesman turned and sat down on a stone.
The other man stood viciously digging his stake into the ground.

"That's just what I am staying for," replied the Bishop. He sat
down on a board that projected from the broken fence.

"You must like our company. It is hard sometimes for people to tear
themselves away from us," and the man standing up laughed coarsely.

"Shut up!" exclaimed the other. "We're on the road to hell, though,
that's sure enough. We need better company than ourselves and the
devil."

"If you would only allow me to be of any help," the Bishop spoke
gently, even lovingly. The man on the stone stared at the Bishop
through the darkness. After a moment of silence he spoke slowly like
one who had finally decided upon a course he had at first rejected.

"Do you ever remember seeing us before?"

"No," said the Bishop. "The light is not very good and I have really
not had a good look at you."

"Do you know me now?" The man suddenly took off his hat and
getting up from the stone walked over to the Bishop until they were
near enough to touch each other.

The man's hair was coal black except one spot on the top of his
head about as large as the palm of the hand, which was white.

The minute the Bishop saw that, he started. The memory of fifteen
years ago began to stir in him. The man helped him.

"Don't you remember one day back in '81 or '82 a man came to your house and told a story about his wife and child having been burned to death in a tenement fire in New York?"

"Yes, I begin to remember now." The other man seemed to be interested. He ceased digging his stake in the ground and stood still listening.

"Do you remember how you took me into your own house that night and spent all next day trying to find me a job? And how when you succeeded in getting me a place in a warehouse as foreman, I promised to quit drinking because you asked me to?"

"I remember it now. I hope you have kept your promise."

The man laughed savagely. Then he struck his hand against the fence with such sudden passion that he drew blood.

"Kept it! I was drunk inside of a week! I've been drinking ever since. But I've never forgotten you nor your prayer. Do you remember the morning after I came to your house, after breakfast you had prayers and asked me to come in and sit with the rest? That got me! But my mother used to pray! I can see her now kneeling down by my bed when I was a lad. Father came in one night and kicked her while she was kneeling there by me. But I never forgot that prayer of yours that morning. You prayed for me just as mother used to, and you didn't seem to take 'count of the fact that I was ragged and tough-looking and more than half drunk when I rang your door bell. Oh, what a life I've lived! The saloon has housed me and homed me and made hell on earth for me. But that prayer stuck to me all the time. My promise not to drink was broken into a thousand pieces inside of two Sundays, and I lost the job you found for me and landed in a police station two days later, but I never forgot you nor your prayer. I don't know what good it has done me, but I never forgot it. And I won't do any harm to you nor let any one else. So you're free to go. That's why."

The Bishop did not stir. Somewhere a church clock struck one. The man had put on his hat and gone back to his seat on the stone. The Bishop was thinking hard.

"How long is it since you had work?" he asked, and the man standing up answered for the other.

"More'n six months since either of us did anything to tell of; unless you count 'holding up' work. I call it pretty wearing kind of a job myself, especially when we put in a night like this and don't make nothin'."

"Suppose I found good jobs for both of you? Would you quit this and begin all over?"

"What's the use?" the man on the stone spoke sullenly. "I've reformed a hundred times. Every time I go down deeper. The devil's begun to foreclose on me already. It's too late."

"No!" said the Bishop. And never before the most entranced audience had he felt the desire for souls burn up in him so strongly. All the time he sat there during the remarkable scene he prayed, "O Lord Jesus, give me the souls of these two for Thee! I am hungry for them. Give them to me!"

"No!" the Bishop repeated. "What does God want of you two men? It doesn't so much matter what I want. But He wants just what I do in this case. You two men are of infinite value to Him." And then his wonderful memory came to his aid in an appeal such as no one on earth among men could make under such circumstances. He had remembered the man's name in spite of the wonderfully busy years that lay between his coming to the house and the present moment.

"Burns," he said, and he yearned over the men with an unspeakable longing for them both, "if you and your friend here will go home with me tonight I will find you both places of honorable employment. I will believe in you and trust you. You are both comparatively young men. Why should God lose you? It is a great thing to win the love of the Great Father. It is a small thing that I should love you. But if you need to feel again that there is love in the world, you will believe me when I say, my brothers, that I love you, and in the name of Him who was crucified for our sins I cannot bear to see you miss the glory of the human life. Come, be men! Make another try for it, God helping you. No one but God and you and myself need ever know anything of this tonight. He has forgiven it the minute you ask Him to. You will find that true. Come! We'll fight it out together, you two and I. It's worth fighting for, everlasting life is. It was the sinner that Christ came to help. I'll do what I can for you. O God, give me the souls of these two men!" and he broke into a prayer to God that was a continuation of his appeal to the men. His pent-up feeling had no other outlet. Before he had prayed many moments Burns was sitting with his face buried in his hands, sobbing. Where were his mother's prayers now? They were adding to the power of the Bishop's. And the other man, harder, less moved, without a previous knowledge of the Bishop, leaned back against the fence, stolid at first. But as the prayer went on, he was moved by it. What force of the Holy Spirit swept over his dulled, brutal, coarsened life, nothing but the eternal records of the recording angel can ever disclose. But the same supernatural Presence that smote Paul on the road to Damascus, and poured through Henry Maxwell's church the morning he asked disciples to follow in Jesus' steps, and had again broken irresistibly over the Nazareth Avenue congregation, now manifested Himself in this foul corner of the mighty city and over the natures of these two sinful sunken men, apparently lost to all the pleadings of conscience and memory and God. The prayer seemed to break open the crust that for years had surrounded them and shut them off from divine communication. And they themselves were thoroughly startled by it.

The Bishop ceased, and at first he himself did not realize what had happened. Neither did they. Burns still sat with his head bowed between his knees. The man leaning against the fence looked at the Bishop with a face in which new emotions of awe, repentance, astonishment and a broken gleam of joy struggled for expression. The Bishop rose.

"Come, my brothers. God is good. You shall stay at the Settlement tonight, and I will make good my promise as to the work."

The two men followed him in silence. When they reached the Settlement it was after two o'clock. He let them in and led them to a room. At the door he paused a moment. His tall, commanding figure stood in the doorway and his pale face, worn with his recent experience, was illuminated with the divine glory.

"God bless you, my brothers!" he said, and leaving them his benediction he went away.

In the morning he almost dreaded to face the men. But the impression of the night had not worn away. True to his promise he secured work for them. The janitor at the Settlement needed an assistant, owing to the growth of the work there. So Burns was given the place. The Bishop succeeded in getting his companion a position as driver for a firm of warehouse dray manufacturers not far from the Settlement. And the Holy Spirit, struggling in these two darkened sinful men, began His marvelous work of regeneration.

Chapter 28

It was the afternoon of that morning when Burns was installed in his new position as assistant janitor that he was cleaning off the front steps of the Settlement, when he paused a moment and stood up to look about him. The first thing he noticed was a beer sign just across the alley. He could almost touch it with his broom from where he stood. Over the street immediately opposite were two large saloons, and a little farther down were three more.

Suddenly the door of the nearest saloon opened and a man came out. At the same time two more went in. A strong odor of beer floated up to Burns as he stood on the steps. He clutched his broom handle tightly and began to sweep again. He had one foot on the porch and another on the steps just below. He took another step down, still sweeping. The sweat stood on his forehead although the day was frosty and the air chill. The saloon door opened again and three or four men came out. A child went in with a pail, and came out a moment later with a quart of beer. The child went by on the sidewalk just below him, and the odor of the beer came up to him. He took another step down, still sweeping desperately. His fingers were purple as he clutched the handle of the broom.

Then suddenly he pulled himself up one step and swept over the spot he had just cleaned. He then dragged himself by a tremendous effort back to the floor of the porch and went over into the corner of it farthest from the saloon and began to sweep there. "O God!" he cried, "if the Bishop would only come back!" The Bishop had gone out with Dr. Bruce somewhere, and there was no one about that he knew.

He swept in the corner for two or three minutes. His face was drawn with the agony of his conflict. Gradually he edged out again towards the steps and began to go down them. He looked towards the sidewalk and saw that he had left one step unswept. The sight seemed to give him a reasonable excuse for going down there to finish his sweeping.

He was on the sidewalk now, sweeping the last step, with his face towards the Settlement and his back turned partly on the saloon across the alley. He swept the step a dozen times. The sweat rolled over his face and dropped down at his feet. By degrees he felt that he was drawn over towards that end of the step nearest the saloon. He could smell the beer and rum now as the fumes rose around him. It was like the infernal sulphur of the lowest hell, and yet it dragged him as by a giant's hand nearer its source.

He was down in the middle of the sidewalk now, still sweeping. He cleared the space in front of the Settlement and even went out into the gutter and swept that. He took off his hat and rubbed his sleeve over his face. His lips were pallid and his teeth chattered. He trembled all over like a palsied man and staggered back and forth as if he was already drunk. His soul shook within him.

He had crossed over the little piece of stone flagging that measured the width of the alley, and now he stood in front of the saloon, looking at the sign, and staring into the window at the pile of whiskey and beer bottles arranged in a great pyramid inside. He moistened his lips with his tongue and took a step forward, looking around him stealthily. The door suddenly opened again and some one came out. Again the hot, penetrating smell of liquor swept out into the cold air, and he took another step towards the saloon door which had shut behind the customer. As he laid his fingers on the door handle, a tall figure came around the corner. It was the Bishop.

He seized Burns by the arm and dragged him back upon the sidewalk. The frenzied man, now mad for a drink, shrieked out a curse and struck at his friend savagely. It is doubtful if he really knew at first who was snatching him away from his ruin. The blow fell upon the Bishop's face and cut a gash in his cheek. He never uttered a word. But over his face a look of majestic sorrow swept. He picked Burns up as if he had been a child and actually carried him up the steps and into the house. He put him down in the hall and then shut the door and put his back against it.

Burns fell on his knees sobbing and praying. The Bishop stood there panting with his exertion, although Burns was a slightly-built man and had not been a great weight for a man of his strength to carry. He was moved with unspeakable pity.

"Pray, Burns—pray as you never prayed before! Nothing else will save you!"

"Oh God! Pray with me. Save me! Oh, save me from my hell!" cried Burns. And the Bishop knelt by him in the hall and prayed as only he could pray.

After that they rose and Burns went to his room. He came out of it that evening like a humble child. And the Bishop went his way older from that experience, bearing on his body the marks of the Lord Jesus. Truly he was learning something of what it means to walk in His steps.

But the saloon! It stood there, and all the others lined the street like so many traps set for Burns. How long would the man be able to resist the smell of the damnable stuff? The Bishop went out on the porch. The air of the whole city seemed to be impregnated with the odor of beer. "How long, O Lord, how long?" he prayed. Dr. Bruce came out, and the two friends talked about Burns and his temptation.

"Did you ever make any inquiries about the ownership of this property adjoining us?" the Bishop asked.

"No, I haven't taken time for it. I will now if you think it would be worth while. But what can we do, Edward, against the saloon in this great city? It is as firmly established as the churches or politics. What power can ever remove it?"

"God will do it in time, as He has removed slavery," was the grave reply. "Meanwhile I think we have a right to know who controls this saloon so near the Settlement."

"I'll find out," said Dr. Bruce.

Two days later he walked into the business office of one of the members of Nazareth Avenue Church and asked to see him a few moments. He was cordially received by his old parishioner, who welcomed him into his room and urged him to take all the time he wanted.

"I called to see you about that property next the Settlement where the Bishop and myself now are, you know. I am going to speak plainly, because life is too short and too serious for us both to have any foolish hesitation about this matter. Clayton, do you think it is right to rent that property for a saloon?"

Dr. Bruce's question was as direct and uncompromising as he had meant it to be. The effect of it on his old parishioner was instantaneous.

The hot blood mounted to the face of the man who sat there a picture of business activity in a great city. Then he grew pale, dropped his head on his hands, and when he raised it again Dr. Bruce was amazed to see a tear roll over his face.

"Doctor, did you know that I took the pledge that morning with the others?"

"Yes, I remember."

"But you never knew how I have been tormented over my failure to keep it in this instance. That saloon property has been the temptation of the devil to me. It is the best paying investment at present that I have. And yet it was only a minute before you came in here that I was in an agony of remorse to think how I was letting a little earthly gain tempt me into a denial of the very Christ I had promised to follow. I knew well enough that He would never rent property for such a purpose. There is no need, Dr. Bruce, for you to say a word more."

Clayton held out his hand and Dr. Bruce grasped it and shook it hard. After a little he went away. But it was a long time afterwards that he learned all the truth about the struggle that Clayton had known. It was only a part of the history that belonged to Nazareth Avenue Church since that memorable morning when the Holy Spirit sanctioned the Christ-like pledge. Not even the Bishop and Dr. Bruce, moving as they now did in the very presence itself of divine impulse, knew yet that over the whole sinful city the Spirit was brooding with mighty eagerness, waiting for the disciples to arise to the call of sacrifice and suffering, touching hearts long dull and cold, making business men and money-makers uneasy in their absorption by the one great struggle for more wealth, and stirring through the church as never in all the city's history the church had been moved. The Bishop and Dr. Bruce had already seen some wonderful things in their brief life at the Settlement. They were to see far greater soon, more astonishing revelations of the divine power than they had supposed possible in this age of the world.

Within a month the saloon next the Settlement was closed. The saloon-keeper's lease had expired, and Clayton not only closed the property to the whiskey men, but offered the building to the Bishop and Dr. Bruce to use for the Settlement work, which had now grown so large that the building they had first rented was not sufficient for the different industries that were planned.

One of the most important of these was the pure-food department suggested by Felicia. It was not a month after Clayton turned the saloon property over to the Settlement that Felicia found herself installed in the very room where souls had been lost, as head of the department not only of cooking but of a course of housekeeping for girls who wished to go out to service. She was now a resident of the Settlement, and found a home with Mrs. Bruce and the other young women from the city who were residents. Martha, the violinist, remained at the place where the Bishop had first discovered the two girls, and came over to the Settlement certain evenings to give lessons in music.

"Felicia, tell us your plan in full now," said the Bishop one evening when, in a rare interval of rest from the great pressure of work, he was with Dr. Bruce, and Felicia had come in from the other building.

"Well, I have long thought of the hired girl problem," said Felicia with an air of wisdom that made Mrs. Bruce smile as she looked at the enthusiastic, vital beauty of this young girl, transformed into a new creature by the promise she had made to live the Christ-like life. "And I have reached certain conclusions in regard to it that you men are not yet able to fathom, but Mrs. Bruce will understand me."

"We acknowledge our infancy, Felicia. Go on," said the Bishop humbly.

"Then this is what I propose to do. The old saloon building is large enough to arrange into a suite of rooms that will represent an ordinary house. My plan is to have it so arranged, and then teach housekeeping and cooking to girls who will afterwards go out to service. The course will be six months' long; in that time I will teach plain cooking, neatness, quickness, and a love of good work."

"Hold on, Felicia!" the Bishop interrupted, "this is not an age of miracles!"

"Then we will make it one," replied Felicia. "I know this seems like an impossibility, but I want to try it. I know a score of girls already who will take the course, and if we can once establish something like an esprit de corps among the girls themselves, I am sure it will be of great value to them. I know already that the pure food is working a revolution in many families."

"Felicia, if you can accomplish half what you propose it will bless this community," said Mrs. Bruce. "I don't see how you can do it, but I say, God bless you, as you try."

"So say we all!" cried Dr. Bruce and the Bishop, and Felicia plunged into the working out of her plan with the enthusiasm of her discipleship which every day grew more and more practical and serviceable.

It must be said here that Felicia's plan succeeded beyond all expectations. She developed wonderful powers of persuasion, and taught her girls with astonishing rapidity to do all sorts of housework. In time, the graduates of Felicia's cooking school came to be prized by housekeepers all over the city. But that is anticipating our story. The history of the Settlement has never yet been written. When it is Felicia's part will be found of very great importance.

The depth of winter found Chicago presenting, as every great city of the world presents to the eyes of Christendom the marked contrast between riches and poverty, between culture, refinement, luxury, ease, and ignorance, depravity, destitution and the bitter struggle for bread. It was a hard winter but a gay winter. Never had there been such a succession of parties, receptions, balls, dinners, banquets, fetes, gayeties. Never had the opera and the theatre been so crowded with fashionable audiences. Never had there been such a lavish display of jewels and fine dresses and equipages. And on the other hand, never had the deep want and suffering been so cruel, so sharp, so murderous. Never had the winds blown so chilling over the lake and through the thin shells of tenements in the neighborhood of the Settlement. Never had the pressure for food and fuel and clothes been so urgently thrust up against the people of the city in their most importunate and ghastly form. Night after night the Bishop and Dr. Bruce with their helpers went out and helped save men and women and children from the torture of physical privation. Vast quantities of food and clothing and large sums of money were donated by the churches, the charitable societies, the civic authorities and the benevolent associations. But the personal touch of the Christian disciple was very hard to secure for personal work. Where was the discipleship that was obeying the Master's command to go itself to the suffering and give itself with its gift in order to make the gift of value in time to come? The Bishop found his heart sink within him as he faced this fact more than any other. Men would give money who would not think of giving themselves. And the money they gave did not represent any real sacrifice because they did not miss it. They gave what was the easiest to give, what hurt them the least. Where did the sacrifice come in? Was this following Jesus? Was this going with Him all the way? He had been to members of his own aristocratic, splendidly wealthy congregations, and was appalled to find how few men and women of that luxurious class in the churches would really suffer any genuine inconvenience for the sake of suffering humanity. Is charity the giving of worn-out garments? Is it a ten-dollar bill given to a paid visitor or secretary of some benevolent organization in the church? Shall the man never go and give his gift himself? Shall the woman never deny herself her reception or her party or her musicale, and go and actually touch, herself, the foul, sinful sore of diseased humanity as it festers in the great metropolis? Shall charity be conveniently and easily done through some organization? Is it possible to organize the affections so that love shall work disagreeable things by proxy?

All this the Bishop asked as he plunged deeper into the sin and sorrow of that bitter winter. He was bearing his cross with joy. But he burned and fought within over the shifting of personal love by the many upon the hearts of the few. And still, silently, powerfully, resistlessly, the Holy Spirit was moving through the churches, even the aristocratic, wealthy, ease-loving members who shunned the terrors of the social problem as they would shun a contagious disease.

This fact was impressed upon the Settlement workers in a startling way one morning. Perhaps no incident of that winter shows more plainly how much of a momentum had already grown out of the movement of Nazareth Avenue Church and the action of Dr. Bruce and the Bishop that followed the pledge to do as Jesus would do.

Chapter 29

The breakfast hour at the Settlement was the one hour in the day when the whole family found a little breathing space to fellowship together. It was an hour of relaxation. There was a great deal of good-natured repartee and much real wit and enjoyable fun at this hour. The Bishop told his best stories. Dr. Bruce was at his best in anecdote. This company of disciples was healthily humorous in spite of the atmosphere of sorrow that constantly surrounded them. In fact, the Bishop often said the faculty of humor was as God-given as any other and in his own case it was the only safety valve he had for the tremendous pressure put upon him.

This particular morning he was reading extracts from a morning paper for the benefit of the others. Suddenly he paused and his face instantly grew stern and sad. The rest looked up and a hush fell over the table.

"Shot and killed while taking a lump of coal from a car! His family was freezing and he had had no work for six months. Six children and a wife all packed into a cabin with three rooms, on the West Side. One child wrapped in rags in a closet!"

These were headlines that read slowly. He then went on and read the detailed account of the shooting and the visit of the reporter to the tenement where the family lived. He finished, and there was silence around the table. The humor of the hour was swept out of existence by this bit of human tragedy. The great city roared about the Settlement. The awful current of human life was flowing in a great stream past the Settlement House, and those who had work were hurrying to it in a vast throng. But thousands were going down in the midst of that current, clutching at last hopes, dying literally in a land of plenty because the boon of physical toil was denied them.

There were various comments on the part of the residents. One of the new-comers, a young man preparing for the ministry, said:

"Why doesn't the man apply to one of the charity organizations for help? Or to the city? It certainly is not true that even at its worst this city full of Christian people would knowingly allow any one to go without food or fuel."

"No, I don't believe it would," replied Dr. Bruce. "But we don't know the history of this man's case. He may have asked for help so often before that, finally, in a moment of desperation he determined to help himself. I have known such cases this winter."

"That is not the terrible fact in this case," said the Bishop. "The awful thing about it is the fact that the man had not had any work for six months."

"Why don't such people go out into the country?" asked the divinity student.

Someone at the table who had made a special study of the opportunities for work in the country answered the question. According to the investigator the places that were possible for work in the country were exceedingly few for steady employment, and in almost every case they were offered only to men without families. Suppose a man's wife or children were ill. How would he move or get into the country? How could he pay even the meager sum necessary to move his few goods? There were a thousand reasons probably why this particular man did not go elsewhere.

"Meanwhile there are the wife and children," said Mrs. Bruce. "How awful! Where is the place, did you say?"

"Why, it is only three blocks from here. This is the 'Penrose district.' I believe Penrose himself owns half of the houses in that block. They are among the worst houses in this part of the city. And Penrose is a church member."

"Yes, he belongs to the Nazareth Avenue Church," replied Dr. Bruce in a low voice.

The Bishop rose from the table the very figure of divine wrath. He had opened his lips to say what seldom came from him in the way of denunciation, when the bell rang and one of the residents went to the door.

"Tell Dr. Bruce and the Bishop I want to see them. Penrose is the name—Clarence Penrose. Dr. Bruce knows me."

The family at the breakfast table heard every word. The Bishop exchanged a significant look with Dr. Bruce and the two men instantly left the table and went out into the hall.

"Come in here, Penrose," said Dr. Bruce, and they ushered the visitor into the reception room, closed the door and were alone.

Clarence Penrose was one of the most elegant looking men in Chicago. He came from an aristocratic family of great wealth and social distinction. He was exceedingly wealthy and had large property holdings in different parts of the city. He had been a member of Dr. Bruce's church many years. He faced the two ministers with a look of agitation on his face that showed plainly the mark of some unusual experience. He was very pale and his lips trembled as he spoke. When had Clarence Penrose ever before yielded to such a strange emotion?

"This affair of the shooting! You understand? You have read it? The family lived in one of my houses. It is a terrible event. But that is not the primary cause of my visit." He stammered and looked anxiously into the faces of the two men. The Bishop still looked stern. He could not help feeling that this elegant man of leisure could have done a great deal to alleviate the horrors in his tenements, possibly have prevented this tragedy if he had sacrificed some of his personal ease and luxury to better the conditions of the people in his district.

Penrose turned toward Dr. Bruce. "Doctor!" he exclaimed, and there was almost a child's terror in his voice. "I came to say that I have had an experience so unusual that nothing but the supernatural can explain it. You remember I was one of those who took the pledge to do as Jesus would do. I thought at the time, poor fool that I was, that I had all along been doing the Christian thing. I gave liberally out of my abundance to the church and charity. I never gave myself to cost me any suffering. I have been living in a perfect hell of contradictions ever since I took that pledge. My little girl, Diana you remember, also took the pledge with me. She has been asking me a great many questions lately about the poor people and where they live. I was obliged to answer her. One of her questions last night touched my sore! 'Do you own any houses where these poor people live? Are they nice and warm like ours?' You know how a child will ask questions like these. I went to bed tormented with what I now know to be the divine arrows of conscience. I could not sleep. I seemed to see the judgment day. I was placed before the Judge. I was asked to give an account of my deeds done in the body. 'How many sinful souls had I visited in prison? What had I done with my stewardship? How about those tenements where people froze in winter and stifled in summer? Did I give any thought to them except to receive the rentals from them? Where did my suffering come in? Would Jesus have done as I had done and was doing? Had I broken my pledge? How had I used the money and the culture and the social influence I possessed? Had I used it to bless humanity, to relieve the suffering, to bring joy to the distressed and hope to the desponding? I had received much. How much had I given?'

"All this came to me in a waking vision as distinctly as I see you two men and myself now. I was unable to see the end of the vision. I had a confused picture in my mind of the suffering Christ pointing a condemning finger at me, and the rest was shut out by mist and darkness. I have not slept for twenty-four hours. The first thing I saw this morning was the account of the shooting at the coal yards. I read the account with a feeling of horror I have not been able to shake off. I am a guilty creature before God."

Penrose paused suddenly. The two men looked at him solemnly. What power of the Holy Spirit moved the soul of this hitherto self-satisfied, elegant, cultured man who belonged to the social life that was accustomed to go its way placidly, unmindful of the great sorrows of a great city and practically ignorant of what it means to suffer for Jesus' sake? Into that room came a breath such as before swept over Henry Maxwell's church and through Nazareth avenue. The Bishop laid his hand on the shoulder of Penrose and said: "My brother, God has been very near to you. Let us thank Him."

"Yes! yes!" sobbed Penrose. He sat down on a chair and covered his face. The Bishop prayed. Then Penrose quietly said: "Will you go with me to that house?"

For answer the two men put on their overcoats and went with him to the home of the dead man's family.

That was the beginning of a new and strange life for Clarence Penrose. From the moment he stepped into that wretched hovel of a home and faced for the first time in his life a despair and suffering such as he had read of but did not know by personal contact, he dated a new life. It would be another long story to tell how, in obedience to his pledge he began to do with his tenement property as he knew Jesus would do. What would Jesus do with tenement property if He owned it in Chicago or any other great city of the world? Any man who can imagine any true answers to this question can easily tell what Clarence Penrose began to do.

Now before that winter reached its bitter climax many things occurred in the city which concerned the lives of all the characters in this history of the disciples who promised to walk in His steps.

It chanced by one of those coincidences that seem to occur preternaturally that one afternoon just as Felicia came out of the Settlement with a basket of food which she was going to leave as a sample with a baker in the Penrose district, Stephen Clyde opened the door of the carpenter shop in the basement and came out in time to meet her as she reached the sidewalk.

"Let me carry your basket, please," he said.

"Why do you say 'please'?" asked Felicia, handing over the basket while they walked along.

"I would like to say something else," replied Stephen, glancing at her shyly and yet with a boldness that frightened him, for he had been loving Felicia more every day since he first saw her and especially since she stepped into the shop that day with the Bishop, and for weeks now they had been thrown in each other's company.

"What else?" asked Felicia, innocently falling into the trap.

"Why—" said Stephen, turning his fair, noble face full toward her and eyeing her with the look of one who would have the best of all things in the universe, "I would like to say: 'Let me carry your basket, dear Felicia'."

Felicia never looked so beautiful in her life. She walked on a little way without even turning her face toward him. It was no secret with her own heart that she had given it to Stephen some time ago. Finally she turned and said shyly, while her face grew rosy and her eyes tender:

"Why don't you say it, then?"

"May I?" cried Stephen, and he was so careless for a minute of the way he held the basket, that Felicia exclaimed:

"Yes! But oh, don't drop my goodies!"

"Why, I wouldn't drop anything so precious for all the world, dear Felicia," said Stephen, who now walked on air for several blocks, and what was said during that walk is private correspondence that we have no right to read. Only it is a matter of history that day that the basket never reached its destination, and that over in the other direction, late in the afternoon, the Bishop, walking along quietly from the Penrose district, in rather a secluded spot near the outlying part of the Settlement district, heard a familiar voice say:

"But tell me, Felicia, when did you begin to love me?"

"I fell in love with a little pine shaving just above your ear that day when I saw you in the shop!" said the other voice with a laugh so clear, so pure, so sweet that it did one good to hear it.

"Where are you going with that basket?" he tried to say sternly.

"We are taking it to—where are we taking it, Felicia?"

"Dear Bishop, we are taking it home to begin—"

"To begin housekeeping with," finished Stephen, coming to the rescue.

"Are you?" said the Bishop. "I hope you will invite me to share. I know what Felicia's cooking is."

"Bishop, dear Bishop!" said Felicia, and she did not pretend to hide her happiness; "indeed, you shall be the most honored guest. Are you glad?"

"Yes, I am," he replied, interpreting Felicia's words as she wished. Then he paused a moment and said gently: "God bless you both!" and went his way with a tear in his eye and a prayer in his heart, and left them to their joy.

Yes. Shall not the same divine power of love that belongs to earth be lived and sung by the disciples of the Man of Sorrows and the Burden-bearer of sins? Yea, verily! And this man and woman shall walk hand in hand through this great desert of human woe in this city, strengthening each other, growing more loving with the experience of the world's sorrows, walking in His steps even closer yet because of their love for each other, bringing added blessing to thousands of wretched creatures because they are to have a home of their own to share with the homeless. "For this cause," said our Lord Jesus Christ, "shall a man leave his father and mother and cleave unto his wife." And Felicia and Stephen, following the Master, love him with a deeper, truer service and devotion because of the earthly affection which Heaven itself sanctions with its solemn blessing.

But it was a little after the love story of the Settlement became a part of its glory that Henry Maxwell of Raymond came to Chicago with Rachel Winslow and Virginia Page and Rollin and Alexander Powers and President Marsh, and the occasion was a remarkable gathering at the hall of the Settlement arranged by the Bishop and Dr. Bruce, who had finally persuaded Mr. Maxwell and his fellow disciples in Raymond to come on to be present at this meeting.

There were invited into the Settlement Hall, meeting for that night men out of work, wretched creatures who had lost faith in God and man, anarchists and infidels, free-thinkers and no-thinkers. The representation of all the city's worst, most hopeless, most dangerous, depraved elements faced Henry Maxwell and the other disciples when the meeting began. And still the Holy Spirit moved over the great, selfish, pleasure-loving, sin-stained city, and it lay in God's hand, not knowing all that awaited it. Every man and woman at the meeting that night had seen the Settlement motto over the door blazing through the transparency set up by the divinity student: "What would Jesus do?"

And Henry Maxwell, as for the first time he stepped under the doorway, was touched with a deeper emotion than he had felt in a long time as he thought of the first time that question had come to him in the piteous appeal of the shabby young man who had appeared in the First Church of Raymond at the morning service.

Was his great desire for fellowship going to be granted? Would the movement begun in Raymond actually spread over the country? He had come to Chicago with his friends partly to see if the answer to that question would be found in the heart of the great city life. In a few minutes he would face the people. He had grown very strong and calm since he first spoke with trembling to that company of working men in the railroad shops, but now as then he breathed a deeper prayer for help. Then he went in, and with the rest of the disciples he experiencced one of the great and important events of the earthly life. Somehow he felt as if this meeting would indicate something of an answer to his constant query: "What would Jesus do?" And tonight as he looked into the faces of men and women who had for years been strangers and enemies to the Church, his heart cried out: "O, my Master, teach the Church, Thy Church, how to follow Thy steps better!" Is that prayer of Henry Maxwell's to be answered? Will the Church in the city respond to the call to follow Him? Will it choose to walk in His steps of pain and suffering? And still, over all the city broods the Spirit. Grieve Him not, O city! For He was never more ready to revolutionize this world than now!

Chapter 30

Now, when Jesus heard these things, He said unto him, Yet lackest thou one thing: sell all that thou hast, and distribute unto the poor, and thou shalt have treasure in heaven: and come, follow Me.

When Henry Maxwell began to speak to the souls crowded into the Settlement Hall that night it is doubtful if he ever faced such an audience in his life. It is quite certain that the city of Raymond did not contain such a variety of humanity. Not even the Rectangle at its worst could furnish so many men and women who had fallen entirely out of the reach of the church and of all religious and even Christian influences.

What did he talk about? He had already decided that point. He told in the simplest language he could command some of the results of obedience to the pledge as it had been taken in Raymond. Every man and woman in that audience knew something about Jesus Christ. They all had some idea of His character, and however much they had grown bitter toward the forms of Christian ecclesiasticism or the social system, they preserved some standard of right and truth, and what little some of them still retained was taken from the person of the Peasant of Galilee.

So they were interested in what Maxwell said. "What would Jesus do?" He began to apply the question to the social problem in general, after finishing the story of Raymond. The audience was respectfully attentive. It was more than that. It was genuinely interested. As Mr. Maxwell went on, faces all over the hall leaned forward in a way seldom seen in church audiences or anywhere except among working men or the people of the street when once they are thoroughly aroused. "What would Jesus do?" Suppose that were the motto not only of the churches but of the business men, the politicians, the newspapers, the workingmen, the society people—how long would it take under such a standard of conduct to revolutionize the world? What was the trouble with the world? It was suffering from selfishness. No one ever lived who had succeeded in overcoming selfishness like Jesus. If men followed Him regardless of results the world would at once begin to enjoy a new life.

Maxwell never knew how much it meant to hold the respectful attention of that hall full of diseased and sinful humanity. The Bishop and Dr. Bruce, sitting there, looking on, seeing many faces that represented scorn of creeds, hatred of the social order, desperate narrowness and selfishness, marveled that even so soon under the influence of the Settlement life, the softening process had begun already to lessen the bitterness of hearts, many of which had grown bitter from neglect and indifference.

And still, in spite of the outward show of respect to the speaker, no one, not even the Bishop, had any true conception of the feeling pent up in that room that night. Among those who had heard of the meeting and had responded to the invitation were twenty or thirty men out of work who had strolled past the Settlement that afternoon, read the notice of the meeting, and had come in out of curiosity and to escape the chill east wind. It was a bitter night and the saloons were full. But in that whole district of over thirty thousand souls, with the exception of the saloons, there was not a door open except the clean, pure Christian door of the Settlement. Where would a man without a new home or without work or without friends naturally go unless to the saloon?

It had been the custom at the Settlement for a free discussion to follow any open meeting of this kind, and when Mr. Maxwell finished and sat down, the Bishop, who presided that night, rose and made the announcement that any man in the hall was at liberty to ask questions, to speak out his feelings or declare his convictions, always with the understanding that whoever took part was to observe the simple rules that governed parliamentary bodies and obey the three-minute rule which, by common consent, would be enforced on account of the numbers present.

Instantly a number of voices from men who had been at previous meetings of this kind exclaimed, "Consent! Consent!"

The Bishop sat down, and immediately a man near the middle of the hall rose and began to speak.

"I want to say what Mr. Maxwell has said tonight comes pretty close to me. I knew Jack Manning, the fellow he told about who died at his house. I worked on the next case to his in a printer's shop in Philadelphia for two years. Jack was a good fellow. He loaned me five dollars once when I was in a hole and I never got a chance to pay him back. He moved to New York, owing to a change in the management of the office that threw him out, and I never saw him again. When the linotype machines came in I was one of the men to go out, just as he did. I have been out most of the time since. They say inventions are a good thing. I don't always see it myself; but I suppose I'm prejudiced. A man naturally is when he loses a steady job because a machine takes his place. About this Christianity he tells about, it's all right. But I never expect to see any such sacrifices on the part of the church people. So far as my observation goes they're just as selfish and as greedy for money and worldly success as anybody. I except the Bishop and Dr. Bruce and a few others. But I never found much difference between men of the world as they are called, and church members when it came to business and money making. One class is just as bad as another there."

Cries of "That's so!" "You're right!" "Of course!" interrupted the speaker, and the minute he sat down two men who were on the floor for several seconds before the first speaker was through began to talk at once.

The Bishop called them to order and indicated which was entitled to the floor. The man who remained standing began eagerly:

"This is the first time I was ever in here, and maybe it'll be the last. Fact is, I am about at the end of my string. I've tramped this city for work till I'm sick. I'm in plenty of company. Say! I'd like to ask a question of the minister, if it's fair. May I?"

"That's for Mr. Maxwell to say," said the Bishop.

"By all means," replied Mr. Maxwell quickly. "Of course, I will not promise to answer it to the gentleman's satisfaction."

"This is my question." The man leaned forward and stretched out a

long arm with a certain dramatic force that grew naturally enough out
of his condition as a human being. "I want to know what Jesus would
do in my case. I haven't had a stroke of work for two months. I've got
a wife and three children, and I love them as much as if I was worth
a million dollars. I've been living off a little earnings I saved up during the World's Fair jobs I got. I'm a carpenter by trade, and I've
tried every way I know to get a job. You say we ought to take for our
motto, 'What would Jesus do?' What would He do if He was out of
work like me? I can't be somebody else and ask the question. I want
to work. I'd give anything to grow tired of working ten hours a day
the way I used to. Am I to blame because I can't manufacture a job
for myself? I've got to live, and my wife and my children have got to
live. But how? What would Jesus do? You say that's the question we
ought to ask."

Mr. Maxwell sat there staring at the great sea of faces all intent on
his, and no answer to this man's question seemed for the time being to
be possible. "O God!" his heart prayed; "this is a question that brings
up the entire social problem in all its perplexing entanglement of
human wrongs and its present condition contrary to every desire of
God for a human being's welfare. Is there any condition more awful
than for a man in good health, able and eager to work, with no means
of honest livelihood unless he does work, actually unable to get anything to do, and driven to one of three things: begging or charity at
the hands of friends or strangers, suicide or starvation? 'What would
Jesus do?' " It was a fair question for the man to ask. It was the only
question he could ask, supposing him to be a disciple of Jesus. But
what a question for any man to be obliged to answer under such conditions?

All this and more did Henry Maxwell ponder. All the others were
thinking in the same way. The Bishop sat there with a look so stern
and sad that it was not hard to tell how the question moved him. Dr.
Bruce had his head bowed. The human problem had never seemed to
him so tragical as since he had taken the pledge and left his church to
enter the Settlement. What would Jesus do? It was a terrible question.
And still the man stood there, tall and gaunt and almost terrible, with
his arm stretched out in an appeal which grew every second in meaning. At length Mr. Maxwell spoke.

"Is there any man in the room, who is a Christian disciple, who has
been in this condition and has tried to do as Jesus would do? If so,
such a man can answer this question better than I can."

There was a moment's hush over the room and then a man near the
front of the hall slowly rose. He was an old man, and the hand he laid
on the back of the bench in front of him trembled as he spoke.

"I think I can safely say that I have many times been in just such a condition, and I have always tried to be a Christian under all conditions. I don't know as I have always asked this question, 'What would Jesus do?' when I have been out of work, but I do know I have tried to be His disciple at all times. Yes," the man went on, with a sad smile that was more pathetic to the Bishop and Mr. Maxwell than the younger man's grim despair; "yes, I have begged, and I have been to charity institutions, and I have done everything when out of a job except steal and lie in order to get food and fuel. I don't know as Jesus would have done some of the things I have been obliged to do for a living, but I know I have never knowingly done wrong when out of work. Sometimes I think maybe He would have starved sooner than beg. I don't know."

The old man's voice trembled and he looked around the room timidly. A silence followed, broken by a fierce voice from a large, black-haired, heavily-bearded man who sat three seats from the Bishop. The minute he spoke nearly every man in the hall leaned forward eagerly. The man who had asked the question, "What would Jesus do in my case?" slowly sat down and whispered to the man next to him: "Who's that?"

"That's Carlsen, the Socialist leader. Now you'll hear something."

"This is all bosh, to my mind," began Carlsen, while his great bristling beard shook with the deep inward anger of the man. "The whole of our system is at fault. What we call civilization is rotten to the core. There is no use trying to hide it or cover it up. We live in an age of trusts and combines and capitalistic greed that means simply death to thousands of innocent men, women and children. I thank God, if there is a God—which I very much doubt—that I, for one, have never dared to marry and make a home. Home! Talk of hell! Is there any bigger one than this man and his three children has on his hands right this minute? And he's only one out of thousands. And yet this city, and every other big city in this country, has its thousands of professed Christians who have all the luxuries and comforts, and who go to church Sundays and sing their hymns about giving all to Jesus and bearing the cross and following Him all the way and being saved! I don't say that there aren't good men and women among them, but let the minister who has spoken to us here tonight go into any one of a dozen aristocratic churches I could name and propose to the members to take any such pledge as the one he's mentioned here tonight, and see how quick the people would laugh at him for a fool or a crank or a fanatic. Oh, no! That's not the remedy. That can't ever amount to anything. We've got to have a new start in the way of government. The whole thing needs reconstructing. I don't look for any reform worth anything to come out of the churches. They are not with the people. They are with the aristocrats, with the men of money. The trusts and monopolies have their greatest men in the churches. The ministers as a class are their slaves. What we need is a system that shall start from the common basis of socialism, founded on the rights of the common people—"

Carlsen had evidently forgotten all about the three-minutes rule and was launching himself into a regular oration that meant, in his usual surroundings before his usual audience, an hour at least, when the man just behind him pulled him down unceremoniously and arose. Carlsen was angry at first and threatened a little disturbance, but the Bishop reminded him of the rule, and he subsided with several mutterings in his beard, while the next speaker began with a very strong eulogy on the value of the single tax as a genuine remedy for all the social ills. He was followed by a man who made a bitter attack on the churches and ministers, and declared that the two great obstacles in the way of all true reform were the courts and the ecclesiastical machines.

When he sat down a man who bore every mark of being a street laborer sprang to his feet and poured a perfect torrent of abuse against the corporations, especially the railroad. The minute his time was up a big, brawny fellow, who said he was a metal worker by trade, claimed the floor and declared that the remedy for the social wrongs was Trades Unionism. This, he said, would bring on the millennium for labor more surely than anything else. The next man endeavored to give some reasons why so many persons were out of employment, and condemned inventions as works of the devil. He was loudly applauded by the rest.

Finally the Bishop called time on the "free for all," and asked Rachel to sing.

Rachel Winslow had grown into a very strong, healthful, humble Christian during that wonderful year in Raymond dating from the Sunday when she first took the pledge to do as Jesus would do, and her great talent for song had been fully consecrated to the service of the Master. When she began to sing to-night at this Settlement meeting, she had never prayed more deeply for results to come from her voice, the voice which she now regarded as the Master's, to be used for Him.

Certainly her prayer was being answered as she sang. She had chosen the words,

> "Hark! The voice of Jesus calling,
> Follow me, follow me!"

Again Henry Maxwell, sitting there, was reminded of his first night at the Rectangle in the tent when Rachel sang the people into quiet. The effect was the same here. What wonderful power a good voice consecrated to the Master's service always is! Rachel's great natural ability would have made her one of the foremost opera singers of the age. Surely this audience had never heard such a melody. How could it? The men who had drifted in from the street sat entranced by a voice which "back in the world," as the Bishop said, never could be heard by the common people because the owner of it would charge two or three dollars for the privilege. The song poured out through the hall as free and glad as if it were a foretaste of salvation itself. Carlsen, with his great, black-bearded face uplifted, absorbed the music with the deep love of it peculiar to his nationality, and a tear ran over his cheek and glistened in his beard as his face softened and became almost noble in its aspect. The man out of work who had wanted to know what Jesus would do in his place sat with one grimy hand on the back of the bench in front of him, with his mouth partly open, his great tragedy for the moment forgotten. The song, while it lasted, was food and work and warmth and union with his wife and babies once more. The man who had spoken so fiercely against the churches and ministers sat with his head erect, at first with a look of stolid resistance, as if he stubbornly resisted the introduction into the exercises of anything that was even remotely connected with the church or its forms of worship. But gradually he yielded to the power that was swaying the hearts of all the persons in that room, and a look of sad thoughtfulness crept over his face.

The Bishop said that night while Rachel was singing that if the world of sinful, diseased, depraved, lost humanity could only have the gospel preached to it by consecrated prima donnas and professional tenors and altos and bassos, he believed it would hasten the coming of the Kingdom quicker than any other one force. "Why, oh why," he cried in his heart as he listened, "has the world's great treasure of song been so often held far from the poor because the personal possessor of voice or fingers, capable of stirring divinest melody, has so often regarded the gift as something with which to make money? Shall there be no martyrs among the gifted ones of the earth? Shall there be no giving of this great gift as well as of others?"

And Henry Maxwell, again as before, called up that other audience at the Rectangle with increasing longing for a larger spread of the new discipleship. What he had seen and heard at the Settlement burned into him deeper the belief that the problem of the city would be solved if the Christians in it should once follow Jesus as He gave commandment. But what of this great mass of humanity, neglected and sinful, the very kind of humanity the Saviour came to save, with all its mistakes and narrowness, its wretchedness and loss of hope, above all its unqualified bitterness towards the church? That was what smote him deepest. Was the church then so far from the Master that the people no longer found Him in the church? Was it true that the church had lost its power over the very kind of humanity which in the early ages of Christianity it reached in the greatest numbers? How much was true in what the Socialist leader said about the uselessness of looking to the church for reform or redemption, because of the selfishness and seclusion and aristocracy of its members?

He was more and more impressed with the appalling fact that the comparatively few men in that hall, now being held quiet for a while by Rachel's voice, represented thousands of others just like them, to whom a church and a minister stood for less than a saloon or a beer garden as a source of comfort or happiness. Ought it to be so? If the church members were all doing as Jesus would do could it remain true that armies of men would walk the streets for jobs and hundreds of them curse the church and thousands of them find in the saloon their best friend? How far were the Christians responsible for this human problem that was personally illustrated right in this hall tonight? Was it true that the great city churches would as a rule refuse to walk in Jesus' steps so closely as to suffer—actually suffer—for His sake?

Henry Maxwell kept asking this question even after Rachel had finished singing and the meeting had come to an end after a social gathering which was very informal. He asked it while the little company of residents with the Raymond visitors were having a devotional service, as the custom in the Settlement was. He asked it during a conference with the Bishop and Dr. Bruce which lasted until one o'clock. He asked it as he knelt again before sleeping and poured out his soul in a petition for spiritual baptism on the church in America such as it had never known. He asked it the first thing in the morning and all through the day as he went over the Settlement district and saw the life of the people so far removed from the Life abundant. Would the church members, would the Christians, not only in the churches of Chicago, but throughout the country, refuse to walk in His steps if, in order to do so, they must actually take up a cross and follow Him? This was the one question that continually demanded answer.

Chapter 31

He had planned when he came to the city to return to Raymond and be in his own pulpit on Sunday. But Friday morning he had received at the Settlement a call from the pastor of one of the largest churches in Chicago, and had been invited to fill the pulpit for both morning and evening services.

At first he hesitated, but finally accepted, seeing in it the hand of the Spirit's guiding power. He would test his own question. He would prove the truth or falsity of the charge made against the church at the Settlement meeting. How far would it go in its self-denial for Jesus' sake? How closely would it walk in His steps? Was the church willing to suffer for its Master?

Saturday night he spent in prayer, nearly the whole night. There had never been so great a wrestling in his soul, not even during his strongest experiences in Raymond. He had in fact entered upon another new experience. The definition of his own discipleship was receiving an added test at this time, and he was being led into a larger truth of the Lord.

Sunday morning the great church was filled to its utmost. Henry Maxwell, coming into the pulpit from that all-night vigil, felt the pressure of a great curiosity on the part of the people. They had heard of the Raymond movement, as all the churches had, and the recent action of Dr. Bruce had added to the general interest in the pledge. With this curiosity was something deeper, more serious. Mr. Maxwell felt that also. And in the knowledge that the Spirit's presence was his living strength, he brought his message and gave it to that church that day.

He had never been what would be called a great preacher. He had not the force nor the quality that makes remarkable preachers. But ever since he had promised to do as Jesus would do, he had grown in a certain quality of persuasiveness that had all the essentials of true eloquence. This morning the people felt the complete sincerity and humility of a man who had gone deep into the heart of a great truth.

After telling briefly of some results in his own church in Raymond since the pledge was taken, he went on to ask the question he had been asking since the Settlement meeting. He had taken for his theme the story of the young man who came to Jesus asking what he must do to obtain eternal life. Jesus had tested him. "Sell all that thou hast and give to the poor, and thou shalt have treasure in heaven; and come follow me." But the young man was not willing to suffer to that extent. If following Jesus meant suffering in that way, he was not willing. He would like to follow Jesus, but not if he had to give so much.

"Is it true," continued Henry Maxwell, and his fine, thoughtful face glowed with a passion of appeal that stirred the people as they had seldom been stirred, "is it true that the church of today, the church that is called after Christ's own name, would refuse to follow Him at the expense of suffering, of physical loss, of temporary gain? The statement was made at a large gathering in the Settlement last week by a leader of working men that it was hopeless to look to the church for any reform or redemption of society. On what was that statement based? Plainly on the assumption that the church contains for the most part men and women who think more of their own ease and luxury than of the sufferings and needs and sins of humanity. How far is that true? Are the Christians of America ready to have their discipleship tested? How about the men who possess large wealth? Are they ready to take that wealth and use it as Jesus would? How about the men and women of great talent? Are they ready to consecrate that talent to humanity as Jesus undoubtedly would do?

"Is it not true that the call has come in this age for a new exhibition of Christian discipleship? You who live in this great sinful city must know that better than I do. Is it possible you can go your way careless or thoughtless of the awful condition of men and women and children who are dying, body and soul, for need of Christian help? Is it not a matter of concern to you personally that the saloon kills its thousands more surely than war? Is it not a matter of personal suffering in some form for you that thousands of able-bodied, willing men tramp the streets of this city and all cities, crying for work and drifting into crime and suicide because they cannot find it? Can you say that this is none of your business? Let each man look after himself? Would it not be true, think you, that if every Christian in America did as Jesus would do, society itself, the business world, yes, the very political system under which our commercial and governmental activity is carried on, would be so changed that human suffering would be reduced to a minimum?

"What would be the result if all the church members of this city tried to do as Jesus would do? It is not possible to say in detail what the effect would be. But it is easy to say, and it is true, that instantly the human problem would begin to find an adequate answer.

"What is the test of Christian discipleship? Is it not the same as in Christ's own time? Have our surroundings modified or changed the test? If Jesus were here today would He not call some of the members of this very church to do just what He commanded the young man, and ask them to give up their wealth and literally follow Him? I believe He would do that if He felt certain that any church member thought more of his possessions than of the Saviour. The test would be the same today as then. I believe Jesus would demand—He does demand now—as close a following, as much suffering, as great self-denial as when He lived in person on the earth and said, 'Except a man renounce all that he hath he cannot be my disciple.' That is, unless he is willing to do it for my sake, he cannot be my disciple.

"What would be the result if in this city every church member should begin to do as Jesus would do? It is not easy to go into details of the result. But we all know that certain things would be impossible that are now practiced by church members. What would Jesus do in the matter of wealth? How would He spend it? What principle would regulate His use of money? Would He be likely to live in great luxury and spend ten times as much on personal adornment and entertainment as He spent to relieve the needs of suffering humanity? How would Jesus be governed in the making of money? Would He take rentals from saloons and other disreputable property, or even from tenement property that was so constructed that the inmates had no such things as a home and no such possibility as privacy or cleanliness?

"What would Jesus do about the great army of unemployed and desperate who tramp the streets and curse the church, or are indifferent to it, lost in the bitter struggle for the bread that tastes bitter when it is earned on account of the desperate conflict to get it? Would Jesus care nothing for them? Would He go His way in comparative ease and comfort? Would He say that it was none of His business? Would He excuse Himself from all responsibility to remove the causes of such a condition?

"What would Jesus do in the center of a civilization that hurries so fast after money that the very girls employed in great business houses are not paid enough to keep soul and body together without fearful temptations so great that scores of them fall and are swept over the great boiling abyss; where the demands of trade sacrifice hundreds of lads in a business that ignores all Christian duties toward them in the way of education and moral training and personal affection? Would Jesus, if He were here today as a part of our age and commercial industry, feel nothing, do nothing, say nothing, in the face of these facts which every business man knows?

"What would Jesus do? Is not that what the disciple ought to do? Is he not commanded to follow in His steps? How much is the Christianity of the age suffering for Him? Is it denying itself at the cost of ease, comfort, luxury, elegance of living? What does the age need more than personal sacrifice? Does the church do its duty in following Jesus when it gives a little money to establish missions or relieve extreme cases of want? Is it any sacrifice for a man who is worth ten million dollars simply to give ten thousand dollars for some benevolent work? Is he not giving something that cost him practically nothing so far as any personal suffering goes? Is it true that the Christian disciples today in most of our churches are living soft, easy, selfish lives, very far from any sacrifice that can be called sacrifice? What would Jesus do?

"It is the personal element that Christian discipleship needs to emphasize. 'The gift without the giver is bare.' The Christianity that attempts to suffer by proxy is not the Christianity of Christ. Each individual Christian business man, citizen, needs to follow in His steps along the path of personal sacrifice to Him. There is not a different path today from that of Jesus' own times. It is the same path. The call of this dying century and of the new one soon to be, is a call for a new discipleship, a new following of Jesus, more like the early, simple, apostolic Christianity, when the disciples left all and literally followed the Master. Nothing but a discipleship of this kind can face the destructive selfishness of the age with any hope of overcoming it. There is a great quantity of nominal Christianity today. There is need of more of the real kind. We need revival of the Christianity of Christ. We have, unconsciously, lazily, selfishly, formally grown into a discipleship that Jesus himself would not acknowledge. He would say to many of us when we cry, 'Lord, Lord,' 'I never knew you!' Are we ready to take up the cross? Is it possible for this church to sing with exact truth,

> Jesus, I my cross have taken,
> All to leave and follow Thee?

If we can sing that truly, then we may claim discipleship. But if our definition of being a Christian is simply to enjoy the privileges of worship, be generous at no expense to ourselves, have a good, easy time surrounded by pleasant friends and by comfortable things, live respectably and at the same time avoid the world's great stress of sin and trouble because it is too much pain to bear it—if this is our definition of Christianity, surely we are a long way from following the steps of Him who trod the way with groans and tears and sobs of anguish for a lost humanity; who sweat, as it were, great drops of blood, who cried out on the upreared cross, 'My God, my God, why hast thou forsaken me?'

"Are we ready to make and live a new discipleship? Are we ready to reconsider our definition of a Christian? What is it to be a Christian? It is to imitate Jesus. It is to do as He would do. It is to walk in His steps."

When Henry Maxwell finished his sermon, he paused and looked at the people with a look they never forgot and, at the moment, did not understand. Crowded into that fashionable church that day were hundreds of men and women who had for years lived the easy, satisfied life of a nominal Christianity. A great silence fell over the congregation. Through the silence there came to the consciousness of all the souls there present a knowledge, stranger to them now for years, of a Divine Power. Every one expected the preacher to call for volunteers who would do as Jesus would do. But Maxwell had been led by the Spirit to deliver his message this time and wait for results to come.

He closed the service with a tender prayer that kept the Divine Presence lingering very near every hearer, and the people slowly rose to go out. Then followed a scene that would have been impossible if any mere man had been alone in his striving for results.

Men and women in great numbers crowded around the platform to see Mr. Maxwell and to bring him the promise of their consecration to the pledge to do as Jesus would do. It was a voluntary, spontaneous movement that broke upon his soul with a result he could not measure. But had he not been praying for this very thing? It was an answer that more than met his desires.

There followed this movement a prayer service that in its impressions repeated the Raymond experience. In the evening, to Mr. Maxwell's joy, the Endeavor Society almost to a member came forward, as so many of the church members had done in the morning, and seriously, solemnly, tenderly, took the pledge to do as Jesus would do. A deep wave of spiritual baptism broke over the meeting near its close that was indescribable in its tender, joyful, sympathetic results.

That was a remarkable day in the history of that church, but even more so in the history of Henry Maxwell. He left the meeting very late. He went to his room at the Settlement where he was still stopping, and after an hour with the Bishop and Dr. Bruce, spent in a joyful rehearsal of the wonderful events of the day, he sat down to think over again by himself all the experience he was having as a Christian disciple.

He had kneeled to pray, as he always did before going to sleep, and it was while he was on his knees that he had a waking vision of what might be in the world when once the new discipleship had made its way into the conscience and conscientiousness of Christendom. He was fully conscious of being awake, but no less certainly did it seem to him that he saw certain results with great distinctiveness, partly as realities of the future, partly great longings that they might be realities. And this is what Henry Maxwell saw in this waking vision:

He saw himself, first, going back to the First Church in Raymond, living there in a simpler, more self-denying fashion than he had yet been willing to live, because he saw ways in which he could help others who were really dependent on him for help. He also saw, more dimly, that the time would come when his position as pastor of the church would cause him to suffer more on account of growing opposition to his interpretation of Jesus and His conduct. But this was vaguely outlined. Through it all he heard the words, "My grace is sufficient for thee."

He saw Rachel Winslow and Virginia Page going on with their work of service at the Rectangle, and reaching out loving hands of helpfulness far beyond the limits of Raymond. Rachel he saw married to Rollin Page, both fully consecrated to the Master's use, both following His steps with an eagerness intensified and purified by their love for each other. And Rachel's voice sang on, in slums and dark places of despair and sin, and drew lost souls back to God and heaven once more.

He saw President Marsh of the college using his great learning and his great influence to purify the city, to ennoble its patriotism, to inspire the young men and women who loved as well as admired him to lives of Christian service, always teaching them that education means great responsibility for the weak and the ignorant.

He saw Alexander Powers meeting with sore trials in his family life, with a constant sorrow in the estrangement of wife and friends, but still going his way in all honor, serving in all his strength the Master whom he had obeyed, even unto the loss of social distinction and wealth.

He saw Milton Wright, the merchant, meeting with great reverses. Thrown upon the future by a combination of circumstances, with vast business interests involved in ruin through no fault of his own, but coming out of his reverses with clean Christian honor, to begin again and work up to a position where he could again be to hundreds of young men an example of what Jesus would do in business.

He saw Edward Norman, editor of the *News*, by means of the money given by Virginia, creating a force in journalism that in time came to be recognized as one of the real factors of the nation to mold its principles and actually shape its policy, a daily illustration of the might of a Christian press, and the first of a series of such papers begun and carried on by other disciples who had also taken the pledge.

He saw Jasper Chase, who had denied his Master, growing into a cold, cynical, formal life, writing novels that were social successes, but each one with a sting in it, the reminder of his denial, the bitter remorse that, do what he would, no social success could remove.

He saw Rose Sterling, dependent for some years upon her aunt and Felicia, finally married to a man far older than herself, accepting the burden of a relation that had no love in it on her part, because of her desire to be the wife of a rich man and enjoy the physical luxuries that were all of life to her. Over this life also the vision cast certain dark and awful shadows but they were not shown in detail.

He saw Felicia and Stephen Clyde happily married, living a beautiful life together, enthusiastic, joyful in suffering, pouring out their great, strong, fragrant service into the dull, dark, terrible places of the great city, and redeeming souls through the personal touch of their home, dedicated to the Human Homesickness all about them.

He saw Dr. Bruce and the Bishop going on with the Settlement work. He seemed to see the great blazing motto over the door enlarged, "What would Jesus do?" and by this motto every one who entered the Settlement walked in the steps of the Master.

He saw Burns and his companion and a great company of men like them, redeemed and giving in turn to others, conquering their passions by the divine grace, and proving by their daily lives the reality of the new birth even in the lowest and most abandoned.

And now the vision was troubled. It seemed to him that as he kneeled he began to pray, and the vision was more of a longing for a future than a reality in the future. The church of Jesus in the city and throughout the country! Would it follow Jesus? Was the movement begun in Raymond to spend itself in a few churches like Nazareth Avenue and the one where he had preached today, and then die away as a local movement, a stirring on the surface but not to extend deep and far? He felt with agony after the vision again. He thought he saw the church of Jesus in America open its heart to the moving of the Spirit and rise to the sacrifice of its ease and self-satisfaction in the name of Jesus. He thought he saw the motto, "What would Jesus do?" inscribed over every church door, and written on every church member's heart.

The vision vanished. It came back clearer than before, and he saw the Endeavor Societies all over the world carrying in their great processions at some mighty convention a banner on which was written, "What would Jesus do?" And he thought in the faces of the young men and women he saw future joy of suffering, loss, self-denial, martyrdom. And when this part of the vision slowly faded, he saw the figure of the Son of God beckoning to him and to all the other actors in his life history. An Angel Choir somewhere was singing. There was a sound as of many voices and a shout as of a great victory. And the figure of Jesus grew more and more splendid. He stood at the end of a long flight of steps. "Yes! Yes! O my Master, has not the time come for this dawn of the millennium of Christian history? Oh, break upon the Christendom of this age with the light and the truth! Help us to follow Thee all the way!"

He rose at last with the awe of one who has looked at heavenly things. He felt the human forces and the human sins of the world as never before. And with a hope that walks hand in hand with faith and love Henry Maxwell, disciple of Jesus, laid him down to sleep and dreamed of the regeneration of Christendom, and saw in his dream a church of Jesus without spot or wrinkle or any such thing, following Him all the way, walking obediently in His steps.